Alice Jolly is a novelist and playwr d ir *Dead Babies*
 *Seaside Towns* won the PE he also won
th P t Me ria y of
Literature in 2014 for one of her short stories, 'Ray the Rottweiler'.
She has written two novels previously, *What the Eye Doesn't See*
and *If Only You Knew*. She has written for the *Guardian, Mail on
Sunday* and the *Independent,* and she has broadcast for Radio 4.
She lives in Stroud, Gloucestershire.

BY THE SAME AUTHOR

*If Only You Knew*
*What the Eye Doesn't See*
*Dead Babies and Seaside Towns*
*Mary Ann Sate, Imbecile*

# BETWEEN THE REGIONS OF KINDNESS

## ALICE JOLLY

unbound

This edition first published in 2019

Unbound
6th Floor Mutual House, 70 Conduit Street, London W1S 2GF
www.unbound.com

All rights reserved

© Alice Jolly, 2019

The right of Alice Jolly to be identified as the author of this work has been asserted in
accordance with Section 77 of the Copyright, Designs and Patents Act, 1988. No part of
this publication may be copied, reproduced, stored in a retrieval system, or transmitted, in
any form or by any means without the prior permission of the publisher, nor be otherwise
circulated in any form of binding or cover other than that in which it is published and without
a similar condition being imposed on the subsequent purchaser.

While every effort has been made to trace the owners of copyright material reproduced
herein, the publisher would like to apologise for any omissions and will be pleased to
incorporate missing acknowledgments in any further editions.

Text design by PDQ

A CIP record for this book is available from the British Library

ISBN 978-1-78352-499-0 (trade pbk)
ISBN 978-1-78352-500-3 (ebook)
ISBN 978-1-78352-498-3 (limited edition)

Printed in Great Britain by Clays, Elcograf S.p.A.

For my son Thomas –
wishing him love and laughter
for the long journey.

# 1

# BEFORE

## Rose – Coventry, April 1941

The dawn must come – that's all that Rose can be certain of now. Fumbling up the steps, pulling Mollie behind her, she sees its band of grey staining the blackness above a jagged line of roofs. She puts a hand against a wall to balance herself, heads for where the gates must be, stops when she gets there, steadies herself once more against their blistered metal. For a moment, the silence is absolute – the streets, the city, breathe out knowing that the night is ending. Rose gulps a deep breath but ash furs her throat, and she gasps, coughs, feels the sting of smoke in her eyes. She puts Mollie down and the child wobbles, clings to Rose's leg, starts to howl. Rose bends down and buttons Mollie's coat, then shakes her to keep her quiet.

The street is white with a frost of broken glass. Rose steps forward into the muffled light, her hand gripped around Mollie's arm. Phantoms start to stumble from the shadows, caked in plaster dust, clinging to one another as though blind. An elderly man comes towards Rose, staggering over broken kerbstones. He has a colander on his head and his bare legs stick out from under his dressing gown. His knotted hands grip the colander and he sings – *Nearer and nearer draws the time, the time that shall surely be, when the earth shall be filled with the glory of God as the waters cover the sea.*

A water main has burst and damp seeps through the soles of Rose's shoes. She reaches down and picks Mollie up, steps out of the spreading puddles. Ahead of her, through the smoke

1

and drizzle, a fire engine is slanted against the jagged outline of a blackened wall. Above, tangled wires dangle from a drunken telegraph post. The sound of bombs still smashes through Rose's head, pounds in her chest, and at every imagined blast the street buckles under her feet. Voices ricochet around her. *God be praised. Where? Where? No All Clear this morning. Wires blown right out the ground.*

People gather around a man standing by the gutter, filling a kettle from a drain and pouring water into glass bottles and mugs. *The trouble with the shrapnel is that it does jam the lawn mower.* Rose's teeth chatter against the edge of a tin cup. The water is clouded and tastes of ash and soap but she gulps half of it down, then bends to hold the cup for Mollie. All the stories are at an end. So what now? Where can we go? The questions form in her mind but she considers them without concern. The mystery is that she and Mollie are alive. Of course, the house has gone, she knows that. It was the Bostocks' house and she'd been staying in the sitting room. At least the Bostocks had left the city and Arthur was out at Division B First Aid. But she'd left her gas mask there, her ration book, her last ten-shilling note. And Frank will, would have...

She turns to a woman standing close by. Shackleton Street? Is this the end of Shackleton Street? Where's the pub? The woman turns, her eyes vacant. She wears red wool socks and pieces of cardboard are tied under the soles of her shoes. Her head shakes, she turns away.

The end of Shackleton Street? The colander man catches hold of Rose and pulls her around, as though he wants to dance. Rose keeps Mollie gripped tightly against her. *The end of the road? It certainly is. Except the end ain't even here, is it? The bloody end and not even any end.* A mountainous woman appears, upholstered into a tweed coat. Taking hold of the colander man, she pushes him away. As the man steps back, his dressing gown falls open, revealing long underpants, a furrow of purple ribs. He pulls the dressing gown back around himself, bursts into tears.

The woman steers Rose and Mollie away. Rose recognises her as Mrs Bartholomew, the butcher's wife, the woman who sold her a steak as green as grass and called her Mrs Von Mayeford. But now Mrs Bartholomew's grip is steady on Rose's arm. You need to get to the Rest Centre, love. At Barkers Butts school. Can you hear me, love? The Rest Centre.

I need to get to the end.

No, Mrs Bartholomew says. No, love. No. Can you hear me?

Mrs Bartholomew is pulling Rose and Mollie back towards the College. Here we are. Butt Street. Can you hear me? You know where you are now, love, don't you? Butt Street. Just keep on going. She pushes Rose and Mollie on.

The morning is arriving now, listless and blank. From an upstairs window an elderly woman shouts at the sky, grips a singed cat. *Seen the worst in November. Wasn't it enough? On and on, not a bleeding brick standing.* Outlined against the bruised sky, a school hat, a pair of field glasses and several pairs of smalls dangle from the blackened branches of a tree. A wooden mangle is hooked over a lamp post and a parachute bomb, like a vast iron coffin, is suspended between the gable ends of two houses. Small boys stand under it, leaping and throwing stones, until a warden drives them away.

A gust of wind sends flecks of ash, shreds of newspaper through the air like giant flakes of snow. Rose knows the Rest Centres will be full. And even if she can find a place they will ask for an identity card. She has Mollie's card but lost her own months back. Perhaps she could walk to Kenilworth or Nuneaton but it'll cost two shillings a week to get any kind of bed and people don't want a woman with a child. From somewhere under fallen beams, a radio plays – *my arm about you, that charm about you, will carry me through to heaven, I'm in heaven.* The sound rises scratchily into the thick air. That was a record Frank loves – used to love.

The road ahead is blocked by a corporation bus, its front and back axles snagged in telephone wires. Men with clippers are trying to untangle the mess. *Apparently they got it. They definitely did*. Raucous laughter. The cathedral went months ago. Others are shovelling bricks, rubble, broken glass off the road. Five bodies lie in an orderly line outside the smoking shell of a house, wrapped neatly in white sheets. Rose turns her head as she passes. A man shouts and comes towards her. Rose recognises the face. Arthur?

Arthur's voice is raw and his shirt and trousers are torn. His black hair is plastered down to his head, his eyes lined red. The port-wine stain which has always covered his chin burns brightly. Arthur reaches out, shifts his weight onto his bad foot and back, takes hold of Mollie, holds her close against him.

Shackleton Street? Rose says. She needs to go back there. Her last ten-shilling note was under the green baize in the knife drawer and she had dry blankets stored in a tarpaulin under the bed. She needs to go back because when Frank comes home that's where he'll look for her.

Rosa. My bella. Arthur's face is close to hers and he shakes her shoulder.

Frank, Rose says. Frank.

No. No. Come on, Rosa. You remember, don't you?

His voice has the usual lilt but the light has gone from it. She does remember.

Rose, you should go to Violet. Rose, can you hear me? Go across Greyfriars Green? You know what I'm saying. You can hear me, can't you, Rose?

Of course, she must go to 34 Warwick Road, to Violet's house. She'd already decided that in the shelter – so close and hot, the air dark and sticky as tar, and then the water started rising and that man's voice singing, *nearer and nearer draws the time*. Yes, she must go to Violet, she'll be safe there. Violet won't mind. Despite everything, she's always said that Rose can go there any time. Rose thinks of Violet's house, at the edge of the Green, imagines Violet with her bright cynicism, her brutal practicality. She longs for that house, for tap water, a fire, a bed with sheets and blankets, an eiderdown.

I'm going to come there later, Arthur says. You go now.

Arthur kisses Mollie, hands her back to Rose, then, taking hold of Rose's arm, pulls the two of them towards Wrighton Street.

Straight ahead here. You know the way. I'll come.

Rose's blood is flowing again now, her eyes are searching through the gritty air, finding her way through these streets which she knows so well but which have been picked up, tossed around, thrown down anywhere. *Violet, I'm coming, wait for me. I'm sorry. I'm so sorry.*

Turning into Wrighton Street, glass crackles under Rose's feet and she smells Sunday lunch. The butcher's shop is ablaze – flames leap up from the area where the counter used to be and smoke billows out through the door. The front window has shattered and a side of pork hangs there, roasting. Some of the other meat has been rescued and is laid out on the pavement. A pool of reddish-brown liquid spreads out at Rose's feet. Blood, she thinks, then sees twisted metal from exploded tins of oxtail soup.

The houses on the corner of Smith Street have gone but that happened months ago. Weeds grow now in the outlines of rooms and along the shattered garden paths. Boards hang and pipes are buckled. Once Rose would have stared in shock but now she doesn't see. The bell of a fire engine rattles, a wall collapses with a sigh. A shopkeeper is trying to boil a kettle on an unexploded incendiary bomb.

Rose comes to the edge of Greyfriars Green, sets Mollie down. From here it used to be possible to see the three spires of Coventry, and the gables of the timbered houses in the centre, but all that's gone now. Ahead is a wall of black smoke and above a crimson sky. As bad as November. Rose sets out across the Green, picking her way around the craters which have punctured the grass. Incendiary bombs still burn like Roman candles and two wardens work with shovels, scooping them up and dropping them into a bucket of water. Sweat is running down Rose's face and so she puts Mollie down, pulls off her coat and cardigan, loops them over her arm.

Now she can see Warwick Road – a white cliff of houses, every one complete, undamaged. Even the Luftwaffe know better than to bomb Violet. Rose hears Violet's voice – *You will kill yourself with all this, Rose Mayeford. Are you listening to me? You will kill yourself.* The houses are three storeys with a great many chimney pots. 34 Warwick Road. Columns, long sash windows, curling iron balconies and three steps up to the front door. A house with two inside bathrooms, the house that belonged to Mr Ernest Whiteley until he gave it to his daughter Violet when she married Stanley Bunton.

Perhaps Violet was right. *Die if you must but do not kill.* Rose wonders now how could she possibly have thought that goodness or reason could defeat this? She and Frank had been children, silly children. Ahead of her, a stream of people stride along Warwick Road, heading out of the city. They carry struggling babies and overflowing bags, they push bicycles or prams piled with cases, baskets, sewing machines, hat boxes, stacks of bedding, boxes of tinned food. A canary in a cage topples on a hand cart and a group of children carry a rolled-up carpet. Toddlers are piled into wheelbarrows. A fat woman has collapsed at the side of the road and an infant clings to her leg. Most of the people walk in silence but, as Rose approaches, a few of them shout at her to go back. Rose stops for a moment to push sweat-soaked hair back off her face but then heads on, gripping Mollie against her, pushing her way through the crowds.

34 Warwick Road. Ernest Whiteley's house, except he isn't here any more. Lost his mind, they say, can't tell the difference between his own daughter and a parrot cage. Rose is unsteady as she opens the gate. The path is zigzagged tiles of red and black brick, and stone lions stand either side of the door. How ridiculous that the lions are still standing up straight and proud. Even now Rose feels as though she must tidy her hair, straighten her cuffs. She rings the doorbell but no one answers. Mollie has settled against Rose's shoulder now, her hands locked over her eyes.

Violet will be out in the Anderson at the back. That shelter was one of the first to be built in the city. The wrought-iron arch – which once rose to a Moorish point, decorated by a pineapple-like knob – and the wisteria were pulled out to make room for it. Arthur and Frank had teased Violet. *Don't be daft. A shelter? There's seven lines of defence before they reach Coventry.*

Rose turns the door handle, steps into the hall, measures the dimensions of this undamaged house, breathes in the shuttered air. A picture has dropped from a wall and lies face down on the floor. Plaster dust is sprinkled across the hall table and peppers the black and white floor tiles but the stuffed eagle is still chained to its perch inside the glass dome and palms still sprout from willow-pattern vases, resting on curvaceous wooden stands. China figurines – shepherdesses and milkmaids – stand unmoved in the glass cabinet beside the fireplace. The stairs sweep down, wide and curving, with their faded green carpet and brass stair rods. The mahogany rail curls itself into a snail shell above the last step and the bevelled glass mirror – spotted and chipped – still reflects the spangled light from the chandelier.

And the giant Chinese vases—

Rose's mind slides backwards. The Chinese vases, the umbrella, that first evening. Two years ago, a half-remembered fairy tale, a Christmas party in the house of Mr Whiteley, the Head of the Accounts Department. Rose had only just arrived in Coventry, had only been working at the factory for three months, had already earned the nickname Red Rose but was still invited along with everyone else. Back home in Lincolnshire, you wouldn't have gone in such a house unless you were in service but Rose had stepped up smartly to the front door, tight on gin, in her silk stockings and her one good pair of shoes, bought in the sale at Owen Owen the Saturday before. The lines of the chessboard floor tiles wavered, vague in the candlelight. The walls glittered with ornaments – silver platters and cigar boxes on glass shelves, candlesticks and salt cellars, photographs in jewelled frames.

And there was Violet, bouncing awkwardly through the sitting-room door – the daughter of the Head of the Accounts Department, in her green-flowered silk dress, with her dull blonde hair perfectly lacquered and her full lips painted bright red. Like a china doll, with eyes too wide open, tiny and plump with awkwardly hinged limbs.

Isn't she beautiful, Rose had thought, although Violet wasn't beautiful. Her face was wide and flat and she had freckles that she'd tried to hide by putting on too much powder. But still Rose couldn't stop looking at her. Violet made her think of confectionery – a sugar-crusted cake, pink icing, twinkling silver balls. Or bread – a loaf newly taken from the oven, smelling of dough and speckled with currants.

As they shook hands, Violet's grip felt hot and fleshy and she held onto Rose's hand too long. And perhaps that was why Rose became flustered and, turning on the tiled floor, put her umbrella in what she assumed was an umbrella stand – except it turned out to be a vase instead. A giant Chinese vase, one of a pair, standing one each side of the sitting-room door. The umbrella poked out of the vase at an awkward angle. Rose was uncertain whether she should pull the umbrella out and try to make a joke, but she judged it best to leave it there.

As she turned back, she saw the slight smirk on Violet's face. Of course, Violet wouldn't tell her that she'd put her umbrella in a vase but that smirk – so very subtle – was enough to let Rose know that Violet had seen through her. A cheap little girl from the country wearing her only good pair of shoes and her hair done in a saucer wave, but only two shillings in her purse.

In the velvet and brocade sitting room everyone made jokes about the names. *Violet, Rose, Rose, Violet. A few flowers more and we'll have a bouquet.* Frank must have been there – perhaps he was serving drinks or playing the piano. There amidst the ornaments – ornamental himself, beautiful even, but part of the background, something to be kept behind glass, admired from a distance. That's what she'd thought of him then, if she'd thought at all.

Later they all played sardines, dashing up and down the stairs, squeezing under beds, behind curtains, into laundry cupboards and attic storerooms. And Rose had dashed into Violet's bedroom – all salmon satin – and looked into the wardrobe, then heard a giggle and found herself pulled into the silk of the dresses, pressed tight against the plump freckled skin of Violet's arm. And it was because they were squeezed in so tight, and had drunk too much punch, and couldn't stop giggling, that they suddenly clung to each other and kissed as though they were lovers, and the wardrobe seemed to tip wildly, turning upside down, and the fur of the coats made them sneeze.

Where is Violet now? She's probably come in from the shelter and gone upstairs to wash. Rose sits Mollie on a red-tasselled chair beside the hall table, notices now that the child smells of urine. Her stick legs dangle high above the floor. She crosses her ankles and folds her hands in her lap, neat and precise, but then her head lolls against the hall table. Rose reaches into her coat pocket, is relieved to find that Bobby the toy dog is still with them, hands him to the child, then takes off her own muddy shoes. Her damp stockinged feet pad on the carpet as she passes the library door on the half landing. At the top, she stops and listens. A faint and regular ticking comes from above, as though a tap has been left on.

She stops at the open door of Violet's bedroom. Everything is just the same – the quilted satin bedspread, the curving oak bedhead, shaped like a seashell, the swagged curtains and lace blinds, the kidney-shaped dressing table top with its skirt underneath and oval mirror above. Violet's shoes are lying beside the dressing table. Such lovely shoes, soft grey kidskin, tiny pearl buttons.

Rose hears a fluttering and looks behind her. The glass has gone from the window at the back. Shards are scattered over the Chinese rug. But Violet is there, asleep in bed with Mollie – the other Mollie, Violet's baby. *Darling. Such fun for them both to have the same name, don't you think?* Violet's head is turned to one side, her hair spread across the pillow, the sheets pulled up to her chin. Her eyes are closed, her lips slightly parted. Cheeks blue-white, lashes spread like a fan. Beside her, tucked against Violet's chest, is the top of baby Mollie's tiny head, the hair flat and lying in neat lines, like the grain of wood. Rose stands beside the bed watching the sleepers.

Again, that fluttering sound, that kindly whisper. A blackbird sits on the shade of the bedside light, which is decorated with a brown fringe, each strand of it finished with a tiny glass bauble. As the bird bobs and hops, the fringe swings from side to side, the baubles knocking against each other. The bird watches Rose, its beak poking back and forwards, its claws rattling as it balances. Again that rhythmic tap, tap, tap. Water is dripping through the ceiling. Tap, tap, tap. It falls onto the sheets, leaving a circular mark, just near Violet's knees.

Pack some clothes for Violet and Mollie, Rose tells herself. They can't stay here until the window at the back is boarded up. They must all go away, at least for a couple of nights. Violet has a car and she probably has petrol, or she can get it. Soon she'll get up and make tea, on a tray with a lace cloth. A committee will be organised, a plan agreed. A note will be written on lavender card with a purple ribbon through the top.

But until that moment comes, it is Rose who must organise. She goes to the wardrobe and pulls open the door. The same sneezing fur coat is crushed in among the silk dresses but no hand emerges to pull Rose in. She closes the door and crosses to the dressing table. A pot of powder is open, and a tube of lipstick doesn't have a lid. A silver-backed brush has strands of Violet's hair twisted into its bristles. *Violet, I told you to get out of the city. I told you. You could have gone to your father in Worcester. I pleaded with you to go.*

One of the drawers of the dressing table is open. A wad of bank notes is pushed down beside a book – ten and fifty-shilling notes, twenty pounds or more in total. Rose lifts the notes out. Violet has always been generous. *Darling, let me buy it for you. No, no. The blue, not the brown. So much better for you. It's my treat. I insist. I absolutely insist.*

In an ebony box a string of pearls is curled around three

military medals. Another box contains cigarettes and a lighter, coins, broken earrings, a needle case and an envelope. Folded inside it, a jaundiced birth certificate carries details written in cramped black ink. Violet Mary Whiteley. Two identity cards lie behind it and a marriage certificate, also a typed letter giving the details of Stanley Bunton's death. *Royal Warwickshire Regiment. Tuesday, 28th May, Wormhout, near Dunkirk. Killed in action.* Of course, it doesn't say they were all just herded into a barn and shot. Rose thinks of them sometimes, grunting and squealing like animals in an abattoir, the hot stench of manure and the blood smeared across the walls.

A creak and a rustle sound at the door. Mollie has walked up the stairs and is watching with eyes like the turning headlights of a car. Bobby the toy dog swings from her hand. Behind her another figure appears – an ARP warden with mud splattered across his cheek. Rose feels her body turn hot, blood bloom towards her skin. She needs to put the money and the papers back into the drawer but it's too late so she pushes them into the pocket of her skirt. Trying to appear casual, she turns back to the dressing table, positions the hairbrush parallel to the mirror and puts the lid back on the lipstick.

You all right, love? the warden says. Take care with the floor.

Yes, of course. Thank you. I'm quite all right. Rose says this as Violet would say it – brisk and certain – but she's terrified the warden will ask her to turn out her pockets. Looters can be shot without trial. Rose looks across at Mollie, who stands staring at her – her headlight eyes fixed on the pocket with the money in. The warden's face is stripped naked. He breathes in sharply and his hand moves up, claw-like, to cover his mouth.

Best to pack a few things, love, he says through his fingers.

Yes. That's what I was just doing. Rose walks to the wardrobe and takes out a suitcase. The leather is smooth as a conker and printed near the handle are Violet's initials. V.M.B. The clips and the buckle are decorated with diamond-like studs. The case was an engagement present from Stanley. Rose remembers

Violet parading with it up and down the hall, practising for being married, that day in September when war was a nightmare from which you might still wake.

Rose pushes the kid shoes into the case, then a rose-pink Fair Isle cardigan, three silk dresses. Her arm glides into a fur coat, a brown brimmed hat positions itself on her head. The names all merge together – *Violet, Rose, Rose, Violet. A few flowers more and we'll have a bouquet.* The lavender smell of the dresses is so familiar that they must belong to her. Behind her she can hear the warden moving towards the silent sleepers. Rose's heart squeezes like a clenched fist. The bird squawks, flutters upwards, lands on the end of the curtain rail. Rose clicks the suitcase shut.

Best to come out now, love. The floor may not be sound.

Rose looks towards the bed, sees the pool of water spreading wider.

Come on now, love. Best not to wait around.

The warden positions himself between Rose and the bed, takes hold of her arm, steers her towards the door.

I was. I wanted.

No, no, love. Best to come away.

The warden picks up the suitcase, pushes Rose towards the door, where Mollie watches and waits. Rose steadies herself against the doorframe. The pattern of the Chinese carpet is moving, the pink flowers twisting into each other, the blue roses growing larger and smaller, as though seen through a twisting telescope.

It's the blast, the warden says. Sucks all the oxygen out the lungs – I've seen it before. Last week – a family of four, all sat at the table and the tea still warm in the pot. Best to come away. Rose feels the warden pinch through to the bone in her arm. Come on, love. Rose stands up straight, takes a deep breath, raises her chin. The warden stops to look at his clipboard.

Name?

Rose stares at him, a lid closes over her throat.

Name? He shakes her arm and her bones rattle against each

12

other like dice shaken in a cup. Listen, love. Can you tell me your name? The warden shakes his head, sighs, looks at the list on the clipboard.

Miss Violet Whiteley?

Rose grips the doorframe, so as not to be washed away.

Are you Miss Violet Whiteley?

With his dusty, cracked thumb, the warden pushes the top sheet of paper aside and consults another list. Sorry, love. Out of date. Married name. Mrs Violet Bunton?

Rose wishes that something would stop her doing this but nothing does. The two identity cards are in her pocket. Of course, it'll only be for a day or two, just while she finds somewhere to live.

Yes, she says. Yes.

And the child – Mollie Bunton?

Yes.

*Darling. Such fun for them both to have the same name, don't you think?* The warden writes on his list and then, with a nod of his head, indicates the bed, whispers so as not to wake the sleepers. Names?

Rose and Mollie Mayeford, staying in Shackleton Road. I don't know the address. Mr and Mrs Bostock.

The warden nods, notes this information. Poor Rose Mayeford. She was always a silly girl with all that anti-colonial talk – equality and the community of nations. The warden takes the suitcase, picks up Mollie and heads towards the stairs. Rose follows him, taking care not to look back. In the hall, the warden makes suggestions about Rest Centres.

It's quite all right. No need to worry. My father lives in Worcester and I'm going there. As she speaks, she sees a vista spreading out before here, a new story unrolling. She stands in a shaft of sunlight, at a post office counter, speaks in Violet's voice, lays the identity cards and the birth certificate out. *No, of course there aren't other papers. A bomb at the back of the house. My husband? Yes, Stanley Bunton. Royal Warwickshire Regiment.*

*Killed on the 28th of May near Dunkirk.*

No point in going to the station, the warden says. But if you can get to Tile Hill you might pick up a train there.

Thank you.

Well, good luck, Mrs Bunton, the warden says, before stepping away across the tiled floor, dissolving through the front door. *Go to Worcester, put on the fur coat, and the kid shoes, and the rose-pink Fair Isle cardigan.* The house shifts – just the slightest movement, but a cloud of plaster dust drops through a crack in the ceiling covering Rose, filling her nose and her throat. Mollie starts to scream. Rose pulls her towards the front door and shakes her to make her stop. Violet wouldn't put up with screaming like that. But still Mollie screams, so Rose claps her hands over the child's mouth and nose until she doesn't have breath to scream any more.

## 2

# Now

## Lara – Brighton, January 2003

Lara checks her bag – laptop, mobile phone, charger, adaptor, five bound copies of the proposal. It might prove necessary to change the estimate for the flooring but she can explain that to the clients when she gets to Barcelona. Everything must be right. She was responsible for bringing in this client. If the project runs smoothly, Craig will have to promote her – at last. She lights a cigarette, inhales deeply and ask herself if she only continues to smoke because Jay has told her so many times how dangerous it is. The flight leaves from Gatwick at ten and she's booked a car for eight. Craig will meet her at the airport.

The morning feels makeshift, perilous. Balanced breathless on an imagined high wire, she wobbles, reminds herself not to look down. During the night she'd been conscious of an electric storm, lightning crackling across the sky and now the air still contains a static fizz. Inanimate objects are not to be trusted. Those copies of the proposal might grow legs and climb out of her bag. Vengeful glasses of red wine might tip themselves onto her white sofas or pale rugs. She can almost hear the blunt buzz and crackle as the hard drive on the laptop suffers a cardiac arrest. Stop. Stop.

Coffee. She needs a coffee but, of course, it isn't possible to have a proper coffee because of the builders. Three weeks waiting for the tiles to be sent and, when they arrive, they're emerald instead of jade. She came back from work on Friday to find the fools had put half of them up. So they'll just have to take them down. All the kitchen equipment – the espresso machine included

– is packed away under the stairs and the kettle is on the floor in the sitting room.

Breathe, remember to breathe.

Lara crouches down to make herself an instant coffee, then heads to the bathroom. Opening the door, she smells Jay's trainers that he's left on the windowsill – again. She picks them up, marches across the hall, pushes them through the door into the darkness of his bedroom. For a moment she stops still, sure that she can hear someone singing. Has she left a CD player on somewhere? She hasn't, but there is a sound – a distant melody, a low, mournful moan. Perhaps it's the wind.

The doorbell rings. She still needs to dress, do her make-up and pack her bag, but it might be the delivery of her new light fittings for the kitchen. Taking her keys from the hall table, she runs down the stairs. As she opens the front door, a blast of January air, stinging with sea salt, rushes in. Lara ties the belt of her towelling robe and shivers.

A girl is standing on the doorstep – a young woman. She's Indian-looking with yards of black hair twisted up onto the top of her head, secured by feathered combs. She wears a purple wool coat stitched with flowers and a shapeless dress, several sizes too big. On her feet, she has jewelled slippers with turned-up toes, like something out of the *Arabian Nights*. Inside them, her tanned feet are bony and bare. Her face is long and mournful and she wears a jewelled stud in her nose. Behind square glasses, her eyes are stinging and red. Lara wonders how a girl who could be attractive manages to make herself look such a mess.

Excuse me. I was just wondering – are you Jay's mum? Is he here?

The voice is soft and suggests a level of education beyond what Lara expects. The girl looks nervous and her skin is strangely luminous. Lara steps back, feeling that if she stands too close, she might get burnt. The girl's eyes are peering behind her, into the entrance hall. For a brief moment Lara remembers when she was young and peered enviously through windows and open front doors into the bright and comfortable houses of people with real lives. Now she's on the inside, just as she always wanted to be. She hopes that the girl on the doorstep hungers for her life, her flat, her job, but the look that trembles in the girl's eyes has nothing to do with envy.

No, Lara says. No, Jay isn't here.

The girl nods and says, I'm sorry to disturb you.

That's OK, Lara says, looking at her watch. I can tell Jay you called round – if you give me your name.

Jemmy, the girl says. I'll write down my number. She digs around in her rainbow-coloured shoulder bag and pulls out a biro and a pink plastic notebook. The pages of the notebook flicker in the wind as the girl writes. A burger box blows along the street and the pages of an abandoned newspaper flap. The people in the top flat have been told a hundred times not to put their rubbish out until Wednesday but they never listen.

The girl tears the page out of the book and hands it to Lara.

It was just – you see – my baby.

Oh yes, Lara thinks. That explains the baggy dress and the red eyes. An unwanted pregnancy. Poor stupid fool, hardly twenty years old. For a moment the thought crosses Lara's mind that the baby could be Jay's but she knows that's ridiculous because Jay has never shown any interest in girls – or boys.

I'll tell Jay you came around, she says.

Thank you but – you see, I was going to...

Listen. Sorry – I've got a flight to catch.

Yes, of course. Sorry. It's just – you don't know where he is?

No, I just said. I don't know where he is. I'll give him the message. Goodbye. Lara shuts the door on those brimming eyes. Only half an hour until the car will be here and she still hasn't finished her make-up, found her suit, brushed her hair. This is her project, everything must be right. She needs to make it impossible for Craig not to promote her. She hurries back upstairs, grabs her personal organiser and her keys from the hall table and stuffs them into her bag. The movement stretches the cracked skin of her knuckles and she winces. *Where is Jay? How the hell should I know? He's twenty, after all. It isn't my business to know his every move.*

Lara applies a thick layer of eczema cream to her hands, then opens her wardrobe. Again, she hears that low mournful melody. Where can it be coming from? She's only going to be in Barcelona for two days but there's a dinner this evening. Her aubergine-coloured wraparound dress needs flesh-coloured tights to go with it. Darkest Nude by Wolford – she doesn't have a pair. The last ones laddered three weeks ago so why in God's name hasn't she bought some new ones? She pushes a substitute pair into the bag although they're the wrong colour and will ruin the look of the dress, make her calves look fat. Everything must be right but already her plans are unravelling.

When was the last time she saw Jay? Sometime early last week? Of course, he's keeping out of her way. Perhaps she had been too harsh but what was she to do? Stand by and watch him throw away every opportunity? Somebody had to say it. She takes several deep breaths. Of course, the man is just a random lunatic. Low lifes, deadbeats, benefit cheats and superannuated hippies. Brighton is full of them. She stretches out her hand and yanks the curtain shut.

She needs to finish doing her face and find the beads she usually wears with the aubergine dress but instead she crosses the corridor to Jay's room. The curtains are drawn and the smell is incense, trainers and bicycle tyres. She picks her way across the room and pulls aside the skull-and-crossbones flag that covers the window. Light falls on a half-dismantled bicycle standing on a dust sheet surrounded by nuts, bolts, a bicycle pump, a spanner. The ceiling of the room is painted black, and books, CDs and videos are crammed onto shelves made out of wine crates. A portable television is suspended from a piece of twisted metal poking down from the ceiling. On the wall is a picture of Che Guevara, a board full of photographs and postcards. The words – *For evil to triumph it only requires that good men should do nothing* – are scrawled in black marker pen across a Stop The War poster. A globe hangs from the ceiling draped with a bicycle chain. *It symbolises the world in chains, of course, doesn't it?* A book about conscientious objectors in the Second World War lies on the desk. Next to it, a pile of brand new philosophy textbooks. Lara had bought them for his course and they had cost over a hundred pounds. Now she thinks, Perhaps I should make him pay the money back?

She opens one of the drawers of Jay's desk. Two years ago, after he was taken to the psychiatric hospital, people had said, *Didn't you know? Didn't you see any signs?* She knew what they thought: single mother, spends too much time at work, neglects her child. Of course, she had known that he was depressed and she'd tried to understand – but she couldn't help but feel angry and she still feels angry now. Because he's tried to do it once, she worries endlessly that he'll try again. A subtle form of blackmail, but infinitely powerful. He's determined to make her responsible. Except that he's better now, or at least he's swapped one form of oddness for another. Still, she should have tried to ring him over the weekend, just to check, but she was at work from nine in the morning until gone ten at night both days. He hadn't come back last night but that didn't mean anything. Often he stayed with his grandparents at the Guest House, just half a mile away.

Lara stops now for a moment beside the chest of drawers and the model of Big Ben. They had made that together, one rainy afternoon, out of cereal boxes. Jay had worked so hard at that, sticking paper on and painting. But he had cried when the pinnacle kept falling off. It is crooked again now. Suddenly Lara longs to hold him, to feel him, to help him stick the pinnacle straight and cuddle the tears away. She moves away before tears can ambush her, picks up a folder that lies on the desk. The truth is that she sometimes feels a mild nostalgia for Jay's years of depression. Of the various Jays she's lived with, Depressed Jay was perhaps the easiest to manage. A photograph drops from the folder onto the desk. It shows forearms and hands with the palms turned upwards. The arms are covered with crooked strips of lint secured by plasters. The lint is stained with patches of blood. Lara knows these photographs. Jay takes them at the hospital, where he works as a volunteer. He has hundreds of photographs like this – bald heads, emaciated limbs, stitched wounds, bedsores and close-up shots of IV lines. But this particular photograph – with those ragged bits of lint – doesn't look as though it was taken at the hospital. Lara's stomach clenches and she shoves the photograph back into the folder.

Beside it, there are piles of paper, printed off the internet. They're all about the effects of the sanctions, Hans Blix and the UN, the need for a Second Resolution, weapons of mass destruction. Yes, this is the latest thing. Since Jay came back from college he's spent most of his time in the Community Centre. That's where the protesters meet, in a cellar room, next to his grandmother's Guest House, at the back of the Church of the Good Shepherd. Making banners, writing letters, planning demonstrations and vigils. All very well, Lara thinks, if you haven't got a living to earn. On the noticeboard above the desk a leaflet about fair trade is fixed by a magnet. A yellow Post-it note is stuck on the magnet with a scribbled name – Oliver Stanmore.

Turning to the bed, Lara finds a plastic folder that contains a leaflet about the Christian Solidarity Movement. A photograph on the cover shows a man kneeling in front of a soldier who points a gun at him. Another report gives information about teams of Christian peacemakers in Palestine who stand in front of buildings that are about to be demolished. Lara puts the leaflet down. She's heard something about that over the last few days. Human shields, wasn't it? On the mantelpiece is a flattened box containing strips of cellophane, curled tinfoil. Jay's medication. He does appear to have taken this pack, at least. But still Lara isn't sure. He's quite capable of dropping the pills down a drain.

She hears his voice – *Mum, I just want to be able to be close to you.* He seems to have the idea that there's some other person inside her, the person she really is, someone who is into yoga and vegetarian cooking and world peace. And he seems to think that it's his duty to reveal that hidden person. It doesn't seem to occur to him that there is no hidden person, only her, just as she is. A single mum of thirty-eight, living in Brighton, who smokes, shops and drinks too much red wine. A woman who works as an interior designer, has an on-off affair with her boss and loves to watch bad crime programmes on television. But that doesn't mean that she doesn't want to be close to him. She has also wanted that and often, together, they have achieved that, haven't they? Perhaps only sometimes, occasionally.

*Mum, I just want our lives to be real.* What does he know about real? When Lara was not much older than Jay is now, she lived on thirty pounds a week, in one room, with a screaming baby – him. Real is to be avoided at all costs. Lara pushes the papers back into the desk. Of course, her parents will probably know where Jay is. Now there's no childcare to be arranged, Lara keeps out of their way, but Jay spends half of his life at the Guest House. But if she calls, she knows what Mollie will say. First something irrelevant such as – *If these young people had lived through the Coventry Blitz then they'd understand what war really is.* After that she'll insist she knows nothing so emphatically that Lara will feel sure she's lying. Then she will become dramatic – *Shall we call the police? Have you rung the lifeboat station?*

Lara picks up an envelope from the desk and finds a receipt for traveller's cheques. Two thousand pounds. She feels a feverish shiver pass across her skin. She puts the papers down and picks them up again. Where could Jay have got that kind of money? She knows, of course. Mollie doesn't have any money herself but that has never stopped her indulging Jay. But two thousand pounds? She remembers now that Mollie did leave a message on Saturday. *Lara, darling. You must call me, urgently. I need to speak to you now.* But everything is always urgent with Mollie.

Lara crosses the corridor, heads towards her office, stops. The copies of the proposal are climbing out of her bag. A glass of red wine hovers over a white rug. Buzz, crackle and the hard drive on the laptop expires. Her flight roars away from Gatwick and she has mysteriously failed to board it. How can she control all these things? Why do objects not stay where they are put – Jay included?

Office, she was heading to the office. Oh yes, material swatches and samples of flooring. She probably won't need those but, if the clients do want the details, then Craig will be furious if she can't produce every last swatch of curtain lining. She's worked so hard for this. She gathers the samples up and puts them on the desk, then picks up the phone and calls Mollie. She imagines her parents sitting in the basement kitchen of their tall town house, which was once the Windsor Guest House but has now subsided into housing-benefit bedsits. The phone will be lying on the floor, or lost under a pile of washing, and Mollie won't even be able to hear it because she'll be busy making tea and toast for one of her non-rent-paying tenants. Or Rufus will be ranting about the state of modern theatre. The phone rings on and on. Lara slams it down – how many times has she told her mother to get an answering machine? But then Mollie has problems remembering her age and even her own name, so what can one expect?

Lara scrolls through the numbers on her mobile and calls Jay. She hears his disembodied voice – soft and scratchy, an unmasculine voice. *Hi, this is Jay. I'm in orbit right now. I'll call you back when I pass by planet earth.* She should ring one of his friends but he doesn't really have any friends, or not ones he's allowed her to meet. In the Community Centre there are those two guys with improbable names – Spike and Wilf. Or was it Wolf? Anyway, Wilf-Wolf's been living at the Guest House for the last few months and Jay has talked about him. And that dippy woman Martha who is old enough to know better.

Lara gathers the sample boards up under her arm. She has prepared answers for every question that the clients might ask. As she walks down the stairs, she forces herself to move slowly because there's no cause for panic. Breathe, remember to breathe. The lights flicker. It must be the storm, she thinks. And then the lights go on and off again and she stops still, hearing a sound at the door. Oh, she thinks, Jay is home. But the sound stops and she's alone on the stairs, listening to the wind.

The doorbell rings and Lara looks at her watch. It's five to eight. She hurries down the stairs and asks the driver to wait. Then she runs back up, pulls on her suit and struggles to close her overnight bag. Her hand slips, her knuckles scrape against the zip and she feels the flesh tear. She hasn't finished doing her make-up. Tallow on the walls, Pointing on the ceiling, she scribbles on a note to the builders. And make sure the jade tiles are ordered today. She underlines the words several times. Maybe she'll be able to get some Darkest Nude tights in Barcelona.

# 3

# Now

## Jemmy – Brighton, January 2003

Jemmy sits back from her desk, looks at her watch. Eleven thirty, only an hour now until lunch. That's how the days are. Counting the time, waiting until the moment when you'll do this, or go there. Except there isn't any point in waiting. Around her phones ring. *Hello, Tiffany speaking, how can I help you? Hello, Monica speaking, how can I help you?* This is Jemmy's first day back at work. Swift Life Investments, Insurance and Pensions were meant to give her three months off but because she's employed on a contract they could only agree to six weeks. Still, it's better to be back at work.

Jemmy gets up and goes to get a coffee. Distant windows are streaked by dusty, January rain. As Jemmy heads back to her desk, plastic cup in hand, Tiffany pushes her chair back. As Jemmy dodges out of the way, she tries not to see Tiffany rubbing her hand over her vast bump. When is Tiffany's baby due? Rona's baby has probably already been born because she isn't in the office, and judging by the pile of post in her tray, she hasn't been in for a while. For a moment a black hole appears inside Jemmy's head and she feels a sudden dizziness, like vertigo.

Strangely the phones are quiet. That never happens on a Monday morning. And Mrs Jarvis, the Section Head, isn't around either so people push their chairs away from their desks, stretch their heads back, roll their shoulders. At the next desk Tiffany turns to Monica. Killing me ribcage.

Oh yeah it does, dun it?

And yer back?

Yeah. Monica has three children under five and is the office expert on all matters relating to babies. She has photographs of her children pinned up all over the board above her computer. Everyone has photographs like that – babies with stripy babygrows, babies propped in pushchairs under fleecy rugs, babies in the bath, bald babies with dummies in their mouths, babies playing with toy mobile phones.

Tiffany and Monica start to look through a catalogue for pushchairs.

Best to get one of those three-in-ones. Do you right through. Pram, Maxi-Cosi car seat, pushchair. How about that one? Not a bad price.

Tiffany groans and rubs her bump.

Sixty centimetres. You need to check that'll go through your door.

Yeah.

Look at this way, love, you've only another three weeks. As soon as it gets to your date, get it induced. You don't want to be hanging around, not in your state. That's what Rona did, couldn't stand it a day longer, can't say I blame her. Oh look at that little Moses basket, isn't it cute? Not very practical, though. The first load of sick down it.

Jemmy can't help but think that all this talk of pushchairs and Moses baskets is aimed at her. Aren't Monica and Tiffany talking more loudly than usual? Don't they turn their eyes towards her as soon as she looks away? The phone rings and Jemmy swivels back to her desk. *Jemmy speaking, how may I help you?* As she takes the call, she keeps an eye on the clock. Half an hour until lunch. But it'll be exactly the same afterwards. Monica and Tiffany are going over the latest redundancy gossip now. Mrs Jarvis has been overheard saying that the company are looking to lay off at least ten people – but when will it be announced? And who will go? Last in, first out, that's the fairest way.

The phones go quiet again and so Jemmy starts to surf the net. It's against the company rules but everyone does it. She types his name into Google – Jay Ravello – but the computer is running slow and nothing happens. She knows anyway – the only thing that comes up is a mention of him under Brighton Friends of the Earth. That was how she found out his address. Perhaps he'll get in touch – if he gets the message – but Jemmy doubts that Jay's mother will pass the message on. Maybe it was a mistake to go around there so early but she'd woken knowing that she needed to go, knowing that she wouldn't get through the door of the office if she hadn't at least tried to find him.

Or perhaps Jay got the message but doesn't remember who she is? After all, she never knew him. He was just a boy from college – a few years younger than her, not part of her group of friends. Everyone thought him a nerd, and girly too. He used to wander around with a notebook, claiming he was writing reports for the college magazine but no one ever saw any of the reports. The rumour was that he'd been shut up in a nut house for a while. But then there was that night he'd followed her home, when she was still wearing thick black cardigans and fingerless gloves. And she'd had those cuts on her arms, which she got from falling into barbed wire walking on the Downs, and he'd helped to patch them up.

And his hands.

But that was two years ago now, before she got married to Bill, before there was Laurie. And yet she's thought of Jay often over the last three months, very often. Sometimes she thinks she sees him – catches a glimpse of his striped scarf on a street corner, sees his curly head in a distant crowd. She talks to him in her head, explaining how her life is now, knowing that he would understand. (Here I am back at work, Jay, and I just thought when I came in this morning that maybe there'd be flowers on my desk, or even a card. Or I just thought someone might mention his name. But no one said anything at all. Silence and silence and silence. And so then I start to think that maybe nothing happened because if everyone else thinks nothing happened then maybe they could be right?)

She types Jay's name into Google again, the computer whirrs and rumbles and a list of websites appears. His name is mentioned in the *Daily Mail*. Something to do with double-decker buses – but that can't be the same person? Jemmy is about to click on the article when the red button lights up. *Good morning, Jemmy speaking, how can I help you? Just let me bring that up on the screen.* Mr Adam Giadini in Maida Vale. She imagines someone who works in the media and wears a flowered shirt. Yes, the payment reached us on the twentieth of this month.

Perhaps she should go around and see Jay's grandma? He used to talk about her all the time and Jemmy knows where she lives – in that fallen-down Guest House on Monmouth Street with a rainbow flag, plastic windmills stuck along the railings, plants growing in wellington boots, grass pushing up between the paving of the front steps.

*Good morning, Jemmy speaking, how can I help you?*

I'd like to see your cunt.

Jemmy takes a deep breath. You'd never believe how many perverts there are out there. Two or three ring every day. Once a caller started telling her about having sex with a roast chicken. She keeps her voice firm and even. *I'm afraid I can't continue this conversation so I'm going to put the phone down.* That's what they tell you in the training. You can put the phone down but you have to warn the caller first.

As Jemmy cuts the caller off, she's aware of movement behind her. She turns around to see Rona coming across the office carrying a Maxi-Cosi. As she looks up, she feels people's eyes swivel towards her like searching flashlights. For a moment she is illuminated – exposed, startled – then the lights turn and drift away. Everyone crowds around Rona and the Maxi-Cosi. Rona kisses Tiffany and starts to open a present wrapped in white paper scattered with pink and blue hearts. She pulls out a tiny babygrow made of pale blue towelling with a train stitched on it. Monica is undoing the straps of the car seat ready to lift the baby out. Jemmy feels her throat tighten and a buzz of panic starts in her head.

She edges away through the desks in the mortgage section and heads for the kitchen. Once there she makes herself a cup of coffee although she doesn't want one. She's fighting with tears, tipping her head back to stop them falling, trying to keep herself calm. She catches sight of her face in a mirror. It seems so strange that she looks just the same. How can that be when she feels as though she's been shot full of holes? A gust of drain-smelling air, rising up from the sink, pushes her stomach up into her ribcage. Why are there so many smells everywhere? Each of them distinct and vicious. Two other women whose names she can't remember come into the kitchen.

Cute, isn't he? Seems the placid type – even then, shocking hard work.

Jemmy stares at the noticeboard. Scraps of paper advertise flats to let, a washing machine free to anyone who will take it away, acupuncture, a bingo evening, finding inner peace. A notice signed by Mrs Jarvis reminds everyone that biscuits are a privilege and will be withdrawn if the kitchen isn't kept tidy. If only someone would say his name. When she arrived this morning Mrs Jarvis did come over and say a brisk good morning but she didn't say, *I'm sorry.* Or, *It must be hard for you.* Instead she said, *The section is under pressure at the moment so it's particularly important for everyone to meet their targets.* Not even Bill says his name. Laurence. Laurie. Instead he says, *Fancy going out for a drink tonight?* Because he's got no idea what else to say. In theory, grief is meant to bring people closer together but that has turned out to be a myth.

Jemmy isn't sure whether she will be able to do this again tomorrow. Bill had wanted her to stay at home for longer but they needed the money and she didn't know what to do with herself at home. She'd been surprised to find herself all on her own. She'd had friends at college but most of them had left Brighton now and she forgot to keep in touch with people after she met Bill. People didn't understand her getting married – *What, married? Now? But you're only twenty-two.* They couldn't understand the pregnancy either and now – well, now – she's adrift, attached to nothing at all, floating, so far away from the shore that no communication is possible. Other people want to talk about clubs and rap and hair mousse and mobile phones that can take photographs. And that guy who used to be on the media course who is just l-u-u-sh. Jemmy wants to talk about death.

As she walks back to her desk, head down, she hears Rona's baby utter a tiny, twisted cry. She dives at her phone and picks up a call. *Good afternoon, Jemmy speaking, how can I help you?* Her shoulders are hunched, her face pressed close to the screen. *Sorry, sorry, can you say that again? Sorry, a slight problem with the computer. Oh yes, sorry, you did say the Premium Policy, didn't you? Yes, just give me a minute, I'm looking at the wrong screen. Sorry, can you give me the policy number again?*

The hands on the clock finally click to twelve thirty. Jemmy snatches her coat and bag and hurries towards the lift. But Tiffany is there and Monica and Rona with the baby. She was sure Rona had gone home – but no. Jemmy walks towards them with her face burning. Every light fitting, every pot plant, every computer screen, every picture of a smiling baby pinned on a board – everything is watching her. She curls up inside herself but keeps walking. (The truth is, Jay, that they've always thought I'm odd. A weird Indian kid with a stud in her nose and too much hair. Most of them are ten or twenty years older than me and they'll be doing this job, or something similar, for the rest of their lives. Whereas I only took the job to get a bit of money so that I could set up my own textile business. You remember I was going to do that? And I will still do it, sometime, although it won't be the same now.)

Now the gaggle of women at the lift are chastened. They do know what happened but they just don't know what to say. (Jay, if only you were here you'd understand. I just want someone to say Laurie's name. That's all that I want. Please, please someone say his name.) Other people are crowding towards the lift but Tiffany, Monica and Rona hang back and say goodbye to her guiltily. *Good to have you back again,* they nod and smile. They say that now but they didn't say it this morning.

You go on down, Jemmy says. Go on. And they all step into the lift. But some of the men from Mortgages have come up behind Jemmy and they don't understand why she isn't moving.

Come on, love, there's room for one more.

No, Jemmy says, I'll wait. You go.

But the men are determined to be polite. Come on love, squeeze in. Room for a little one here. They jostle and laugh. An opportunity to get to know each other better.

No, Jemmy says. No. But she's hustled into the lift. Tiffany has her head turned away and is recounting the story of a friend's labour. *Nightmare, absolute nightmare. Had to stitch her up from the nape of her neck right round to her chin.* Jemmy finds herself pressed against that bulging stomach. Tiffany turns her head, notices Jemmy, looks away again. The lift fills with a tight and itchy silence. Jemmy is conscious of the baby inside that bump, just an inch away. A live baby, all curled up there, ready to be born, ready to cry out with that piercing, mournful, newborn cry. The lift stops at the third floor. More people push in. Jemmy is close to the Maxi-Cosi now. She can see the white cotton blanket, the tiny sleeping face.

The lift has dropped straight down its shaft. The baby looks so like Laurie. Exactly the same. (Jay, if only you could have seen him. You would understand. I know you would. But what was it that happened then? That one night and then I was well but I've never known how or why.) The lift clanks and hisses down towards the centre of the earth. Jemmy feels sweat sticking her T-shirt to her back and she struggles to draw breath.

The baby starts a grisly, spluttering cry which soon rises to a note of shrill anguish. Jemmy ducks her head, grits her teeth, presses her eyes shut. (Exactly the same, Jay, exactly the same. Because Laurie looked like every other newborn baby – smaller but absolutely complete. All of him tiny and perfect – fingers, toes, lips, eyelids, his ribs spread like a fan, his head as round and smooth as a billiard ball. And he was all curled up and sleeping, just as Rona's baby is. And it wasn't possible to understand – it wasn't possible at all – to understand why – because he looked exactly the same.)

# 4

# Now

## Mollie – Brighton, January 2003

A bitter cold morning but bright enough. La-la-la-la, Mollie sings as she goes upstairs to get dressed. Should she wear the pink court shoes or the wedge-heel boots? Best to leave Lara alone for a while, let her calm down. It *is* upsetting, of course, but Jay is twenty and he's got to lead his own life. At least he *cares*, at least he's taking responsibility – which is a good deal more than can be said for most people of his age.

Mollie and Rufus live in a flat at the top of the Guest House, nearly eighty stairs up, but Mollie's always liked the views from up here, the jumble of roofs and aerials, the crooked chimneys and somewhere beyond – the sea. Not that it's possible to catch a glimpse of it but you can feel it. Definitely. In her bedroom, Mollie takes a bottle of whisky from the windowsill, pours some into a tooth mug, and drinks it down. Good for the creaking joints, these cold mornings.

Mollie would never say so to Lara but she'd enjoyed going to see the buses off. Vintage buses they were, Routemaster '67s, owned by such a cheery man and good-looking too – the kind Mollie might have fancied for herself if she'd been the age for all that. And even though the weather was pitifully cold, still it was like a carnival with singing, a band, lots of people from the papers and all those dirty-looking young people with their dreadlocks, studs, tattoos and guitars. Bunting and anti-war banners everywhere and a bubbling feeling of hope. A lovely old man was reading the poems of Gerard Manley Hopkins and wept as he got onto the bus. More like people setting off for a day trip to the seaside rather than a war. Stupid, really, but you couldn't help but feel quite tearful at the courage of it all.

Mollie puts on her black velvet dress with the white collar and cuffs and pulls the pink court shoes out from under the bed. Hey-ho, the wind and the rain. Standing stork-like on one leg, she pushes her foot into fishnet tights. This is one of the things she's learnt in life. In difficult times – and times do always seem to be difficult – make sure to dress up absolutely your smartest. In ten minutes she's off to London, going to see one of Rufus's rehearsals and then drive him home. Poor soul, he's stayed with Baggers up in town the last two nights, can't get the train back because his back is stabbing pains every time he moves even an inch. Mollie pours more whisky into the tooth mug and swigs it down.

She's worried about Rufus. He's given up drink and that's never a good sign. Ah well, it's unlikely to last, never has before. Just let's hope that bloody car starts. If it doesn't then she'll have to take Rufus's Daimler. Had it for more than forty years now, ever since they first met. Worth a fortune now. Mollie's scared senseless to drive it in the rushing and hooting London traffic because he'll kill her if it gets scratched. When she gets back she must get on with sorting out the flat in Roma Street. The tenants there have left and she needs to get it cleaned up before she can let it again. Always the same, always too much to do.

La-la-la-la. Mollie wraps a feather boa around her neck and heads back down the endless stairs, passing Mr Lambert on the third floor, and next door to him, Wilf and the shuffling Chinese whose name Mollie has never really grasped. On the next floor down, there's Stan and Stan and Stan, the Polish builders who are away in Croydon this week. And Ahmed, from Iraq, who washes up in a hotel when he's not campaigning against the war. Mollie met him in the park, sitting on a bench and she had to give him a room because where he was living, in Brunt's Court, they called him a fucking Paki and posted dog muck through his letter box. Mollie tries her best to take care of him although it's difficult given he's so very quiet and so painfully polite. His room, as she passes the door, smells of cheap aftershave and something else. Loss? Despair? Do such things smell?

As Mollie descends the stairs to the basement kitchen – take care in those toe-pinching shoes – she takes a few deep breaths. Remember that lightning rods play an important role in storms, she says to herself. But Lara's anger has subsided and she's sitting at the kitchen table writing things in a notebook. A beautiful coat, she's wearing, Mollie thinks. Slate-grey sheepskin. Must have cost hundreds of pounds, that. Hopefully she'll tire of it soon, Mollie thinks, then maybe she'll pass it on to me, although I'll have to chop the bottom off.

I need to speak to the Foreign Office, Lara says. And I need to find a way to contact Jay.

Yes, dear, but I don't think there *is* any way.

Don't be ridiculous. There must be – but I've got to go to Barcelona again today. When I'm back, I'll go up to London and talk to the people who organised this stupid escapade and I'll ring the Foreign Office or a lawyer.

Mollie can't help but feel a pang of pity for those whom Lara intends to contact. And no good will come of it. Like father, like daughter. Both of them antagonise, arouse suspicion. The worst motives will always be attributed to them, no one will ever give them the benefit of the doubt. Ah well.

And you, Lara says. What you need to do is to go around to the Community Centre and speak to – whatever his name is – the one who lives upstairs.

Well, I would do, dear, but I've got to go to London.

Mum.

To help your father. This new play's got a very short rehearsal period.

Mum. For God's sake.

Yes, I know, dear.

Reaching for the teapot, Mollie knocks a saucer onto the floor. It goes down with a bang but doesn't smash and she reaches to pick it up. Of course, all of the vile things Lara says about her father are absolutely true but Rufus is a man with a creative vision and you've got to have some respect for that.

Mum, are you listening to me? This isn't about Dad and a play. It's about real life. It's about your grandson and the fact that...

No, love. No. Just calm down and let me get you some tea. The buses and all that, it's just a publicity stunt. There isn't going to be a war – of course there isn't. That Tony Blair isn't such a fool – but he's got to pretend because of Bush. And anyway, they'll never let those buses into Iraq. Listen, love, I'm sorry. I just wish I had a bit more time. Why don't you come around for supper tonight and then we can have a good chat and sort things out?

Lara is pacing the kitchen again now. She's taken off her gloves and Mollie can see the livid red of her knuckles and fingers where her skin has peeled. Mollie blames it on the job. Rush, rush, rush. Mobile phones, computers, websites, secretaries, proposals, clients, flights to catch. Lara looks exhausted all the time. And she doesn't look after herself properly, she could look so much better than she does. Although it's always been hard on her, Mollie thinks, that she inherited Rufus's looks rather than mine.

Who is Oliver Stanmore? Is he the vicar?

No, not the vicar but – well, now you come to ask, I don't exactly know. Would he be the churchwarden? Or some sort of caretaker for the Community Centre?

No. What I'm saying is...

But he would certainly be a good person to talk to. He would pray for Jay, I'm sure, and you know prayer can achieve great things. Apparently Mr Stanmore has cured people with terminal cancer.

No. I'm saying – do you think he persuaded Jay to go to Iraq?

No, dear. No. I don't think anyone did.

La-la-la-la, Mollie sings to herself. She finishes making tea for Mr Lambert – piles causing agony, or so he claims, skiving old hypochondriac – and pours a cup for Lara, taking care not to listen to what she's saying. Blaming Spike and Wilf and the other peace protesters when they're good sorts really. Mollie goes around to the Community Centre – it's at the back of the church, not a hundred yards from the house – most days, takes them some cakes and sandwiches. And after Jay got involved in the campaign, she was there even more, making banners, writing letters to MPs, making a giant papier-mâché model of George Bush which was meant to be burnt in front of the Houses of Parliament but the flour paste didn't dry so he wouldn't light. Ah well. You've got to do your bit.

Mind you, it's all different nowadays with the technology they've got. Very unreliable, those computers, it seems. All those young people in that office talking to her about the evils of mankind, as though she hasn't lived long enough to know plenty about that. Suez, Vietnam, Afghanistan – she marched for them all, not that it made a blind bit of difference, although she doesn't say that to them, of course. Warmongering men – you can't stop them. Not enough competitive sport and not enough women doing their marital duty. Sex on every billboard and breasts on the television every time you switch on. But not many people having a good old-fashioned screw, when you get down to it.

Just popping up to take this tray for Mr Lambert, Mollie says, and heads for the stairs. La-la-la-la. Usually Mollie would have a chat with Mr Lambert but this morning she keeps things brisk and heads back downstairs. God knows why she's dragging trays upstairs to the likes of him, grumpy old queer that he is, and hasn't paid the rent in months. But he did help her to put the ceiling in the second-floor bathroom back up. Quite a double act, they were, with the bucket and the plaster, swinging around on the ladder, high up near the ceiling. Then painting it all over, lumpy as it was, and toasted teacake and a glass of whisky to finish. So she might as well get him breakfast as a bit of a thank you. She used to get breakfast for twenty or more every day but she can't do it any more. And there isn't the business. Newer smarter places opening up all the time and everyone expecting en suite and a television in the room.

When Mollie arrives back in the kitchen Lara's anger has turned to despair. I just don't understand how he can do this to me. I can't believe he would do something so stupid. I mean, why would he do this?

Mollie lays Rufus's shirt out on the board and puts the iron on, says nothing. Over the years she's had plenty of practice at dealing with Lara. Just ride the levels, as the surfers say, and try not to take too much notice. And Mollie can do that most of the time – but not when Lara starts criticising Jay.

You know Jay is very intelligent. You can be sure he would have thought it all through, she says.

Mum, don't be ridiculous. Of course Jay hasn't thought this through. He never thinks anything through. He's irresponsible and unbalanced. That doctor said he could be bipolar, or even schizophrenic. He's meant to be on medication. A boy in his condition can't go to Iraq.

Mollie fizzes steam from the iron and noses the point of it between the shirt buttons. How dare Lara say that? Jay isn't mentally ill. He's just different, that's all. Doctors want to label it manic depression, or schizophrenia, but maybe it's just goodness. It's so hard, so very hard. The hatred, the opposition, the manipulation that people meet with when they're just trying to do the right thing.

All this is just attention-seeking, Lara says.

Mollie takes a deep breath, presses the iron down hard. Best to keep the peace with Lara, that's what she's worked out over the years. After all, Mollie already has Rufus to deal with and it's never wise to fight on more than one front at the same time. But attention-seeking?

No, love. No. Jay may be young and idealistic and perhaps he does get confused but he knows what's right and wrong – and what more does he need to know? In my generation people knew how to make sacrifices, and many of them sacrificed their lives. Your own grandfather, his regiment herded into a barn near Dunkirk and shot. Now you can't even persuade people not to buy

Nestlé coffee even though they know about those mothers in the Third World not breastfeeding their babies.

Mum, listen. Listen. I'm not saying he can't do something to help. He could volunteer in the local Oxfam shop.

I don't think—

Or spend more time at the hospital, if that's what he wants. But why is he doing this? And why now?

La-la-la-la, Mollie sings inside her head. Of course, it isn't just Lara, it's all the women of the new generation. What did feminism achieve? A woman's right to scented candles, pedicures and a psychotherapist. Mollie wonders whether she should take some sandwiches with her and a flask of tea. Bound to be quite a lot of waiting around. Would Rufus like corned beef? That's really all she has in.

Oh because I'm such a bad mother. Because I threw him out of the house.

I didn't say that – but you did tell him he'd have to move out.

Well, yes. But not to Iraq.

Mollie smells burning and pulls the iron away from the shirt.

People of his age are very sensitive, she says. He, in particular, is very sensitive. He was upset. I mean, *you* may have wanted to go to university but he never did. He came around here in floods of tears, bless him. And then as luck would have it your father had a go as well. Honestly, I could have whacked him over the head with a brick – ranting and raving about how people protesting against the war are supporting Saddam Hussein, when only a week ago I heard him saying to Baggers that they should be marching. But that's how he is, isn't he? But Jay can't see, takes it all personally.

Oh right. Fine. So it's Dad's fault and it's my fault?

No. That's not what—

And you won't do anything to help me get Jay back?

Lara, he'll be back in no time. Those buses didn't look fit to go to Catford, let alone Iraq. But, of course, you're worried – and I am too and I'm available later today. In fact, I thought – well, there's old Bobby Marsden, you know, and his son works for one of the big American newspapers. Your father worked with Bobby at the Sheffield Crucible – oh, 1975 it would have been, in *Hamlet* where that poor girl who played Ophelia really did finish up banged up in the local mental hospital.

Mum, I don't want to hear about you and Dad at the Sheffield Crucible in 1975 – OK? For Christ's sake, Jay is vulnerable and confused. Things happen to Jay – you know that. But you just don't want to see it, do you? Here you are doing your fluffy mother act. *And at least I reminded him to pack a hat and some sun cream.* But a war might be going to start and people will die.

Lara, don't tell me about death. Perhaps you don't remember that I lived through the Coventry Blitz – people with their lungs blown out and a dog running down the street with a child's arm in its mouth.

Fine, Lara says. Well, if you want to spend your time talking about something which happened sixty years ago, which you can't even remember anyway, then you do that. I'm going to bring my son home. I had hoped you would help me. But since I'm obviously mistaken, I'll go around to the Stop The War office myself.

Lara goes to the door and then turns back.

But you be sure to get in touch if you hear anything.

She picks up her coat and bag, marches towards the kitchen door. Mollie watches her as she stamps away up the area steps, her head disappearing first, then her bag and finally her sheer tights and office shoes. Let her go, Mollie thinks. Let her strike out on her own – yet again. It won't last long, she'll soon be back. Mollie draws herself up tall, feels a sudden surge of energy. The times they are a-changing and the worms they are a-turning. *If you hear anything* – because Lara knows, of course, that when Jay rings he'll call her rather than Lara. And Lara will never ask herself why that is. Maybe she actually doesn't know because she wasn't there. She didn't see the child standing over there at the window staring up the area steps. *Will Mummy be home soon? When will she be back? When?*

For a moment she thinks of Jay, remembers his face as he stood by the bus. He'd hugged her until her feet came off the ground. She can smell him still, and feel him, loose and bony, pressed against her old, stiff bones. He'd looked so young, wearing those falling-down trousers and his jacket all torn.

Mollie looks at her watch. Hell's bells, she should have left half an hour ago. Pulling on her velvet coat, she takes a bottle of perfume from the back of the draining board, sprays herself. The cats do smell. Perhaps she should have worn those wedge-heel boots. These shoes are shockingly hard on the corns, but she's not having the cast of the play thinking that Rufus is married to some old crone.

Looking in the mirror, her eyes widen, shocked, as she sees the stranger staring back at her. Who is that old woman with watery eyes and a sagging jawline? Mollie still expects to see one of her other selves. Perhaps Mollie Fawcett – Worcester schoolgirl, going to see Ludo for that first audition, hurrying through the cramped streets near the canal, with rain lashing down, water gathering in the gutter of her school hat and that wretched school satchel banging against her hip. Or perhaps Mollie Mayeford, that woman she invented, stepping out of the stage door, with a diamond-glinting smile and a fox fur, tiny teeth and glass eyes shining, wrapped about her neck. Where are those people now? Gone, gone and forgotten. Ah well. Old age has got much to recommend it when you consider the alternatives.

# 5

## BEFORE

### Bertie – Worcester, April 1941

Bertie Fawcett drums his fingers on the varnished mahogany of the bar. The barman wears a stained apron and his chilblained fingers fumble – doubtless some poor old chap called out of retirement now all the young men have gone. The bar smells of hair oil, coal smoke, wet wool. In a distant corner, under the leaves of a crooked palm, a gramophone turns, scratchily playing some jazz tune. The Feathers Hotel is just in front of Foregate Street Station and, as a train pulls in, the bottles and glasses lined up on their mirrored shelves shiver and the gramophone stutters. Bertie drums his fingers once again.

A good day at the Works – signed a government contract for aircraft parts worth more than ten thousand pounds. The war provides many opportunities. Where is that drink? The hotel lounge has a claret carpet and matching velvet chairs, their arms worn through to the thread, stuffing bulging out. Brass lamps glimmer along the oak-panelled walls and lace mats float in the middle of low tables. An elderly man sneezes behind a newspaper, snorts and coughs up phlegm. Bertie often comes to the hotel for a drink after work now he's alone. Later he'll eat cutlets and boiled potatoes cooked by his housekeeper and then deal with some paperwork – the building contract for the extension to the Cottage Homes for orphaned children, one of his charitable hobbies.

Finally the elderly barman, using two shaking hands, places Bertie's bourbon on the bar. Bertie takes a sip, turns to find himself a seat. Seen through the glass of the revolving doors, the street is blurred grey and the rain is beating down. A stately black car rolls past and shadowy figures skitter along the pavement, gripping bucking umbrellas. Only quarter of an hour now until the blackout. Bertie feels the bourbon spread through his veins. The man behind the newspaper rattles phlegm in his chest and the bottles behind the bar tremble as another train passes. A porter with a coal scuttle builds up the smouldering fire.

The revolving door swings around and a young woman comes in, pulling a tiny child behind her. Her brown brimmed hat is dripping wet and her crocodile-skin suitcase sticks against the turning door. She tugs at the suitcase as though her life depends on getting it into the hotel. The fur coat she's wearing looks as though it must once have belonged to some much shorter woman but it's an elegant coat, with a high collar and wide sleeves. She's damp and dishevelled, exhausted and tearful, her hat and the shoulders of her coat smeared with wet plaster dust. One sees people like this often now. Victims of the bombs, waifs and strays with no place to go.

Bertie watches as she stops, hesitates. The suitcase looks brand new and must have cost a fair penny. Despite the dripping hat and the plaster dust, she draws the eye. She's much more beautiful than Deirdre ever was. She, poor soul, was good-looking when Bertie first met her but she'd faded so fast. Thank goodness she didn't live to see the war. He hears a mention of Coventry and shuts his eyes, taking care not to think. The show started there again last night. There had been talk of it at the Works. A deliveryman had seen it as far away as Kenilworth. Once again the horizon burning red as a hot coal – God save their souls. It's hard to imagine that there can be anything left there to bomb.

Bertie watches the woman as she sits down, pulls the tiny girl down beside her, keeps the suitcase close. She has a beautiful face, he thinks, strong and fine but also veiled and private. Despite the disorder of her hair and clothes, she manages to appear neat and precise in a way that is infinitely satisfying. Perhaps she is not so much beautiful as well-designed? Under the low lamps, he sees her fingers fumble in her purse. She pulls out identity cards. The child leans against her legs, clinging, unstable. In her hand she grips a dirty toy dog.

Idly Bertie thinks of his home – the sleek white house on Langley Crescent, one of the finest houses in Worcester, bought with his own money, all of it made himself. A house perched on the hill, with a view over to the cathedral and the Malvern Hills. And at the front a wide terrace, sloping lawns, terraced beds, a line of trees hiding the road below. He can see the woman there, in his house, sitting on a white iron garden chair on the terrace, or walking in through the French windows, standing beside the marble fireplace in the sitting room, the delicate tilt of her head, the slow upward curve of her lips, reflected in the tall gilt mirror above the mantelpiece.

And a child as well. Bertie feels that old, jagged ache. Deirdre was too ill, of course, and he couldn't put her health at risk but he hears the laughter of those shadow children sometimes – children who leave their toy skittles in the hall and their tiny shoes, wet from the garden, at the back door. Other men want sons but he's always wanted a daughter. The face of this little girl makes him think of a coral necklace that he bought for Deirdre once when they were on holiday in Capri. Pale and intricate as a miniature garland of flowers. So very fragile to look at – and yet impossible to break.

He thinks of the things he could buy for this mother and child, once the war is over. Whatever he wants he can afford, order it from abroad if it isn't available here. Pink and white bedroom furniture for the child and shoes for the mother, something to replace those delicate kid slippers, entirely ruined by dirt and rain. Another train passes and, just for a moment, the lights dim. On the gramophone the record jumps as a porter passes.

At the reception desk there seems to be some difficulty. Voices are raised and Bertie understands that soon the woman will cry. He stands up, moves towards her. The man at the reception desk – skin stretched tightly over the jutting bones of his face – looks down at the pristine buff-coloured card that the woman holds in her hand. *National Registration Identity Card.* That man, Maurice Heaton, damn him. Dry little pedant, charmless. Bertie moves closer. He knows the manager of the hotel, will be able to sort out any difficulties.

Born in November? Five months? The reception man stares at the child.

Sorry. Sorry. Wrong card.

The woman raises her chin, produces another card, this one scuffed and creased.

Mollie Mayeford? But *your* card says Bunton.

My friend's child.

Bertie knows his moment has arrived, dusts dandruff from the lapels of his overcoat and does up his buttons to hide the curve of his stomach, swoops.

Everything all right, Heaton?

Yes, sir. Only—

Friend of mine, no need to worry. Drink, my dear?

Yes, please. How kind. The woman's face is fixed into a desperate smile but she plays her part well, pushes all the papers away into her purse, follows Bertie towards the velvet armchairs, the low tables. Her eyes move briefly around the room but then settle on the floor, as though she can't trust herself to see too much.

Bertie Fawcett, he says and stretches out his hand.

She raises her face to him and he sees terror. His eyes run over her, taking in the smoothness of her calves, like turned wood, the dark hair which has fallen down under her hat, the firm, smooth line of jaw and chin. Briefly she puts her tiny, cold hand in his. He indicates a chair and, as she sits, a flicker passes through him as he understands that this woman will not be like the others. She will not be a question of a few drinks, a generous present or two, a dinner and a goodnight kiss.

A train comes into the station behind the hotel. Even here – in the sealed space of this hotel bar – it seems as though they feel the displacement of air, the hiss and rattle of the engine, the slamming of the doors. The woman stares around, reaches a hand out towards the threadbare arm of the velvet chair. Her tongue runs over dry lips. Her eyes are searching for something, spinning from the mirrored glass shelves, to the dusty palm, the hotel reception desk, the revolving door.

You have to be careful, she says. There are many buildings which appear to be stable but then there is bomb damage.

She stops, smiles brightly, as though this is all some hilarious joke.

Bertie smiles, agrees with her that one must take care. Then asks her, gently, whether he might buy her a drink. She's like a small animal, hesitant, the beating of her heart so violent that he imagines he can hear it. She looks up at him, her eyes bright blue and blank. Her cheeks are oddly flushed and the whites of her eyes flash as though she has a fever. She agrees that she would like a drink. A whisky, if they have one. Bertie goes to the bar to order. The barman is quick this time, as though he knows how important this is. He puts the whisky on a miniature silver tray, with a white napkin beside it. As Bertie walks back towards the woman, he feels the air light beneath his feet. Of course, she's too young for him and too pretty but her situation is desperate and Bertie isn't a man who fails to grasp an opportunity.

He sits down beside the woman and places the whisky on the low table in front of her. She says thank you but then is silent. He had hoped she might initiate some conversation but she continues to stare at her hands. The bar is suddenly filled with a sound like a sudden gust of wind as a train pulls into the station. The woman seizes the child, disappears into the collar of her coat, squeezes her eyes tightly shut.

A train, Bertie says. A train.

The woman sits up straighter, stares around her.

You know many buildings appear to be stable but they aren't.

Bertie is uncertain how to reply to this.

The child wraps her toy dog in the lace mat on the table.

Don't, her mother says.

The child snatches her hand away, shivers. She has the same black hair as her mother's and it is swept to one side, held with a scrap of red ribbon which must once have been tied in a bow but now hangs loose. Her coat is blue tweed and worn at the sleeves but she wears it with pride. Her mouth is broad, her lips full. The face is too savage for prettiness, too brazen for beauty. She has the same gaze as her mother but without the veil, without the fear. She watches Bertie with shamelessly determined eyes, daring him to speak.

Bertie asks the woman her name. She looks up at him and her eyes are full of confusion. Something has gone wrong, badly wrong. He thinks briefly of her fingers fumbling with the identity cards, the mumbled story of a friend's child. But he doesn't want to know, is more than ready to understand her as the woman she wishes to be. Eventually she speaks, her voice almost a whisper. Violet, she says. Violet Bunton.

The girl pulls at the too-short sleeve of her mother's fur. The woman – Violet – pushes the child back from her. The gesture is strangely brusque but Bertie understands that the woman is frightened that the child might be judged as badly behaved.

The child has no such concerns and tugs at her mother's sleeve again. Violet is sleeping, she says. The woman looks up, shrugs. It looks as though she might burst into tears but then she laughs too loudly, a sudden, high-pitched mirthless giggle.

Bertie laughs loudly as well since that's the only way of making her behaviour seem natural. He leans over, picks up the glass of whisky, hands it to the woman, noticing the pitiful smallness of her hands, their secrecy. It looks to me, he says, as though Violet hasn't had a good night's sleep in a long time. It looks to me as though that's what she needs. That – and a hot bath and a good dinner. Wouldn't you say? He addresses this to the child, although she has lost interest in the conversation and is folding and re-folding the napkin on the tray. Briefly he watches the movements of her tiny, creased hands. That old jagged ache. He wants her as much as the woman.

Violet takes a sip of the whisky and smiles uncertainly. Bertie settles himself into his chair. Don't worry in the least about finding a room. They may have said they're fully booked but I know the manager here. I'll make sure something is organised.

Thank you, she says.

Bertie drains his glass, feeling again the flush of the bourbon as it settles in his veins. Ah, so I have her now, he thinks, even though he knows the game is only just beginning. She's too proud and too clever to surrender easily and Bertie is glad of that. But still it's only a matter of time – and he will enjoy every minute. Violet. Perhaps that isn't really her name? But no matter, Bertie has always liked that name. Violets are one of his favourite flowers. The steeply sloping front lawn of 48 Langley Crescent is thick with them in spring.

# 6

# Now

## Lara – Brighton, February 2003

The builders didn't turn up on Thursday or Friday last week. No phone call, no apology, nothing. Lara wonders if they've been today. As she enters the flat, plaster crunches beneath her feet and a breath of icy air blows into her face. Flicking on the hall light, she sees that the kitchen window is swinging out into the creaking night wind. Rain has blown onto the new work surface and the freshly painted wall above the new cooker. She catches hold of the swinging window, slams it shut. Will the rain have marked her new work surface? Damn the builders. She turns, pushes open the sitting-room door and finds two bags of cement propped against the wall. A map of Europe, which was spread out on her desk, has slipped to the floor.

It's a week since Jay left but that week has felt like walking through glue. She picks up the map and wonders where he is. The buses split up in Paris, some heading down to Italy and some taking a detour via Amsterdam and Germany. Apparently the German bus stopped off at Dachau, as though the peace protesters, not content with taking on the sorrows of modern Iraq, also felt the need to take on the historic trauma of the Jews. Lara hasn't even been able to find out which of the buses Jay is on. Her desk is scattered with papers listing telephone numbers – the Iraqi Embassy, the Foreign Office, lawyers, MPs. She pushes them aside now, goes to the kitchen and pours herself a large glass of white wine – what else is there to do?

She's on a nine o'clock plane to Barcelona tomorrow and she's hopelessly behind with preparations. Breathe, remember to breathe. She pulls the floor-length white curtains across the bay window, shutting out the swirling trees in the square and the glitter-sprinkle of the town lights. If it was just floor plans that she needed to take to Barcelona then that wouldn't be a problem but no one who is anyone in the world of interior design uses floor plans now. Instead they use a new computer programme called Room Space which enables the creation of a three-dimensional space, one which can be adjusted endlessly. Lighten the colour of the carpet, substitute curtains for blinds, change the position of the fireplace or the pictures. In the office Kylie, Sarah and Shuna – all in their twenties with flamingo-like legs, ballet pump shoes, thin jewelled belts – can all work the programme with a few flicks of their pale pink nails. Lara, who is so much more senior, pretends she can as well but, despite a three-day training course, she can't. Surely thirty-eight is too early to become obsolete?

The answer machine blinks green, showing that three messages are waiting. The first is from her friend Annabel. *Good news*, the disembodied voice shrieks. *You know that blue silk dress you liked in Maya-Maya? Well, it's reduced now by forty per cent. So I thought that we—*. Lara wipes the message. The next two messages are from journalists. The press are interested in Jay because he's the youngest of the peace protesters and because he's Rufus's grandson. The journalists' voices wheedle. *Miss Ravello. Miss Ravello.* Lara has never liked the name Ravello, never feels that it belongs to her, which is not surprising because it's the stage name Rufus invented at the beginning of his career. He wanted to be thought Italian. Tricky when you have red hair and are over six foot tall. But then it's better than Nigel Dalking, which is his real name. Dalking – a town south of London, or an illicit sexual activity?

Laura plugs the computer into the phone line and it burbles and squeaks as it tries to connect. She needs to start on Room Space straight away but she can't stop herself checking her email first. Various messages have arrived from others who have relatives on those buses. A wife from north London, a sister from Illinois, a friend from Sydney, a family in Ghent worrying about a grandfather who left without his neck brace. Lara reads these messages as they circulate. Clearly these relatives actually receive news, calls, emails. Lara has posted messages asking for news of Jay but no one has heard anything. Something about the chatty, positive tone of the messages leaves her feeling cold. She has no wish to be part of this jolly little group, who, like Mollie, seem to have mistaken this Iraq fiasco for a day trip to the sea.

Also many of these relatives seem to actually support the peace protesters. Lara doesn't and won't. She moves the mouse to open the first of the messages. But just as she does so a message arrives from Alan at Truth, Justice, Peace – Human Shields Action to Iraq. Doesn't that name say it all? Lara takes two large gulps of wine, opens the email.

*Dear Collaborators and Colleagues,*

*We have received news that both buses arrived at the rendezvous point just south of Rome. However, one of the buses has now broken down. I spoke to Ken by phone and he also adds that one group of peace protesters have decided to go home – however, Ken is glad that they're going as they aren't committed to our cause. Attempts are being made to fix the bus, something to do with the starter motor maybe, and it's hoped that the convoy will move on soon. I will let all you good people and supporters of our movement know as soon as there is more news. Yours in Truth, Justice and Peace – Alan*

Maybe Jay is among the people who have decided to come home? Someone must know who those people are. Lara grabs her list of phone numbers and rings the Stop The War office in London. No answer. Then she rings the phone in the peace protest office in the basement of the Community Centre. Engaged. Then she rings Mollie. No answer. Lara reads the email again, goes to the kitchen and pours more wine. She tries to ring Alan but, as always, his phone is engaged.

Alan is supposedly responsible for press and communications in the UK. Lara has called him repeatedly since Jay left but she's only managed to speak to him three times and he doesn't respond to her messages. A retired librarian from Southend, Alan is apparently reasonable, considerate, professional – but Lara knows that deep down Alan is a man enjoying his moment in the media spotlight, a man indulging some fantasy of the nerve centre, the clandestine operation, the tiny group of heroic individuals standing against the great tides of history – and she hates him with a passion.

She wanders up and down the hall, into her bedroom and out again, lights a cigarette. It's not the prospect of war that's frightening, because everyone knows it won't come to that, but if those buses do go into Iraq then anything could happen to their passengers. A dull bleep sounds. Lara pushes her hand into the pocket of a duffel coat which hangs on the coat rack. Jay's mobile phone. Gripping it tightly, she takes a drag on her cigarette. So all those calls she made to him have been going nowhere except to a mobile phone a few feet away across the hall. But there's more. Her hand goes back into the pocket and pulls out a flattened box, containing cellophane strips of pills. The drugs which the doctor prescribed and which Jay promised he would take regularly.

Lara picks up her coat and bag. The peace protesters in the Community Centre deny any knowledge of Jay's departure, which of course they would do – but they might have some scrap of information and Lara needs to do something, anything. She can't possibly sit at a computer trying to work out how to exchange a chandelier for a spotlight in a virtual restaurant in Barcelona. Later she will have do that but she can't do it now.

The night is alive with a restless energy. Rain comes down in sudden squalls. The branches of the trees in the square shuffle and sway and the lights from cars and houses blur in the rain. Lara stops for a moment under a striped awning outside a newsagents. Lights shine out onto the pavement and two young men stand at the door, drinking beer. Lara's eyes wander over the newspapers and magazines displayed in the window. *Iraq allows full inspection. Truth about life with Michael Jackson. Invasion comes closer. New clue in Thames boy murder. Doubts cast on information dossier.*

*Girl, eight, crushed by tree.* She has already read all the newspapers and none of them tell her what she wants to know.

She pulls her coat collar up and heads on, her legs aching and tears gathering briefly. She should have eaten something before she came out. If only everything would stop, just for a day, or even an hour. She worked all weekend trying to catch up because she'd taken Thursday and Friday off last week to go to the Foreign Office, the Iraqi Embassy, the Stop The War office in London. Every door had been slammed in her face. No, no, she reminds herself. Don't exaggerate. Not slammed but gently, politely, with bone-china teacups or Styrofoam coffee cups, with forms to fill in and words of reassurance, closed against her, with a sharp and decisive click.

I'm sorry, Miss Ravello, but there's nothing anyone can do. Jay is an adult.

Well, only twenty.

Yes, Miss Ravello, an adult. So his life is his own.

Perhaps a lawyer?

No, I don't think there would be any point in talking to a lawyer. No, not unless you get him sectioned and I don't think there's really any evidence to suggest that he's mentally ill, is there? And you really mustn't worry too much because there won't be a war. As each door closed – gently – what Lara had seen was blame. As a mother, it seems you're responsible for everything your son does but if you actually want to take control of him then there's no way you can do it.

Lara turns into Monmouth Street. Everything is quiet. Up ahead, at the end of the street is the Guest House, a staunch bulwark against gentrification. In Lara's mind, it squats like a toad, dark and deformed, menacing. The rainbow flag stretched across one of the balconies, the wellington boots filled with dead plants, the plastic windmills and wheel-less bike hanging from the front railings, the rotten window frames and blackened brick – all of it threatens to drag her in like quicksand. For Lara, her own flat – polished oak floors, white curtains, built-in cupboards – is a vital line of defence in her fight against the Guest House and all it contains. Or it was until the builder arrived.

As she comes closer, she sees that the basement kitchen at the Guest House is dark. It seems that Mollie – so assiduous in packing Jay's hat and sun cream – has now lost interest. She continues to leave messages on Lara's phone, insisting that nothing will happen, that the buses will never go into Iraq, but she hasn't done anything to bring Jay back. Initially Lara had agreed with Mollie's view on the buses. *They'll never go into Iraq.* But that was before she went to the Stop The War office in London. There a young American woman with pierced lips, dreadlocks and a startlingly sharp mind had explained to Lara the level of contact that had been established with groups in Iraq. *You think Saddam is going to pass up a publicity stunt like this?*

The church is next door to the Guest House – a vast and spiky mass of blackness. Outside there are posters – *Christ has died, Christ has risen, Christ will come again. Family service, 11.00 a.m. All welcome.* Two elderly drunks are sitting on the steps passing a roll-up between them. As a child, Lara used to go to the church with her mother sometimes but she can't remember the interior – it merges with the interiors of too many other childhood churches. Lights are on in the road which runs along the side of the church, towards the Community Centre car park. Lara turns down this road, heading towards the glass doors of the Centre – a ramshackle jumble of red and black brick buildings tacked onto the back of the church. As she pulls the door open, music thumps from a piano and a smell of trainers and sweat floats towards her. Through a half-glazed door, she sees rows of girls bouncing up and down in leotards. *Time, time, time. The moment is coming soon. Time for you, you, you to make your mind – up.*

Lara hurries on to the end of the hall and down the stairs to the basement. Lights are shining dully, voices buzz and a dog barks. She knocks on the flimsy, half-open door and steps down into the office, a large room, half underground, with a low polystyrene ceiling, crowded with strip lights and edged by thick pipes. The carpet is grey nylon with brown stains. Through a line of high windows, the street is visible, or at least the lower sections of bicycle tyres, parked against the railings. A lurcher with a red and white spotted scarf tied round its neck is curled up in a cardboard box. The room smells of electric heaters, cold coffee and dog.

Although it's past nine o'clock, they're all still here – Wilf, who lives at the Guest House, Spike and Martha, and in the corner, with his back turned, Ahmed, the mysterious Iraqi who never seems to look up, or speak. Lara knows that Ahmed lives at the Guest House but she's only encountered him once. He had been standing in the kitchen, worried about nineteen pence, which he owed to Mollie for a second-class stamp. He'd explained to Lara that he was worried that Mollie might not find the money on the table so he'd taped the coins to a small piece of card with Sellotape to make sure.

All the low life of Brighton seems to pass through the Guest House at some time, so it can be hard to keep up. She wonders whether, when Jay was round at the Guest House, he spent time talking to Wilf and Ahmed. She would like to accuse them directly but knows she might do better to wait. That tabloid headline – *Mum slams irresponsible peaceniks* – didn't help, even though the mum in question wasn't her but the parent of a 25-year-old woman from North Yorkshire.

Good evening, she says now, trying to sound friendly.

Spike nods briefly, Wilf moves closer to his screen and Martha starts to get up and then reaches out to answer a ringing phone. Lara has come across people like this before, they have a talent for being oppressed. She should have changed her clothes. Her corporate look – wool overcoat, black trouser suit and cashmere scarf – might be understood as provocative.

Spike is the person who Lara has spoken to before. He isn't friendly or helpful but he can put a sentence together. In his mid-twenties, he's plump with sandy bristly hair, a crumpled black shirt and baggy trousers. A dragon tattoo spreads up his right forearm and both his earlobes are crowded with studs. On his feet he wears sandals and thick wool socks. Something about the droop of his shoulders, and the length of his arms, makes Lara think of monkeys.

Sorry, I know you're busy but an email just came through. Did you get it?

Spike is trying to wrestle crumpled paper out of a printer. He looks up at Lara, his pale blue eyes blank and weary. About the buses? Yeah, we got it.

Oh good. Right. So have you spoken to Alan?

Not today – no.

No. I realise not today – but you did speak to him last week? As we agreed.

Yeah, I did. And I gave him your message for Jay – and he said he'd speak to Jay and phone back.

Oh – right. But he didn't phone back?

No.

And you didn't phone again?

Spike presses buttons on the computer, the printer whirrs and the paper starts to move. But then a sound of crackling emerges as the paper crumples and the printer jams again. Listen, I'm going to have to copy this to another computer because this printer keeps on blocking.

No. No. You can't do that, Wilf says. If you put the Compaq on it'll blow all the fuses. We tried it twice this morning and it blew both times.

Yeah, then what can I do?

Let me have a go.

Wilf is in his forties and is all bone and tanned leathery skin. He wears a tight denim jacket, jeans, a large silver crucifix on a shoelace around his neck. An indication of religious belief or a piece of gothic jewellery? His head is shaved and his face is narrow and sharp. He looks to Lara like the kind of man who might carry a knife or swing a bicycle chain. Gothic jewellery – surely? Now he bends down and pulls paper from the recalcitrant printer. A plate lies on the table with crumpled tinfoil and the remains of a cake. Lara knows the blue willow pattern on the plate. Mollie is forever cooking cakes. One would suppose that if you baked enough cakes then eventually your fruit loaves and vanilla cupcakes would improve but it seems that's not the case. And anyway how can Mollie be making cakes for these people when they were responsible for encouraging her grandson to go to Iraq?

Excuse me. I know you're busy but I just want to check – you didn't ring Alan back again after you gave him my message?

Listen, Ms Ravello, Spike says.

Lara. You can call me Lara.

OK. Could you give me a minute? Do sit down – if you can find anywhere to sit.

The only available chair is close to Ahmed. Lara moves towards it reluctantly. Something about Ahmed's back unnerves her – maybe it's the fact that his shirt collar is still crisp and white, his navy blazer uncreased, despite the fact that Mollie has said that he often works for eight or ten hours without stopping. Or perhaps it's the way that his black hair is cut in such a very neat line across the back of his neck, leaving the skin too exposed beneath it. Lara's eyes run over a press release on the desk beside her.

All of this is pointless. Why ever did she come here? She should just go to Italy and fetch Jay back. But what if he refuses to come? For a moment, she remembers trying to push Jay – three years old and stiff as a plank – down into a pushchair. And she remembers battling to get him out of the car. It was like dealing with an octopus, as soon as she managed to unclasp one tentacle another stuck fast to the door. But those kind of battles had been rare and she had always won them, eventually. Jay wasn't a fighter at heart, or not in that way. Instead, as he grew older, he became slippery and shiny. Things bounced off him, or skirted around him. Or he slipped away, put up the shutters inside his eyes, refused to see her, or to talk to her. He had done that more and more as the years went on – probably it was to do with his condition.

For a moment, Lara imagines standing beside a double-decker bus at a service station in the Rome heat. Watched by a bus full of grubby peace protesters, she tries to get Jay to come home. She's wearing the clothes she wears now – the black tailored trouser suit – and she's hated for it. She issues orders but they're ignored. So then she wheedles and pleads, tries to reason. The day is coming to the boil, the tarmac melting. The place smells of tyres and engine oil. And all the time she's watched by a sneering group who sit around on the verges or loll against the bus, many of them babbling in languages she can't understand. The image is so humiliating that she moves her mind away from it.

At the weekend she'd called a shrink in London – a man she used to go and see herself on a regular basis and who she has consulted before about Jay. At least he had understood the seriousness of the situation. Why is he doing this? Lara had said. I don't understand why he is doing this to me? Dr Charmain had been clear about that. Jay doesn't have proper boundaries, he said. He doesn't have a clear idea of what he is responsible for and what he isn't. He's taking on an international problem which has nothing to do with him in order to avoid addressing the real issues in his life – such as why he has dropped out of university and why he finds it difficult to establish normal social contacts.

Lara looks around the office and wonders about the people here – what issues are they avoiding? It certainly looks as though they might have difficulty establishing normal social contacts. She's met these kind of people before. In Lara's childhood, Mollie was always surrounded by the professionally oppressed. Of course, this threat of war is a gift for them. If it didn't exist they would need to find something else to get angry about, some other force of oppression to battle against.

It seems that Wilf has succeeded with the printer. The paper is running through it smoothly now. Spike turns back to Lara, running his hand briefly across his shaved head.

Sorry, Ms Ravello. Listen, it's like I said last week. I know Alan has given Jay your message – several times. And I do understand you're worried but I can't really do more. You know the people in this office were not even in support of the buses.

And you don't know anything about these people coming home?

Martha has finished her phone call and sidles along beside Spike's computer with an enthusiastic, spaniel-like smile. She's a round woman in her fifties who wears tight black leggings and a vast pale pink jumper. Straggly grey plaits hang over her shoulders, tied at the ends with pink flower bobbles. Cup of tea anyone? Spike. No? Wilf? OK. Fine. I can do a coffee instead. She turns to Lara. Ms Ravello. How about you? Stressful for everyone, isn't it? Let me get you a cup of tea.

No thank you.

Oh right. Well, good to see you anyway. And how's your mum? We haven't seen her for a day or two. She's such a fantastic lady, isn't she? We're always so grateful for her help.

Lara can think of nothing to say. She's spent her whole life being the large and sullen daughter of lovely, sparkling, little Mollie – daffy, dotty, dear little Mollie, out saving the world in four layers of mascara, bright red lipstick and a stringy feather boa – and she grew tired of it long ago. Martha smiles uncertainly and twists her fat hands together. A phone rings and she picks it up, then presses a button on a fax machine. With a groan, and then a high-pitched squeal, a fax begins to emerge. The dog raises its nose, sniffs, shuffles out of its cardboard box and adds its whine to the noise.

He's a rescue dog, Martha says. Nerves are bad.

She bends to stroke the dog but is distracted.

Oh my God. Look, have you seen this? Martha's head is bent down sideways to read the fax as it comes in. About the hospital in Baghdad, the lack of drugs. Some journalist took photos.

Everyone here is very fond of Jay, Martha says.

People assume that your son knows what he's doing, Spike says. And OK so Jay is young and he was quite new to all this but that doesn't mean he doesn't care. Jay knew a lot and he talked to people, people like Ahmed here.

Yes, I had assumed that.

Lara notices that Ahmed's back has tensed, that his hand has stopped still on the computer mouse. She feels that those neatly cropped hairs just above his collar are bristling. His back sends a message of accusation but he doesn't turn around. Lara looks again at that blue willow-pattern plate. She wishes that she were a small and good woman, helpless and wide-eyed, a fragile woman who people would want to protect and support. But all her attempts to be that woman have failed. She's too tall, has too much dry red hair, too many freckles and a chin that suggests opposition. She feels herself to be a giant Alice in Wonderland, crashing around in the world, dangerous and awkward, accidentally breaking things. Now she thinks, as she often does, that since she's destined to be that awkward woman, then she might as well play the part to the full.

Listen, excuse me. I know you're busy. But I just need to be clear. Does anyone here know anything about who is coming home?

Wilf is reading the fax.

The bastard. That's appalling.

Excuse me.

What? Wilf turns around, his narrow eyes turn to steel.

I was just asking.

Yep, I heard your question, Ms Ravello. I think we all heard your question several times before.

Hey, come on, Spike says. Peace, Wilf, peace. Be part of the solution.

OK. OK. But I think what you need to understand is that this isn't about you or about your son. It's about what's happening, about how we're going to stop this war.

Ms Ravello, are you sure you won't have a tea or a coffee? No, right. Sorry. But I was just going to say – I think you were looking for Mr Stanmore, weren't you? You said last time you came.

Lara wonders if she should respond to Wilf but there's no point. She feels energy draining from her as though someone has pulled the plug out. She knows she should be at home, wrestling with Room Space. For a moment she imagines a miniature image of Jay on the computer. A new programme has been developed which allows you to control your child. Lara can use the programme to create a room for Jay – a very stylish room, grey and black, perhaps – and then she can just put him in it and keep him there. But Jay – even the virtual Jay she imagines – will not yield to her virtual fantasy. Instead he slips away, laughing, and not a mark is left on his stain-resistant surface.

I could go and see if Mr Stanmore is here, Martha says. He often is when the hall is in use. I could show you where his office is. Well, it's the vestry really.

All right. Thank you. Yes.

Martha rolls towards the door and Lara follows her. She's defeated and she knows it, hates Jay for putting her in this position. How can she be routed by this bunch of losers? But she has no choice but to follow ghastly, cheery little Martha up the stairs. She knows she won't find Oliver Stanmore. No one has even been able to tell her exactly what he does – something to do with the church and the keys to the building? Or is he some kind of alternative healer? *Mr Stanmore has cured people with terminal cancer.* Apparently, he doesn't have a telephone but Lara is sure that isn't true. Music vibrates from behind glass doors. Shuffle, shuffle, crash. *And soon you will find that there comes a time for making your mind up.*

Martha knocks on the vestry door. No response. She tries the handle but the door is locked. Oh dear. Of course, I suppose he could be upstairs.

Upstairs?

Yes, he has a flat up there.

Through this door?

I don't think you're supposed to.

Lara pushes open a door in the corner marked Private and finds herself in another, smaller, tiled hallway, a place crowded with mops and buckets. The fact that Oliver Stanmore is hiding from her means he knows something. If he's some kind of fake healer, then maybe he suggested to Jay that he should stop taking that medication. Lara's feet move soundlessly up the dusty wooden stairs. At the top a door is open and Lara peers in. The room is narrow with one arched stone window. The paintwork is dirty and a strip of stained beige carpet fails to cover raw boards. A Formica table with metal legs is piled with books and a man's jacket hangs from the back of a plastic chair. A piece of paper taped to the wall reads – *He who saves the life of one man, saves the whole world*. Above the desk hangs a large and gruesome crucifix. Blood runs down from the crown of thorns, from Jesus's furrowed ribs and from his feet. Lara has always hated crucifixes.

Surely no one actually lives here? It looks more like a storeroom than a flat although through a door by the window she can see a kitchen sink and the edge of an antiquated cooker. Lara steps into the room and immediately her eyes are captured by a line of vases set on a shelf. They're not large but they dominate the room. The colours vary – indigo, sea green, heather, jade. The shapes are organic. They must be hand-blown glass and Lara knows them to be worth hundreds of pounds. Mentally she begins to design a room around them – placing them close to a window to ensure that light falls on them, and through them, choosing fabrics and paint which will echo those turquoise and sky threads of light. Then her eyes alight on a photograph which is propped on the desk. She knows the image – the thin wrists turned upwards, the bandages and the lint, the stain of blood. One of Jay's photographs. Lara thinks again of that abandoned packet of pills in Jay's coat pocket.

From outside the exhaust of a motorbike backfires and then the engine roars away, the sound splitting the night. Lara pulls her eyes away from the photograph and finds that she's out of breath. She must go, she must get away from here. The crucifix, the horrid metal-legged table, the man's jacket. Something about this room offends her – not the brutality of the bare boards, the squalor of the paintwork – something else which she can't name. As she pulls her coat around her, and heads back down the stairs, she feels sure she's being followed or watched. Her hands jitter as she turns the doorknob at the bottom of the stairs.

Voices still rise up from the basement office but thankfully

Martha has gone so Lara turns and heads for the door of the Community Centre. She would like to slam it behind her but it's on a spring and refuses to respond to her violent tug. The rain is coming down harder, blown sideways by gusts of wind, and the night is icy but she's glad to be outside again and gulps down the wet air. For a moment she looks up but the stars and moon are lost behind cloud. She's sure now that Oliver Stanmore knows something. Those pills. He is responsible. And she will come back and find him – no matter how hard he tries to avoid her. As she passes the Guest House the lights are on but she crosses the road and walks on.

# 7

# Now

## Jemmy – Brighton, February 2003

Nearly time for lunch – another morning gone. Jemmy drinks coffee from a brown plastic cup and stares out through the dappled grime on the office windows. She mustn't stand by the window long otherwise Mrs Jarvis will see her. The offices of Swift Life Investments, Insurance and Pensions are six storeys up and look down onto a roundabout, bus stops, the entrance to a multistorey car park. Today sleet slops down from a dishwater sky and the traffic looping around the roundabout below merges together into an endless ribbon of beige. The phone rings and Jemmy heads back to her desk.

Hello, Jemmy speaking, how may I help you?

I bet you like it up the bum.

Jemmy swallows and her fingers tighten around the plastic of the phone. I'm afraid I can't continue with this call. She tries to say this firmly but her voice comes out sounding tight and prim. She presses the red button to cut the caller off. Bloody creeps. That's the third she's had today.

It'll happen any day now, Tiffany says, leafing through the *Daily Mail*.

You reckon so?

Yeah, sure to.

What, you got cramps?

Nah – the war. Dunno why they didn't get on with it sooner.

The phones have gone quiet again. The office smells of clandestine cigarettes, burnt dust and nylon carpet. To Jemmy, it seems that each of these smells is separate and specific. She can almost see them moving through the office, like threads of smoke, curling around the computers, the coat stands, the potted palms and filing cabinets. Each smell makes her stomach lurch. A taste like the sole of an old shoe lingers in her mouth and her lips are dry. Am I hungry or I do I feel sick? Jemmy doesn't know the answer to that question.

Finally, lunchtime at last. She pulls sandwiches wrapped in tinfoil from her bag and turns her mobile on. Bill has left three messages. He calls up all the time to talk about nothing – whether she wants him to buy ginger tea or cinnamon, whether the rain which has been forecast for the weekend could delay the trip they might make to Eastbourne. The evening before they'd had a row – another row – except that they never actually do have a row, just vicious little skirmishes conducted in cold, short sentences. Eventually she hadn't been able to stand it any longer and so she'd gone out and walked down to the seafront, walked there for a long time, she didn't know how long. It helped to hear the sound of the sea, to see the distant lights of ships, blinking in the blackness. Often she says to herself, *I can't do this any more, I can't do it for a moment longer.* But she knows that these words are pointless because there is no other option. *Lie down and die* – that's the expression. But you can lie down for a long time and you won't die.

Now Jemmy calls Bill back and he answers. They have the same conversation they always have. How are you? Fine, fine. *Well, actually, miserable, desperate. What do you expect?* And how is work? Fine, fine. *Work? This bloody awful job. I'd have given it up by now if it wasn't for Laurie's death.* I thought that when you get back we might pop out somewhere? Oh yes. Well. We could do. If that's what *you* want to do. Yes, I suppose so. Why not? *Go here. Go there. What does it really matter? Laurie will still be dead.*

At the Support Group they tell her that men and women grieve differently. Just because a man plays loud music, drinks too much, stays at work late, goes out all the time, then you can't say he doesn't care. That's his way of grieving and you've got to respect it. Could endless discussion about domestic trivia be grief as well? Jemmy isn't sure. She agrees with Bill that they need a supermarket shop. He volunteers to go if she writes the list. After that she says goodbye – then finds that she misses his voice at the end of the phone.

It's so hard to understand why Bill won't talk about Laurie, why he won't even say his name. Because he's the one who is interested in gravestones, church registers, family trees. He has books about genealogy and he's a member of a local history society which helps people to trace their ancestors. But now it seems that he isn't interested in the branches that wither. Would Laurie even make it onto a family tree? Probably not. He didn't have a birth certificate because he was too premature.

You know there's some local boy gone, don't you? Monica says. It was in the *Argus*. Didn't you see? You know that dirty, old guest house on Monmouth Street.

Yeah, but what's the point? Tiffany says. I mean, how stupid can you get? Why would it help for some load of wasters to go there in a bus? You know, one of the people is off *Big Brother*.

Jemmy remembers when she found out that Jay had gone to Iraq. It wasn't as much of a surprise as it should have been. *Jay in moon landing. Jay walks to North Pole. Jay wrestles with crocodile.* Any of it could be possible. And he's right about the war, of course. Absolutely right. Jemmy doesn't know anyone who supports the war.

Shouldn't be allowed, Monica says.

Jemmy checks the anger rising in her throat. (Don't you listen to them, Jay. You do exactly what you want.) She remembers that intense stare and those hands – small and white but firm, decisive. Turning her palm upwards, she traces with her fingernail the line of a white scar which runs across her forearm, as thin and straight as the string of a guitar. Probably Jay will take photographs and write things. He'll see through all the media lies and try to show things as they really are.

Just attention-seeking. That's all it is.

Jemmy takes a deep breath, pulls a packet of coloured pens and her sketchbook out of her bag. She's written Laurie's name in curly writing across a whole page of the sketchbook and now she starts to decorate it, outlining each letter in a different colour, sketching in a ring of stars to surround his name. Once she's done that, she tears the page out and starts to cut around the edges of the stars.

Then she pins Laurie's name up on the board above her desk. With the flowers and stars, it looks like an advert for a circus. She opens her bag and takes out her photographs. These are not the original photographs, only copies. After she got back from the hospital, she'd had five copies made and hidden them in different places and she'd got Bill to get a safe box at the bank and put one set of copies in there. (That's all I've got, Jay. A packet of photographs. You think you're going to come home from the hospital with a baby and instead they give you photos, blurred photos and nearly all the same – Laurie wrapped up in the hospital cot, the sheet with the tiny blue cars on pulled up to his chin. Just like all the other baby photos except a flower lies in the cot, near to Laurie's head.)

Jemmy holds the photographs up, considering how to arrange them. Finding scissors in her drawer, she begins to cut at the photographs, making them into different shapes, arranging them on the desk so that they fit together like crazy paving. Once she has a design she likes, she pins each individual photograph to the board, overlapping the edges. She stands back and admires the effect. In Ship Street there's a shop which can put a photograph on a T-shirt, a mug, or even a canvas bag. Jemmy begins to consider the possibilities, envisages Laurie's photographs on one hundred household items, the name Laurie stretched across her desk in neon lights.

Other people are coming back from lunch now but no one says anything – have they not noticed or are they embarrassed? Even if no one will say Laurie's name he definitely exists. He must do, because his photograph is there in front of her and his name.

Laurence James Aldridge – 3rd of November 2002. She knows that Tiffany and Monica are watching but she doesn't care. She might even get told to take the photographs down. But Laurie is her son and she wants his photograph on her board. (I won't ever forget, Jay. I won't forget what you did for me. You made it all possible. No more black cardigans and fingerless gloves. Look after yourself now, won't you? And when you come back I'll show you the photographs of Laurie, my beloved boy.)

# 8

# Now

## Lara – Brighton, February 2003

The church is open this evening. *Christ has died, Christ has risen, Christ will come again. Family service, 11.00 a.m. All welcome.* It's more than twenty years since Lara has been inside this church. Now it all returns to her – the plain, square interior, the brown ceiling. The shadowed spaces are cavernous, echoing. A drunk is propped, sleeping, in one of the pews. Rain beats against the high windows and someone is playing the organ – a few breathy, mournful notes. In the distance, candles flicker on the altar and low lights glow above the choir stalls.

Lara walks up the aisle, hearing her office shoes click on the floor, staring up at the lectern, in the shape of an eagle with its wings spread. A grimy picture on a distant wall is crammed with falling angels, moving gracefully down through the air, feet first, eyes rolling heavenwards. The smell brings back those other churches of her childhood. Cross-stitch kneelers, incense, Sunday school palm crosses, slack-mouthed old women singing out of tune, endless smiling strangers. Mollie liked churches so she and Lara went every Sunday in whatever town they were living in. But it couldn't be just any church – Mollie picked them carefully, choosing those that were ancient and atmospheric, thick with incense and bleeding plaster saints. So many churches in so many different towns.

Lara moves through the shadows, pushes open an arched wooden door into the Community Centre. An aerobics class is taking place and a light shines up the stairs from the peace protest office but once again there is no sign of Oliver Stanmore. Lara has been told by Martha that he would be here this evening and so she sits down to wait. She checks her phone and finds two voice messages. The first is from Annabel. *Listen – I just read this magazine article about water in rivers in the Middle East. This bug – you've no idea you've swallowed it until worms bore deep inside your intestines. They even dig out through your skin so you must warn—*

Lara slams her finger down onto the red phone, heads back to the church. The next message is from the phone at the Windsor Guest House. Rufus's voice is so loud that Lara imagines the mobile exploding in her hand. She imagines him – six foot, flaming red hair, booming voice. Like a dormant volcano or a ticking bomb. When he's in the room there isn't enough air for other people to breathe. Usually Lara hates him but Jay's departure has left her with no energy for the normal hatreds. I have decided, he bellows, that I must go after him and bring him home safe. It's the only way. Your mother agrees, she'll come with me. Not this week, of course, because of the play. And your mother has been in touch with this guy Greg Marsden, son of an old friend, journalist, out in Iraq. So once the play is over. It's the opening night. You know that, don't you?

Rufus is Biblical, Shakespearean. *And gentlemen in England now a-bed shall think themselves accurs'd they were not here, and hold their manhoods cheap whiles any speaks that fought with us upon Saint Crispin's Day.* Of course, Rufus doesn't actually say this but Lara imagines he does. And he is magnificent. It would bring tears to your eyes, if you didn't know better.

That's the problem with all this, Lara thinks. It's so easy to be swept up in it. Because at least what Jay is doing isn't small. It's extravagant, it's bold, it's courageous. Even Lara feels the draw, finds herself tempted by the luxury of life being narrowed down to a single purpose – stop the war, bring Jay home safe. So much easier to do that than carry on in the drab and dreary little days of the journey to work and back and the decision as to whether it should be moussaka or lasagne for supper. She could become the mother of a saint, the brave woman fearlessly sacrificing her son to the noble cause.

But despite the grandeur of Rufus's voice – and he does have a fantastic voice – Lara is not suborned. Years ago, around the time that Jay was born, she understood the importance of keeping things small. Jade tiles rather than emerald. This isn't Henry V at Agincourt, it's a mentally disturbed boy on a bus somewhere in Italy or maybe Turkey, about to blunder into one of the most complicated political situations possible.

A man emerges from that arched wooden door which leads to the Community Centre. His eyes immediately fix on her and he moves towards the chancel, stands in front of the altar. He's tall and solid but well-proportioned and strangely light on his feet. Although the space he occupies is large, he nevertheless seems to fill it. With his heavy shoulders, thick neck, big head, there is something of the bull about him, of the Minotaur in the labyrinth. And yet he's nervous, uncertain.

His clothes are unexceptional – jeans and a dark T-shirt which he wears under a loose denim shirt – but somehow these clothes seem inappropriately modern. Should he not be wearing a robe of some kind? He's neat and clean and yet he has the hidden desperation of a derelict, a down-and-out, the kind of person you might find sleeping in a doorway, or begging outside a shop.

Lara knows – although she can't say how she knows – that this is Oliver Stanmore – the man who, in the twenty-first century, apparently has no landline, no mobile and no email. The man who might be a vicar, a churchwarden, a caretaker, or some kind of alternative healer – but no one seems quite sure.

Good evening. Are you Mr Stanmore? Lara speaks loudly and definitely, wishing to emphasise that she's not in the least intimidated – although that isn't quite the case. The truth is that Oliver Stanmore isn't at all what she expected. In Lara's view, church people are usually unattractive, misfits, failures. There's something odd about this man – but he's none of those things.

I am Oliver Stanmore, he says. His voice is strangely sonorous. He says the words as though he finds it difficult to confess to his own name. It's clear that he doesn't wish to speak to Lara, or anyone else. His eyes are unpleasantly direct, dark and unmoving. Lara puts her hand on the side of a pew to steady herself. Mr Stanmore's eyes move to her knuckles – red, cracked and raw. She pulls her hand away and conceals it inside the pocket of her coat.

I need to speak to you about my son, Jay.

Ah yes. Of course. Perhaps we could find somewhere rather quieter?

Yes.

I'm sorry, he says. The hall is in use and the café is closed. Would you mind if we went into the office? At least it will be quiet there.

She follows him back through the door to the Community Centre. The door which leads to the stairs and the peace protest office is open and Lara hears voices from down below. She has spent the last three days in Barcelona and so she hasn't spoken to anyone in that office. Even if she had been in England, she probably wouldn't have spoken to them. Aerobics has changed to ballet. Feet shuffle and thud in time to rattling piano notes. Lara follows Mr Stanmore up a short, steep flight of stone steps and through another arched wooden door into a room with high arched windows, a dark wooden desk, filing cabinets, a box of keys on the wall. Mr Stanmore moves towards a chair, indicates that they should sit down.

No thank you, Lara says. She isn't interested in a comfy chat.

Oliver Stanmore sits down and watches her closely. I think I know your mother? She runs the Guest House next door?

Yes, she does. And I know that you met my son – that you spoke to him?

Yes, I did speak to him on two or three occasions.

So you knew that he planned to go to Iraq?

I'm afraid that the contents of my conversations with your son are private.

Lara had not expected to be so clearly and firmly rebuffed. This man unnerves her and the strange silence he carries with him makes her uncomfortable.

But you knew he planned to go to Iraq?

No. Iraq was never mentioned.

Then what did you speak about?

As I just said, my conversations with him were private. However, I would say that he did seem rather upset when I last saw him. He seemed to find things very – noisy.

Noisy?

Yes?

What? So you're telling me he went to Iraq to get a bit of peace and quiet?

Oliver Stanmore is silent again but the quality of the silence has changed. Lara is aware that, at some deep level, he is angry. His will, which has been so firmly bent towards kindness and reason, is beginning to fail. She's frightened by his anger, but determined not to let that show.

You love your son? Oliver asks.

Lara stares at him coldly. Only a man could ask such a stupid question. How could he possibly understand? Understand what it is to be eighteen and unmarried and pregnant, abandoned and under pressure to have an abortion. But she'd refused to do that and she'd brought up her son and made money and bought him everything. Sent him to private school, spared nothing in order that he should have something better than she had. She's close to tears. Oh God, she says to herself – I've become such a cliché. I didn't want to become this person saying – *where did it all go wrong?*

She looks at Oliver and realises that she hasn't answered his question. He's making a fool out of her. With a sudden weariness, she says, Of course I love my son.

Sometimes if you love someone then you have to watch them making mistakes.

No. That may be your version of love but it isn't mine. I've fought long and hard for Jay. And I'm not prepared to see him throw it all away. Jay has suffered from serious depression but I got him through that, and I helped him to get a place at university. To me, that's what love is.

She expects him to argue but instead he nods his head as though he understands. Lara realises she should keep quiet but knows also that she can't resist this man, will surrender to him, even though he doesn't sympathise, would rather not hear.

Even now I'm trying to understand him, she says. But I just don't know why he's doing this to me, why he is so ungrateful. Why does he have to do something so thoroughly self-dramatising? The situation in Iraq doesn't have anything to do with us. I spoke to a psychologist about this, a professional, and he said that of course people care about other people's suffering but they have to have some limit on that. They have to realise that some things aren't their responsibility.

Rubbish, Oliver Stanmore says, rubbish. He pronounces the word definitely, spitting it from his lips. Of course, what's happening in Iraq has to do with us. The truth is that we're all much too good at deciding that something isn't our responsibility, too good at cutting off from other people. The whole way in which we live, here in the Western world, depends on the suffering of others.

Yes but if we all cared about everything then our hearts would break.

Then they should break, Oliver says.

But...

Overhead, the strip lights go out with a click and the office drops into darkness. Lara hears a shout from the corridor. Around her the space is suddenly limitless even though a dull light gleams in from a high window. Feet clatter and a door bangs. Lara stretches out her hand, hoping to find the back of a chair, but her fingers fish through emptiness. She can sense Oliver Stanmore, a patch of darkness, blacker than the other darkness.

Oh no. Not again. I'll just go down and deal with the fuse box.

She feels him move and then something feathers against her cheek. She brushes at it but it touches against her again. She backs away – what can it be? A moth perhaps? She feels Oliver Stanmore pass her in the darkness and hears the door open. Surely now some more light should come into the room? But it doesn't. An image flashes in her mind, an image she saw earlier in the day on the internet. A cancer ward in a hospital in Baghdad, a place where they have no drugs, no equipment. A child blown up like a balloon and one of his legs black and twisted. She tries to push the image away but it won't go, she presses a hand against her mouth, turns, uncertain now where the chair is, the door.

Again that feathered flutter but against her lips this time. She flaps her hands through the darkness, stops herself from calling out. Feeling her way forward, she stumbles against a chair, finds her hand gripping wood. This must be the door frame. Below her she hears voices and sees a haze of light, which shines through the glass entrance door. She stretches her foot forward into the darkness, and begins to feel her way down the stone stairs. Her hand scrapes against the wall and she winces. Her foot wavers, searching for the next step, but it isn't there. She loses her footing, pitches forward. For a moment, she's connected to nothing and that moment seems to go on and on. She has a vision of herself going over the side of a cliff, falling and falling into the darkness, gliding down the air. She lets out a cry as her arms flail.

But then unseen hands grip her and break her fall. She stumbles against him and it's like hitting a tree trunk or a brick wall. As she tries to right herself, his hand grips hers. She winces, ready for the pain from the eczema on her knuckles, but the hand which holds hers is strangely fluid and she feels no pain. She pulls away and stands straight again. The lights flash on. All that has happened is that she has fallen down four steps. And yet the shock on Oliver Stanmore's face suggests that she fell from a great height. It's as though some great salvation has taken place. For a moment they might hug each other and shout for joy. But it was only four steps so both of them look away, embarrassed. Lara straightens her blouse and jacket. Oliver moves his hands swiftly to the side as though to brush the whole incident away.

He knows it all, Lara thinks. Everything. He knows about the drugs, and the doctors, and the shame, and the way that she hates Jay yet can't stop loving him no matter how hard she tries. And she can never be free of him, never, and none of it was her fault really, and she has tried so hard to make it right but nothing has ever been enough. He knows all of that and so Lara raises her hand to shield herself from him.

He is staring at her hands. She steps away, peers down at her fingers. His eyes meet hers and his face is shocked, appalled. She pushes her hands down into the pockets of her coat and keeps them there. She pushes the door to the church open and hurries away from the angels and the lambs and the sickening smell of incense, her shoes clicking down the aisle, her head bent down, looking at nothing. Pushing open the door, she emerges into the space of the night and snatches a deep breath, which becomes a sob. As she passes the Guest House the lights are on but she doesn't slacken her pace. She's at the end of the street before she stops and turns back to look at the church. In some part of her mind, she expects to see Oliver Stanmore staring at her from the steps. But, of course, he isn't there.

She walks on to where a street light draws a fuzzy circle of yellow onto the pavement, the brimming rubbish bin, then she draws her hands out of her pockets. She wants her hands to be red and covered in scabs – as they have been for the last twenty years, ever since Jay was a baby. Creams, diets, supplements, soya. Nothing has had any effect but now her skin is perfectly smooth and clear, golden in the light from above. Tiny hairs on her fingers glitter white. *Mr Stanmore has healed people with terminal cancer.* She looks back at the spiky outline of the church on the hill, remembers the strange silence in the office. She can still feel his fingers touching hers. She stretches her hands up to the street lights and they float through the darkness with the gliding grace of white swans.

# 9

## BEFORE

### Rose – Coventry, March 1939

Sunday lunch at 34 Warwick Road – and spring has arrived today. The light of the sun is white and wavering but already it's drying the grey-green grass of Greyfriars Green. Birds hop on the park railings, sing loud and uncertain, unable to trust that the winter might finally be ending. A breath of wind catches at the grass, rustles through hedges and the bare branches of trees, but then is still.

Rose slows her bike and comes to a halt outside the house. For a moment she looks up at the towering façade – columns, long sash windows, curling iron balconies and a great many chimney pots. Then she crosses the red-brick tiles, passes the stone lions and steps up to the front door. As she raises her hand to press the bell, the door swings open and Violet is there. Half of her hair is twisted into pin curls and secured by bobby pins but the other side hangs loose. Her freckled skin is powdered and touched with a blush of pink.

Oh disgusting. Violet rolls her eyes. You even smell of socialism.

Rose laughs, drops her bag onto the red-tasselled chair beside the hall table and kisses Violet. The chessboard floor tiles enclose their miniature territories. The Chinese vases still stand beside the sitting-room door but have lost their power to deceive, humiliate. The stuffed eagle winks at her from his perch inside the glass dome.

And pray what does socialism smell like?

Violet shudders and crumples up her nose. Drains, coal houses, lard.

Rose raises her hand to give Violet a pantomime slap, then kisses her again.

Red Rose. Violet's voice is a mixture of contempt and affection. Briefly Rose remembers that first night, shut in the wardrobe together, sneezing among the fur coats. Violet had decided they would become best friends that night and so it is – although Rose has never quite understood why.

Mr Whiteley shuffles out of his study on his sticks. As always, he wears a stained green-velvet smoking jacket which has gone shiny on the lapels and cuffs. Good morning, my dear. Good morning. Rose goes to kiss him, feeling his whiskers against her cheek, tasting his smell of hair oil and decay.

And Happy Birthday. Twenty today – isn't that right?

Father has a present for you, Violet says. Well, *I* bought it but it's *really* from father. She produces a package from the drawer of the hall table and hands it to Rose. Rose's fingers close around the rustling pink tissue paper. Violet always manages to choose the best presents. A pale blue cardigan slides out of the tissue paper and lies in Rose's hands as soft as clouds. The edges of it are lined with turquoise silk ribbon and the buttons are covered in velvet of the same colour.

Put it on, Violet says.

Rose pulls off her own cardigan and her arms slide into the cloud. She pulls the new cardigan straight, then turns to smile at Mr Whiteley. She would not have chosen pale blue for herself – too much fine summer's day and not enough thunder – but still the cardigan is perfect. Quite different from the only two she has, which are covered in pills and darned around the cuffs.

Just right, Mr Whiteley says. Just right.

Thank you, Rose says. She kisses him again and feels his crabbed hand touch her back, pulling her towards him. She yields to him and kisses his cheek once again.

Dreadful news, isn't it? Mr Whiteley says. What can Mr Chamberlain do now?

Oh father, don't start, Violet says. Come on, look in the mirror. She pulls Rose up onto the first step of the curving stairs and Rose looks at herself through the chips and spots of the bevelled mirror. The cardigan is just what Violet would have chosen for herself and – for a moment – in the mirror, Rose sees herself as Violet, scrubbed clean and glistening, pale and doll-like but awkward and stiff in the joints. Violet's hand, hot and fleshy, pulls Rose on up the stairs. Come on, I haven't finished getting ready. Come and talk to me while I'm finishing my hair. You know, Stanley Bunton is coming to lunch as well. After golf with Frank.

Violet's bedroom is decorated in pink satin and a cream-coloured Chinese carpet covers the floor. Swagged curtains make the window look like a stage. The bedhead is made of curving oak and the kidney-shaped dressing table has a salmon satin skirt underneath. Rose loves every detail of this room – and hates herself for loving it. She changes the words of St Augustine in her head. *God give fairness and equality to the world but not right now.*

Rose kicks off her shoes and collapses on the bed, gliding her hands across the slippery satin quilt. She worked overtime at the factory yesterday, sang in the Folly Night Club until midnight, spent the morning delivering copies of *Peace News* and helping to put up posters for a concert to raise money for the German refugees. Her feet ache and her arms are heavy but she's still full of energy. She rolls onto her stomach, cups her chin in her hands, swings her feet in the air. Her shoulder aches where a man stubbed out a cigarette on it at the club. She'd been lucky to get away with only that. Of course, Violet has told Rose on numerous occasions that singing at the Folly is common, and that no decent man will walk out with a girl who does that, but Rose suspects that Violet's disapproval is tinged with jealousy. Anyway she loves singing at the club, loves the scratchy feather costume, and the bright lights and the faces in the shadows, turned up, watching her. Now she turns her cheek, touches it against the fluff of the cardigan. Of course, she won't wear the cardigan to the factory. *Cheap little gold-digger.* She hears the whispers but cares nothing for them – and yet she is fascinated by her own duality, by her ability to balance her different worlds.

So tell me, she says. Has Frank said anything more?

Violet sits at the dressing table, securing her hair with pins. Not really. Well, he hopes I'm thinking it over.

But you don't need to think it over, do you?

I don't know, Violet says. I just – I'm never quite sure.

Oh come now. You mustn't disappoint Aunt Muriel.

Violet and Rose chant together – Because she's already got the hat.

Laughing, Violet takes cigarettes and a lighter from the dressing-table drawer and comes to sit on the bed. She takes two cigarettes out of the pack and passes one to Rose.

What's the problem? Rose says. You've wanted to marry him since you were ten.

Violet lies down on the bed, pulls Rose's arm around her.

Go on, tell me why you're not sure.

Oh no. I couldn't. Violet blushes pastel pink, hides her face.

Go on, Rose says. Tell me.

Violet pulls Rose's head close to hers and whispers. Her breath is hot and her words rustle in Rose's ear. He might be a pervert.

Rose laughs. No. Why?

Well, I don't know. It's just— You know, sometimes when he kisses me. Violet pushes her head closer to Rose's and whispers again. Rustle, giggle. Puts his tongue in my mouth. And once on the Green. Put his hand up my skirt.

Rose pushes her head down into the satin eiderdown, trying not to laugh.

Yes, I know you think it's funny.

Violet, men do that.

Not until they're married.

Yes, they do.

Violet gets up from the bed and goes to the dressing table. Putting her cigarette down, she clips on earrings and loops a string of pearls around her neck. Rose. I know that in your sort of world. Well, I know that the girls in the factory would think nothing of it but I expect Frank to show some respect.

Rose opens her eyes wide, making a silent objection.

Oh Rose, really. Don't be offended. You know I didn't mean it like that.

Downstairs the gong sounds so Violet stubs out her cigarette and Rose's as well, and pushes them back into the packet. Mr Whiteley doesn't like women smoking and particularly not in the house. Now he's so ill, he doesn't seem to notice but it isn't worth taking any chances. Violet links her arm through Rose's but on the landing she stops. Should I?

Oh don't ask me. You know, I don't believe in marriage.

Rose.

I don't. It's a capitalist institution for the subjugation of women. The desire for reproduction is the force which destroys the female. Rose starts this sentence in a serious voice but halfway through she begins to laugh.

Is that what Mrs Watson says? Violet asks. The one who wears men's trousers and smokes cigars and has lice leaping in her hair?

Rose slaps at Violet who catches hold of her hand and they fight for a minute before bursting into giggles and lolling on down the stairs. Frank has just arrived and stands by the fireplace in the hall. Frank Fainwell. His pale hair is neatly combed into a side parting. His porcelain perfection illuminates everything around him. But on his neck a rash burns where his shirt collar has chafed. Violet throws herself towards him, kisses him, then takes hold of his hand and swings it back and forth. Frank comes to lunch at 34 Warwick Road every Sunday, has done since his childhood. He and Violet are second cousins and their faces are remarkably similar – Frank has that same sugar-crusted brightness and the same dull blond hair, sullen mouth. The same slightly insect-bulbous eyes, surrounded by mauve shadows. But whereas Violet is tiny and awkward, Frank is tall and lithe, beyond improvement or comparison. The two of them stand together now, joined, the one a mirror image of the other, indivisible.

Frank stretches out his free hand to Rose and says good afternoon. Rose knows that Frank's mother, Aunt Muriel Fainwell, refers to her as *Violet's common little friend* but Frank always waves across to her at the factory, even though he's in Accounts whereas she's on the Works floor.

Beautiful weather, Mr Whiteley says, appearing at his study door. The sap is rising? Can't you feel it?

The doorbell rings and Stanley Bunton bustles into the hall in his homburg and tweed coat. Rose knows him from the factory where he's employed in the Company Solicitor's office. Although Stanley is the same age as Frank, he appears to be of another generation. Portly and precise, he has a clipped black moustache and hair slickly oiled back. Rose wonders why he's been invited – perhaps the management have mentioned him to Mr Whiteley as Promising. Mr Whiteley may have retired but he is still a major shareholder. Stanley shakes hands with Rose briefly, giving her an awkward half-smile. Rose knows that men like Stanley find her unnerving and she's glad of that. The fact that she's taller than Stanley doesn't help, disrupts the proper hierarchy.

Violet and Frank head into the dining room, hand in hand, legs moving in time, and Stanley follows. Mr Whiteley has got his stick wedged in a threadbare patch of carpet near his study door, so Rose goes to release it and then guides him across the hall. The dining room is at the back of the house with French windows that open into the garden beyond. Through those windows Rose sees a glimpse of a wrought-iron arch. It must once have been painted white and rises to a Moorish point, decorated with a pineapple-type knob. Wisteria twists through the ironwork but is not yet in flower. The dining-room furniture is all mahogany and so tall that it feels as though it's leaning in on them. Lace encrusts the blinds, the edges of the shelves, the tablecloth, suffocating. In one corner, a parrot in a tall brass cage puffs up his grubby feathers and shrieks at them.

So where is Arthur? Violet says, with a sigh. Was he at the – oh what's it called? Delivering stuff with you?

He was there first thing, Rose says. But I don't know where he went after that.

Typical, Violet says. He probably won't even come.

He will come, Frank says.

But always late. Violet isn't keen on Arthur. He's another cousin but he was brought up in Italy and has only just returned. Mr Whiteley found him a job at the Works and always asks him to Sunday lunch, despite Violet's complaints.

Rosie, dear, come and sit near me, Mr Whiteley says, as he always does, and Rose gives him a kiss before settling herself down next to him. The cardigan suits you, my dear, Mr Whiteley says and runs his purple hand down her arm, stopping to give her hand a squeeze. Rose looks across at Frank and Violet, together. Violet raises her right hand to her glass and Violet expects Frank to raise his left hand at exactly the same moment even though it doesn't happen quite like that. But their eyes sidle together, meet, and they smile secretly, excluding everyone else. Rose knows that when they were children they used to play at being twins.

A housemaid arrives and serves braised beef, swede, peas and boiled potatoes. Mr Whiteley pushes down pills from a china box which stands beside his water glass. Stanley makes a comment about Chamberlain's speech on the radio and the situation in Czechoslovakia – a place which, apparently, no longer exists. Violet groans and pleads with him to stop. Frank suggests to Violet that they might head out to Binley Woods later for a walk and Violet approves this plan. Rose raises her eyebrows at Violet, and runs her tongue along the top of her lip. Violet tries not to be amused.

Well played, the parrot shouts. Well played.

The front door opens and rolling footsteps – clump, shuffle, clump, shuffle – sound across the hall. Arthur enters, out of breath and sweating. He's older than Frank, older than Stanley. His skin is pockmarked, his face long and lugubrious. His nose wobbles over thick lips but his small eyes are intense and humorous. Today he looks tired but every man in Coventry looks tired at the moment, with the factories running six days a week and into the evenings as well. I'm sorry, Arthur says, waving his hand. I'm very sorry.

Rose loves the exotic lilt of Arthur's voice, the way that he stresses the beginning of every word and raises his hand in operatic emphasis as though drawing the words out of his mouth. Arthur shakes hands with the men and then kisses Rose three times. Rosa, my bella. How wonderful to see you.

Violet waves to him vaguely across the table. Arthur sits down, knocking a knife from the table but catching it deftly. His black hair is plastered to his head by sweat and the port-wine stain which covers his chin burns brightly. Although Arthur is neither particularly tall nor abnormally large, something about his compact and blunt body looks out of place among the polished mahogany and tissue-thin china of 34 Warwick Road. He looks up, catches Rose's eye and smiles. The smile says – *We may be outsiders but we know how to play this game.*

The parrot bounces up and down on his perch. Cunt, he shouts. Cunt.

Violet winces, exchanges a brief glance with the housemaid who hurriedly produces a black cloth and places it over the cage.

I have some new books which you might want to look at, Mr Whiteley says. Rose says she'd love to see the books. Mr Whiteley has a vast library and, since he retired, he spends most of his day reading political books and articles. He often lends Rose books and she's grateful for that. In her childhood, few books were available and most of them were silly romances. *You're an advanced young woman, Rose Mayeford,* Mr Whiteley often says. *Very advanced.* Now Mr Whiteley puts a pea on his side plate and flicks it at Arthur who is talking to Stanley about Czechoslovakia. Arthur tries to flick one back but it only goes as far as the salt cellar. Stanley chokes on his beef and reaches for water. Pea-flicking is a regular activity during Sunday lunch at 34 Warwick Road but it seems that no one warned Stanley.

But we have to act, Stanley says, wiping at his moustache with his white linen napkin. And Britain *can* win a war now, thanks to the work of companies in Coventry.

Rose quotes Mr Chamberlain's speech at Kettering. In war, whichever side may call itself the victor, there are no winners but all are losers.

Pudding is served – jam suet roll and custard. Mr Whiteley prevents the housemaid from taking the dish of peas, lines one up on his side plate, flicks it towards Frank's water glass and laughs gleefully. Violet is sitting up straight, her lips pressed together. She doesn't like politics or pea-flicking. The housemaid will complain about the mess.

It's about capitalism, Arthur says. Exploitation. And people don't think that so much arms production is good for the future of the city. Of course the contracts keep on rolling in, and now even more shadow factories will be built but Coventry shouldn't be based entirely on one industry.

Violet sniffs, turns her head away. Rose feels a momentary pang of pain on Arthur's behalf. So many people are affronted by him or suspicious. Partly it's his club foot, dark skin and foreign name – Arthur Bonacci – but it's more because he isn't as humble as a plain-looking foreign man should be. A spick, Violet says. But it is exactly Arthur's pride that Rose likes. She also loves his voice – that swooping, surprising, spacious voice. Often at the factory she and Arthur sing together, just to lighten the atmosphere, although they have to watch out or the Foreman complains. Sometimes they sing English folk songs – 'The Oak and the Ash', 'Afton Water'. Sometimes modern songs like 'Paper Moon', 'A Tisket, a Tasket' or 'Cheek to Cheek'. Rose loves to hear Arthur's voice joining hers, blooming into the air. She stands close to him, feeling exactly when she needs to start and end each note. Arthur's exotic accent makes the words sound extravagant. Afterwards everyone claps and the other girls on her line – Beryl, Ivy and Win – plead for more and Win says, *You don't hear better even on those broadcasts from Carnegie Hall.*

Well, yes, Mr Whiteley says, blowing his nose into a large handkerchief and then lining up another pea. In theory that may be right. Yes, in theory. But my thought is that marriage might be the answer. All you young people should be married by now. One has to find an outlet for one's natural instincts.

Arthur flicks a pea that bounces across Frank's napkin and says – but despite all the money coming into Coventry, wage levels are not rising.

Yes, in theory.

People will resign from the arms factories, Arthur says. They feel strongly that the more military production there is, then the greater the chance of war.

Oh don't be so silly, Violet says. Haven't you listened to the radio, Arthur? There *is* going to be a war. There has to be.

No, Rose says. Chamberlain is negotiating at the moment. If they manage to bring together the Pact of Five—

Oh really Rose, Violet says.

Rose feels a twinge of anger but it soon subsides. Why does Violet never question anything? Is she very stupid or highly intelligent? Rose listens to her voice. Light and bright, languid and listless. She's talking to Frank about clothes, voluntary work, golf, the cinema. Such jolly good fun. Rose should be irritated but she knows that, in truth, if she were ever to discover another dimension to Violet then their friendship would be finished. Violet must remain as she is, an intricate surface.

Frank, reaching to flick a pea, upsets a jug. It falls across Violet's plate splashing water and jam suet on to her dress. Violet jerks her chair back and Frank rights the jug.

Oh Frank, look. Honestly.

Sorry.

A housemaid appears with a cloth. Rose knows that she is expected to help clear up the mess and does so gladly enough. She knows how to feign a feeling of social inferiority although in reality she has never experienced such a feeling herself.

Frank, my dress is stained. Look. And it's new. You could at least help.

Frank jumps to his feet and tries to look useful, although the housemaid is now in charge. Rose catches Frank's eye. She's hardly ever looked at Frank before, never seen him properly. He's always been part of the background, ornamental, something to be kept behind glass, admired from a distance. As she moves a plate, his hand – blue-white and transparent – catches against hers. His eyes are darkest blue but strangely shallow. Once he's married to

Violet, he won't even be able to flick a pea, let alone express a political opinion.

People promised, Arthur says. We all promised.

Promised? Promised what? Violet wipes at the mark on her dress.

We signed the Peace Pledge, Rose says. Two million people signed it.

She remembers all the postcards. And the words on them. Two million people had sent off their cards promising that there would never be another war. Even in Lincolnshire, where Rose had been brought up, people who thanked the squire for lowering their wages still sent off their postcards. That had been the beginning of the Peace Pledge Union and at one time it had had more than a million members and the meetings had been crowded out. Rose knows that even Violet signed one of those cards but now she, like so many others, tries to forget.

It's a matter of conscience, Arthur says.

Oh these young men and their consciences. Mr Whiteley lines up another pea.

Arthur, please don't encourage father with the peas. You've already ruined my dress. I'll have to go upstairs and change.

Frank jumps to his feet to open the door for Violet.

Rose my dear, Mr Whiteley says, let's escape from all these temperamental people and retire to the library for a little peace and quiet. What say you?

Oh yes, of course, Rose says.

Arthur and Frank stand up and Arthur says that he has to go. He's on his way back to the Peace Pledge office. Rose gives him a wave and promises to see him in the office later. There's a meeting tonight and papers to prepare.

Rose offers to take Violet upstairs to rinse the dress but Mr Whiteley is keen to get on with his books and so she follows him to the library. He closes the door behind them, takes the key from the mantelpiece and locks the door. The library is on the ground floor, looking down onto the Warwick Road and Greyfriars Green beyond. It's a high-ceilinged room with bookshelves on every wall from floor to ceiling. Only the marble fireplace and the tall mirror over it are bookless. The room smells of lavender and bottled air. Mr Whiteley, who is always concerned that the spines of his books might fade, draws the blinds down and switches on the lamp on the desk. Rose moves over to the shelves at the back where Mr Whiteley always puts his most recent acquisitions, ready for cataloguing. She opens a copy of *The Limits of Economics* by J. F. Broadbent.

Of course, in England we find it difficult to have a real class war, Mr Whiteley says, because no one can decide who is on which side. He snuffles, shakes his head. As for Violet, he says, I would consider Arthur. He may be no matinee idol, gammy leg and all that, but still.

Rose turns the pages of a book, waits.

After all, one has one's natural instincts, Mr Whiteley says.

Rose feels Mr Whiteley's breath rasping on her neck. Should be interesting, that one, he says. Although perhaps you'd prefer something more political? Why do we all live so safely? That's the question I ask myself.

Rose picks up another book, flicks through the pages. She feels Mr Whiteley's head against her as he leans down to put his hand up under her skirt. A tingling starts between her legs as his gnarled hand touches the inside of her thigh. Putting down the book, she rests her head forward against the cool of the bookcase, takes a deep breath, moves her legs apart. Mr Whiteley's hand fumbles at her smalls and his fingers press up inside her. His breath against her neck rasps in sharp gasps. She feels his tweed-trousered groin against her side, as he rubs himself against her in a hopeless attempt to arouse himself. His fingers dig deeper and his other hand reaches round, pushes up her blouse so that the buttons come open. Fingers grip at her nipple as he rubs himself furiously against her.

Rose always worries that he might give himself a heart attack but he has surprising energy for a sick man. She feels her curled hair descending, falling across her eyes. Book titles blur in front of her eyes. *The Limits of Economics* by J. F. Broadbent. *The Failure of Paternalism* by Roger Derek.

Mr Whiteley has exhausted himself and staggers back from her, supporting himself against his desk, wiping his hand on his handkerchief. Rose turns around and moves towards him, lays her head against his chest, feels his arms around her. His whiskers touch against her cheek.

You're a good girl, he says. A very good girl.

Rose pulls back from him and smiles, lays a finger on his lips. She's fond of Mr Whiteley but glad that he's too old to do anything much. She wouldn't want to take her clothes off for him but these Sunday afternoon library sessions, which began as soon as she became Violet's friend, are not unpleasant. Mr Whiteley is an old man who may not have long to live. He's sorting through his wallet. A little present, he says, and gives her ten shillings. Rose smiles at him, raises her eyebrows. Mr Whiteley draws another ten shilling note out of his pocket and Rose kisses his cheek as she pushes the money into her pocket. There are many ways in which wealth can be more fairly distributed.

Mr Whiteley turns the key in the lock and, as he guides her through the door, he squeezes her bottom. She turns to him, laughing, as the door closes. Moving towards the stairs, she raises her hand to push her hair out of her eyes. Frank is standing in the shadows of the landing, staring at her. His eyes are hollow, helpless. Rose swallows, clasps her hands against her half unbuttoned blouse but forces herself to meet Frank's eyes with a calm gaze. Frank has turned bright red and he's sweating. His collar rubs against that patch of spots on his neck. Rose coughs awkwardly, straightens her blouse.

I thought you and Violet were off to Binley Woods?

Frank tries to speak but his voice doesn't come. He coughs, pulls at his collar, breathes deeply and tries again. No. Violet doesn't feel too well.

Oh I am sorry, Rose says. How disappointing for you.

And she has to look after her father. He hasn't been at all well this week.

Rose is aware of the gossip that Mr Whiteley is losing his mind but she suspects that for the first time he might be taking possession of it.

Frank's voice croaks again but no words come.

Oh well. I'm sure you'll go to Binley Woods another time, Rose says, and tries to move past him. But Frank stands close, blocks her path. All this is very nice for you, Rose, isn't it?

Yes, it is. Her eyes meet Frank's and she pities him. Wearing that too-tight collar, being bossed around by Violet and his mother. She wonders who Frank really is, if there is any Frank. She marvels at the way in which education and wealth leave people with no idea how to operate in the world.

You could come with Arthur and me tonight, if you like? she says. We're going to the Peace Pledge Union meeting in the City Hall.

As soon as she has said these words, Rose wonders why she asked. She needs to offer Frank something but not that. Frank has no interest in politics. He went to grammar school and is part of the management or will be soon. Violet would be furious if Frank even thought of it. He's still standing very close and she can hear the snatching of his breath.

I might do that, he says. Yes, I might.

You'd be very welcome.

From below she hears the Sunday afternoon sounds of the house – the ticking of the clock in the hall, the clatter of a plate, the murmur of a radio. A door opens and shuts, unseen. Frank is still close to her, red in the face. She wonders why he doesn't move. The thought comes to her that he is a small and frightened boy in the body of a tall and confident man. He has no idea what to do with his beauty. As yet, it is merely burdensome, an embarrassment. She swallows, looks down at that open button on her blouse, then up at Frank. Perhaps he has been drinking? It's rumoured that he does drink although Rose finds this hard to imagine. But still his eyes are thunderous, he might suddenly hit her or shout.

You won't spoil my happiness, will you, Frank?

He breathes in deeply, takes a step back.

No, Rose. I won't spoil your happiness.

Thank you.

She walks on down the stairs, feels his eyes clinging to her.

See you tonight perhaps? she says.

# 10

# Now

## Jay – Istanbul, February 2003

Dear Granmollie,

I'm sending you this from Istanbul which is a really cool city although we're only in the outskirts and so I haven't seen much. Really friendly people here all crowd round the buses and cheer and push food and drink on us even though we can't understand a word they're saying. Also a guy took me into his house last night and so I slept in a proper bed for the first time and that was really, really good. I have to be quick because someone lent me this computer just for a while but they need it back and actually I'm not sure the message is going to send but I just hope it does.

It is hard to hear yourself think with all the arguments going on, so much talk about peace but it's certainly hard to get any here. There's this stupid prat who has managed to offend everyone in this whole town. Too many nutcases on this bus, one with food intolerance and he can't eat anything with grain which is pasta and pizza and he obviously hasn't noticed that we left London some time ago. And all these journalists saying that all this is a complete waste of time and a stupid publicity stunt because Saddam is hardly going to take any notice of what a bunch of wacky-baccy smokers from Hampstead think, even if they are standing in front of a school waiting to get bombed. And part of me agrees with that and part of me doesn't but anyway there is no other way to get into Iraq right now so that's why I've come with them.

And this guy he was in Vietnam and he talks about how it was the worst experience ever but then he's turned up here – he can't keep away. I don't know. You probably heard that our self-appointed leader Ken O'Keefe who you've probably seen on telly decided to burn his passport because he doesn't need it any more. He's a citizen of the world. Only problem is that the Turkish authorities have decided not to buy that shit and so he's stuck at the border and can't get anywhere. What I know is that the proper story is not being told and no one is actually listening to the people in Iraq. No one is consulting them or asking them what they want. So I just want to spend some time looking around, understanding what it's really about, what the real story is, and writing it down, not for the press because they never publish the truth but just for some people, somewhere, who might want to know. I just think we've all got a duty to try to understand. Say to Mum – it's just about Iraq, that's all it's about. As usual she's got some big theory, as she always has and she's been getting in touch with everyone and telling them that I've got to come home, that I'm mentally ill, ringing the frigging Foreign Office and then leaving four messages a day. All I'm asking is that she should just let me exist. I'm not going to come back. Somebody has to do something about this. It's not OK just to let this happen. IT IS NOT OK. The morons and bullies who are doing this for their own ends, for oil and accusing everyone of having WMDs when they've got piles of the bloody things themselves. One rule for them and one for everyone else. There is this very good website called Voices of Truth you can look at. Wilf and Spike will show you and it has real stories from Iraq, written by ordinary people there, and then you can begin to understand. And Mr Stanmore. You know him? He says empathy is the only hope for changing the world and for healing people. I know she's a very good mother, I know she's made every sacrifice for me, I know that she only wants what is best for me and all that shit. I love you, Granmollie, and I don't want you to be frightened. You and me both know that what I'm doing is the right thing. Even if what I do is only helpful to one person then one person is enough. Yeah and there's a guy called Kevin who is probably looking for this CD I borrowed and I left it on the dresser in your kitchen underneath the radio. Got to go.

Love you. Jay

# 11

# Now

## Oliver – Brighton, February 2003

So the Great Trickster has appeared again, like a travelling salesman with a bag full of cheap temptations. But why now? And why that woman with her clicking high heels, swinging handbag and shrill voice? Every time he shuts his eyes, he sees her hands. Those hands, which looked as though the skin had been peeled from them but then were clear and smooth as rainwater. In the church he polishes brass, mops up the water that drips in through the roof, juggles with bookings and keys, tries to forget.

But it's no good because The Dying are back as well. Oliver sees them everywhere and they cry out to him endlessly, calling for help. *You are our last chance. If you can't save us, who will?* He knows The Dying well. They first appeared after Grace's death – balanced on balconies, stepping down perilous stairs, hanging in stairwells, feet dangling, kicking and twitching, desperately trying to secure a foothold. But after a while they had receded. Or he had forced them away, by keeping his mind steady, sticking to the simple, the material, believing in nothing, hoping for nothing. But they too saw that woman's hands.

He needs to be vigilant. One never knows when or how they will appear. There are such varied ways to die. The world bristles with risk. Now, standing at the window of his room, up above the church, Oliver looks down into the street and watches as a young man decides to cross the road. The night is treacle black and slippery with rain. The young man wears dark clothes and a wool hat pulled down over his ears. Oliver watches him slide between two parked cars and he sees the battered white van, which is speeding to meet him, to run him down. It glides down the street, splashing through puddles, its headlights glittering funnels. Oliver hears fear beating inside his head, imagines a screech of brakes and the thump of metal on bone. But the van passes and the young man – unaware of Death beside him – saunters across the road.

Oliver turns away from the window and goes into the kitchen, pours himself a glass of wine, grips the stem firmly to stop his hands shaking. Then he presses his head against the wall, feels the plasterwork against his forehead and nose, breathes deeply.

But when he opens his eyes, hands are outside, clinging to the windowsill – thick-fingered brown hands which grip like claws to the stonework. His heart bashes against his ribs, he opens his mouth to cry out. Someone must have fallen from higher up the building and they're hanging on here, about to drop to the pavement below. The bones and muscles of the hands strain, struggling to maintain their grip. Oliver knows that he should pull the window open, try to catch hold of the man, lean down and grasp his arms, haul him to safety. But instead he shuts his eyes, breathes deeply again and moves away from the window. When he dares to look back, the hands have gone. But The Dying still wait in the shadows. And he is responsible – responsible for them all – and now for the boy as well.

In the sitting room he starts to read, trying to calm his mind. His book is called *Facets of Time* and it examines several theories as to what time is. Oliver has read several times the pages about concurrent time – a theory which suggests that everything is actually happening simultaneously. Time is a construct in the minds of men, a system that they invent in order to organise events and make sense out of them. Oliver is aware that the arguments put forward in favour of this idea are all spurious, but at another level he suspects that the theory is right.

He reads a few sentences but he can't settle. An image comes to him. It is one he knows well. A great ship lurches in a tempestuous sea. The waves rise as high as the ship, crash down around it.

The wind rips, the ship tosses and bucks, tipping wildly, deluged with water, barely staying afloat. The crew of the ship cling to railings and ropes. The captain is absent, no one is in control, the wheel spins wildly, the ship will soon go down. Oliver pushes the image away.

He thinks of that boy – the one who has gone to Iraq, a boy whose soul lay close up under his skin. Of course because he's only twenty, he doesn't really believe in death, has no sense of the love that others have invested in him or how they would be damaged by his loss. Thin, with a shock of curly red hair, with an old corduroy jacket and baggy trousers, a striped scarf, a ring through his ear. Oliver tries to imagine that boy in Iraq and allows himself a frivolous moment of feeling a little nervous on the Iraqis' behalf. Have they not problems enough? The boy's grandmother comes to the church often. Tiny and elegant, she makes her responses passionately in a deep and resonant voice and lights a cigarette before the service is over. She's determined that everyone should understand her as dotty and dim but Oliver isn't convinced. Wilf says that the boy has been in touch with her now but Oliver knows no more than that.

He should never have talked to that boy, of course, but he couldn't leave him alone there, sitting at the table in the Community Centre café, weeping damply. The habit of caring is hard to shake off. And so he'd gone up to him, sat down. The boy's eyes were startling – so that Oliver had asked himself whether those wide pupils had some chemically induced significance. He talked as though words were a currency fast being devalued. The normal catalogue of teenage grievances expressed in the clichéd language of the young. I can't understand my family, he said. Why are they all acting their lives rather than living them?

All Oliver had to do was listen. He'd had years of practice at that.

That's the problem with the world we live in now, the boy had said. We've got too much information and everything is too interdependent. You just want to buy a packet of green beans from Kenya in a supermarket but suddenly it's a life-and-death issue. If you buy the beans then you're responsible for ruining the environment and causing earthquakes, famine and floods. But if you don't buy them then people in Kenya will lose their livelihoods.

Yes, Oliver had said. Uuum. Yes. I do see. Yes, I understand.

Then the boy had stared at him, pinning him down with those aching eyes.

But it doesn't matter, actually, does it? Any of it, I mean.

Oliver had considered this question, made an effort to speak the truth. No, it doesn't matter. It's just a question of how to fill the time, and if you live in this part of the world then you might have some pleasure, but if you live in some other part of the world then you'll have a lot of pain.

So it might be worth trying to reduce some other person's pain?

Yes, that might be worth it.

He felt uncomfortable with this conversation. This boy was too young to know these things. He felt frightened by him and for him. Once again he regretted ever having engaged with him.

That's what I want, the boy had said. That's all I want. But no one believes I can. They think you have to be a doctor or someone to do that. But I do help people. Only in small ways but still... Why don't they believe I can help?

Oliver considers the boy. He must not lie to him. He must tell him that no one can help anyone else, that to think otherwise is a dangerous delusion of power and control. But there was something so plaintive in the boy's voice that Oliver couldn't resist offering a little comfort, although he'd promised himself that he wouldn't. Of course you can help people, he said. Of course you can. The ability to empathise has a tremendous power to heal. There may be professionals – doctors and hospitals – but every day, through empathy, we all have the power to heal.

After the boy had gone he'd found the photograph lying on the café floor. Had it dropped from the boy's bag? It showed forearms and hands with the palms turned upwards. The arms were covered with crooked strips of lint secured by plasters. The lint stained with patches of blood. Something about the photograph attracted Oliver. Its honesty, perhaps, for these were certainly real arms, real wounds. Oliver had kept the photograph, meaning to return it to the boy when he saw him again. But then the news came about Iraq. And Oliver had propped the photograph on his desk, for reasons he couldn't explain.

Now he turns to the photograph, looks back on that conversation with a rising feeling of horror. Why had he sold that boy the cheap philosophy of the power of empathy? Why had he spoken to him at all? Usually he takes more care. People are always looking for him. Bald cancer victims, the mothers of disabled children, people with chronic skin conditions or twisted by arthritis. He avoids all of them, hides in his room upstairs, never answers a letter, or returns a phone message. It's best that way. Oliver gets up from his chair, paces across the room, remembers the boy's mother. Maybe he should get in touch with her again? But there is no need. She's moving towards him as certainly as the bullet moves towards the boy heading to Iraq. Both will find their target. It's only a matter of time.

*I'm trying to find out why my son would do this* – that's what the mother had said. Oliver knows the answer. It's because the boy lives at the extremes, at the edges, where there is only hope or despair. He can find no middle ground. It's so hard to find the middle ground, there is so little of it and one is pulled to the edges all the time. All this has nothing to do with me, Oliver tells himself. Nevertheless, he supplied the boy with hope and that is crime enough.

## 12

# BEFORE

## Rose – Coventry, June 1939

The day is sunless but swathed in damp heat. The sky is a low fluff of grey. The Saturday crowds in Broad Street move slow as treacle – women push prams, fathers shepherd small children. A man plays a mournful Irish jig on a violin. Rose sits behind a table strewn with leaflets with Mrs Watson beside her, smoking a cigar. Mrs Watson has removed the pinstripe jacket she usually wears and pulled her braces down off her shoulders. Frank, Arthur and Mrs Bostock are handing out leaflets explaining the details of the Military Training Act. Mr Bostock addresses the crowd from a kitchen chair, sweating in his suit and wiping at his horn-rimmed glasses with his handkerchief, his voice slow and momentous.

War has never solved anything and it will not solve anything now.

Rose undoes her sandals and releases her swollen feet while Mrs Watson pours lemonade from a flask. Above her a yellow and green Peace Pledge flag hangs limp. A banner reads – *War will cease when men refuse to fight. What are YOU going to do about it?* Through the crowds she sees a tram passing and the façades of the building opposite – Owen Owen and the Provident Insurance. A boy pushes his sister and is cuffed by his father. The air is greasy and swells with the sound of bicycle bells and the jangle of an ice-cream van. Rose nudges Mrs Watson, indicates a man in a tweed jacket with thick glasses who has just arrived. He claims to be a PPU supporter but everyone knows he's a detective. Detectives have been watching them now for several months, turning up at meetings and hanging around the office. Detect the detective is a game which has kept them all amused.

The capitalist system is pushing the people of Germany and this country towards a conflict which neither wants.

Mrs Watson puffs on her cigar. Even if there are Germans stamping down the street with their jackboots I'm not shiftin. I'm getting under me bed.

I thought I might do better on the bed, Rose says.

Mrs Watson throws back her head and guffaws, revealing blackened teeth, then dissolves into a bubbling cough. Rose looks around, checking that Mrs Bostock hasn't noticed. The Bostocks are concerned that no one should bring the Peace Pledge Union into disrepute and Rose has been reprimanded before for inappropriate levity. Frank has turned to look at her so she gives him a bland smile. Ever since that day on the stairs at 34 Warwick Road, Frank has been looking at her. Even at the factory he comes to stand nearby asking questions about nothing. Does he need her approval for handing out leaflets? Rose knows it isn't only about leaflets and enjoys her power.

A nice piece of flesh, Mrs Watson says. I'll say that for him, I certainly will.

Sssh. Rose kicks at Mrs Watson's leg. It's quarter to two and her stint ends at two. Frank finishes then as well and they're going to see Violet who is stuck at 34 Warwick Road because Mr Whiteley is too ill to be left. Rumour has it that he's lost his mind, can't tell his own daughter from a hatstand. Someone said they went round there and he was shouting obscenities – but probably that was the parrot. Rose watches Frank, sees how even his perfection is melting wax-like in this heat. His shirt is soaked with sweat, the top button undone, his waistcoat creased. The dull blond of his hair is dusty, his sullen lips cracked, the mauve shadows around his eyes darker than ever.

Mind you, my thought is he'd be easily thrown off balance that one, Mrs Watson says. But you enjoy yourself while you can, love. The time is short enough.

Oh do be quiet, Rose says, but she's laughing.

Frank is here every Saturday now and he helps deliver *Peace News* in the evenings as well, raises funds for the victims of German fascism. Rose is glad because the Peace Pledge Union needs all the support it can get – but was she responsible for this change in Frank? At first she had thought so but now she isn't so sure. She feels mildly offended. She'd thought it was only that Frank was sweet on her, she didn't think he was seriously interested in politics. She'd also assumed that Violet would be furious but she doesn't seem much troubled. Perhaps if Frank's busy with politics he doesn't have time to get his hand up her skirt.

A man with neatly trimmed hair and a ginger moustache is asking questions – Do the PPU care nothing for the plight of the Jews in Europe? Is it not the case that people like Mr Bostock – while doubtless well intentioned – are actually serving to weaken the British armed forces? Surely activities of this kind can only serve to strengthen Hitler's position?

Helmut and some of the other German refugees who work as volunteers for the PPU are restless, their strings pulled tight. Soon they'll be accused of being German spies, again. Mr Bostock silences Helmut and his threadbare friends, and from the height of the kitchen chair makes his usual replies – The peace treaties of one war contain the seeds of the next war. If the British government were prepared to reconsider the question of their colonial possessions, and their economic policy, then peace could still be possible.

Next time we want to position ourselves outside the Employment Exchange on a week day, Mrs Watson says. Catch 'em as they go in to register.

Rose nudges Mrs Watson and indicates the two policemen standing near the door of the Council House. They've been there now for a while, watching Mr Bostock with their arms folded, their faces insolent. Of course, they could have Helmut and the other refugees thrown out of the country but they won't. For a moment, it looks as though they might move forward but then they settle back into their former position. The detective in his tweed jacket looks towards them, nods his head. Rose finds all this ridiculous. Could they not at least be a bit more subtle?

They'll not dare, Mrs Watson says. Not with so many people around.

There've been scuffles before. The police don't dare object to the leaflets, or the speeches, although they can always clear people away on the grounds of public nuisance. So far it hasn't happened much in Coventry but it's happening in London and Manchester. Refugees have been sent back for making public statements against the Reich.

A group of young men are crowded around Arthur. It's not legal, is it? Men just won't agree to do it. They've got no right. The government can't force us.

That's what everyone thought but the Act went through a week ago and now any man between the ages of twenty and twenty-two has to go for six months' military training. Rose wipes sweat from her face and dreams of iced water. A young man is boiling over, rolling up his shirt sleeves, yelling, caught somewhere between violence and grief. It's like this everyday now. The air is tight with hysteria, people laugh, scream or cry for no reason. Spies are everywhere – in garden sheds, attics, posing as standard lamps with large fringed shades covering their heads. At the boarding house where Rose lives a jug jumped off its shelf one morning and smashed to the floor, quite of its own accord. Beryl at the factory tells of a child bitten by a fox in the middle of the street and hordes of rats chasing across the floor of the council chamber. And Win comes into work every morning with stories from her sister who works at the hospital – a baby born with six fingers, another with a tail.

Rose doesn't believe any of it. She watches Arthur calm the weeping young man. Why does he always seem so much older when the difference is only a few years? At least that means he won't be called up, although no one would want him anyway because of his gammy leg. Frank won't turn twenty-two until July so he'll have to go. All week the Peace Pledge office has been full of young men asking questions about what will happen if they refuse but no one knows the answer. Most of them will sign up in the end. It's only training and it won't come to anything, they say. But Rose understands that this is how war starts. A few rocks shifting on the high slopes, the landslide long and slow.

Bloody murdering bastards, Mrs Watson says. They'll not be the ones that die. You mark my words. It'll be the poor buggers like us that gets it.

Frank pushes his way through the crowd towards Rose. Are you coming then?

Rose gathers up her bag and says goodbye to Mrs Watson, waves to Arthur and Mrs Bostock through the crowd. Others are arriving now to take over but Mrs Watson says she'll stay, as she's nothing better to do. Rose gives her a peck on the cheek. She wonders if Violet is right about the head lice. Mrs Bostock is beckoning to Frank who pushes his way back towards her. Frank is a great favourite with the Bostocks. Of course, they favour him because he's a grammar school man and so can be relied on not to indulge in inappropriate levity.

Arthur pours himself some lemonade. The sweat on his face makes the pockmarks and the port-wine stain more obvious. He fixes Rose with those small, mocking eyes. You and Frank off to Violet's then?

Rose nods. Arthur hasn't been invited. Now that Mr Whiteley is sick, Violet decides who is and isn't invited to the house.

Well – take care, won't you.

Care of what?

Arthur raises his eyebrows. Rose feels fire rise to her cheeks.

Oh really, Arthur. Surely you don't listen to gossip.

Don't be silly, Rose. You know me better than that.

What then?

Just – you underestimate Frank. Like the pendulum of the clock. If it goes very far one way, then it must swing back the other.

Arthur, nothing's happened. Frank has got interested in politics.

Beware the weak man who finds a cause.

Frank has returned and, as Rose follows him through the crowds, she looks back at Arthur but he's disappeared. Why would he say that when he and Frank are such close friends? Rose and Frank find their bicycles and sidle away down Meadow Street, slow with the heat. The crowds ease and the air seems to stir a little. Rose feels it move against the stickiness of her skin. She can't think of anything to say to Frank, although usually they talk easily enough.

I need to go home and change my shirt, Frank says.

That's all right. I'll head to Violet's and see you there.

Yes. All right. Fine. Yes.

Rose turns to go.

Or you could walk with me – since the weather is so good.

Rose stops, looks at him, calculates. Then she shrugs her shoulders and agrees. After all, it's up to him. She's not going to worry, not on a day like this. She chats to Frank about nothing but inside her head she's calculating her happiness. She's been in Coventry for a year now and she earns three pounds and ten shillings a week at the factory and often she had two extra shillings for working an evening or a Sunday. She also has two shillings for singing at the Folly Club. She has had her hair done in a permanent wave. She owns three wool skirts, two pairs of new shoes and several pairs of silk stockings, which Violet had bought for her.

Not bad really when she'd never even intended to come to Coventry. Climbing into the back of that potato truck, she'd thought it was headed for Lincoln. When she heard she was in Coventry, she expected smoke and grime and machinery so it surprised her, that first evening, to walk through a green and leafy city. She loved the higgledy-piggledy streets around the cathedral and marvelled at the hundreds of small workshops operating from courtyards and alleyways. She leapt aside as crowds of bicycles rushed past, their bells ringing. And later she saw the crowds of new houses springing up all the time around the outskirts of the city.

Frank asks her about her family. Rose knows that he's only asking to be polite and because he doesn't want to look like a snob. Rose tells him the usual story of bucolic rural life back home in Lincolnshire, happy children and happy families making the hay in summer and cuddling up by the fire in winter. Every time she tells this story she embellishes it but she's always careful to remember each new detail. It's important to tell consistent lies. Something brushes against Rose's face. She raises a hot hand to wipe it away.

No wait, Frank says and she looks down, sees that a butterfly is caught in the front of her dress. Its wings – russet decorated with white spots, edged with black – flap gently but it doesn't move. She raises her hand towards it but although its wings rise and fall it doesn't fly away.

Frank props his bicycle against his hip, leans in towards her. His blue-white hands are clumsy, they fumble against her chest. The butterfly moves but settles again, lower down. Frank leans in close, she feels his breath on her forehead. His hand touches against her again and then the butterfly is gone. Rose straightens her dress, laughs awkwardly. Frank's bike falls and he jerks his hand down to catch it. Rose looks for the butterfly, hopes to see it fluttering above but there is no sign of it. She can still feel the place where Frank's hand touched her.

They walk on, pushing their bikes. The silence is determined, taut. Soon they enter Fitzmaurice Street. The house of Aunt Muriel Fainwell is solid and tidy, red brick with a half-timbered gable. Standard rose bushes are clipped in the front garden and two bay windows shine brightly on either side of the dark green front door. A wisteria twists up from the porch, wrapping itself around ornate balconies on the first floor.

There's no one home, Frank says. My mother's gone to visit my brother.

I'll wait here.

Frank and Rose leave their bikes against the wall. Frank goes through the gate and it swings shut, but still they talk over it, babbling about anything. Frank swings the gate open and shut, open and shut, as though he might invite her in. Rose puts her own hand on the gate, near to his, and rocks the gate as he does, until gently she begins to push it further and further open. For a moment they stop and look at each other. And Rose remembers that she really mustn't do this because Frank is going to get married to Violet. But together they hold the gate open and Rose follows him up the path.

Much better to wait in the shade of the hall, Frank says.

I'm hoping to go to the cinema with Violet tonight, Frank says. The house is still, the air heavy and smelling faintly of bleach. I'm very fond of Violet, of course.

Yes, of course. I'm very fond of her as well. Of course.

The hall floor is polished parquet. A watercolour of an English landscape hangs slightly crooked above a walnut desk. Frank's mother's gloves are lying on a chair. Aunt Muriel Fainwell who refers to Rose as *the common little friend*. Aunt Muriel who has apparently already bought her hat for Frank and Violet's wedding. Frank says something about tea. The pale skin of his face is red and mottled, the shadows under his eyes darker than usual. He hovers at the bottom of the stairs, muttering about changing his shirt. Rose thinks of Violet. How can she love Violet so much and yet feel such a desire to damage her? Or maybe she is doing Violet a favour?

Come on then, Rose says and stretches out her hand. Frank turns, and heads up the stairs, his feet whispering on the carpet, and Rose follows. Frank's bedroom is full of old school photographs, cricket bats and the smell of clean sheets and linseed oil. The furniture is dark wood and polished so that Rose can see their reflections move on the chest of drawers. Three pairs of his shoes, neatly polished, are lined up beside a trouser press. He has a Thorens Excelda portable gramophone. Rose has only seen one once before and bends now to examine the tiny machine, no bigger than a large book and shaped like a Kodak camera with a gramophone arm sticking up out of it. The case has a green crackle finish and a little leather carrying handle. Frank shows her the shield he won at school for playing tennis, then pulls open the wardrobe door and takes out an ironed shirt.

Can I put this on? Rose says, looking through records.

Yes, of course.

Rose slides a record from its cover, positions it carefully, drops the needle. A thump, a rustle, a squeak and then the voice comes clearly. *Paradise here, paradise close, just around this corner. The place happiness is for me.* The music turns the air in the room to silk. Frank is flustered, moves towards Rose, starts to stretch out his hand, then stops and turns aside.

I might see if Violet wants to play tennis later, he says.

Rose considers the bed – it's narrow and will almost certainly be lumpy.

This is a beautiful house, she says, do you mind if I look around? She heads back to the landing. The house is conspiratorial, can be trusted with secrets. It whispers behind cupboard doors, watches from clock faces and the glinting glass of pictures. Her feet are muffled by the yielding carpet; she pushes open a door. Aunt Muriel Fainwell's bedroom is broad and spacious with a bay window looking out over the back garden, nodding trees, an ornamental pond, glimpses of other gardens beyond.

Rose feels heat rise inside her and shivers. She's aware of her body moving under her dress. The room is flowered wallpaper, a matching quilted bedspread, a dress hanging shapeless from the wardrobe door, photographs in silver frames on the tall chest of drawers. Some devil in her wants to desecrate this house. Frank comes into the room wearing a clean shirt, and stands awkwardly by his mother's bed. Yes, he says, it is rather a nice house. We are lucky.

So hot, Rose says, puts her foot up on a button-backed chair, undoes the buckle of her shoe. Frank is icy white, drips with sweat. She unclips the top of her stocking, peels it off, measures her feelings for Frank. Curiosity, that's all, really. But it's impossible not to want to touch Frank, to share some part of his perfection. Impossible not to want to know what it would take to break him.

She doubts that Frank has ever been with a woman before and she feels tenderness towards him, and pity. Winning the school shield for tennis is no help to him now. He comes to stand close beside her, his eyes bulbous and shallow blue. She can hear his breath heaving in the silence of the house, feel his blood pulsing. He watches as she unhooks her other stocking and slides it down her leg.

About Violet, Frank says. It's rather difficult because she can't go out in the evenings much – because of Mr Whiteley's illness.

Yes, Rose says. Very difficult.

As she reaches towards him to undo his belt, he stands absolutely still, helpless, resigned to his fate. She undoes the front of his shirt to reveal the white expanse of his chest. His skin is shivery and looks too tender to touch. The least pressure and he will bruise. She reaches out her hand, slowly bumps her finger down over the furrows of his ribs. When she lays her hand flat on his stomach he gasps, and leaning forward he begins to undo her dress, snagging at it clumsily. So she pulls the dress off herself and takes off her liberty bodice as well. Then she reaches her hand into the front of his trousers and takes hold of him.

Pushing himself at her, he yanks off his shirt and pushes down his trousers, then pulls her against him, roughly. She pushes back the snow-field covers of his mother's bed and lies down. He climbs on top of her, his hands fumbling, his knee digging into her thigh. His hand catches in her hair and strands tear away, stinging, from her scalp. She knows that there is a part of him that hates her. He scrabbles between her thighs, pushes her legs apart. Then he exhales sharply several times, makes a sound like a sob and falls against her. Her thighs are wet. He draws back with a look of panic, sits on the side of the bed, his head buried in his hands.

I'm sorry, he says. I'm so sorry.

Rose reaches out and touches him, strokes the skin of his back, tells him that it doesn't matter. His shoulders heave and sob. From the bedside table an alarm clock ticks. Through the window Rose sees the top of distant trees, a tiny aeroplane motionless in the sky.

Beside her, he tries not to cry and she tries not to feel tenderness for him but does. How weak men are, she thinks. Everything is left to women, finally. She slides off the bed and kneels beside him. Somewhere in a distant bedroom Violet is howling but Rose shuts the door of that room, silences her.

It doesn't matter, she tells Frank.

Then she eases his legs apart and takes him in her mouth, works on him with tenderness until the moment when he is ready to enter her. And she shows him how he should do it – gently, while looking into her eyes. And she looks up at his blond hair, and the whiteness of his skin, and she feels for a moment that she might want him to touch her forever.

Afterwards he rolls away from her and she goes to open the window. Cooler air touches against her skin. A breeze is rocking the branches in the garden now. The aeroplane has left a trail of silver across the sky.

Wait a minute, she says and heads down the stairs. She finds a box of cigarettes on the sitting-room mantelpiece, sherry and glasses on a low table. Another gramophone stands on the sideboard – two in one house – and Rose looks through the records. All of them are classical or military. She puts on a Beethoven symphony, turns the volume up loud. Gathering the sherry and cigarettes, she stops for a moment, enjoying the feeling of being naked in this neat room where every piece of furniture, every picture, turns away from her in shock. The inappropriate grandeur of the music makes her want to laugh as she crosses the hall and hurries back upstairs. Sitting on the bed, she pours Frank a sherry and starts to light a cigarette but Frank pulls her to him.

And so they make love again – for longer this time. Rose loves to touch him, to feel the length and smoothness of his limbs. He is so white, clean and smooth as marble. Rose pulls herself against him as she feels him reach his climax. Frank gasps for breath and grips her arms too tightly. Rose, I want you to marry me.

Rose laughs, pulls herself away from him, digs her toe into the side of his leg. Oh Frank, for God's sake. She sits up and pours herself sherry, feels the burn of it on her lips. Frank has pulled the sheets up over his body, hiding himself. Rose knows he feels a little ashamed of what they've just done and she pities him. She pours him sherry and tries more laughter but he refuses to be amused. Instead his white face is hot with anger.

Don't be silly, Frank, she says.

Rose, you're not listening. I want to get married to you.

Rose looks away, annoyed. She had thought Frank understood the rules. She can't believe how stupid rich people can be. Spoilt little boy, she thinks. Isn't it time that someone should deny him what he wants? She hopes he isn't going to make trouble.

Rose, are you listening to me?

Frank, I don't want to be married – not to you or to anyone else. Not ever. I've got better things to do. She reaches out for the cigarettes, lights one for Frank, but he refuses and so she places it between her own lips. All the while Frank watches her, his eyes pressing against her skin. She blows out smoke, looks down at him. Anyway you can't get married to me because you're engaged to Violet.

No, I'm not.

All right – but as good as.

Frank's face is iron and storm. He sits up, turns away from her, pulls on his shirt, then turns back to face her. I'm not marrying Violet, he says. She's a frigid cow and I'm not marrying her. And anyway, she doesn't love me.

I'm sure she does.

Perhaps not as much as she loves you?

Don't be silly, Frank. I don't know what you're talking about.

And the other thing is – I might as well say – I'm not going to sign up.

What? Why?

What do you mean – why? You know why.

But Frank – you'll be sacked.

Then maybe I should save them the trouble and resign.

Rose says nothing because she knows he's beyond reason.

What's the matter? he says. You know that's the only thing I can do. You know that's the right thing for me to do. And I thought that surely you'd approve.

Approve? What does my approval have to do with it?

Rose gulps down the sherry and reaches for her dress. The air of the room floats blue with cigarette smoke. The thumping, yearning music from downstairs is beginning to irritate her. Its cadences shout veiled warnings. She feels a shudder pass through her like the beginning of fever. Frank is being childish but he'll have forgotten about all this tomorrow. She picks up her cigarette, strides over and slams the window shut. The trees in the garden appear strangely crooked, the pond an ugly scar in the earth. That silver line still cuts the sky in half. Rose watches the smouldering tip of her cigarette. How very silly of Frank to ruin the afternoon – but there's nothing to worry about.

# 13

# Now

## Oliver – Brighton, February 2003

Oliver hears her voice – that brassy, intrusive voice. She's downstairs in the Stop The War office. He could go out, walk down to the sea, walk anywhere, but there's no point. He opens the door that leads up to his flat. As he ascends the stairs, the body of a man dangles in the stairwell, suspended by his neck, silent. A suicide, a preventable death. Oliver turns away, closes his eyes. He enters his flat, pulls the bolts, turns the key, although he knows that no lock or key can keep out the waiting future. In the kitchen, he pours a glass of wine, identifies that point on the soothing white of the wall, presses his head against it, feeling the familiar imperfections of the plaster against his skin.

He wonders what has become of the boy – perhaps he's dead? He doesn't have to be in Iraq to die. One of those buses could be involved in an accident, he could leave the group, wander into a dangerous part of Istanbul – or whatever city he has reached by now. Oliver presses his head against the wall. Even when the vicar first suggested letting the peace protesters use that downstairs room, he had sensed pain stalking him. Time passes – minutes, hours? Time is only a construct in men's minds. All that will ever happen has already happened and will keep happening forever now. Perhaps she's gone home? But no, he hears footsteps on the stairs. Then an insistent knocking. At the door, he steadies himself before he pulls back that redundant bolt.

She looks quite different – no business suit or high-heeled shoes. Instead, a knee-length blue coat, a pale blue cotton shirt, jeans, hair which is tangled and wet. She smells of something sweet and expensive – a hint of lemon, or perhaps lime? Shivering, she stands with her arms wrapped around her. I need you to help me, she says. She swallows and pushes her damp hair out of her eyes. As though illuminated by a sudden flicker of white light, he sees her hand – the skin sand-coloured and smooth. His heart stumbles and then rushes on.

Have you heard from him? Oliver asks.

No – yes. Just an email which came – but that was over a week ago. And now they're at the border – they may even have crossed. I don't know.

So they will go in?

Yes, I think so. There are all these messages going around from the other relatives but still no one actually knows. Apparently they're likely to have all communications equipment confiscated at the border.

You better come in, he says.

She steps into the room, her eyes picking out Grace's vases. He should have hidden them away somewhere. He's never invited anyone into this room before. It's achingly cold, he realises, although he hadn't noticed before. He gestures to a straight-backed chair which is close to the broken gas fire. He moves the only other chair and sits opposite her. Her face might once have been attractive but it's been obscured by so many layers of want and disappointment that he can't see who she really is at all. Her wet hair drips onto the shoulders of her coat, stains her shirt with drops of darker blue.

She's staring around her at the white plastic shelves and a former tenant's attempt at a paint effect that might once have suggested marble but now looks merely grubby. The strip of beige carpet, marked by the last tenant's furniture, and the vacant curtain rails present themselves for his consideration as they've never done before. A faint and persistent buzzing comes from somewhere – perhaps the fridge or a fly trapped somewhere? He waits, confident that silence will prove dangerous.

Her eyes return to the vases on top of the cupboard. They're not large but they dominate the room. The colours vary – indigo, sea green, blue-purple. The shapes are organic. Inside the glass – so small that she cannot see – tiny bubbles float and glitter, held in stillness. As she tilts her head, the light on them changes, figures appear dancing in their shadows. For a moment he shuts his eyes and sees Grace, as she was when he first saw her. Eight years old. The cleanly drawn jawline and the swing of her strawberry-blonde hair. Her head turned away from him, she sits in the pew in front of him in the church of St Mark's, Falmouth.

The Gulf War, Lara says. You know, in 1991. You remember that British soldier they took hostage. His photograph was all over the papers. Well, they never said what was actually done to him, did they? That was never revealed, was it? She stops to catch her breath. I need to find a way of getting him back. I need you to help me.

Of course, I'll do anything I can.

I know you can help me. She holds out those indecently smooth hands. You can pray – or whatever you do.

I don't understand, Oliver says, although he understands only too well.

Please, she says. I know that you can bring him back.

He shakes his head, looks away from her. I don't know what you've been told but none of it is true.

She says nothing but her hands are still stretched out towards him. He shuts his eyes for a moment, as he does when he sees The Dying, hopes that when he opens them she might have gone. But she remains solidly there, absolutely present, drips of water still seeping into her pale blue shirt, her hands innocent in her lap.

You make a mistake. I'm sorry about your son but there is nothing I can do.

She is deflated, shrugs her shoulders stiffly, stares down at her fingers. He sees how alone she is. People like her, with money and good taste and family living all around them, are often lonely. She stands up, shrugs, picks up her bag. I'm sorry, she says. I'm upset, I shouldn't have come, I'm sorry.

Quietly she starts to cry. She's a woman who isn't used to crying and the sound is quiet and strangled, tight with shame. She is ripe, overdue. Her despair touches against his own. He feels angry that temptation has been placed so squarely in his path. This isn't a man walking out between two parked cars or a phantom dangling from a windowsill. It isn't a woman lying on the tarmac at the side of a motorway bleeding to death. This is easy, very easy.

Her sobbing is pitiful. She seems to have shrunk. He has to take away her despair before it raises his own to an unmanageable level. What he can bear for himself, he cannot bear for others. She turns to look back at him and he sees the yearning in her eyes. Of course, she thinks that it's all high drama, a mumbled incantation, a whiff of smoke, a fizz of electricity, a miracle, but usually it's invisible, subtle, impossible to quantify. A subtle and silent switch that flicks somewhere. You can feel your way to it, just by concentrating, listening. It's happening now and he isn't in control. He hates the fact that it's so random, fickle. The captain is back at the helm of the ship, at least for this moment. Just let the process unfold.

I'm sorry, he says. I didn't mean to be unkind. Please, sit down.

She sits down again awkwardly, wiping tears from her eyes.

You know in his letter he said – I want to exist. That's what he said. But nobody has to go to Iraq in order to exist.

She catches a sob in her throat, wipes at her eyes again.

You know, he's always said that none of it has anything to do with not having a father but it must have something to do with that. I mean, his father abandoned me when I was seven weeks pregnant and never wanted to see him. That must have had its effect but he never wanted to talk about any of that. And now it's too late.

Oliver is fascinated – perhaps even a little envious – of how absolutely self-centred she is. For her the war in Iraq is about what happened to her twenty years ago. But he must push these thoughts aside, concentrate.

No, he says. No. It's not too late. It's never too late. That's the opportunity that you're being offered here – the chance to have a different relationship with your son. This isn't a random event – nothing is. There are reasons why this has happened.

Punishment? I suppose that's what it is. I mean, that's what people like you believe and I've never accepted that but now... I was only an averagely bad mother.

One mustn't be scared of confrontation. Conflict and healing aren't opposites but lie close together. I don't believe in punishment, he says. But I do think you may be being offered a possibility, an opportunity to understand something. And it might take twenty years for you to understand it but you will understand it if you want to. You need to find some meaning in this. That's the only thing you can do. That's the only way you'll cope.

He dislikes himself for saying this because he doesn't believe it. He's selling her a line. But what else is one to do with the despairing? One shouldn't underestimate the value of cliché in times of disaster.

But I don't know where to start, she says.

Maybe begin by doing nothing. By making some time – see what comes along.

I can't do nothing. I work full time. I've always had to work full time just so I could do the best for Jay.

I can see how difficult that must be, he says. These words, he has discovered over the years, are often all one needs to say. Empathy, that's what he talked to the boy about. Another cliché he questions – but sometimes, sometimes, the mere fact of being understood can heal.

You know I don't believe in God or prayer, she says. And yet now I find myself praying all the time. And endlessly making bargains with God. I keep asking – what do you want? What do I have to do? Anything, anything for him just to come back safe.

Oliver is familiar with this talk about God, about bargains. People always fall back on that, even people who have no religious education, no faith. Deep in us all, imprinted there from the beginning, is the idea that if we are good then we will be rewarded. Even in this secular age, it's a language people understand. He doesn't bother to argue with her. If it's going to help her get through the day then what does it matter? He had thought her stupid and shallow. Now he realises that although she may be shallow, she isn't stupid.

As I said before, I think it might just be a question of a bit of quiet.

I know what you're saying. But I just don't have any support. My mother and father. They don't understand. All my mother cares about is the first night of some play. And my job, it's the one thing I have which is mine. It's me, it's who I am.

But Oliver knows that soon she will break – maybe not now, maybe not in the way that he expects – but it will happen. It's already happening. When he looks at her now, she's quite different. Something has dropped away from her. The layers of want and disappointment are breaking up so that her face is now, distantly, visible. He doesn't want this power over her. He should have left well alone. If someone is desperate then you can get them to believe absolutely anything. As he looks at her, and sees how she's changed, he's frightened for her.

I must go, she says. I suppose that the only thing I can hope for now is that there won't be a war. The peace protesters may be my best hope. Thank you.

That's quite all right.

Her eyes move up to the vases again.

They're beautiful – really extraordinary.

Yes.

Do you mind me asking where they came from?

They were made by my wife – Grace.

Even now he finds it improbable that the word wife should be used in relation to Grace. The fact of her being married had always been ridiculous.

And she's an artist glass-blower?

No. No. She's dead.

Oh. I see. Sorry. I'm very tactless – always have been. One of my few talents.

No need to worry. It's quite all right.

He says this calmly but he feels his bones grating inside him, presses his teeth together in case he should give her an idiot grin. He has seldom needed to actually say that word – dead – and so now it's as though he's hearing it for the first time. After she's gone, Oliver stands still in the middle of the room, measures the space that she occupied, feels the tension she has left in the air. He's light-headed, tired, strangely elated. He aches for Grace now, for any woman, for human flesh, for comfort.

That first day comes back to him – a day far back in childhood, the garden in Falmouth, the frost still thickening the mossy grass, the tall, crooked fences, made of black, half-rotten wood. The flattened flower beds and the row of straggling Scots pines whose intricate shadows shiver on the grass. The children playing, their breath rising in white clouds around them. And Grace sitting on the garden bench, with her legs swinging, wearing a lilac-coloured beret and a matching scarf. Her eyes are widely spaced and a cool shade of green. Her face mysterious as the moon and full of questions.

He lifts one of the vases down and runs his finger up the side of it. The glass is infinitely solid and dense. As he moves his finger, it sticks just a little to a tiny, unseen flaw. He moves his finger, runs it along the vase's lip, a sensual curve. He hears her voice, her adult voice. *You and your arrogance. How can you believe that? It isn't anything to do with you.* He often hears this voice, taunting him.

But now he answers – *Yes, but it's happening again. It does happen. Perhaps not on the hard shoulder of the motorway with the blood draining away but it happens, in small ways, it happens.* A wave of electric energy surges through him. He's back into the flow of this again. A feeling he hasn't had in years. A warm tingling, a firing-up of engines somewhere deep inside, a desire to touch, to hold, to laugh. If only it could last, if only he could be sure.

# 14

## BEFORE

### Rose – Coventry, September 1939

The house in Warwick Road smells of restless waiting and illness now. The maid has told Rose that Violet is upstairs with Mr Whiteley and that she's to wait in the hall. In the past, Rose would have gone up to Violet but now she doesn't dare. Instead she sits on the red tasselled chair by the hall table and folds her hands in her lap, pressing down against her knees as though to ensure that her body, at least, stays in its proper place. Frank is alive on her skin – the slight burn on her chin where his stubble scratched her, the touch of his tongue against hers, the dampness between her legs and the tenderness of her breasts.

Too many things are happening too fast. The earth is unstable, the air itself is rattled and shaken. What will she say to Violet? She's sure Frank is wrong. Violet wouldn't have got him sacked, even though she does have cause to feel aggrieved. The lines of the black and white floor tiles march steadily from the front door to the foot of the stairs. In the evening shadows, those treacherous Chinese vases stand guard at the sitting room door and the china shepherds and shepherdesses still frolic in their glass case. It's houses like this – and the people who own them – who have caused the war, Rose knows that, but she can't help but love this house. Except that now those who are not for are against. Rose looks at her watch. She's agreed to meet Frank at seven thirty at the Peace Pledge office.

From above a door clicks open, a rustle of fabric, the click of shoe on a polished board, and Violet appears at the top of the stairs. Mr Whiteley's illness has tarnished her pale perfection but still her silk dress is ironed and her hair is neatly rolled, her lipstick bright. She wears a string of beads and swings the end of them in her hand as she sweeps down the green-carpeted stairs, her orchid hand coming to rest on the mahogany snail curl at the end of the balcony. Rose, my darling. I'm so glad you're here. You'll never guess what. I've got news. Big news.

What? Let me guess.

No, I want to tell you. Stanley asked me – and I said yes. Violet gives an awkward bow, sweeping her hand down and then up, waving it high in a circle above her head. So we're engaged.

Oh, that's super news. Absolutely fantastic.

Rose isn't surprised. It was only two months ago that Frank finally managed to ease himself away from Violet but it was always unlikely that Violet would play the role of jilted woman for long. Rose feels an intense gratitude to brisk and portly Stanley with his stubbly little moustache. He has erased Violet's disappointment, her own guilt.

Congratulations. Rose catches hold of Violet and hugs her, feeling the soft wool of her pale pink scarf and the touch of powder on her cheek.

Last weekend we went away to the Foremans together – you know, to Backley Grange because, of course, Stanley was at school with George Cunningham. Stanley says you can come with us any time. Of course, we're going to marry as soon as we can. So that if – when – Stanley has to go away. Hopefully father might be well enough to come. You will be bridesmaid?

Yes, of course.

I must show you. Look. Violet opens a cupboard under the stairs, pulls out a fur coat on a hanger and holds it up against her. Then she reaches into the cupboard and pulls out a suitcase as well. Holding the suitcase beside her, she models the coat and case, flouncing her curls and making a pouting, film-star face. Rose touches the coat. It's so soft that it hardly seems to exist at all.

Look. Violet opens the suitcase, which has tiny jewels fixed into the catches. Inside the lid, the oyster satin is gathered up to make a separate compartment and above it a tiny mirror is held in place by an extra layer of satin. Initials have been engraved into the leather. V.M.B. Violet Mary Bunton.

Super, Rose says. Beautiful.

Violet twirls around again, holding the coat against her but then starts to put both back in the cupboard. I'll have to go back up in a minute. Father is having a bad day. But let's have a cup of tea – and maybe a sandwich. Is it seven already?

Violet goes to the kitchen door, calls for tea, leads Rose into the drawing room. There she sinks into a chair, eases off her shoes, wriggles her toes, lights a cigarette. Through the French windows, amidst the gathering shadows, Rose can see where the garden has been dug up to accommodate the Anderson shelter. The Moorish arch with its pineapple knob has disappeared – probably they took that when they pulled up the railings outside. The remains of the wisteria, broken and hacked, is piled in a flower bed.

Violet draws on the cigarette, tipping her head back. I knew straight away, of course. Even that first day when Stanley came to lunch – you remember, back in March – seems like another world, doesn't it? We won't be able to have much of a honeymoon, of course – but we might go to the Lake District or Pembrokeshire. And Stanley is going to come here, at least to start with, so that I can look after father. I'm just so happy. I couldn't have wanted anyone better than Stanley. He's been so good over the last two months. Such a support with father so ill.

Rose looks out again at the wreck of the garden and now, suddenly, the scarred earth and the lumpy roof of the shelter seem unbearably sad. That strange hysteria which has inhabited the city all through the long summer months has ceased now and often a strange stillness descends. Everything is braced, ready. Surely something will happen now – but nothing does. Although fines are issued to anyone not carrying a gas mask, and on the outskirts of the cities the factories crank and grind all night, their lights dazzling, their smell of oil heavy in the air. And the men emerge white-faced into the dawn, bicycling home, only to go back again at lunchtime.

And how are you? Violet asks.

Fine. Well, bitterly disappointed, of course. I did know it would come, but all the same. People have worked so hard. I just can't believe it – and I'm frightened, and well – not exactly excited, but—

Yes, I am too. Dreadful, isn't it? I'll be all right until Stanley goes.

All the alarms sounded at the factory the other day – this wailing, screaming noise, and everyone thought the Germans were rattling at the gates, ready to shoot us or kick us to the ground. But no one really says anything. Apparently they're going to evacuate all the children.

No. Surely not. Why would they do that?

The maid brings the tea, her eyes red and her hands shaking as she pours. As she puts the teapot down on the tray, it smashes against the milk jug and both Rose and Violet move to right it. The maid snuffles and disappears.

Really, Violet says. As though she's the only person whose husband is going away.

Rose knows that she needs to ask Violet about Frank soon. To her, it doesn't really matter why Frank has been sacked but Frank himself is furious, absolutely furious. Rose saw him two nights ago. He stayed at the boarding house – climbing up a trellis and across a roof – because both of her roommates were away. Rose had been looking forward to that night – so much better to be in a bed rather than the cellar at the Peace Pledge office or sharing a blanket in Binley Woods.

She remembers now lying in bed, watching him dress. At the open window the grey light was lifting, revealing the familiar outline of roofs and chimneys, the branch of a stunted apple tree. In the half-light, Frank pulled his braces up over his shoulders, lifted his foot onto the wooden end of the bed to tie his shoelace – his movements musical, sliding like dance. Allegro, piano, fortissimo. Rose doesn't know the meaning of any of these words but they describe Frank as he moves. When he'd done his shoes he came to kneel beside her, twisted her hair, bit at her lip.

But then he spoilt it all by ranting yet again about Violet. She was responsible, he was sure of that. She'd been in to see her father's friend, Mr Cardew, and persuaded him. But why, Rose asked herself, had Frank not seen this coming? He's a conchie, he's jilted the daughter of a powerful man and there are rumours, endless rumours. But no – Frank did not see it coming because he stubbornly believes in decency, fairness and the triumph of love. Rose had found herself caught between irritation and tenderness.

I suppose you've heard? Rose says. That Frank has lost his job?

Yes. I did hear.

Rose can never be sure what exactly Violet knows. She's too proud, too discreet for confrontation and Rose admires that.

Of course, as you know, I was never really interested in Frank, Violet says. We've always been friends but it was never going to be anything more than that.

No. Absolutely. He was never right for you.

I never really thought of it. I know other people did. Just because we look rather similar people seemed to like the idea. And then Aunt Muriel with her hat. And, of course, I am fond of Frank because he's my cousin. But now I'm concerned about him. Very. I've been talking to Stanley and he thinks Frank is having a mental crisis. It's to do with chemicals in the brain. Stanley has read all about it. Or it could be a depression. Apparently, a depression is sometimes a refusal to participate in society – and that would certainly fit with the way that Frank is behaving, wouldn't you say?

Rose wants to ask, *Are there not some so-called societies that we should refuse to participate in?* But she keeps silent, feels herself playing out the rope, seeing how far Violet will go. And she thinks of Frank – his drink-crazed eyes and his anger. She'd never thought that he'd refuse to sign up. Others had but they were Quakers, committed to conscientious objection from the womb. Many of the young men in the Peace Pledge office had signed up finally and there were no hard feelings about it. Everyone understood. But Frank had been one of the few who absolutely refused and has kept on campaigning, working late into the night, writing up the minutes of meetings, sticking up posters, handing out leaflets.

At the Tribunal the judge had said that Frank was lucky to be registered as a conscientious objector when he has no religious background and described him as *a fit and able young man who could easily serve his country had he not been infected by the poison of communism.* And then, of course, his name had been published in the papers, and at the factory Ivy, Beryl and Win had said to Rose – *Surprised you're still talking to him. Bloody traitor.* In the bar at the Socialist Workers' Club a man hit him over the head with an empty bottle of beer. Then the police had arrested him for causing a Public Nuisance and he'd been released the next day with his eye black and swollen. At the factory it was suggested to him – politely – that he would no longer be required for the tennis team. The man who crossed the floor. But he has borne it all – the jibes and the bitterness and his mother's tears. Now what will happen to him? He's a fool, Frank, but truthful and right. Does no one have any respect for that?

Although really – why should I care? Violet says, pouring a second cup of tea. Frank is an adult and can do what he wants. But I'm worried for you, Rose. Very worried. Because I know what a pest Frank can be and I don't want your reputation ruined. If Frank wants to go to the dogs then he's welcome but you really mustn't let him take you with him.

So you got him sacked?

Violet flushes crimson, licks her lips.

Rose, you must understand – at the factory they've got to be very careful. They have already been incredibly tolerant towards Frank. Most companies would have sacked him the day he refused to sign up. And it was only the influence that your Mr Bostock has with the Tribunal which meant that he kept his job and only had to move to a different department. Well, I don't know. But now everything is different. They can't afford to have someone with those kinds of political views and it isn't only politics. I talked to father once about this and he understands. It's also – well, you know I told you about Frank and his – instincts.

So you got him sacked?

Oh Rose, for goodness' sake. Do let's be civilised.

You did? Didn't you?

Rose, really. I did it for you, dear. Because I care for you. I felt I had to and I don't know why you mind. He was going to lose his job anyway. And it's not as though you would be silly enough even to think about it – and neither would Frank. And anyway, now that he doesn't have a job, he certainly can't marry. And he'll have to go back to the Tribunal and I doubt they'll be so lenient again. And so he'll find himself sent away to do some filthy agricultural job or even sent to prison and perhaps at the end of all that he'll see sense.

Rose feels her jaw tighten, her throat contract. Blood is burning under her skin. But there's no point in saying anything. Violet holds all the power, has always held all the power, and she can dispose of them all as she wants. The hypocrisy of this is dazzling. How is it possible to live in a world where weakness and strength are so dangerously confused? Rose puts her teacup down. She's trying not to be like Frank – not to be angry or surprised – because she's only discovered what she always knew. She stands up, heads to the door.

Oh Rose, really. I'm sorry. Please don't go.

Rose stops at the door and turns back but only because she's interested to observe the charming way in which Violet will negotiate this little difficulty.

He'll bring you down, Rose. All this silly stuff with the Peace Pledge Union. He would never have done all that if it wasn't for you.

Violet, you don't know.

Yes, I do. Frank is weak. He'll do anything for – that. Well, you must see. If you tell him to do something then he'll do it. You don't have to waste your time on him. There's a hundred other people you could marry.

The tragedy of this is that Violet is right. Rose has made no commitment to Frank and she doesn't want to marry a man with no job. A minor matter of missed monthlies and morning sickness might have to be dealt with but Rose has talked to Mrs Watson and she knows a woman who can organise it all. Frank's enthusiasm had punctured the membrane of her Dutch cap and she'd neglected to send off for another one. But it isn't even certain that Frank is the man responsible for the pregnancy. Rose knows that she should finish with him, then she and Violet could go to house parties at Backley Grange.

She looks around the sitting room now, recording the details because perhaps she won't come here again. The stained-glass panels at the top of the window, the potted palm on its lace mat, the dark wood fireplace with its green-patterned tiles, the dark little oil painting of a landscape – Holland it must be, with those windmills. Her eyes fix on the lower part of Violet's legs, slanted neatly to one side. The pale stockings she wears are wrinkled at the ankles above the buttoned strap of her shoes. Something about those flesh-coloured wrinkles is unbearably childish, pitiful.

Rose, please. Don't leave me. I thought you might come and live here – once Stanley has gone. We've got to stick together, haven't we?

I'm sorry. I've got to go.

Please, Rose. Please. I was trying to look after you.

Violet is on her feet now and catches hold of Rose's arm.

Rose, please. I love you. You know that.

Rose finds herself swallowing back tears.

Rose, you will come back later, won't you?

Yes, of course.

Rose takes Violet in her arms and holds her tight. Violet's small hands grip against her shoulders and her tears soak Rose's blouse. Why is it so difficult just to leave? Violet is nothing but prettiness and frivolity, her moment has passed. And yet Rose finds herself clinging to her, stroking her hair. She's tried so many times to dislike Violet, to dismiss her, but she's never been able to do it. Wasn't it always Frank she wanted, not Violet? Or was it the other way around? The two are indivisible, or should have been. Even though Violet is standing up now the wrinkles of those stockings still pucker at her ankles. Rose pulls herself away and turns to go.

I must go. I'm due at the Peace Pledge office.

Honestly, Rose Mayeford. You will kill yourself with all this. You will kill yourself. Do you hear what I'm saying?

Outside Rose draws in deep breaths of the September evening but even the air tastes different now. It carries the dull sting of conscription, First Aid, gas masks and sandbags. Rose turns back to look at 34 Warwick Road with its white-cliff façade and its many stacks of chimneys. Violet is at her bedroom window, tiny and pale, a doll in a doll's house, waving and waving. Of course, she isn't really there but Rose can't get that image out of her mind, Violet's white dress and that tiny waving hand.

As Rose walks on everything looks so normal – the trees lining the Green, the families trailing homewards with prams and baskets containing the remains of picnics, and the three spires of Coventry glimpsed in the distance. Except that as Rose looks across the restful city, its image is overlaid with another, blurred black-and-white shadows from newsreels and newspapers – an impression of the Spanish cities after the aerial bombardments. Rose shuts her eyes, shivers, walks on. The day is sliding towards the grey of evening and lights flicker on in the windows of houses, which are turned in on themselves now, guarding their safety, watching, waiting.

Rose hurries on towards the Peace Pledge office – although the office isn't actually there any more. Everything of importance has been packed up, hidden underground, the bank account closed, the records and leaflets hidden away in people's houses where the police can't find them. *Peace News* continues to be produced but the name of the printer has to be kept secret or he'll lose his business. Rose still has a key to the basement of the building. So when she arrives, she goes around to the back, looks around her to check that no one is watching, slides the key into the lock of the back door and enters the corridor with its dustbins and ragged noticeboard. Frank comes up the cellar steps to meet her. He wears a navy roll-neck jumper and his shirt hangs out of the bottom of it. He's thinner now and his face has lost its shine.

She steps into his arms and he holds her against him, kisses her. Then he turns and pulls her down the cellar stairs after him. A gas lamp burns from a nail and Frank has laid a sheet across the rusty iron bed which is wedged in a corner. He takes hold of Rose, kisses her again. Rose pulls back, her eyes join with Frank's and suddenly she understands. It comes at her with the acid sting of truth. Frank loves her. She herself has never been interested in love, had entirely discounted the possibility of it, but now here it is, unwanted.

Rose undoes the front of Frank's shirt, presses her head against the flat of his chest. His skin is pale, blue-veined. Of course, if she married him then his body would be hers, permanently. And he's a possession that she can't help but covet. A painted shepherd she can put in her own glass cabinet. Frank turns to the gramophone. He insists on keeping it here even though Rose has told him that it'll get damp, that someone will hear. A thump, a throb, a rustle. *Paradise here, paradise close, just around this corner. The place happiness is for me.* Frank undoes the buttons of her dress. She kicks off her shoes, lies down, shuts out the waiting city. Shuts out the throbbing factories, the bicycles, the stamp of boots.

Afterwards she lies with her head against Frank's back, rests her hands on his hip. The record has come to its end, the gramophone throbs and crackles. Rose gets up to switch it off. Frank probably wants her to play the record again but she's bored by those sentimental old songs. Her mind moves back to an evening earlier in the week. She and Arthur had been pushing their bikes back from the factory and she'd said to him then, Arthur, how do I come to be in this mess?

127

And he'd said, Ah well, Rose. No point in asking, is there, who betrayed you? You did it to yourself.

Oh Arthur. Why don't I marry you instead? It would be so much easier.

Rosa. My bella. You have only to name the day.

Now she runs her finger along Frank's hip and wonders what will happen to him. Hopefully he will avoid prison. He might even get sent to a farm that isn't too far away. The two of them are on a rock in the sea with the water rising around them, less and less space to stand on. What happened to Frank? How did he change? Violet says that he did it for her but is that true? And must she marry him to thank him? No. Frank simply saw what is true and evident and has held to it. Now he turns over, holds her close.

Rose, when we're married, promise me one thing.

When we're married. The words are sonorous as a church bell tolling at a funeral.

Promise me you won't ever see Violet again.

But Frank. You and Violet.

Rose pictures them for a moment, standing in the hall at 34 Warwick Road, the mirror image of each other, Siamese twins; when Violet moves her right hand, his left hand echoes her movement. That which should have been indivisible has been divided and she was the one who broke it apart. And she had done it for no reason except that she could. And now she will have to marry Frank because although he was educated at the grammar school, and lives in Fitzmaurice Street, he will be nothing without her. He isn't a brave man and yet he's being brave. He can't be left alone in this.

Frank, listen. It doesn't have to be like that.

No, Rose. I've decided – and now it's time for you to do the same.

Those who are not for are against. Rose has run with the hare and hunted with the hounds for long enough. She turns her face towards Frank, kisses him, feels that familiar shock run through her body. She would rather die than accept that this world in which they're living is all that is possible. What Violet said will prove accurate – Frank will bring her down. But finally it doesn't feel like her fault, or Violet's, or Frank's. It feels like some larger force has taken over. Not war, or love, those clichéd levers of destiny, but something older and deeper, something infinite and ancient, far beyond human control. She touches Frank's face, holds him tight. Will he be a partner or a millstone? She knows the answer to that question but remains defiant. She is strong enough for both of them – and this is their moment. Frank will be sent away – maybe he won't come back. Maybe the city will be invaded and soon they'll all be under German rule. But here under the gas light, lying on this narrow bed, with its clean white sheet, they can lie flesh against flesh, and hear the city all around them, its muscles tense. And beyond that the darkness of the skies, the heavens, indifferent.

# 15

# Now

## Mollie – Brighton, February 2003

It's early but Mollie prefers to get up. Best not to spend too long in bed, people die in bed. In the kitchen, she yawns, pours a slug of whisky into her coffee. Her face is dry with yesterday's make-up and her throat sore with last night's cigarette smoke. In a corner, a pool of cat piss is spreading across the tiles so she drops two sheets of newspaper over it. Picking up the remote control, she turns the sound up and flicks through the channels. The picture on the screen is dissolving into zigzags so Mollie wobbles the wires at the back. Nothing was said on the television yesterday or in the evening papers but surely there will be something today? It's three whole days since they heard that the buses had gone into Iraq – but now nothing and nothing and nothing. But Wilf or Martha will come around straight away if they find out anything.

Although Rufus is not at home, Mollie can feel his rage. The reviews of his play come out today and he's gone for the papers. The rage always starts before he's even read them. Usually Mollie ignores most of what Rufus says but, with Jay gone, she has fewer defences against him. La-la-la-la-la. A grey old day but it's sure to brighten up. She needs to do some tea and toast for Mr Lambert. Plunger. She needs to take one up to the third floor to unblock the sink. After she's got the breakfast, she'll give Lara a call and then pop around to the peace protesters. It worries her that Lara hasn't visited. Occasionally she leaves a message with some news but nothing more. Of course, she was furious about that message Jay sent, bless him. Mollie realises that soon she might have to apologise to Lara although God knows what she's done wrong. Anyway, no point in thinking about that. Hand it over to the Good Lord and hope for the best.

Two empty champagne bottles stand on the table and Mollie throws them into the bin, then she fills a china vase and unwraps a wilting bunch of flowers. She should have tidied up last night but they all stayed up too late and drank too much. After the show there was a party backstage, then Mollie drove Rufus home, and the stage manager came back as well, and it was four o'clock before they got to bed. The music from last night still tingles in her ears. On the sideboard there's a cake, which Martha brought around yesterday, bless her. She's a good soul. Mollie lifts the cake. Ah well, could be useful as a doorstop or something to smash over the head of a burglar. Or feed it to Stan, Stan and Stan. Turns out that lot haven't got any papers so they're in no position to be fussy.

Upstairs the front door bangs. Oh God, spare us, Mollie thinks. Now it begins. There won't be more than one or two write-ups, if that, but still Rufus will have bought every paper. Last night he talked long and drunkenly about how it's totally and completely unimportant what critics think.

The buggers. The buggers. Just look at this. He stamps down the stairs and into the kitchen, wrestling with a newspaper. Sections drop from his hands and float to the floor. Mollie hurries to scoop them up, looking for the news pages, hoping that she might see something about the human shields.

Will you turn that bloody television off? Rufus says.

Mollie presses her finger onto the volume control.

Rufus finds the right page. It says, 'Dreary subject matter. Failure to grip.'

Oh dear. But that's only one.

Listen, just listen to this. Rufus starts to read. He's wearing pyjama trousers, brogues and a large wool jumper. His face is red and stubbly, his thick hair stands on end and his eyes are bleary from last night's drinking. Mollie wonders why age has mellowed everyone except her husband.

Last night...

Just be quiet, will you? Listen. Bugger. God, my head hurts. Where is it? It says 'Dreary subject matter.' Dreary bloody subject matter, my arse.

Pearls before swine.

Rufus pours himself a whisky. Can't bloody win. What do these people want? Nice little middle-class drawing-room dramas. You try to put a proper play on. You try to actually make people think. Tossers. Arse-licking teenage cowards making a living by spitting on other people's creativity.

Why don't I get you some bacon and egg?

Are you listening? He stamps around the kitchen, shuffling through the papers again and again, reading sections, waving pages at her in disgust. Mollie nods her head, drinks her coffee, clears up, starts on the bacon and egg. The play is called *Going Nowhere*. Mollie had always thought it an unfortunate title but hadn't liked to say so.

What did Rufus expect? He knows quite well that no one wants serious theatre any more. They want a When-Did-You-Last-See-Your-Trousers farce. Or they want big sets, purple lighting, dry ice. It isn't possible just to put two people on a blank stage any more and let them speak the truth. But Rufus won't give up. He may have done his voiceovers and his television ads but he always goes back to the theatre and Mollie respects him for that. Oh but the price is high. She's lived with Rufus's creative vision for nearly forty years and she's tired. How much rejection can anyone take? So hard to be endlessly misunderstood. She thinks of that comment Lara always makes – *There's no curse worse than minor artistic talent.* Lara is a bitch but what she says might be true.

Mollie catches sight of George Bush on the television, turns the volume up.

Leave that alone, Rufus shouts and, picking up a book, hurls it at the television. As the book sails through the air, it catches against the vase of flowers on the table and sends it crashing to the floor. Mollie stares at the pieces of the vase and the wilting flowers spread across the tiles. From next door, banging sounds. It's the gossip of the street, of course. That mad actor shouting at his wife and throwing plates. Well, they can sod off, the whole lot of them.

Why does everything have to be about that boy? Rufus says, gesturing towards the television. What do you think? That lot risking their lives, that lot having the courage to actually do something which might be some use. Finding out what war is. I don't think so. An absolute bloody waste of time. One thing you can be sure of is that none of that lot's going to get killed. And nothing they do will make the blindest bit of difference. Just a bunch of bloody towel-head savages. A lesser phase of evolution, that's all. So why the hell doesn't he just come back? Attention seeking. That's all it is. Not surprising really. I mean, look at his mother. Her son is risking his life and she won't even take one day off work.

Rufus.

Hardly surprising the boy's got problems, is it? Brought up believing he's less important than curtains?

Rufus, you know quite well that Jay has never been neglected, Mollie says.

No, of course not. That's the whole point. Like mother, like son. Spoilt them both rotten. All very handy for her, forcing you to do all her childcare while she's off in London working every hour that God sends for that ridiculous pink-faced toad. But what about me? When I worked in London people respected me.

You go to London all the time.

Shut up, will you? Christ, you don't even get any support from your own bloody wife. Lara, Jay, the bloody lodgers, everybody else except for me. That queer upstairs even gets given his breakfast before me.

I'm getting your breakfast now.

Mollie drops slices of bacon into the sizzling fat. La-la-la-la-la. There will be better days soon. They should be kind to each other now that they're old. At least the play has provided a distraction over the last couple of weeks. Better than sitting there all day watching the phone. Mollie knows that, deep down, Rufus is terrified that something is going to happen to Jay. That's partly what all this shouting is about. Rufus wouldn't have been doing this play if it wasn't for Jay. Jay had needled him – telling him to stop wasting his time on bad-quality television, questioning his values and ideas. If only Jay were here now, he'd find a way of sorting Rufus out.

She remembers Jay, four years old, standing on a chair in the kitchen, saying to Rufus, *You talk too much and you make too much noise.* Mollie was terrified that Rufus would hit the boy but instead he waltzed him around the kitchen in his arms, laughing, and told everyone the story for days afterwards. And often Jay would stand by the sink with a bottle of Rufus's best whisky. *Help Granmollie get the boiler going again or this lot is going down the sink.* And Rufus would swear and curse but he would get the boiler going again. Mollie has never achieved the same and Lara certainly hasn't. Baghdad appears on the screen, low rise and dust coloured. Mollie picks up the remote control.

Switch that television off, Rufus roars.

Mollie sees sandbags in the streets and boarded-up shop windows – but no news about the human shields. Rufus comes up behind her, swipes at her, catching the side of her head, so that inside her head, her brain smashes against her skull. She ducks, hears his rasping breath and smells stale smoke and alcohol clinging to his shirt. But still she keeps her eyes fixed on the television.

Turn it off, Rufus says, raises his hand, swipes again. Mollie screams and, pulling away from Rufus, collapses at the table. Rufus reaches for the remote control but Mollie keeps it gripped tight in her hand. Turning, she points it at the television and switches the volume up so loud so that the whole kitchen is filled by the bellowing voice of the newsreader.

Rufus is shouting as well and although Mollie can't hear what he's saying, she can guess. He's going to London, he's not coming back. That's what he always says. She watches him now, stamping away towards the stairs, turning back to shout one more insult at her. As he goes, she turns the volume down and presses her hand to side of her head, easing the pain. Rufus always says the same – *I'm not coming back*. Then he stays with his friend Baggers in Golders Green for two or three weeks until the car breaks down on the motorway, or he loses his wallet, or strains his back, then he's home again.

She pushes the frying pan from the hotplate and, kneeling on the floor, eases fragments of the broken vase into the dustpan. Her head throbs. She stops to pick up one large piece. The vase was white with a blue willow pattern. The fragment is diamond shaped and bears the mark on the back – English Willow, Stafford. She bought the vase in some northern town – Sheffield or Bradford? Rufus was in *Look Back in Anger* or was it *All My Sons*? They were lodging in a suburb somewhere, near a church. Lara must have been ten or thereabouts. Long white ankle socks and second-hand patent leather shoes, a smocked dress. No matter what clothes she dressed Lara in, they always looked too short. One morning they went out to a jumble sale in the church car park. And Mollie bought the vase just because she fancied it, even though the rim was chipped. She'd never had many things of her own, what with the lodgings, and moving all the time. It's a wrench now to see it go in the bin but she makes herself throw it in briskly. Ah well, nobody's dead.

Rufus comes down with a holdall. He's still shouting his way through all the old arguments. Why do we have to live in this dump? Why did we ever come to Brighton? How can I be expected to do my work when I don't have five minutes' peace and quiet? We should sell up before the entire place falls down. Rufus always says 'we' although the Guest House isn't his, not one penny of it. It's Mollie's inheritance, all that she's ever had, and over the years she's kept a tight grip on it, despite Rufus's many attempts to wrest it from her. Wiping the table, she judges his performance – overplayed, obvious, lacking any real sense of pace.

Don't get any support even from my own wife, Rufus says, his voice weakening.

Mollie knows what she's meant to do. She's played the part often enough before. She's meant to wring her hands and plead with him. Rufus, Rufus, don't leave me. I love you, I love you. I can't live without you. She looks across at him and sees that he's poised ready, waiting for her. He needs someone to play the scene against but she can't be bothered now. Her shoulder hurts and she's tired. All she can think about is Jay. It's three whole days now since those buses arrived.

Rufus stands near the door, uncertainly. If Mollie won't fight then he doesn't know what to do. She looks him in the eye. Let him go. She can't even be bothered to hate him any more. She always used to say that twenty per cent of her marriage was fantastic, and eighty per cent was hell, but that the twenty per cent compensated for the eighty. That ceased to be the case years ago. She's bored by him. She's spent enough time bending and twisting her life in order to make it fit the shape of his needs. He will never forgive her for the fact that he has damaged her.

Right, I'm going then, Rufus says, giving it one last try.

Mollie sits in silence, staring at him. She should tell him that the fact that Jay has gone to Iraq is his fault – because it is. Jay was sitting at the kitchen table, right where she's sitting now, and he was upset about Lara and her stupid threats. And then Rufus comes home, in a roaring temper because the bailiffs are threatening to seize the Daimler, and takes it all out on Jay. She should say all this to him but there isn't any point. When one thing goes wrong why do several other disasters always have to follow?

Rufus picks up his bag and heads to the door. Don't bother to call, he says. I'm not coming back. It's finished. You understand?

Rufus looks back at her, angry that she's ignoring the script, unnerved by her silence. For a moment, he looks as though he might start shouting again but instead he just shakes his head. She hears him stamp up the stairs and bang out of the front door. The plate of bacon and egg is slowly going cold. Never mind, give it to

Mr Lambert. Mollie moves her shoulder as far back as she can in order to feel the comforting twinge of pain that movement makes. She pours whisky into her empty coffee cup and gulps it down. Bugger him. She's too old now to be left alone. Usually at least Jay is here most days. There are tax forms from five months ago and the window has jammed open in Wilf's bedroom and so he's sleeping on the landing. She hasn't paid the builders' bill from last time so she can't ask him to come in again.

Ah well. KBO. Keep Buggering On. That's all you can do. That flat in Roma Street still isn't let despite the fact that she had the boiler fixed and the sitting room repainted. She needs to go out and get some shopping, and there's a chicken carcase to be boiled for stock, and a sick cat that ought to go to the vet. Life is only courage, nothing else. In two weeks it will be her birthday. No doubt Rufus will be back by then. Sometimes they go dancing at the Grand Hotel in Eastbourne. Which birthday is it? Her November birthday or her February birthday? Really she was born in February 1940 but her birth certificate says November 1940. Some administrative mistake she's never managed to sort out. Rufus always insists that she should celebrate both of her birthdays.

Ah well, time to pop around to the peace protest office, see how they're doing this morning. She might see if they fancy some sandwiches for lunch. Mollie finds her coat and purse, a string bag for shopping, and hurries up the area steps. The air is crystal sharp and seagulls wheel. Brushstrokes of sunlight feather the façades of the houses opposite and glitter on last night's rain. She sets off down the street but then stops.

A man is standing on the opposite side of the street, watching her. He's a youngish man, swarthy, with dark hair. Something tells her he isn't English – Italian perhaps, or Spanish? He's wearing a long overcoat, an army one, like the soldiers used to wear in the war. And he's got a strange mark across the bottom of his face, a birthmark or a scar? He doesn't stand straight, one shoulder is higher than the other. No, he isn't the same. Of course not. But all the same.

In Mollie's mind, years slide away. He does look like him, the man who came to the house in Worcester. She remembers him exactly, although it was over fifty years ago. He was called Arthur. She looked for him, after he'd gone. She can't walk on down the road with him still standing there, watching. Of course, it isn't the same man, not after all these years. The shopping can wait until the afternoon. She stumbles back down the steps into the kitchen. Jay. I need you. The house is too quiet without Rufus. Time to deal with that chicken carcass. She turns the radio on and then the television. La-la-la-la. Carrots for the stock – celery and garlic and a teaspoonful of mixed herbs.

# 16

## BEFORE

### Oliver – Falmouth, February 1961

Grace the glass-blower. Grace his wife. How typically perverse of her to pick a profession which depended on breath when breath was the very thing she could not depend on. He remembers the first time he saw her. The pale blue line of her jaw and the swing of her strawberry-blonde hair. Her head turned away from him, she sits in the pew in front of him in the church of St Mark's, Falmouth. He's ten years old and she's three years younger. His father stands in the pulpit. *But I will punish you according to the fruits of your doings, saith the Lord: and I will kindle a fire in the forest thereof, and it shall devour all things round about it.* The church windows are caked with ice, inside and out, and Oliver's fingers are numb, despite wool gloves. After the service Grace will come back to the vicarage for lunch. Oliver plans what he will say to her, how he will behave. He has never needed to consider such things before.

When they all arrive back at the vicarage, Oliver's mother sends all the children out into the garden to play while she's getting lunch. She tells Oliver that he's in charge, that the children mustn't make too much noise, mustn't stand in the flower beds, mustn't push or hit. Oliver keeps close to Grace as they all go out through the back door. The vicarage is on the outskirts of Falmouth, several miles back from the sea, but the faintest trace of salt still sharpens the air. The remains of a morning mist hovers low. It's nearly midday but the light is dull and frost still thickens the mossy grass. The garden is surrounded by tall, crooked fences, made of black, half-rotten wood. The flower beds are flattened. To one side of the lawn a bank rises, topped by a row of straggling Scots pines whose intricate shadows shiver on the grass. From beyond the bank come the occasional muffled grumbles from passing cars. The children are stiff with coats, hats and scarves and their breath rises in white clouds around them. They stand in the garden, waving their hands around awkwardly. They know that they must play but are uncertain where to begin.

Oliver is considered to be in charge because it's his parents' house and he's one of the oldest. A boy called Andrew suggests playing tag but Ian Harris wants stuck in the mud. Ian's sister Emily protests, because they'll be in trouble for getting their Sunday clothes dirty. Emily is right but Oliver can't be bothered to argue with Ian. He already accepts that this will end badly, that he will be blamed, that his parents will be disappointed in him for not supervising the younger children better. As a punishment, he will be required to sit in his father's study and write the Ten Commandments out thirty times. This is what usually happens on a Sunday. Oliver doesn't care. He has a relationship with God that his parents can never understand. He has been chosen.

As the other children organise themselves for stuck in the mud, Oliver suggests to Grace that perhaps it would be better for her to sit on the bench and watch. She agrees to this and Oliver is pleased with himself for taking care of her, for saying the right thing. She sits on the garden bench, with her legs swinging and her hands folded in her lap. She wears a lilac-coloured beret and a matching scarf. Her coat is green and underneath it she wears a Fair Isle jumper and a kilt. Her hair, which sticks out from under her beret, is a pale tint of peach and her eyes are widely spaced and a cool shade of green. Her face is mysterious as the moon and full of questions.

As Oliver runs he feels blood warming his veins. The children dodge away from reaching hands and dive, tumbling, between each other's straddled legs. Oliver appears to participate in the game but, whenever possible, he runs close to Grace so that he can study her. He's puzzled by how slight she is, almost transparent, and yet luminous as well. He's never seen anyone else who looks anything like her. He doesn't have a sister but, if he did, he would want her to look like Grace. Oliver feels sure that Grace has been chosen by God as well.

Ian Harris is soon bored by stuck in the mud and wants to climb trees instead. There are two or three in the garden which are possible. Oliver has always been forbidden to climb them but he does it when his parents aren't watching. He tells Ian that he shouldn't climb the trees but only so that later – when there is trouble – he will be able to point out that he did try to prevent the tree climbing. Emily also tries to stop him but he's enjoying being the centre of attention and doesn't listen. It may be that today Oliver will have to write out the Ten Commandments fifty times.

They all stand at the bottom of the large oak and watch Ian start to climb. Grace gets up from the bench, and comes closer. Oliver positions himself behind her so that he can watch her without being seen. The beginning of the climb is not difficult because the oak has two low branches but after that it gets harder. Ian already seems dazzlingly high, in a different world. The mist in the air turns him into a black spider moving up through the tree. He shows off, swinging up through the branches. The children at the bottom of the tree stand with their heads tipped back. They shout encouragement and Ian shouts back. Their voices swell with a cut-glass echo in the icy air. Oliver watches the way that Grace's hair curls so neatly over the back of her coat. He noticed that in church – the way her curls swung forward gently as her head bent over her hymn book.

A shout and then screams. Oliver looks up to see Ian cartwheeling downwards. The black branches hiss and crack as his body scrapes through them. He seems to be falling for hours. Emily is pressing her hands against the sides of her head and screams again and again, the sound cracking the stillness of the garden. Oliver catches sight of Grace with her mouth open and her face crumpled. Ian lands, his body like a wet cloth thumping down. They all move forward but do not touch him. Oliver looks back and sees coatless grown-ups spilling through the back door onto the lawn. He can't imagine how many lines he will have to write for allowing this to happen. He runs forward and looks at Ian's twisted body lying on the sparse winter grass. His father is suddenly next to him calling out Ian's name.

Then Ian moves, coughs, and stands up. He has a large grin on his face and mud all over the shoulder of his coat. He draws in a deep breath, pulls at his wrist and laughs. Oliver's father starts to shout about not climbing the trees, he quotes the Ten Commandments at them. Honour Thy Father and Thy Mother. God will be sure to punish such disobedience. But despite these words everyone relaxes, nods their heads in amazement. Someone slaps Emily on the back and laughs at her for screaming. A mood of exhilaration is in the air. Oliver's father continues to quote the scriptures but his voice sounds strangely exuberant.

And so it is that no one except Oliver notices that Grace is lying on the grass. Strangely she looks quite natural there, as though she has just laid down to take a rest. Oliver kneels down beside her but she doesn't move. Her breath comes in short, whistling gasps. He stretches out a hand and touches her fingers as they lie inert in the grass. He says her name but she doesn't seem to hear.

And now the others have turned their attention from Ian to Grace. Oliver's mother pulls him out of the way and kneels beside her. It seems as though Grace is just playing but the grown-ups shake her and she doesn't get up. Grace, Grace. They call her name, sure that she will wake up any minute from her sudden sleep. Her breath still whistles but gently now. Mrs Harris comes running from the house and everyone stands aside because she's a ward sister at the hospital. She leans down over Grace and pulls at her eyes.

Call an ambulance, she says. Call one now. Oliver's father runs to the house. Mr Harris brings blankets and they put them over Grace. Emily is crying noisily. Ian stands beside her in his mud-covered coat, the grin gone from his face.

Oliver had seen the rolling white of Grace's eye as Mrs Harris pulled it open and knows that Grace is going to die. Perhaps she was always going to die – on this, the first day he met her. That was why he looked at her so intently in church this morning. Because he knew. And that's why Grace has that strange transparent look about her and those cool, unfocused eyes. She doesn't seem to be breathing any more now and her lips and eyes are swollen. On her neck bumps have appeared like nettle rash. But she can't be allowed to die when he hasn't even said one word to her. She was going to be his best friend, his sister.

Mrs Harris bends down over Grace and pulls her mouth open, then she pulls Grace's head up and begins to breathe into her mouth. She stops after each breath, counts and then dives again. Oliver feels now that the whole world has become distilled into this back garden. And he sees the scene from high above. Mrs Harris – in her woollen Sunday dress – kneeling on the grass beside this tiny figure who is somehow no longer there. Emily crying and Ian with mud on his coat. Oliver's father hurrying back from the house. Mrs Harris breathes into Grace again and again but nothing happens.

We'll have to wait for an ambulance, she says, but tears are flooding down her cheeks. Oliver's father is shouting at the children, wanting to know what happened. But none of them know. She was suddenly just lying on the grass.

Mrs Harris is standing back from Grace now. Oliver's father says several times that he's called an ambulance. The garden is quite silent and Oliver feels that, yes, this is how death will be. This silence and stillness and a circle of people with their faces clean of everything. Then his mother says that they must all pray, and she drops down on her knees in the frosty grass. The children follow her, folding their hands together, lowering their heads. *Our Father, who art in heaven, hallowed be thy name.*

But Oliver can't let it happen so he runs forward to her. Mrs Harris tries to pull him back but he smashes his fists against her arm. Kneeling beside Grace, he pushes aside her green coat. God is love, not punishment, not sin, not writing lines. Oliver knows that God won't let Grace die because she has been chosen. He looks down at his own hands and notices for the first time how alive they are. *Give us this day, our daily bread.* He won't need to breathe into her body. All he'll have to do is to put his life into her. God will help him to do this. Grace can't be allowed to die when she hasn't even lived. There should be so much more for her than just this Falmouth garden with its half-rotten wooden fence and flattened flower beds. He wants her to be down on the beach, in the sun, running out towards the water.

*In the name of the Father, and of the son, and of the Holy Spirit.* He lays his hands down on her heart, gently. He knows that if she dies then he will die as well. He needs to pull them both through. He shuts his eyes and takes a deep breath. Something moves inside him, a force which comes up from his stomach into his throat. It may be a sob, a shudder, a shout. He feels other faces close to him. *Amen, Amen, Amen.* And then suddenly he opens his eyes and Grace's green eyes are staring up at him as though she's just been born. Then she coughs and turns on her side, and gasps and draws in a deep breath. When he looks up he sees faces all around him, mute and staring. He stands up uncertainly while Mrs Harris comes to kneel beside Grace. He shrugs his shoulders, moves away.

When he looks up again, he finds every eye fixed on him. His mother is still kneeling and his father moves to join her, dropping to his knees. Oliver knows that although they are bowing down before the power and mystery of God, they're also bowing down to him. There will be no line-writing this afternoon, or ever again. He has them in his power. And not just them – the trees, the rising bank, the crabbed branches of the Scots pines. Everything now radiates from his outstretched hands. He feels the power twitching through them, crackling like static, firing life into everything he touches. When he looks back at Grace she's lying on her back with her scattered eyes turned towards him.

# 17

# Now

## Jemmy – Brighton, February 2003

Hello, Jemmy speaking, how may I help you? As Jemmy listens to the caller, she watches Monica and Tiffany. Jemmy feels sure that, as soon as she takes her eyes off them, they turn to look at her – or at the photographs of Laurie, or the mug which Jemmy has had made with his photograph on. Or perhaps at the T-shirt she's wearing which has his name on it and that one date. Laurie, Laurie, Laurie. His name is everywhere now. But no one ever says his name, no one speaks to her, no one says anything at all.

Jemmy puts down the phone and it rings again.

Hello, Jemmy speaking, may I help you?

What if England is attacked? Will my insurance cover me?

Jemmy starts to explain. War is ruled out of insurance policies because it's considered to be an act of God. No insurance policies can protect you against God.

Then I need to take out another policy, the caller barks. What kind can I take?

I'm not aware that Saddam Hussein is planning to invade Brighton.

Listen.

No, Jemmy says. You listen to me. I've got a friend who is actually in Iraq right now and no one even knows where he is and he hasn't got any insurance at all. So why don't you just grow up and consider yourself lucky?

She puts the phone down, looks around, praying that Mrs Jarvis hasn't heard. The phones have gone quiet. She licks at her dry lips, feels that sick and hungry feeling. She can't possibly be pregnant again. She can't be. Those dry fumblings couldn't produce new life. Those failed encounters she has with Bill – and Laurie there as well, his tiny cold body lying between them in the bed. No, it isn't possible that some other baby could possibly have the audacity to think that it might take Laurie's place. She doesn't want another baby, ever. She has Laurie and that's enough.

Jemmy imagines telling Bill she's pregnant again. He might smile and if he does then she'll kill him. Or he'll want to go down to the pub and announce the news. And then it'll be congratulations from everyone. A round of drinks, raise a toast for the new baby. How lovely, how wonderful. Problem over then. Jemmy won't allow that. No one bought a round of drinks for Laurie, or raised a toast for him. And because Laurie never had any of that, then no other baby is going to have that either.

It's five thirty and time to go home. Jemmy has clicked the red button but she doesn't get up. Instead she sits on at her desk, staring at her photographs of Laurie. The day seems to have lasted for weeks. Before Laurie died she hadn't understood that grief is physically exhausting. She wishes that, just occasionally, she could wake up in the morning and be someone other than a woman whose baby has died. But there is no respite.

She should go home but she can't do it. She thinks this nearly every evening but where else is there to go? She's considered moving somewhere else, just for a while. But where would she go? She thinks again of Jay, wishes that he was in Brighton, wishes that she could call him. (Jay, I know that the mug and the T-shirt are silly and over the top – but I just want Laurie to have a place. And I want his name to be known, to be said. And I thought that this might be the way to do it but it hasn't worked. And if Bill found out he'd be furious. He'd think it macabre and disrespectful and perhaps it is.)

She remembers Jay's hands – white and thin but surprisingly strong and certain. And they had talked about how when someone touches you then that's the only way in which you can be sure you do exist. Certainly Jay's hands had brought her back to life. She thinks of that evening – so hot it was like being shut inside an oven – when he came back to that room where she used to live. Sitting on a floor cushion, his long legs bent up awkwardly in front of him, talking some meaning-of-life rubbish. That's what she thought, until she knew better. Only that one evening.

Of course, most people knew Jay by sight because he was odd and noticeable. His shock of red hair, his long mournful face, his uneven teeth and those weird clothes. All the other boys of his age wore baggy jeans, and sweatshirts with hoods and trainers. But he wore tapered trousers that looked like they belonged to some grandpa, and braces, which performed no function as his trousers still hung down too low. And his lips were a girlish red, somehow too exposed, and he wore long striped scarves and jackets which had once been formal but now had holes in them. His clumpy boots seemed too heavy on the end of his thin legs.

His camera was always around his neck but it wasn't a modern, silver, digital camera. Instead it was a big old-fashioned camera with a leather case. He would stand around the college with it, endlessly lining up a shot that he never seemed to take. And he didn't take photographs of people, only of things. Curious things. Like puddles, or doorframes or the branches of trees. Jemmy's friends had called him the Camera Boy. The general view was that he might be a bit simple. Most people didn't believe the stuff about drugs because his face had the clearness and depth of undisturbed water.

As well as taking photographs, the Camera Boy was involved in every college campaign. Famine in Africa, destruction of the environment, traffic calming outside the college, collecting money for orphans – he was always there shaking a tin, putting up a banner, asking people to sign a petition. When Jemmy saw him around the place, she noticed that he stared at her. She didn't find that unusual. The younger boys at college often blushed red when she passed, or stumbled into her, asking if she had the time, and then failing to listen when she told them. The Camera Boy didn't do that but he did watch her. She didn't like him – felt the venom towards him that the marginally excluded feel towards the thoroughly excluded. And his eyes on her always made her feel uncomfortable. It was as though he could see right through her thick black cardigan, as though his eyes peeled off the fingerless gloves that she always wore. Somehow she had the feeling that he knew.

From somewhere close by, a phone is ringing continually. Tiffany is nowhere to be seen and another desk is empty as well. Usually the phone rings four times and then switches into silence and joins the queuing system but something has gone wrong because this phone rings on and on. Jemmy looks at her watch. Her shift has finished but she reaches over, clicks buttons, takes the call.

Hello, Jemmy speaking, may I help you?

The voice is slow and gentle – the voice of an old man. His name is Mr George Waldron. He makes several enquiries about a policy. When was it first started? What is its value? What will he need to do to make a claim? Jemmy has to give him the information several times. She looks at her watch. She shouldn't have taken this call. Bill will be wondering what's happened to her.

You see, she died. My wife. Two weeks ago. At the doctor's surgery they said it was only flu and it'd be gone in a day or two. She took out this policy years ago, wondering what I'd do if anything happened to her. Silly, I said. But she was set on it and maybe she was right. In any event, I need to be sure to get the money because she would want that.

Jemmy feels a rush of tears gather in her eyes. Oh. I'm so sorry. I'm so sorry.

Thank you, dear. That's kind of you.

Jemmy looks at the details on the screen.

Joyce – her name was Joyce, wasn't it?

Yes, love, that's right.

Joyce is a lovely name, Jemmy says. If someone is called Joyce then you just know they must be really nice.

Thank you, dear. I always thought it a lovely name.

I'm very sorry she died. It must be very hard for you.

Jemmy says this because it was a promise she made to Laurie. Everyone left her alone when he died but she'll never do the same to anyone else.

Thank you, my dear. I do appreciate that. Quite a shock at my age.

Yes, it must be. A terrible shock.

Jemmy looks at his address on the screen. 8 Wilmlow Gardens, Harringbourne, Sevenoaks. She knows that place – not the exact place but those towns south of London, which are only really housing estates, spreading faceless for miles and miles across the featureless earth. She grew up a few miles from there. Endless detached red-brick houses – and always autumn. Damp leaves, threads of mist floating through the air and the curtains drawn early. People smothered by the fear that something might happen. Her parents – the cramped house, the closed windows, the carpet-slipper shuffle, the television endlessly spewing fake laughter, lace everywhere and the smell of tinned food. All that bottled desperation. Each evening they congratulated themselves on their narrow escape from life. Don't let anyone speak too loud, or ask for too much. The endless waiting for some Awful Thing to happen, the day drawing ever closer.

And no one seemed to see that the Awful Thing had already happened, was happening every day. But Jemmy saw it and left there determined that whatever the Awful Thing was, she would go out and face it. But then so much had happened, too much. She'd finished her college course, got married. Her parents didn't like that – not because they objected to Bill but because of the Bollywood, Indian kitsch wedding, the fact that Jemmy wore a sari. They'd spent their whole lives trying to leave India behind and couldn't understand that Jemmy might want to rediscover it. And then she got pregnant, lost Laurie – and now? Other people might go home to their mother. She won't ever go back to hers. What had happened would be her fault, she had wanted too much.

Mr Waldron is talking about Joyce and her cross-stitch. She was very good at it – very. Went on courses, taught at the local college, filled the house with all sorts of pretty things.

Jemmy knows she needs to be careful. All the calls at Swift Life are taped and the aim is not to spend more than four minutes on any call. General chat should be responded to in a friendly manner, but then the caller should be firmly drawn back to the reason for their call. That's what they tell you in the training. Perhaps Mr Waldron senses her worry because he says, Oh I am sorry, my dear, I'm taking too much of your time.

No, no, Jemmy says. It's quite all right. I've got time. I've got plenty of time. Please tell me about Joyce. I'd like to hear about Joyce.

Jemmy can imagine the manicured front garden, the floral curtains, the British Racing Green garage door, which Mr Waldron has recently repainted himself, using masking tape to make sure it doesn't smudge. The streets of her childhood. And inside the walking stick on the back of the chair, and the seaside souvenir ashtrays and the Royal Worcester figurines. The days must be silent for Mr George Waldron – and long. She would like to go around and have a cup of tea with him, chat about Joyce. Hear the stories of the various figurines, the occasional trips to the sea, the time they went on a coach to that place in Austria by the lake – the name escapes him. Jemmy will never go back to that world but she's surprised to find comfort in hearing a voice from there.

Sorry, dear. I've gone on too long, he says. Yes, too long. How kind of you to talk, it does me good.

That's all right, Jemmy says. You can call any time. I'd like to hear. I'd always be pleased to hear about Joyce.

# 18

# Now

## Lara – Brighton, February 2003

Lara types an email with one hand while speaking on the phone to a client. In her head she makes lists. Get in touch with the suppliers about the paint, chase up the builders for a price on moving that door. Beside her Kylie, with her flamingo legs, ballet pump shoes, pale pink nails, hovers, waiting for Lara to check a letter. Lara finishes her call and puts the phone down but it rings again immediately. She waves Kylie away, takes the call while still typing the email to the builder. Why has the new gas cooker still not been connected? Yes, sorry. Yes, I realise we had promised. Yes, I'll make sure that it's done by the end of the day.

An email from Press and Communications Alan pings onto the screen. Lara shuts her eyes, clenches her teeth. She knows that the peace protesters are all in the Andalus Hotel in Baghdad and she's rung there every day. People she speaks to are friendly, helpful, tell her that Jay is doing fine but she's still never managed to speak to him. Alan hasn't been in touch for nearly a week but now finally – news.

So when will it be possible to make these adjustments? the voice on the phone says. Lara leans forward, stares more closely at the computer, feeling that she might be able to absorb the contents of Alan's email without actually opening it. Please, please, God. Make this message say that it's all over, that the buses are coming home.

Hello? Are you still there? I'm just trying to ask.

Sorry. I'll have to ring you back. Lara puts the phone down, stares at her hand on the receiver. Then she looks back at the screen, clicks on the message. Information has been cut and pasted. *The arrival of the buses in Iraq has been welcomed by the Iraqi people. Since that time the human shields have been in negotiation with Iraqi officials about how they can best try to prevent war. These conversations have been difficult.*

Lara already knows this from her conversations with the Andalus Hotel and from emails that have been forwarded by other relatives. *As you know, the aim was to protect Iraqi hospitals, schools, civilian facilities. This will not be allowed. Human shields are being asked to protect key infrastructure such as water-treatment centres, bridges, telecommunication towers, power plants, factories and oil installations. So discussions have taken place.*

Lara's eyes move down to where the pasted message ends. In a different typeface at the bottom a message records that Jay is with a group of twelve other peace protesters who will be stationed at the Baghdad South Electrical Plant. A letter is being written to the Joint Chiefs of Staff with a request that they recognise the fact that targeting these sites would be in violation of Article 54, Protocol Additional to the Geneva Convention.

Lara feels a silent wail rise in her throat. Already other emails from outraged relatives are pinging up. *This was not the plan, it's time now for the protesters to come home, they're nothing but political pawns.* She tries to shut one of these emails down but her hands fumble and she opens another instead – something about site meeting dates. Yes, she does need to confirm that she can make the first of those dates. Her phone is ringing, the sound of it battering inside her head. She pushes her chair back from her desk, stands up, walks a few steps towards the kitchen, then turns back. She looks around at the other people working. Should she announce this information to them? What would be the point? They don't know Jay. They do know he's in Iraq but nothing much has been said – or at least nothing much has been said to her face. She picks up the ringing phone, puts it straight down, goes to the machine to get a coffee but can only stand, staring, unable to remember how this ritual is performed.

She'd always known that this moment would come but still the shock is like an assault. *This was not the plan.* The human shields only ever intended to protect civilian infrastructure. Why has Jay allowed himself to be positioned in front of a power plant when surely facilities of that kind will be the first to be hit? She can barely stand because of the knots that have gathered in her chest. She tries to ring Alan but the number is engaged. Then she tries to rings the peace protesters in Brighton but that number is busy as well. *This was not the plan.*

Lara notices a message on her mobile and clicks to listen. Mollie's voice crackles into her ear. Yes, of course. Lara should have known. Rufus has left. He bloody well would, wouldn't he? The critics always say that his timing is excellent. Lara thinks of him as one of those small children who, whenever there are visitors, falls down the stairs. Of course, he'll be back within a week or two. An artistic crisis – that'll be the story. An artistic crisis involving too much drink and younger women. Lara sits staring at the phone. Mollie, a child of war, so incredibly tough about everything except Rufus. How can Lara ring up and say – *I'm so sorry, what a disaster, you must be devastated?* It's no secret that she's been longing for Rufus to leave since she was ten. And why does anyone care what Rufus is doing? A play, reviews, a bad back, a petty domestic row. Lara no longer occupies a world in which such things are worthy of any consideration.

Craig is striding towards her. He's wearing a plum-coloured tie, which isn't a good idea considering the pinkness of his face. I need to have a word with you.

She follows him to his office. She's worked for Craig for eighteen years and slept with him on and off. He's married with three children but Lara doesn't mind. The plate-glass windows of his office look out over Berkeley Square. The branches of the trees rustle and umbrellas bob beneath them. Benches line up beside curving gravel paths. A sculpture of two hares, on their hind legs, dancing, stands on a slab of concrete. The building opposite is like a vast ocean liner, soon to set sail. For a moment an image of

Jay flashes into her mind. *Yes, this is what is happening in my life*, she tells herself, but she can't take the measure of the information she's received.

Lara, I'm concerned about this situation with Lonsdale. I've had James Wright on the telephone three times this morning and I'm not surprised he's frustrated.

Lara is lost in the maze of his voice. Briefly she remembers how she first came to work for him. The Employment Agency with the pink candy-striped armchairs and Ms Carver with her red-rimmed glasses, and black suit with Channel-swimmer shoulder pads. At the time she hadn't understood that she was Ms Carver's present to Craig, or that Craig only tolerated her initial incompetence because he intended to get her into bed. But overall she's never ceased to feel gratitude to Ms Carver, the author of her liberation, her escape.

Lara tries now to concentrate on Craig's voice but her head is foggy and sounds come to her as though from another country, over a crackling phone line. She wonders if she might be going down with flu. For some reason the scene in front of her – Craig, his desk, the branches of tree waving in the square – none of it looks right. It isn't that the scene appears blurred, and neither does it appear exaggerated. It's simply that nothing seems to fit together properly any more. There used to be some hidden logic behind Craig, and his phone, and his chair, and his potted palm, but now that logic has gone. So there's no reason for all of these things to be in the same room. The desk could be substituted for an elephant or a petrol pump and it wouldn't make any difference.

Lara, are you listening?

Yes, that potted plant could be an elephant, Lara thinks. And Craig could be anyone – an astronaut, a snake charmer, a traffic warden. Lara becomes aware that Craig is shouting but even his shouting doesn't make sense. What in God's name is he doing? Does he have any idea how ridiculous he is? How irrelevant?

I'm sorry, Lara says. But you see, my son.

Your son?

Yes, my son. Jay. You remember.

The astronaut is shaking his head, his face closed. And then suddenly Lara understands. Although she's worked for this astronaut for eighteen years, and she's explained the situation about Jay several times, he's nevertheless totally forgotten that Jay is in Iraq. Forgotten, in fact, that Jay exists at all.

I can't have people working for me who aren't committed.

Lara shuts her eyes, cutting out the astronauts and the elephant and whatever else is in the room. She'd never expected anything from Craig. Although perhaps if you put a man's penis in your mouth on a regular basis then inevitably you do hope for something. Just a few words of kindness. But – she admits to herself – it isn't that he's made a decision to ignore her difficulties, he simply hasn't seen that she has any. Hasn't seen, in fact, that she exists. When she opens her eyes, she looks up at the astronaut and understands that he requires the answer to some question.

I'm sorry, she says. I'm going to have to take a couple of weeks off.

The astronaut begins another series of puppet-like movements. He says things about complaints, about a fax that needs to go out by the end of the day. It just isn't possible, he says. Do you understand me? You can't just take time off work for no reason at all.

I won't be here for the next two weeks – at least, Lara says. She feels the finality of this, hears doors slamming all around her. But what does it matter? Given that the office has turned into some kind of zoo, what exactly is there to leave? The pieces of the jigsaw are not going to go back together again.

I can't believe you're letting everyone down like this, the astronaut says. This company has spent years building up a reputation and a client base.

Lara imagines turning a dial inside her head that switches Craig off, tunes him out. She smooths down her skirt, relieved to find that it's still a skirt, that she is still the person she thought she was. It seems miraculous now that her foot connects to her leg, that her hand connects to her arm, that her head sits firmly on her shoulders. The astronaut is still talking but she turns away from him and heads towards the door. He's saying something about terms and conditions, employment law.

Reaching the door, Lara turns the handle – which is still mercifully just a handle – and opens the door. She keeps her head up as she walks towards her desk. Behind her she can hear the astronaut shouting at one of the giraffes. Suddenly it occurs to her that the astronaut is just like her father. How strange that she worked for him for so long  and it's only now that she sees this entirely obvious fact.

Everyone in the office knows something has happened because they've heard the shouting. As Lara reaches her desk, she thinks about that fax she needed to send, and examines a phone message left on her desk. But she doesn't have to send the fax or return the message. Instead she can go home – sleep, eat, organise. Sarah and Shuna – with their young, empty faces, their twenty-something purity – are watching from their desks.

Family Difficulties, she thinks. For the first five years working for Craig, Lara never mentioned having a son and she's never, in all her time at the office, asked to leave early due to a childcare problem. Even when Mollie's car had broken down on the way to the scout camp and the irate organiser was shouting down the phone at her, even when Jay had been rushed into hospital for his appendix, even when he was at the police station because of the drugs. In all that time she'd never mentioned Family Difficulties. In fact, she'd always felt a robust contempt for those women with nappies and bibs in their sagging handbags, women who couldn't even meet for a coffee without explaining all of their childcare arrangements in wearying detail. But now it seems that Family Difficulties are bound to get you in the end. The only mystery is how she survived so long.

She thinks of friends she could call. Annabel? She doesn't want another conversation about killer bugs in Middle Eastern rivers. And neither does she want Annabel to ramble on for half an hour about her teenage son and his mysterious new mobile. He claims he was given it. But did he actually steal it? Lara is used to all that now – the speed at which her crisis is instantly translated into someone else's angst.

The truth is that no one is really interested in anyone else's problems. Two or three people have sent cards with confused messages. What does one say? Jay's departure doesn't fit into the usual catalogue of death, divorce, bereavement. People don't know whether to express support, regret or outrage. Lara knows that people only send cards and flowers in order to maintain their own idea of themselves as good people. Or else they do it because they want their piece of the drama. Everywhere they go they'll be saying – *Oh yes, of course, we know his mother. Dreadful, dreadful.*

She could try speaking to some of the other relatives but their numbers have dwindled over the weeks. They disappear almost immediately once they know that their sister, son or friend is now coming home. All they want to do is forget and how can you blame them? The only person who might understand is Oliver and he doesn't have a phone. Maybe she'll go around and see him when she gets home.

Unsteadily she picks up the file of letters on her desk. *Jay is in Baghdad and he's heading towards a power plant that will be a key target if a war starts.* The information rises up and catches at her throat. Lara starts to choke, her whole body rocked by coughing. Tears run down her cheeks. She reaches for tissues and then finds herself laughing – a shrieking, mirthless laugh which turns into a sob and then a cough. Kylie is coming towards her with a box of tissues. She can't bear to become a person who is offered tissues.

Kylie is followed now by Sarah, both of them wide-eyed. For a moment Lara sees Sarah's hand, with its pastel-painted nails, stretched out in what can only be genuine kindness. It would be so easy to take that hand, to accept the trip to the coffee shop across the square that is being suggested. But Lara has no place inside her to put such kindness. And she can't allow Jay's danger to become a question which will yield to coffee and nods of understanding. So, hurriedly she takes a tissue, mutters in a strangled voice that she's fine, turns away.

Files, books, stapler, the tube on her desk full of pens. She should take everything because she may need some of these things when she goes to a new job. Logistics – she needs to hire a car, find boxes, sort papers, explain to Kylie and Sarah, say a proper goodbye. Then the knowledge comes to her that she can just walk out. On her desk there's a photo of Jay and she wants that – and her laptop. It belongs to the office but she's taking it anyway. She reaches her hand out towards it, but it is still plugged in. Kylie dives under the desk and pulls out the plug. Sarah takes the photograph from Lara's fluttering hands and packs it into her bag. Thank you, Lara says. Thank you. And goodbye. She waves her hand in an awkward regal wave, loops the bag onto her shoulder. Why does she feel nothing at all?

## 19

## BEFORE

### Rose – Coventry, November 1940

Rose nudges the pram along the road towards the cemetery, guiding it through the crush of black overcoats, dripping hats and umbrellas. The rain has been coming down since dawn, washing the ash and soot into the gutters. An ivy-covered wall near the cemetery gate has fallen down but the bricks have been stacked up to keep the pavement clear. Water has seeped into Rose's shoes, and her fingers, gripping the handle of the pram, ache with cold. Mollie tries to sit up, starts to wail but Rose takes no notice of her.

It has to be a mass funeral, everyone understands that. Not enough wood or carpenters can be found to make the coffins, and anyway carpenters are needed to repair houses for the living rather than make boxes for the dead. One hundred and seventy-two so far and there'll be many more to come. They can't even identify all the bodies. Fighter planes are in the sky because the talk is that the Luftwaffe might bomb the funeral. That seems possible now. No one says anything much. Instead they stare and stare, their eyes gasping, as they take in this new world. And the cathedral. Although the tower still stands, and the tower of Holy Trinity looking down on them now.

The gate of the cemetery is thick with mud but two men lift the end of the pram and Rose raises it as well, struggling to keep a grip, as her feet squelch and slip. The men put the pram down on firmer ground and Rose pulls a handkerchief from her pocket and leans into the pram to wipe at Mollie's streaming nose, takes a bottle of milk from her bag and pushes it into the child's outstretched hands. Why is she always moaning and screaming? What can be the matter with her?

Rose presses on past cypresses and yews, past the bomb craters in the older part of the cemetery. Diggers have been brought in because of the number of holes to be dug. They stand in the background, against the cemetery wall, their dinosaur outlines black against grey smudges of sky, a line of roofs, the smoking chimney of a factory. Duckboards have been laid across the mud and people queue to step across them and look down into the long trenches dug for the dead. The crowds of people standing in those queues seem themselves to have become part of the mud and the colourless sky above. Calloused hands grip handkerchiefs or the brims of hats. Everyone has found black to wear, even if it is only a black raincoat over stained dungarees. No one pushes or complains. Other than the rattle of the rain and squelching of the mud, an occasional muffled sob, everything is silent, hollow.

Rose tries not to think of Mrs Watson – her toothless grin and her hair done in a plait like a little girl. Mrs Watson had always understood. *Bloody murdering bastards. They'll not be the ones that die. You mark my words. It'll be the poor buggers like us that get it.* It'd been her choice, of course, but she should have gone to the shelter and everyone had told her that. But she'd been adamant. *Nursing on the front two years in the last war. They didn't get me then, they won't get me now. At least I'll die in the comfort of my own bed.*

Three hundred copies of *Peace News* had gone up with her when fire ripped through the backs of three houses in Back Street West – and fold-up chairs and tables belonging to the Union as well. Not that it mattered much because no one had time now to distribute leaflets. Except it would have mattered to Mrs Watson. Mercifully, Rose's own things – the few things which remained – had been in the front bedroom and were left more or less untouched. Ivy and Win had come after work to help. They'd both tried to persuade her to go home to her mother although she's told them a hundred times that she'll die before she does that. And then Mr Bostock had arrived and said straight away that she must move in with them and he'd come with a team of others from the Peace Pledge. And with barrows they picked up everything and carried it away, while Mrs Bostock found a camp bed and blankets for the sitting room.

Rose knows she'll never get the pram across those duckboards – and anyway she doesn't know where Mrs Watson's body would be. Instead she stands watching the crowds as they wobble and stumble, filing past the gaping trenches, which are surely dug a mile deep into the earth. A line of black wool overcoats, leather-gloved hands, grey hair loosely pinned, stockings full of holes, shoes with cardboard tied on the soles. Some drop flowers down onto the dead. Those trenches must be filling up with water, Rose thinks. One vast woman collapses crying into the mud and lies there flailing, her hand waving, seeking purchase on something, anything until her husband and his friend come to heave her up. One side of her coat is caked in mud, her dentures have come loose and so she spits, coughs, pushes them back in.

Rose wishes that she had picked flowers but where would she have put them? It seems wrong to go without having done anything at all – but what is there to do? At least Mrs Watson wouldn't have expected anything, being staunchly atheist. *Well, if there is a God he'll have a bleeding lot to answer for when I get to those pearly gates.* There are so many dead that after a while it becomes hard to know how to apportion grief. Rose thinks of the ARP warden sitting in the street. He was one of the people who had gone into the elastic factory – forty women and children were in the cellars there and because of the elastic the heat like an inferno.

Rose heads back to the entrance, shoving the pram through the mud, but the gate is blocked by another digger coming in. A man catches hold of the end of the pram and helps to lift it aside. Something in the man's swift movement makes her think for a moment of Frank and his letters. She finds those letters to be full of self-pity but they also frighten her. She has learnt that what

161

doesn't bend will break. A gust of bitter wind drags at Rose's hat and she moves to the side of the pram, sheltering by a shack with a corrugated-iron roof and canvas sides. She will miss living at Mrs Watson's, although what Violet had said about the lice had turned out to be true. No doubt they will have survived the blast.

The wind is sour with the smell of bleach and Rose rubs her hands together as she waits. Behind her, the canvas of the shack rattles in the wind. Rose turns around just as the flap of the canvas blows to the side. Inside the shack, lumps of tarpaulin are stacked on makeshift racks. Rose draws in a short breath as she realises that the tarpaulins cover lines of bodies. At the lowest level there are no shelves so the bodies are lying on the ground, in the mud and the inch of water that has accumulated. Lime, like a dusting of snow, is sprinkled over everything.

The sound of the digger roars as it struggles through the mud. The canvas sheet blows again in the tugging wind. The tarpaulins don't completely cover all of the bodies and so there are feet sticking out – purple feet, tiny and shrivelled with the toes scrunched up like animal claws. Each pair of feet is tied with a metal tag around the ankle. Rose feels her head sway and catches hold of the handle of the pram. Mollie is screaming now, her tiny face bright red. Rose swings the pram around and pulls it behind her, tugging at it, the smell of lime stinging her mouth and throat. A hand reaches out and pushes the pram forward. A woman steps aside, pulling two tearful children with her. Rose finds herself back in the road, still tugging the pram behind her.

She stops for a moment, shakes the rain from her hat and then puts it back on. Finding Mollie's bottle of milk, she tries to settle the child down although her hands are so cold that she can't feel the blankets as she straightens them. Despite the milk, Mollie still wails. Rose sometimes wishes she could just park the pram in a doorway somewhere, run off and leave it there, never go back. Wind rushes down the street, slapping against cheeks and tearing at hair. A car engine splutters and dies. Somewhere behind Rose, perhaps in the churchyard, a man is keening like a wounded animal. Rose grips the handle of the pram and steps on down the road. Ahead of her she sees a tiny woman, a neat ghost, moving towards a parked car. The woman wears a fitted black coat with a grey fur collar and cuffs and a saucer black hat, perched to one side of her head. On her arm she carries a square black bag. The woman turns and looks back down the crowded road and her eyes fix on Rose. Rose sees that face – that familiar face, paler but otherwise unchanged.

Rose. Oh, Rose.

Violet reaches out her arms and Rose, abandoning the pram, walks straight into them, holding Violet close. It's been more than a year but that time means nothing now.

The baby? Rose says.

She's quite all right, Violet says. Quite well. Born three weeks ago now.

Oh, I am pleased. Because I did hear.

A spasm passes across Violet's face but she forces a wintry smile.

It'd been on the radio, somewhere near Dunkirk. The Royal Warwickshire Regiment. An image appears in Rose's head of men in a barn, in the half darkness, the flash of torches, a smell of hay and manure, and then the sudden thud of bullets in flesh, and the screaming.

And you? Let me see. Violet approaches the pram and peers in at Mollie.

Oh isn't she beautiful. Arthur told me she's beautiful. And, darling, you know what? I called my baby Mollie as well. I just wanted to – such fun for them both to have the same name, don't you think?

Rose nods her head and smiles. Fun? She had forgotten that word.

I'm so sorry, Rose said. About Stanley. I did write at the time.

Yes, I know you did. It was very sweet of you. I appreciated it very much.

And now you're here?

Cook's uncle. He used to work in the garden when I was a child.

I'm sorry.

Well, yes. And you?

Mrs Watson.

Oh no. Trousers and lice? Oh but Rose.

I was living in her house. If we hadn't gone with the trekkers out of the city.

So where are you living now?

Rose explains about the Bostocks. Arthur is there as well. Didn't he tell you? We all three of us share the front room.

Oh Rose, why don't you come and live with me? Or we could both go to Worcester, to my aunt. Father is there, of course, although last time I saw him he thought I was his mother. Poor soul. But my aunt's got a super house and we'd be welcome there.

No, thank you, Violet. No.

Oh Rose, really. Why?

I have to consider Frank.

Rose, really. I think the time has come. We must be honest.

Rose views Violet's brimming eyes with distaste. She's noticed that this is one of the effects of war. People start to allow all sorts of things that would be better left unsaid to spill from their lips. It can be embarrassing. Rose is disappointed in Violet. She'd always thought that Violet would know better.

Frank. Violet says, through twisted lips. When has he ever considered you? I've heard from Arthur. Twenty shillings a week. And giving money away to get people out of prison.

Frank is much better placed now, Rose says. Working in the Hackney Hospital.

He shouldn't have done this to you. How does he expect you to live?

I would get a job, Rose says. If I could find anyone to look after Mollie.

Frank has a duty. You're married. Why doesn't he organise for you to go to Aunt Muriel in Norfolk?

Violet knows the answer to that question. Frank would be too proud to ask his mother for help, and even if he asked, his mother would never take her in. She came to the wedding wearing a mean little purple flowerpot hat. Surely not the one she had reputedly bought for Frank's wedding to Violet? And she'd brought a silver teapot but made no effort to hide her disappointment.

Violet, I'm sorry. But I have to go.

Oh Rose, please. Please don't. Please, I'm all on my own. And I've got a nurse to look after my Mollie and she would help you as well. Please.

I'm sorry, Violet. I have to go. And you must go, you must leave the city. Go to your aunt's in Worcester. Really, you must.

No. I can't go, Rose, unless you come with me. I can't.

How very awkward. What has come over Violet?

I'm sorry. Rose walks away, her hands locked on the handle of the pram, tears streaming down her face. Her mind is drawn back to 34 Warwick Road, as though pulled by a magnet, back to the wide curving staircase with its worn green carpet, the leaning mahogany furniture in the dining room, the photographs in jewelled frames on glass shelves. The arch crusted with wisteria in the back garden. It isn't the house that she wants but the world that she inhabited when she visited that house – so much of it gone now. And what does it matter what they rebuild? Now there is no road back.

Rose pushes the pram back to the Bostocks' house, through the blackened streets and mountains of rubble. A convoy of vans pass by, mobile canteens arriving from America, God bless them. Cardboard and plywood float on the wind. Most of Hendry Street has gone and the houses in Warmington Road have been evacuated although most are still standing. Victoria Street is closed because of a gas leak so instead she cuts along Butt Street. A barrage balloon has come down on some houses, and bobs about there, like a wounded elephant. Curtains flap at broken windows and the street is littered with beams, bricks and broken telephone wires. Beds, curtains, books, shattered light fittings, bathroom sinks all lie on piles of rubble. Fire hoses twist across the street. The city looks like Ypres in 1914.

No one had expected a raid such as this. When Rose left the city with Mollie on the bus, with the other trekkers, Arthur had said – *Not too bad tonight, moon as thin as a nail clipping*. And later Rose, unable to sleep, had got out of the bus, and walked through the thin stretch of woodland to the road. From there she'd seen the usual pillars of white light cut upwards through the darkness, crossing and meeting, forming overlapping circles. And occasionally, far away, the slant of a roof, or the edge of a chimney pot, caught in an instant of light.

But still she hadn't known – until she was back in the bus and the sound of the bombing went on and on and on without stopping, the rhythm of it beating through hearts and heads, on and on and on until finally dawn had come. Then the bus hadn't been able to get back into the city and all they could see was red on every side. And men everywhere stripped to the waist, and drenched in sweat, for the whole city had become a furnace and everything was alight. And it wasn't until evening that Rose had got back to Mrs Watson's house and found it gone.

Best not to think of it now. She's alive – and so are Mollie and Arthur, Mr and Mrs Bostock. That is miracle enough. She turns the pram into Redmond Street, longing now to get home and stoke up the range. The only good thing to be said for the bombing is there's plenty of wood to be burnt. But without Mrs Watson there won't be so much food. Mrs Watson always had extra because when her elderly neighbour died of a stroke, Mrs Watson got her identity card and ration book and used them. Initially Rose had been shocked but soon enough she didn't care. Everyone else did the same. Win at the factory is claiming rations for her great-aunt and she died before the war even started.

As she comes to the house, Rose sees a man standing aimlessly near the gate, a man whose coat drops as though from a coat hanger, square at the shoulders and yet loose. Then she realises – the man is Frank. She stops for a moment, staring, feels her hands tighten on the pram handle, then moves on towards him. She hasn't seen Frank for more than six months although he's written often. She knows that she should run towards him, throw her arms around him, kiss him and keep on kissing him. But he doesn't look the same. His skin is bone white and the circles around his eyes are so dark that for a moment she wonders if he's been in a fight. And he's grown a wispy moustache which doesn't suit him. But worse than that, he looks ordinary.

She stops the pram and he looks up at her. His eyes are lit by a blank brightness. The pram seems to have swelled to the proportions of a house and neither of them know how to get around it. Frank moves towards her and he's seen the disappointment in her eyes. So she hurries towards him, throws herself against him, kisses him. He's all angles and bones and he smells damp. His lips are cold and that new moustache spikes against her face but she kisses him firmly. Then she goes back to the pram, picks up Mollie, forcing her on to Frank, trying to cover up the awkwardness – or fear – which lies between them. Frank holds Mollie against him although the child is squirming to get away.

How did you get here? Rose asks.

I walked.

What – from London?

No. Don't be daft. Not all the way. But – I'm sorry. It's only one night. I've got a new job in the Ambulance Service. You know, I wrote about it. But everything here – the cathedral and all that – it's all been in the paper and I saw a newsreel. And they said I could come to see you, start one day later.

That's good – about the job.

Frank grips Mollie in his arms, and looks up and down the street.

It's the same in London, isn't it? Rose says.

Frank continues to stare. Rose pulls him up the path of the Bostocks' house and elbows the door open. Frank follows her inside, sees the piles of furniture in the hall and the patch of green mould on the wall by the staircase but heads on past, asking nothing. Rose tells him that they must have supper as soon as they can because the bus goes at seven o'clock. She's written to Frank about the bus but he doesn't seem to understand.

Where are Mr and Mrs Bostock?

Doing ARP. We'll see them at the bus. Arthur's usually over at Division B First Aid but he's got a night off so he'll come as well.

In the kitchen, she adds coal to the range and puts the kettle on. She's glad that at least she has some food to give him.

So how are you, Rosie?

Rose can't answer that question. She pours milk into a pan for Mollie.

I went to Mrs Watson's house – so I thought...

Rose looks over at Frank and the image of that house seems to shine out of him. The blackened walls at the back, the shreds of torn wallpaper, the wires dangling down, the pots still on the dresser but streaked black. Mollie is patting her father's cheeks with her tiny hands and chattering to him wordlessly but Frank doesn't appear to feel her touch or hear her voice.

I'm sorry. I did write but it wouldn't have reached you yet. We'd gone out on the bus. And we did say, but she wouldn't go to the shelter.

Rose clutches the top of the kettle, shuts her eyes.

The front door crashes open. Fra-a-nk. Arthur's voice sounds in the hall and he lurches into the kitchen, throws his arms around Frank. It's strange how news loops its way through the city even though most of the phone lines are down. Arthur shakes Frank by the hand, slaps him on the back.

Isn't she grand? Isn't she just grand? Frank says, kissing Mollie and turning her around, displaying her to Arthur. Frank and Arthur have gone through to the front parlour, pushing past the dressing table and chairs stacked in the hall. Where's the gramophone? Frank says. Let's have some music.

Sorry, Rose says. I packed it away.

Oh well, Frank says. Oh well. What does it matter? What do we need a gramophone for? We can sing, can't we? You can sing, can't you, Mollie? We have Arthur here and your mother and they have the best voices in all of Coventry. Anyway, where is it?

In the sideboard, Rose says.

Frank spins Mollie round, sings to her, pulls the green crackled case from the sideboard, assembles the tiny Thorens Excelda gramophone. In the kitchen, Rose unpacks pork chops from sheets of newspapers. The meat has a silver-green sheen to it, like the skin of fish. Mrs Bartholomew, the butcher's wife, always gives Rose the worst meat. *Ah there we are, Mrs Von Mayeford. Still trying to tell us there's no harm in them, are you?* Rose wonders if they might get poisoned but she smears the chops with lard and puts them in the range anyway.

Arthur shuffles into the kitchen. You all right, Rosa?

Yes, fine. And you?

Fi-i-ne. Nothing doing at Division B last night except a man who trapped his finger in a ladder. But the paint shop went at Alvis Shadow Factory at Canley. Anyway, come on.

We must leave by six thirty, Rose says.

Yes, I know. I know. But first.

Rose follows Arthur through to the sitting room. Frank has wound the gramophone up. *Paradise here, paradise close, just around this corner. The place where happiness is for me.* He picks up Mollie and swings her around, dancing with his cheek close to hers, as though they are moving through a white-pillared ballroom. Rose knows that she should feel happy – Frank is home, Arthur is with him, Mollie is smiling. They're all together again, all of them alive. Rose opens her mouth and tries to join the singing but no sound comes out. Arthur is holding Mollie up, showing her the record which turns on the miniature turntable. Rose goes back to the kitchen to find the range smoking. The pork chops won't cook and time is going on.

Wonderful to be home, Frank says, appearing at the kitchen door. His voice is tight and thin and he coughs. Come and dance with us, Rosie.

No. No. Look, I'm trying to…

But then she looks at Frank and knows she needs to follow him to the sitting room. Mollie is sitting on Arthur's knee, clapping her hands and singing tunelessly to the music. Frank takes Rose in his arms and their bodies remember how to move together. *The place where happiness is for me.* Rose feels the movement of Frank's back under her hand – the rough wool of his shirt, the muscle tightening beneath as he turns. She pulls him closer, feels his leg press against hers. *Paradise here, paradise close, just around this corner.* The carpet – patterned red and blue – flows under their feet as they dip in and out of the shadows. The sideboard, the bookcase, the mirror over the fireplace, all kaleidoscope into each other. The wall lights, shaped like swans' necks, blink, the line of silver tankards on the mantelpiece swirls past. The pink rosebuds on the tired wallpaper are bursting into bloom. Mollie's eyes flicker like candles, her hands no longer clapping but stretched out, motionless, as though ready to gather the dancers into her tiny arms. Rose lays her head on Frank's shoulder, feels the whole house, the whole city, standing still to watch them.

But then Frank catches his foot on a stool, stumbles, and she has to hold onto him tight to stop him from falling. He laughs loudly, claps his hands, tries to pretend that the moment hasn't shattered. Rose stands beside Arthur, desperate. He reaches up and lays a hand on her arm.

Good to have him back, isn't it?

Yes, good.

Rose goes back to the kitchen, clings to the handle of the pan.

Look, we've got to go and these are only half cooked. I don't think we should.

Oh don't be daft, Frank says. We can eat them like that.

You'll get poisoned.

Course we can.

He butters bread, picks up a half-cooked chop.

Delicious, he says. Delicious.

Rose tries to laugh while Arthur slices more bread. Frank has eaten the green chop and the bread in half a minute. Here, he says. Here, Arthur. Rose.

Oh no, Arthur says. Oh no, Frank, I've had my supper.

I'm not hungry, Rose says. You eat it, Frank. Mollie and I prefer bread.

Best get on this bus, Arthur says. Neither of them look at Frank while he eats. Frank asks if he should go with them because he needs to find a lift to a station early tomorrow. Rose reassures him that they'll get back in plenty of time for that. It's better than the shelters, safer and more friendly. Most of the shelters won't withstand a direct hit and often you have to stand up all night. So they pack up their things – a flask, cushions and blankets. Rose has all of this ready in the hall.

We won't need all that, Frank says. It's a mild night.

Yes we will.

No. No.

We will, Rose says. We will.

For a moment it seems as though the atmosphere might snap. Frank might cry, the roof of the house might fall in, she might start screaming.

Don't worry, Arthur says. I'll take it. I'll carry everything.

Frank sweeps up Mollie and they start to walk. Frank is talking all of the time, stuttering over words. It's nearly dark now and soon the sirens will start. Seven thirty every night the bombing starts. The Germans are so regular you can set your watch by them. Wardens are going around checking the blackout. Rose, Frank, Arthur and Mollie stumble in the waning light. As they cross Greyfriars Green, Rose looks across towards 34 Warwick Road. The house is in darkness, its white façade, its crowd of chimney pots merging into the grey of the evening. Rose remembers Violet in her black coat with its grey fur collar and cuffs. Perhaps she should have gone home with her?

She'll have gone, Frank says. Moved out months ago. Gone to live with her father and her aunt in Worcester. Rose can feel Frank bristling with contempt.

No, Arthur says. Still here. Pretty brave really. Don't know why she doesn't go.

They come to Newsome Street. The stationer's at the corner was bombed out in the big raid three nights ago but he continues to operate from a stand in the street. Frost is gathering and his breath is white. A light hangs crookedly from the top of his stand and he bangs his hands together trying to keep warm. A sign above the stall reads, *Don't let the Bosch beat us.*

Evening, love, the stationer calls. How are you?

Fine thank you – and you?

Fighting back, he says. Fighting back.

Many of the shops are out on the streets now. Some of them have nothing to sell as lorries haven't been able to get to the city. But perhaps it doesn't matter because most of the customers have left as well. Rose saw them all trailing out of the city three mornings ago. The people who could go had gone before. Now even the people who have nowhere to go are getting out. People are living under bridges and in ruined buildings but you can't survive like that for long, not with this cold.

In the London Road, the bus is waiting. Mr and Mrs Bostock clap Frank on the back and pour him tea from a flask. Then everyone crowds onto the bus and it rumbles out through the outskirts of the city. Arthur takes Mollie and sits her on his knee. Rose and Frank crowd into a seat together. The sorting of bags and the jostling of seats stops and a weary silence falls. In the dimming light Rose sees rows of crouching red-brick houses, feels the marching beat of lines of unlit lamp posts, hears the grind of the arms factories like distant thunder. The sirens wail and the bus judders and struggles, engine roaring, over the broken surfaces of the roads.

Watch out. Jerry's getting started.

Send Adolf a line, ask him to give us a night off, we haven't had one all week.

Send him to Birmingham – must be their turn now.

People try to laugh but the sound is vacant. Rose watches Frank staring out at the city. His face is suddenly frozen, his breath quick and shallow. He swallows again and again, his Adam's apple sliding up his stalk-thin throat.

It is like this in London? Rose asks.

Yes, Frank says. Like this.

Then he tells her about fire watching on the roof of the Hackney Hospital. You see them coming over, far up high. And then, when you spot where the fires are, you radio instructions. Sometimes they come low – so low you can see the swastikas painted on the undersides of them.

One went into the building next door, he says, and then we had to run for cover, down twelve flights of stairs in the dark with glass blowing in all over us. There are eight of us in the team and we work in shifts. Most of the others are good guys. I've got to know them pretty well because most shifts nothing happens. For days and days nothing happens. Then for several hours it's all hell let loose and radioing again and again. And seeing five or six fires sometimes all at one time. And just watching them burn because, although we've given the information, the fire engines can't get there because of bomb craters or flooding.

Frank is talking too fast and too loudly. Rose nods her head, looks as though she's listening. She would like to lay a hand on Frank's arm, calm him, soothe him, but she knows if she does that, he might break. Two boys at the front of the bus play mouth organs. Their mournful tune fills the crowded air. It starts to rain, heavy drops beating down on the roof of the bus. Crowds of people are walking out of the city, tramping along the London Road, in an endless stream. Like refugees, Rose thinks, and that's what they are. These trekkers – the thousands who walk out of the city every night with their bedding, and food and flasks, loaded into prams and wheelbarrows, or balanced on bikes. Some rich people go in cars to cottages they've rented in Binley Woods or Canley. Poor people take their tarpaulin sheets and sleep wherever they can – in barns, or churches, under bridges or hedges.

The bus passes arms factories and Rose sees piles of bikes, black and spiky, parked at the gates, armed guards, smoke puffing from the chimneys. Then the bus is in open country, passing through sloping fields, their dark roll appearing black against the lesser black of the sky. Through the smeary window Rose sees the wood, a tangle of black lace, and the outline of a gate. This is where the bus is always parked. Someone jumps out to open the gate, the bus rocks on the uneven ground. Rose thinks of the hours ahead. Of course, they'll try to sleep but there will be little chance of that. Arthur suggests that she and Frank should take the back seat. This is a kindness to Frank because the back seat is the best place. So they sit down there and Rose makes a bed on the floor for Mollie, spreading out blankets and a sofa cushion. Mollie moans and kicks her legs against Rose's shins but stops when Rose moves to slap her.

A bomber sounds overhead.

Don't worry, love, it's one of ours, a man shouts from the front of the bus. Others guffaw and by the time the laughing dies down the noise of the plane has evaporated. Sheets of black paper are stuck up over the windows of the bus and candles are lit. Their light flickers over the black paper, flares across the ceiling. Frank talks to Mr and Mrs Bostock, the others crammed into the seats around them. They're all pacifists of one kind of another, or they have pacifists in their family. They pass around whisky and beer, talk about the news of the war. Arthur starts to sing and Rose concentrates on the sound of his voice as it swoops and falls. The sound should be comforting but it exists far away, in another world, and Rose can't draw it to her. Mollie is asleep on the floor now. Rose sits above her, propped in a corner, in the darkness. She feels stiff and her stomach heaves. Her feet are still wet from the rain earlier. Although it isn't yet eight o'clock she lays her head down on a cushion and tries to sleep. She can't understand where Mrs Watson is. Three days ago she lived a few streets away and now she's gone. Rose doesn't believe in the afterlife. Only stupid people believe such things. So then it's just nothing. But even nothing is something, isn't it?

The men are repeating those tired old phrases from before the war – you must listen to your conscience, war isn't the answer, a capitalist conflict created by the economic structure of Europe and the colonies. Rose can't believe they're still saying these same irrelevant things. The individual conscience is all – but do they never consider that view to be selfish or arrogant, do they never consider the wider good? Frank's insistent voice kindles her resentment. He has colleagues to work with, people to talk to, and he doesn't see what it's like for her. His voice is quavering, lit with a bright intensity. What a fool he is. For what he is saying – what all these people are saying – doesn't reflect the reality of the furnace city, of the women digging in the rubble with their bleeding hands, screaming for their children. Why do they not talk about death? Rose knows the answer. No one here can afford despair. But still anger churns inside her.

Frank comes to the back of the bus, swaying a little. Come on, he says. Come out for a bit. The rain's stopped.

She doesn't want to get up but goes with him and they walk into the woods, stumbling in the blackness. A nudging wind moves through the blackened branches above. It's a thin moon again but still, in the distance, they hear the rattle and whine of the planes coming in, and far away, at the edge of the city, pillars of light appear, cutting up through the air. Frank has been drinking and his voice is slurred. He asks her about the Peace Pledge Union, what's going on, what they've been doing.

Nothing, she says. Very little. People haven't got the time. It isn't possible.

You will do soon, he says. You will.

He stands close to her and she smells whisky.

I love you, Rose, he says. I love you.

He reaches out his hand, touches her shoulder.

You're not frightened, are you, Rosie? You mustn't be frightened.

I'm not frightened.

I love you, Rosie. I love you.

He strokes a curl of her hair but she doesn't respond.

You need to get out of Coventry, Frank says. You need to go.

Rose stares down at the ground. He knows there's no way out.

You mustn't lose hope, Rosie.

Why not? What's wrong with losing hope?

You're someone who does the right thing. You've always done that.

Yes, but what does it matter now? What does any of it matter?

Rosie, there's still good you can do. There are people who need help. Small bits of kindness. Keeping humanity alive. You can still do that.

Rose knows how badly Frank needs her to agree with this, how badly he needs her support. She also knows what he's saying is true. The bigger struggle has been lost long ago but there are still those daily choices to be made, right or wrong, compassion or cruelty, making sure not to walk by on the other side. Frank kisses her, his hand runs across the front of her blouse, touching her breasts. She feels nothing except irritation.

Well, at least at the end of all this your conscience will be clear, Rose says.

Rose feels Frank shrivel, knows the depth of the wound.

Come on, let's go back. I'm tired, she says.

They feel their way back to the bus and Frank makes Rose lie down and then sits next to her, rests her head on his lap. They're both wide awake. Mollie cries out in her sleep, thrashes and twists. Rose prays that she isn't going to start screaming and wake everyone up but the child turns on her side and settles again. Rose knows that she should stretch her arm out, pull Frank towards her, talk to him, stroke his cheek. But she lies awake, burning with a silent anger. An old man coughs again and again, clearing phlegm from his lungs. People snuffle and shift, curled awkwardly on the seats or spread out on the floor. The air smells of candle wax, and engine oil and wet wool and leather. From above her, Rose hears Frank swallowing again and again, then his hand goes up to wipe at his face. Rose reaches out, encloses his cold fingers in her colder hand.

# 20

# Now

## Jemmy – Brighton, March 2003

Jemmy stares at the bowl, which contains penne with tomato sauce. She cooked as soon as she got home but she's only managed to eat four spoonfuls. Now she's hungry again and pulls the bowl towards her – but no, the smell of it makes her feel sick and the sauce is just – too red. The evening is uncertain, the details of her kitchen, usually comforting, are not to be relied upon. The front window of the basement flat is steamed up but a dull glow shines in from the street lights outside. Sounds travel from far away, down on the seafront, the muffled bangs and whizzes of fireworks, some Gay Pride celebration.

The news will be on in five minutes so she flicks on the radio. Outside feet scrunch on the steps and Bill's shadow appears at the half-glazed door. Jemmy picks up a patchwork quilt she's been finishing off. She likes the way the colours work together, their echoes and resonances, each one changing the others. She sits down to sew, wanting Bill to see her, just for a moment, as peaceful, contented. She would like, at least, to give him that.

Hello there, he says.

Hi. Her fingers wobble as she tries to thread a needle. Bill drops his briefcase on the floor, takes off his coat, notes the uneaten bowl of pasta, starts to sort through post. Tell him, she says to herself. Go on, tell him. Every evening she promises herself she'll talk to him about the new pregnancy but the risk is too great.

Bad day? he says.

No, not particularly.

He reaches over towards the radio.

No, no. Don't turn it off. I'm waiting for the news.

Oh, Iraq, you mean? Your friend?

Jemmy wonders why Bill doesn't use Jay's name.

Yes. I didn't show you – there was an article in the *Guardian* last week. Jemmy reaches into her bag and pulls out a blurred photocopy of a newspaper article with a photograph. Protesters are lined up in front of a high barbed-wire fence, wearing matching black and white T-shirts. A banner above them says – *To Bomb This Site is a Violation of the Geneva Convention Article 94.*

He isn't there, though, Jemmy says. I looked at the faces. So I went around to the peace protest office and they said they could put me on a list and forward any emails.

Bill fiddles with a knitting needle lying on the table. For the first time, Jemmy wonders what Bill thinks about Jay. Perhaps he's jealous? He could be because all he knows is that Jay is someone Jemmy knew around the time that they met. Maybe she should try to explain but where would she start? *He was a boy I didn't know. He saved my life.* If she explained that then she'd have to explain about the thick black cardigans as well. Bill looks at his watch, the action a veiled threat. OK, so you just listen to the news, then we'll be off soon, shall we? Or do you need to get changed?

Listen, sorry. I just don't think I can. I know that you wanted me to go.

Tony will be really disappointed.

Jemmy wonders why she should care about what Tony thinks.

Are you sure it's good for you to stay in so much? Bill says.

No, not really, Jemmy says. But it isn't good for me to go out either.

She sees him wince. OK, he says. OK. Jemmy waits for him to go because that's what he usually does – gives her a kiss, disappears, doesn't come back until gone midnight. But now he sits across the table watching her. Her sleeves are rolled up and she feels Bill's eyes touch the silver lines that run across her wrists and forearms. Those scars are something else they've never talked about. The radio continues to murmur. *The rapidly growing trade in derivatives poses a catastrophic risk for the economy. Such highly complicated measures are time bombs.*

I like that wool, he says, nodding towards a jumper that she's been unravelling. She unpicks old jumpers and makes them into scarves with patterns of flowers and butterflies, which will sell for over eighty pounds in the Lanes because they're recycled.

You know, James and Rachel would really like to see you, Bill says.

No, they wouldn't. They don't like having me around. I smell of death.

For God's sake. Don't be silly, of course you don't.

She knows that she isn't being fair but she's tired – so tired – of having these conversations, night after night. She looks up and sees the familiar frustration on Bill's face. This man – she married him, she loves him and she knows he's working hard and that he likes to go out for a drink in the evening. And there's nothing wrong with that – but then why doesn't he go?

Bill turns the radio down. Jemmy gives him a warning look.

Yeah. I know. But I can't hear myself think. And there isn't going to be anything more about Iraq. Most of those people on the buses have left now anyway. And it isn't our problem.

Jemmy continues to sew in threads, anger quickening her fingers.

You could do the patchwork another evening, Bill says.

It's not the patchwork. The problem is that I want to talk about Laurie because he's what's going on in my life but no one else wants to talk about him. So finally there isn't any conversation to be had.

Bill is staring down at the table, keeping tight hold of his determination to be reasonable. This is how these conversations go. They involve long silences. She sees Bill trying to decide what he can and can't say. But he is slipping on the cliff face and his fear curdles the air. Getting up from the table, he strides towards the door, purposefully, then moves back again, standing with his back against the sink. Of course, she could rescue this conversation. She could tell him about the new baby. They could hug and kiss, celebrate.

Actually, Bill says. Actually – you won't even let anyone try and help. People would talk to you but they just don't know what to say. People are frightened, don't you understand that? They're frightened because if our baby can die then so can theirs. And it's the thing that people fear beyond anything else.

Yes, I know. I understand all of that. And I'm sorry that other people find it difficult. But what do they think I feel like? Do I have to keep quiet about my dead baby so that they don't feel upset? When does someone put my feelings first? Because this happened to me.

And to me as well.

Yes. I know. I know.

Jemmy says the words with conviction although the truth is that, despite the fact that she understands Bill entirely, she's unable to feel much sympathy for him. She's tried to help him but he refuses every offer she makes. She's said that she'll make a special album for him containing the photographs of Laurie, she's suggested that they should go and visit the grave together. They could make a tiny garden there, the vicar wouldn't mind. But Bill doesn't want any of that. If she presses him he says that he doesn't find it helpful to talk, talking doesn't change anything, the situation is what it is.

At the Support Group they say that you mustn't judge the quality of other people's grief. And Jemmy does understand that Laurie's death is probably more difficult for Bill than for her. He's someone who's always been lucky. Things work out for him. A life of ladders rather than snakes. He did well at school, qualified as a surveyor, got a job in the best firm in Brighton, bought this flat for far less than its real value. So now he's shocked to find that he too is vulnerable. No client of his will ever find that they've bought a house with dry rot, a leaking flat roof, or rising damp. So how come his life has suddenly been revealed to have a major structural problem? A problem that can't be solved – ever. At the Support Group they say it's worse for the woman than for the man but Jemmy doubts that's true. She suspects that women do heal eventually – but men don't.

You can't go on like this, Bill says. Sometime you've got to let go of him. You've got to move on.

As soon as the words are out, Jemmy sees him measuring the size of the error. At the Support Group nobody uses those phrases. It isn't about moving on, only about finding the right place in your life for the baby you've lost. Jemmy knows that Bill doesn't mean what he said but she can't stop herself from exploiting this advantage.

Why would I move on? she says. I mean, Laurie is not a roadkill, is he? Why does anyone move on from their child?

I didn't mean that. You know I didn't mean that. What I'm trying to say is – you can't have a relationship with someone who is dead.

Of course you can. I do. I am. People who are dead are very important. It's only this fucked-up modern world we're living in which tries to tell us otherwise.

Jemmy can't understand why she needs to explain this to Bill because he's the one who's got books about gravestones and is interested in drawing up family trees, sorting back through the dead, linking them one to the other, tracking down every last child, grandchild, great-grandchild. But now that he's actually confronted by someone who's dead his only response is to refuse to see. Impossible to understand – except that similar things have happened to Jemmy again and again over the last four months. In the places where one most expects understanding and comfort, it isn't there. Like diving into the deep end of a swimming pool and finding that the water is only two foot deep.

The point is, Bill says, still staring at the table, that if you try to have a relationship with a person who's dead then it's a one-sided relationship, isn't it?

In what sense?

Well, he can't participate in the relationship, can he?

Yes, he can. Of course, he can. For me he's quite different at different times. I understand him differently and his effect on me is different. You just can't understand that because you're stuck with the idea that you can, and should, leave the dead behind.

This is what the people at the Spiritualist Church tell Jemmy and she knows they're right. Jemmy looks at Bill and for a moment she hates him. At the Support Group they say – *You mustn't turn your anger against each other.* But where else can it go? There's no one to blame. The hospital was not at fault. She sometimes thinks it might be easier if they had been. They had said when Jemmy was four months pregnant that Laurie might not live and that there was nothing they could do. But still they'd monitored and tested and prescribed pills, and then later they'd taken her into hospital, and she'd been there a whole week. And the hospital was so new and clean and there was so much technology and everything so shiny and bright that Jemmy never really thought Laurie would die, not even right at the end. Because it just didn't seem possible with all those white coats, and machines and dials and knobs. It just didn't seem possible that anyone could do something as old-fashioned and vulgar as dying.

Bill picks up his coat and heads for the door.

I don't get it, he says. I don't get it. Why would you want people in the pub to spend their time talking about. Something which. Hurts so much?

Because I want people to know I had a baby. If I could, I'd take his dead body into the pub and put him down on the bar. Because he's a person, because he existed, because everybody else shows off their baby. He's what we made. I want him to have his place.

Yes, but the point is, Jemmy, that he's dead. That's the point.

Oh so you think I'm in doubt about that, do you? You think I'm confused? I mean, if I'm holding a dead baby in my arms then I know absolutely how dead that baby is.

Jemmy, please. Please. Don't do this. I just wanted to go out for the evening and have a break, think about something else. If that's really too much to ask then what's the point of being married?

Bill picks up his coat from the back of a chair and heads out into the hall. Jemmy follows him, stands watching as he hesitates. Silence crowds the hall. Jemmy knows that what she's said is unforgivable. Only fifty per cent of marriages survive the death of a baby. She never thought she would end up in the wrong fifty per cent but somehow, by accident, just like that, she finds herself heading in that direction. Bill is quite right – what is the point of being married? She should go and put her arms around him and tell him that she loves him, tell him about the new baby. That's what she would have done before Laurie died. And she does love him still – absolutely and completely. But strangely that is irrelevant now.

Bill says, The truth is— the reason why you hate Tony and James and Rachel and the others so much is that they sent Christmas cards and they didn't put his name in them. You wanted his name in the cards, didn't you? That's what this is all about, isn't it? You blame them for that. But that isn't reasonable, Jemmy. I'm sorry. I'm trying to be sympathetic but that just isn't reasonable. People do not write the name of someone who's dead in their Christmas cards.

Jemmy sits on the stairs, nods her head. She's too tired to say any more. He's right, of course, she was angry about that. This is what Bill says all the time – you're not being reasonable. But he doesn't seem to understand that in this situation the comforting geometry of reason is as powerless as the deepest love.

Jemmy longs for Bill to leave, but he stands there still, bright and fragile as a glass ornament. Also, he says, I just wanted to say that I've made some arrangements about the pushchair.

They've been discussing the pushchair ever since Laurie died. Bill wanted to take it to the charity shop straight away. After all, they don't need it, and it's making them feel bad. But Jemmy didn't like the idea. Some other mother would buy that pushchair and she wouldn't know that it belonged to Laurie. So what are we going to do with it? Keep it. Why not? Jemmy had spoken to the lady at the Support Group and she'd said, *Listen, love, you keep it just as long as you want and don't let anyone tell you otherwise.*

Someone at the office is about to buy a new pushchair so I offered to lend it to them, Bill says. Not give – just lend. So I'm going to take it into the office with me tomorrow. So I just thought I'd tell you that's what I've decided.

Jemmy nods her head, unable to speak. She watches Bill slam uncertainly out of the house, pulling his coat on. She sinks down on the stairs, bloodless. She remembers the man at the Support Group who suddenly started shouting, *If I'm strong and do all the cooking, washing, cleaning then I'm a heartless bastard who doesn't care, but if I sit down and cry then I'm not offering her enough support. So what the fuck am I meant to be doing?* After he'd stormed out of the meeting, Jemmy had looked up to see other men nodding their heads.

She would cry but she's cried so much over the last three months that she hasn't got any tears left. She can't say, *I'm pregnant again*, because Bill will not remember what they said in the hospital. Jemmy had asked the question, saying the words slowly and clearly, when they went for the results of Laurie's post-mortem. *If we have another baby then will that baby die as well?* And the doctor had buried her face in the computer screen and said, *It's very rare, most unusual, it would be unlikely, I would certainly hope not, but unfortunately, yes, sometimes, yes.* Bill will not remember that conversation.

She wanders into the bedroom. Movement is easier than stillness. Laurie's pushchair is parked in the corner. She knows that Bill won't really get rid of it. He only said that because he was trying to move the situation forward, to break the deadlock. He'd done it in the worst way possible but it was kindly meant. She moves back to the kitchen and sees all that is familiar suddenly newborn. She goes to the draining board, starts to put away pots and plates, longing for simple actions to bring comfort. A long knife emerges from under a plate, its wide blade is eloquent, its point provokes. Jemmy picks it up, lays her wrist down on the draining board, places the blade of the knife across her skin. Positions it on the exact line of one of those pale, criss-cross scars. The action feels welcoming, but no, she doesn't want to do that now. Sometimes she used to want to feel pain as a way of checking that she existed. But now she's in such pain – burning, hurting, aching, longing – that she doesn't need physical pain in order to prove anything. It's so strange. She was mad when she had no cause to be mad, back in the thick black cardigan days. But now she does have cause, she's frighteningly clear-sighted and sane. Madness has become a luxury she can't afford. She lays the knife down and looks around her. Vegetables to make into soup before they rot, stale biscuits to be thrown out, a credit-card bill to pay.

But she can't do it any more. She just can't. Who should she call? Perhaps Hannah from the shop in the Lanes, but Jemmy doesn't know her well. She'd like to call Mr George Waldron of 8 Wilmlow Gardens, Harringbourne, Sevenoaks. It's proved more difficult to sort out his policy than Jemmy expected. She's had to call Mr George Waldron back on a number of occasions and he's called her as well. She's never told him about Laurie but she knows that, if she did, he'd understand. If she could hear his voice then she'd feel calm again. Finding her phone, she calls his number and listens to the burr-burr-burr of the ringing tone but no one answers. Jemmy listens for a minute, maybe two, three – finally flicks the phone off.

If she waits up for Bill then they'll talk, and say sorry, and they'll have got through another day. But tomorrow will be the same, and the day after that. Sometime she'll have to tell him about the pregnancy. Then he'll want to go down to the pub and tell everyone. When the new baby is born – if it is born alive – then everyone will send cards. And they'll be so pleased. Problem over, then. A happy ending. Well, aren't you lucky? A lovely new baby. Cuddly toys and babygrows and mobiles to hang on the ceiling. That she absolutely cannot bear. Laurie didn't have any of those things so no other baby is having any of that either. And yet she knows that the baby – the size of a strawberry now – is quite innocent and has no choice but to nudge its way into the world. A death can't be allowed to ruin a life – but she can't attach any love to this new baby. The risk is too great.

Getting down on her knees, she pulls a rucksack out from under the bed. The canvas in her hands sings of escape. She won't go for long, of course, just for a few days, while she thinks things over. It'll be better for Bill that way. All she's doing is making him unhappy. Their relationship isn't over, it never will be, because he was there when Laurie was born. He saw what happened. And so they are locked together in some silent pact that goes far deeper than the mere fact of marriage. But twenty-two is far too young to spend your life with someone who doesn't understand. If she and Bill can't share Laurie's death then what is their relationship worth? And then there's the shame – the shame of what she said earlier, the shame of having failed Bill, the shame of not being able to pretend everything is fine.

She finds her jeans, her patchwork jumper and purple boots. She'll miss the flat – the curtains she made, the wooden floors she and Bill sanded and waxed together, stopping off at some point to make love amidst the sawdust and shavings, the wire of the electric sander pressing into her shoulder. She unplugs her laptop, pushes another jumper into her rucksack, finds the charger for her mobile, puts her camera into its bag, scoops underwear off the radiator in the bathroom. She'll take the pushchair as well because she can use that to transport her sewing machine. It only takes ten minutes to pack. Surprising how quickly a life can dissolve.

She should leave a message but she can think of nothing to say. Carrying her bag up the area steps, she thinks – I must be careful. Don't run, don't lift anything heavy, don't eat undercooked meat or unwashed salad, don't get your hair highlighted. But she was careful last time and it didn't do any good. She bumps the pushchair up the steps. She's no idea where she's going. It doesn't matter. Siberia, Patagonia, Timbuktu. She could live to be one hundred and ten but she'll never stop being a woman whose baby died. Wheeling Laurie's pushchair, she sets out down the street. She's never steered a pushchair before and she likes the feel of it.

As she walks, she hums to Laurie and moves carefully, picking out a route where the paving stones are smooth, taking care not to jolt or bump, in case he wakes.

## 21

# Now

## Jay – Baghdad, March 2003

Hi Mum, Granmollie and friends back home,
Hope you are all OK. It's kind of weird here. I'm looking out of
the window and this city is all the same colour, sand coloured,
concrete coloured and big pictures of Saddam everywhere.
And huge palaces which belong to him on every street corner
but you're meant to pretend that they're not there. And what
I'm writing to tell you is that I'm not coming back – or not
right now anyway. No big decision, just I need to be here a
few days more. But still I know you're going to be upset about
this so that's why I'm writing to explain. I'm not quite clear
myself. All I can do is tell you about what happened to me
yesterday and hope you'll understand.

A doctor I met here took me to a hospital, a really cool
guy, really high up, who speaks very good English and trained
for three years in Edinburgh and talks about how cold
Edinburgh is and walking in the Highlands. And it's funny
because he speaks English with a slight Scottish accent and
says wee instead of small. The people here are really great but
none of them will say a single critical word about the regime,
not one word, however hard you try to get it out of them, so
that in the end you start wondering if actually that really is
what they think.

Anyway, this doctor took me to the hospital where he
works and he took me to one of the wards and they have
no drugs there, and no drips and no bandages and not even

clean sheets. And people there are just crying in pain and slowly dying – children, old people, a boy with his legs and feet all shrivelled up to half their proper size. And after that I was just crying and crying and I felt so ashamed because, of course, the doctor I was with doesn't cry at all. He hasn't got the time or energy for that. All he does is stand around all day and watch people die and he can't even give them a fucking aspirin.

But he was really kind to me and didn't mind that I cried. We just hung around in this side room where there were blood-covered dressings lying around the place, and they're washing syringes in sinks in case they should ever get any drugs to put in them. And then the Iraqi doctor thanked me for looking around the hospital and I thanked him – and both of us wanted to have this conversation about what we could do. He wanted to ask me if I could get drugs or medicine but he knows I can't. And I want to ask him what he thinks should be done but actually there's nothing to say, nothing at all. Even if George W called off his war and sent some massive load of aid then it's still too late for the people here. For them the only hope is that they'll die quickly. I wondered if the doctors here ever kill people to put them out of their misery. And I asked the guy in a roundabout sort of way and suddenly he laughed and said, we don't have the drugs to do it with.

And the point is that I know, in a sense, that I've been set up for this. Every journalist here has been taken on a horror tour of a hospital and it's all a huge propaganda thing to show how terrible the sanctions are – and the journalists tell me that really it's nothing like as bad as people are making out. And actually it's true that the TV makes it look worse than it is. When you're here it's attractive – like some place you'd go on holiday. Well, grottier than that but not bad really. I mean everything is broken and people are queuing and they're drinking water from pipes in the street and apparently it's contaminated. But I don't know. It's hard to explain. It's just different. Simpler, harder, basic but not necessarily worse than the excess and lethargy and mindless consumption where we come from. I'm not trying to romanticise what is going on here. That would be the biggest insult to the people who live this every day. But still in this place you do find an energy, a clarity, a purpose which is amazing.

But the point is you can come up with all these fancy arguments and you can debate into the small hours and you can suggest this idea or that idea, and you can blame that person or this person, and you explain it away by saying this and that and the other but at the end of the day those people in that hospital ward are there. And actually all the conversations that you have are just a means of trying not to see, or trying not to face up to how many people here have died, are dying, will die.

I guess you know that most people who came out on the buses have flown home now. Most of them weren't doing much except playing cards. A few of them I miss but some I'll be glad never to see again. Anyway, I met this guy called Greg Marsden who apparently knows you or Granmollie and he's going to stay but most of the journalists are going. I also met a Spanish journalist called Patricia and a German mate of hers called Hans. Patricia cooks tortilla for me and says I can stay on the floor of her room. I love her, she's really great.

The truth is that I don't really know what I'm going to do. There's nothing I can do but maybe if I'm lucky something will emerge. All I know is that this is the right place for me to be. It sounds kind of strange but I like it here. It works for me. Some human rights people who got out a few days ago left me this really flash camera and told me I could document human rights abuses. I'll certainly give it a go, though I think the photographs I take will not be the ones they want. But I could talk to Voices of Truth as well. They might be interested. Perhaps what I'll do is just say sorry to people.

Take photographs and say sorry. After all, somebody has to say sorry. Just to see is something. Just to see – I don't know what good it does but it does do something.

And I know that you don't agree with me but you do know that I'm right. You know it really. And you mustn't worry about me. Not at all. I'm really fine. I love you, Mum, and I wouldn't say these things if I didn't love you. But you can't keep on living the way you live. I can't keep on discussing with you whether we should have salmon or lamb for supper, whether we should go on holiday to Italy or Spain, whether it's time to invest in a new stereo. Life has to be about something other than consumption. And I know what you're going to say. You're going to say that you are no worse than anyone else. And you are right about that. Definitely right. But I'm afraid it isn't enough not to be bad.

Anyway I have to stop writing now because I want to carry this letter over to the Palestine Hotel before it gets dark. I'm going to give it to Greg because he knows someone who is trying to leave tomorrow and they'll take this letter with them. Greg is going to email you the number of his satellite phone. It's an American number and it doesn't work well but he can get a signal from the back of his hotel. But please, please, don't use either his phone number or email unless you really need to because Greg can get thrown out of the country. No one is meant to use any equipment except the stuff that is at the Ministry of Information. Just two days ago a journalist got thrown out for using his private phone. I love you. Don't be frightened. Only good people die so I'm certain to be OK.

Jay.

# 22

# Now

## Lara – Brighton, March 2003

Lara wakes and turns over. Will she be late for the train? But then she remembers, checks her watch. It's six o'clock in the evening. She went to bed at four intending to sleep for half an hour. Often now it's easier to sleep in the day than at night. More than a week has passed since she left her job but still her mind keeps snapping at her – *Time to get to work.* Strangely, she misses Craig. Her tarnished love affair with him, the vague anger he always stirred in her, are proving difficult to leave behind. That anger was her fuel and without it she can't seem to get started.

She pulls herself up from the bed, takes care not to think. Instead – *What can I do now? This minute?* She's spent the last week clearing and sorting, doing all of those jobs that never got done because she was too busy. Now she goes down to the sitting room, starts to make yet another list but it fizzles out after item number four. Oliver said to do nothing but Lara isn't quite certain what that would involve. She rubs her eyes, tries to quell that lurching disorientation which always follows daytime sleep.

She thinks of calling Mollie. Over the last few weeks Mollie has called most days but Lara has only replied once or twice – and has limited her conversation to the exchange of vital information. But now – briefly – she misses Mollie. Christ, things must be bad if she misses her mother. Would it be comforting to sit at the table in Mollie's basement kitchen and drink tea? No. The milk will have gone off and will float in puddles of oil on the surface of the tea. Lara adds Mollie to her list of things to do. But the list won't fill an evening, or even an hour.

So strange, she thinks. Jay was meant to be the problem in the family, the person who caused trouble, who needed looking after, who was irresponsible. The scapegoat. But maybe it wasn't like that at all. Maybe Jay was the keystone, the brick that held the arch together, because now he's gone everything is coming tumbling down. She had thought that Jay needed them but maybe it was always the other way round.

Lara flicks on the radio. *Stock markets and investors around the world have enjoyed record gains but the storm clouds are gathering.* Her hand smacks the off switch. On her desk a file is stuffed with post that she's received over the past three weeks. Some of the letters are carefully typed with correct spelling – hatred presented neatly. Other letters are written in sprawls of green ink on crumpled paper. One letter consists only of three illegible words scrawled on the back of an advert for a window cleaner. Traitor, betrayal, tyrant. Lara stares at the letters trying to understand their sizzling anger. These people have gone to the trouble to find out her address and write to her just because they've found Jay's name in the papers. Why does anyone care enough to do that? Of course, there are some letters of support as well. Jay the hero, Jay the martyr, Jay the good Christian.

Where is he now? *I need to be here a few days more.* That could mean anything. The red buses left Iraq two days ago and are now stranded on the Lebanon–Syria border because no diesel vehicles are allowed into Lebanon. Lara feels sure that he won't be with those buses but is equally sure that he'll be home soon now. All the reports say that everyone is leaving. Lara has a phone number for Greg Marsden now and she's been in touch with him, knows that he has seen Jay and spoken to him. Of course, Lara had felt annoyed that, after she'd spent weeks trying to find a way of getting in touch with Jay, Mollie seemed to have managed it with no trouble at all. Mollie who always knows someone, always charms them, always gets what she wants without apparently trying.

But it had been a relief to have some way of getting in touch. Last night she'd left a message for Greg, pleaded with him to try to get Jay home but she's heard nothing. And she's tried everywhere to find a phone number for Patricia, the Spanish journalist.

The only person who does understand is Oliver. She's been back to see him several times over the last two weeks and she would go now but he's busy at some church meeting. She still doesn't know what or who he is. Often he treats her as a vicar might, a shepherd tending a lost sheep. But sometimes she sees beyond that to some other person who is uncertain, frightened, too lost himself to look for the lost. Her mind drifts back to those vases that float on the shelf in his makeshift flat. All she does know is that he doesn't mind if she goes around, rants for an hour or more, and then leaves. She's embarrassed to remember what she said last time she saw him.

Do you have any idea how difficult it is being a mother? The yawning boredom, the tedium. Food shopping, meals, clothes washing. Clean your teeth, wash your face, hang your coat on a hook. Again and again and again. You know, every house you go to there's the wedding photo. Such beautiful girls – full of power, and ambition and hope. And three years later they're all the same. Pushing a pushchair up and down the street, the whole damn lot of them lost to motherhood with their waists gone slack and their hair greasy and saying – *I never was much interested in a career.* And society sells them the idea that they have the ultimate compensation. A beautiful child who loves them. But is that compensation enough? When their husband leaves, and their child stops speaking to them, starts taking drugs, fails every exam. Even if the child does grow up happy – is the mother compensated for what she's lost? Of course, the theory goes, that through all that self-sacrifice you find your true self. But I doubt it. As a mother you're nothing more than a venue where other people are living their lives. There were times when I could easily have bought a one-way ticket to Australia. But those times exist for every mother. The women who deny that are simply lying.

After she'd said all that, she looked over at Oliver, massive and still, sitting on his uncomfortable upright chair and waited for him to argue, but instead he said that he understood and something about the look in his eyes told her that this was true. But that only made her feel ashamed because, in truth, she hadn't made the sacrifices that other women make. She'd escaped, gone back to work, handed over half of the drudgery to her mother.

But I still maintain that I was only an averagely bad mother, she'd said. And then she'd started to laugh and strangely he'd joined her, his laughter like the clanking of an ancient machine. A machine which hadn't been used in many years, which was rusted up and overgrown with weeds but had now, mysteriously, come back to life, wheezing and straining but alive, definitely alive.

If only Oliver was at home tonight. She never expected to become friends with a church warden, or a failed vicar – or is he a failed faith healer? But that's what seems to be happening. Passing the table in the sitting room, she picks up Jay's letter. He can be surprisingly articulate for someone who has failed so many exams. She wanders into the kitchen. At least the builders have nearly finished now – just the painting to be done. And it does look good – very good. Although if she was doing it again she would choose a lighter coloured splashback and perhaps a slightly darker wood. In her head she makes the normal bargains. Dear God, if you bring him home safe then I'll be good and kind forever and I'll do whatever you want. But what does God want? Lara has no idea and anyway she doesn't believe in God. But God is in her life now whether she wants him or not because it simply isn't possible to believe that whether Jay comes home is just a matter of chance. Human life can't be saved or lost on the toss of a coin. Someone, somewhere must be making a decision. It must be possible to strike a bargain, there must be a right of appeal.

Standing at the window, Lara sees a shower of pink sparks whizzing into the seeping blackness above the pier. All day bands have been playing and loud speakers blaring. And occasionally men have passed in the street wearing dustbin liners or pink rabbit ears. Lara listens to the scream of a firework, then to the silence that follows. Kicking off her shoes, she heads upstairs to her study. Green box files are lined up on a shelf and she examines these carefully. Have they been moved? One of them sticks out slightly further than the others. She wonders now why she ever kept that letter.

In some distant storeroom of her mind, she's always worried that one day Jay would start going through her files. But had he done? Lara lifts the last of the files down and, kneeling on the floor, opens it. The piece of paper is buried behind all the other letters and papers. It lies to one side of the file and she wonders now – has it been moved? But there's nothing to suggest that. The paper is furred but Lara still remembers the writing – that green copperplate swirl and the London address, just an address, no name. Lara pushes the piece of paper back into place and shuts up the file. Jay has always claimed that none of his difficulties have anything to do with not having a father. But can that really be true?

Why? Why? Lara says as she pushes the file back into its place. But the power of these words to obliterate all else is fading. They were a rope bridge constructed to reach across some vast abyss in her mind. But the ropes are straining and creaking, the wooden slats cracking. Standing still for a moment, on the landing, she stares at Jay's bedroom door. Only a week ago she'd been thinking she'd clear up his room, reorganise things a bit, ready for him coming home. A great wave of something – fear, grief, shock – rises in her throat. She goes to the bedroom door and pushes it open.

Staring at the room, she realises for the first time that Jay has gone. It's ridiculous, of course, because he's been gone for six weeks but now she feels it, in her joints, the tips of her fingers. His absence is so tangible that it's present. His trainers are still lying near the door and now she knows that she must never move them. They've become exhibits in a museum, evidence of some irrecoverable past. As she stares at them, he suddenly appears. His height and shape, the way he stands, weight on one leg, his thick glasses and tousled hair, his young man smell and those eyes which never turn away, which continue to ask questions without answers. The shivery white blemished skin, the unchanged socks, the movements clumsy and raw. The great wet footprints which he leaves on the carpet as he crosses the landing. The soaked towel on the bedroom carpet. The banana skin pushed into a half finished glass of milk on the bedside table.

Staring at her son, who isn't there, she sees that he's someone quite different to her, quite separate. Stupid, of course. She knows that. And yet this is the first time that she's really understood that his eyes don't see the same world that her eyes see. She stands beside his bed, stares around his museum room. His books, his tapes, his half dismantled bike, his clothes still piled on a chair. That book about conscientious objectors in the Second World War. She wants to kneel down and touch the wheel of the bike, trace her finger on the place where his name is written on the front of a notebook. Jay. My son.

If only she could hold him, or talk to him. If only he would walk in through the door then she could make it different, she could heal the wound. She remembers this room as it was when they first moved into this flat – blue trains on the curtain, a blue patchwork duvet cover, a rug with ships sailing on a wavy blue sea. She'd bought him a little bed, painted blue, and she used to kneel down beside him as he slept. His tiny head would be sweaty, his arms stretched back beyond his head, abandoned to sleep, his closed lids fanned by the longest lashes. And then she'd wish that she'd never had a child. It had been wrong of her, she was sure of that. Life is not something one would wish on anyone else.

But the little blue bed and the patchwork duvet cover have gone long ago. It'd all moved too fast, she'd been too tired. Often Jay had been an interior design problem – a bookcase too big for a particular alcove, a cushion that clashed with the carpet. And then the university place – that had been the breaking point. She'd given up her university place for him and then he gave up his for no reason at all.

She kicks off her shoes, lies down on his bed, smells the sheets. Even after six weeks they do still smell of him. She pulls the duvet close to her face, wraps her arms around the pillows. Slowly and quietly, she starts to cry, as she lies in the darkness, her tears soaking into the place where his head should lie. The tragedy is not that she misses him now but that she's missed him always. *I love you, Mum, but I can't keep on discussing with you whether we should have salmon or lamb for supper. Life has to be about something other than consumption.* No doubt he's right. But what? What?

She thinks back to his childhood and remembers winter afternoons, on her own, pushing him on a swing in a park. And it had seemed the saddest thing in the world – the child, the park, the trees bare of their leaves and the light melting. Somewhere in the background the mournful music of an ice-cream van. She asks now, *Why does childhood – any childhood – seem loaded with loss?* Balloons and teddy bears, mobiles swinging from the ceiling, alphabet friezes. All of those things, which are meant to be so full of happiness, speak to her only of something fractured. Perhaps she was never a mother to Jay, only to the child that she once was.

Another memory. Jay as a toddler, in a park, with a balloon. He's bundled up into a navy blue duffel coat and his tiny face is alight with wonder. He's staring up at the balloon – a large, green balloon dancing on the end of a string. But then older children come, a boy and a girl, well dressed and sure of themselves. They must be eight or nine – and they take the balloon away, snatching it out of his tiny starfish hands, laughing, dancing away insouciantly, not caring that the child in the blue duffel coat has started to wail.

Lara is filled with sudden and violent hatred. She wants to shoot those children, or stab them, pummel their faces with her fists. She hurries towards them, shouts at them, grabs the balloon, threatens to find their parents, to report them to the police. She's shocked at her own venom, has never felt such anger before. She goes to Jay and tries to give him the balloon but he won't take it.

He's wailing so much he can't even see the balloon. Lara's head is thumping with hatred for those posh little children. How could they do that? She tries again to give the balloon to Jay but he won't take it. Lara can't bear him wailing. She hugs his stiff, duffel-coated little frame but that doesn't work. He's still crying and the sound seems to fill the whole park, to rise up high into the air, to press against her bones. Please, please, make him stop.

She wants to get away from him then, to run from the park, to silence him somehow, anyhow. She grabs him and shakes him into silence, his small head rocking back and forwards as she yanks his shoulders. Then she hates herself for doing that, and hugs him tightly. She cries all the way home and all the time he toddles beside her saying — *Sorry, Mummy, sorry.* And she says she's sorry as well, but she can't stop herself from crying even more. She can't bear his innocence – so fresh and sharp and dangerous – she can't bear being responsible for that. He can't be allowed to walk through the world as naked as he is. Perhaps she's always been frightened of Jay.

# 23

# Now

## Mollie – Brighton, March 2003

The sound of the doorbell rattles through the Windsor Guest House followed by a crash. Bugger, Mollie says. One of the cats knocking something off the table? She sets off downstairs. Rufus must be home, she thinks, and feels a familiar tingle pass across her flesh. But pulling open the front door, she finds only a girl holding a suitcase, her face olive green under the accusing porch light. At the bottom of the steps, in the shadows, other bags are stacked against a pushchair. Mollie has seen the girl before, wandering the streets, or in the corner shop.

The old story. The displaced and dispossessed of Brighton. They knock on her door because the stained paintwork and rotten window frames suggest that the Windsor Guest House might be cheap enough even for them. She considers the girl – an Asian girl, with long black hair, wearing a gypsy skirt, footless tights, jewelled shoes. Some young mum thrown out of the house. Probably the husband – if there is one – can't cope with the baby.

The girl clears her throat and starts to speak. Her voice is surprisingly refined for a girl of her type. Mollie remembers all the things that Rufus and Lara have told her. You're not running a hostel for the homeless. Make sure you get a deposit in cash. Don't allow children or dogs. Make it clear that this isn't a guest house any more. Anyone who rents a room needs to do their own cleaning and get their own breakfast.

Excuse me, do you have a room? Just for one night.

Mollie stares down at the shadowy pushchair. It would be wrong to refuse a woman with a baby. Dangerous for it to be out on the streets. Mollie imagines talcum powder, nappies, bottles, all the soft and scented baby things in that bag in the bottom of the pushchair. She knows what it is to wander the streets looking for a place to stay. More than forty years ago now, but she doesn't forget. Rooms with other people's stains on the sheets. Doors banged in her face. Middle-aged men with beer-smelling breath standing too close. *Yes, yes, yes. Of course, my dear, you must come in.* The creaks and strains of other people's houses, flock wallpaper, the expressionless faces glimpsed through half-closed doors. What right have Rufus and Lara to tell her what she can and can't do?

I'm a friend of Jay's, the girl says.

Oh, well, of course.

Sorry to disturb you.

No. No. I was looking for something. Nothing important. You better come in although the rooms aren't ready and I've had a problem with the window – but I'm sure I can organise something.

Thank you, the girl says. She carries the suitcase into the hall. Mollie puts a wedge under the front door while the girl goes to get her other bags. I better go and help her with that pushchair, Mollie thinks. Cotton wool and a white blanket wrapped around the sleeping child. A tiny, wrinkled hand stretched out and locking around her finger. She hurries down the steps, lifts a bag. The girl spins the pushchair around, and there's no baby, only a sewing machine. Her heart shrivels inside her. She had wanted to see the baby – but never mind. She'll tell the girl she can bring the baby around tomorrow. Probably left it with her mother.

So have you heard any news of Jay? the girl asks.

Not much. But on Sunday we did hear that the buses were coming back.

Together Mollie and the girl haul the bag and pushchair up the steps.

I'm not sure what you know, Mollie says. This man, somebody Al-Hashimi, he's part of the group which invited them to Iraq, but now he's telling them that he's deciding what sites they can go to – and sending them to places not approved by the UN. So some of them are being turned out of the country and the others are coming back. Well, they've got to, haven't they?

Yes – because there will be a war now, won't there?

I fear so – yes. Spike says soon. I just hope they get out.

But you haven't spoken to Jay?

No, but we have this friend, a journalist called Greg Marsden, and he's in Iraq and if his paper orders him out, which they will do soon, then he won't leave without Jay.

Must be awful.

Yes, just the waiting and waiting. Hard to know how to get through the day.

In the hall light Mollie sees that the girl is shivering and sallow. Probably she's the victim of one of those Muslim family feuds. Mollie's read all about those in the newspaper. Only the other day the body of a young woman was found chopped up in a suitcase in the Left Luggage at Heathrow. All she did was marry the man she loved.

Let's get a room sorted out, Mollie says. Then I'll make you a cup of tea.

Together they haul the bags and the pushchair up to the first floor landing. Mollie enjoys the struggle, the brief bubbling of laughter as the wheel catches in the torn stair carpet. Thank goodness for company. Mollie hates it when the Guest House is empty and it is tonight. Stan and Stan and Stan have all left for a job in Croydon and won't be back until early next week. Ahmed is at the peace protest office and Mr Lambert has gone off down to that Gay Pride march on the seafront. Mollie's got nothing against them, of course, but no one over the age of fifty should be allowed to wear pink lycra shorts.

I'm sorry, Mollie says. About the window – but don't you worry because I'll be able to get it sorted out soon enough. I'll put some clean sheets on and get you a hot-water bottle.

As Mollie goes up to her own room, she passes stacked piles of boxes and bags, the open door to the store cupboard under the eaves. Boxes. Stuff. More stuff. That's what she was doing when the doorbell rang, sorting and searching. How emotion accumulates around physical objects. Over the years Mollie has pushed so much away into the cupboard under the eaves.

Some of these boxes belong to people who are now dead. Physical things are so robust, their owners fragile. Mollie should doubtless throw out those boxes but she hesitates because the objects they contain were significant to the people who owned them, even though the stories which made them more than mere junk can never be recovered now. Most of this stuff has accumulated while she's been at the Guest House but there are two or three boxes that come from before, one of which might contain her birth certificate. Rufus burnt a copy when she first met him – but did she get another one later? Of course, it's always had the wrong date but she could still use it to apply for a passport. In the past she'd always borrowed someone else's but that might not be so easy now. All that new technology. She probably won't need one now that Jay is on his way home.

La-la-la-la-la. Deal with all that later. She goes into her bedroom, takes a brightly coloured patchwork bedspread out of the wardrobe. If the girl wants to bring the baby here then she hasn't a cradle for it. She gave the one she used for Lara away, couldn't stand to have it in the house. But she'll borrow one if the need arises or get one down the charity shop.

The girl tucks the corner of the sheet under the mattress. So how did you come to know Jay? Mollie asks. The girl explains about the college. Leave that now, dear. Come downstairs.

Let me.

No. No. No need. I can do it.

Sorry, I realise I don't know your name?

Mollie laughs – A good question, that. I've so many names I forget myself. Bunton, that was my father's name. Stanley Bunton, killed in the war. Fawcett, stepfather. Bertie Fawcett. I learnt my cheerfulness from him. He was forever laughing. What else could he do married to my mother? And stage name – Mayeford. Married name – Ravello. That's a name you might know. My husband's an actor.

Mollie points out pictures of Rufus on a board in the hall. Doing a show in London, she says.

The girl nods but Mollie has the impression she isn't fooled.

This is him in *She Stoops to Conquer*.

As she looks at the photographs, Mollie thinks again of how she hates Rufus and how she misses him. He's been gone nearly three weeks. Left a heap of unpaid bills and uncancelled appointments. The bailiffs have been around twice. Mollie leaves messages with Baggers, and she knows Baggers passes them on, but Rufus doesn't ring back. She was sure – totally sure – that he'd be back for her birthday. But that was ten days ago and he didn't even call. Bugger him. No doubt the whirligig of time will eventually bring in his revenges but Mollie is tired of waiting.

The curious thing is that her longing for him is physical, even sexual. Earlier in the evening, leaving the Rose and Crown, she'd even thought of going home with Bobby Bellows. She's done that before – with Bobby and with other men. You've got to keep your vaginal fluids from drying up. If you don't use it, you lose it. She never tells Rufus, of course, but she enjoys the silent power it gives her. Helps to even things up. But really she's past the age for all that now – and it wouldn't be any good with Bobby Bellows anyway. For all the trouble she's had with Rufus, at least she's always known that she could never have had better sex with another man. Thank God for his manifold mercies, Viagra included.

Sex was always there, through the laughter and the tears. And even at the times when she hated Rufus with a black passion, she had still lain awake at night, waiting for him to come back from the theatre, her body hot with longing while her mind was filled with contempt for him. Of course, it was sex as a substitute for love, as a substitute for intimacy, but she had valued it all the same. The sex – the whole extreme, brutal performance of it –

made them like two people who have committed a crime together. It created a bond between them that went far beyond mere love.

And this is your daughter? the girl asks.

Yes, Lara. Yes, there – and somewhere in the back row here. Yes, she was at Frencham Heights, you know. You've heard of it? One of the best schools in the country. Won a scholarship and now she's very successful in the interior design world. Or she was but she's taking a break.

Mollie doesn't say that she'd thought it stupid of Lara to give up the job. After all, there are still bills to be paid. Plenty of bills given all the fancy renovation which has gone on in that flat. When Lara had first taken the job, eighteen years ago, Mollie had been set against it but surely this isn't the moment to give it up?

I do hope he will be home soon, the girl says.

Mollie looks up into the girl's face and wonders what friendship she had with Jay. Girlfriend? Mollie hopes she was. Jay didn't mention her but he'd have been shy.

In the kitchen Mollie puts the kettle on and pulls the armchair forward. The table is littered with envelopes for the MPs' letters but now Mollie pushes them aside. Washing is hastily moved from a chair and urine-soaked newspaper picked up from the floor, stuffed into the bin.

Let me, the girl says.

No. No. No need.

The girl has seen the cake on the table and the cards. Your birthday?

Well, it was last week. Or at least one of my birthdays, Mollie says.

One of them?

Oh yes. I have two. Don't you? Everyone should.

Quite right, the girl says. I think I'll decide on another for myself.

Brightening up now, Mollie thinks, and cuts the cake. A bit old but it'll taste all right.

Usually Rufus is here and we go over to Eastbourne. You know the Grand Hotel? Rufus has a Daimler Dart – vintage – from the sixties and we drive over in that.

Mollie remembers all the times they've been to the Grand, rolling along the coast road in the Daimler. Palm trees in the ballroom, and a proper band, long windows looking out over the seafront. She and Rufus glide over the parquet floor with perfect timing, twisting and turning against each other. People turn to watch because you don't often see people dance like that now. Give it another day or two, she decides. If Rufus isn't home by then, she'll go and get him. What other choice does she have? She might have gone to fetch him sooner except the car is so unreliable.

Mollie hands the girl a cup of tea, tips a cat from a chair, bats another from the hearth. Oh they do smell. Mollie makes a mental note to give the kitchen a good airing tomorrow if the sun comes out.

Leave the baby with your mum, did you?

No, no. He was— I mean...

What's his name?

Laurie.

Oh what a lovely name, Mollie says. Laurie. Lovely. Like Lawrence of Arabia or Laurie Lee. A gentlemanly-type name, but soft as well. Very romantic. Still cold are you, love? I'll get the fire going a bit. Still a few sparks left.

Mollie looks over at Jemmy, sipping her tea. Got a bit of colour in her cheeks now. But her eyes glow too brightly, and there is some aura about her, almost as though she's ringed by a circle of red. You wouldn't want to touch her, she might burn you.

Some men don't adapt well to babies, Mollie says. Makes them jealous.

No, Jemmy says, sitting forward in her chair. Sorry. No. I didn't explain properly. I felt a bit awkward because of the pushchair and everything. But Laurie is—

Mollie feels something shift in the air. Of course, she thinks, I should have known. But still she feels the loss inside her. She had almost held that baby in her arms. She'd wanted to wash the babygrows and buy some wooden bricks and one of those baby walkers.

Oh love, she says. I'm so sorry. Poor little mite. Born into God's arms, was he?

Jemmy nods.

Oh I am sorry, Mollie says.

Yes. It was. The girl breaks off and stares into the distance, her eyes wide and brimming. That explains it, Mollie thinks. She would like to go and give the girl a hug but she isn't that kind of girl. She's private, rigid and fighting all on her own.

Tell me, Mollie says. Was he beautiful?

Yes, Jemmy says. Yes. Very beautiful. Smaller than the other babies but all quite perfect and complete. Tiny hands and feet, each nail perfectly formed. Thin and his head perfectly round like a globe. And his eyes tight shut just as though he was sleeping. She wipes at her eyes with her sleeve. As she does so the material of her shirt folds back at the wrist and Mollie sees a fine skein of silver marking the flesh.

Thank you very much for asking. You're the only person who's ever asked.

Oh it's a bugger, Mollie says. An absolute bugger. But what can you do? Milk, love? You comfy there? Didn't live even for a few hours then? Shove that chair up a bit closer to the fire.

I'm expecting another baby now, the girl says. But I can't.

No, you can't feel any confidence, Mollie says. Of course you can't. But it'll work out right this time. You'll see.

I've got some photographs, Jemmy says. If you'd like to see?

Mollie knows she mustn't back out now. Yes, love, of course I'd like to see. She searches for her glasses, finds them on the back of the sink, takes the album of photographs. Might do better without her glasses. It's a pocket-sized album with a cardboard cover decorated with pictures of daisies. Mollie opens it, considering what the right reaction might be, calculating the response that's needed. But then she's ambushed by the images, blurred and crooked but you can see baby Laurie there, in a little plastic cradle, with the sheets, patterned with tiny blue cars, pulled right up to his chin. His perfectly sculpted head poking up above the sheet, his eyes closed. Just like every other baby except a flower lies beside his head.

Could just pick him up and hold him against you, couldn't you? Mollie's voice creaks, as she turns the pages. The photos are all similar, some taken from a slightly different angle, some clearer than others. In one she can see the rubber boots which the man taking the photographs must have been wearing in the morgue. At the back of the album are photographs of a churchyard and a grave. The church is in the countryside, surrounded by a hedge, with a lych gate and low hanging yews. The tiny grave is decorated with a teddy bear and a glass vase full of field daisies.

Thank you, she says. Thank you. They're lovely. Breaks your heart, doesn't it? Mollie turns away. I'll find a cosy for this pot and we'll be able to have another in a few minutes. You know, I lost four myself. We had Lara, my daughter, that's Jay's mother, when I was twenty-eight. I lost them early, not like Laurie. But all the same.

I'm sorry, Jemmy says.

Well, yes, but they were miscarriages. Although – it isn't just the flesh and blood that goes, is it? It's the dreams and the hopes, a whole idea about the future. At least I'd one that stayed alive, but I still think of the others. Planted a tree for one. And one buried in a beautiful meadow, a shady spot under some trees, on the banks of a river.

You know, early or late – there aren't any easy ways to lose a baby.

You're right, love. Put them in the hospital rubbish – that's what they do. Which is no way to treat a human being, is it? Even a human being two inches long deserves better than that.

Yes. At least we got a grave. And it does help, to know where he is.

Mollie goes to pour more tea. Her hands are numb, and cold has taken hold of every inch of her body. I love your coat, she says. With those flowers on it.

Yes, the girl says. It's Laurie's coat. I made it to remind me of him.

Ah yes, Mollie thinks. Everything does come back to that.

How did you learn to sew like that?

That's what I do, the girl says. Textiles. I mean, that's what I'm going to do.

I used to be good with the sewing machine, Mollie says. And, in fact, I'd been going to get it out because I fancy some new curtains. The cats have scratched the bottom to rags. You probably know where to get some good material?

Yes, the girl says. Yes. Of course I'll find you some.

That's better, Mollie thinks. Find her something to do. Don't let her sink into all that grief. The girl starts to talk about fabrics and she brightens a little. But still she isn't really here. Although intently present she also looks as though she's listening for something else, some sound that might come from far in the distance.

I was going to set up a textile business, the girl says. But then Laurie died.

North Laine? Would that be a good place for material?

The thing is, the girl says, about Laurie. I know he's quite close. I feel him with me. Sometimes I hear him crying but sometimes he's peaceful, nestling just beside me. I know people think it's mad, but he hasn't really gone, not completely. I've been reading about it. You know that the Spiritualist Church think the dead are all around, just invisible.

Oh really? Mollie says.

Oh yes. I've been quite a few times. And when you're there you can feel the dead – and the influence they have on our lives.

Mollie thinks, Best not to mess with the dead. But who's to say? There are more things in heaven and earth than are dreamt of in our philosophy.

Of course, I'm always hoping for a message from Laurie. Well, not from him, of course, but just someone telling me he's all right.

Mollie looks at the girl – her wide staring eyes, her taut thinness, her small hands gripped into tight fists. Tomorrow she must get out the sewing machine, get her started on the curtains, that'll bring her out of it.

You could come along to the church with me if you like. Anyone can.

Perhaps I should. Maybe someone would know where my birth certificate is.

Mollie cuts herself another slice of cake.

Look, the girl says, you know my photographs. Look. She opens up her bag and pulls out a T-shirt with one of the photographs printed on it.

Lovely, Mollie says.

No. It's nutty but it's just – I suppose the question is – how do you make the dead live? The girl stops for a moment, takes a deep breath. Don't you feel the dead are very close?

A tap drips, a cat scratches at its fleas, music plays from the end of the street. Mollie feels herself suddenly bitterly cold, drained of blood. The silence brings with it a sensation like vertigo. Mollie's hand grips the arm of her chair.

I don't really know anyone who is dead, she says, trying to laugh. This girl isn't what Mollie wants her to be. She'd imagined someone simple and smiling, full of laughter and energy, straightforward and obliging. A girl with a chubby, smiling baby. Someone who would be easy to help, someone full of honest gratitude. But that's not who this girl is at all. Mollie feels that she's taken an irreversible step which she will later regret.

But what about your parents? the girl asks. I mean, sorry – but presumably they're dead.

Oh yes, but I never knew my father. He was killed in the war – at Wormhout, near Dunkirk. And I didn't keep in touch with my mother. Never got on with her – but I loved my stepfather. They died within a few weeks of each other. He had lung problems, I was told, and she had a heart attack although she was no age.

Even if you didn't keep in touch, she must have a grave.

Mollie has never thought of Violet, her mother, as having a grave. She knew when Violet died, of course, because that was when she came into money, bought the Guest House. Of course, there must be a grave, in Worcester probably. *The dead are all around us, so close that you can nearly touch them.*

Mollie thinks of all those letters she sent from London after she left home. Not Known At This Address. Except that Mollie had checked, and Violet and Bertie did still live at that same white house on the hill in Worcester – 48 Langley Crescent. A stately white house, high up on a green hill, above the railway line, the allotments, the red-brick grime of the city. From the top rooms you could see the cathedral, standing on the banks of the Severn, and even the distant Malvern Hills. One of the finest houses in Worcester, her stepfather always said. Turning to look at Jemmy, what Mollie sees is herself. She remembers being that age, wanting everything to be a grand drama, too young to know that most of the dramas turn out to be sordid little accidents.

Didn't you ever want to know?

The girl asks too many questions.

No, dear. I left when I was fourteen and never went back. And now there's so much I can't remember. It used to worry me that I couldn't remember. But now I can't even remember what it is that I can't remember – so I don't worry at all.

Sorry. Perhaps I shouldn't have asked.

No, dear. No. But it was a long time ago. You know – it was the war.

Mollie thinks, Why are young people nowadays obsessed by the past? All that psychotherapy rubbish about exploring years gone by in order to understand the present. All those stories of the diaries found in the attic, the sepia photograph, the love letter hidden in the back of the photograph frame. Usually there is no mystery, only muddle. Mollie finds that life is too short for all that one needs to forget.

When she tries to picture her mother, she finds only absence. The world around her – the white house on the hill, the railway line and the allotments, laughing Bertie Fawcett with his endless presents, violets on the sloping front lawn – all that is there, but her mother exists only as a woman endlessly departing – in a fur coat, carrying a neat little leather suitcase, smooth as a conker, the clips and the buckle decorated with diamond-like studs. Although she never did carry a suitcase like that. The curtain rises but the stage is empty. A round of applause, expectant waiting, but her mother never emerges. Not every wound heals.

It wasn't the war – that had been over for almost ten years by the time she left home. And she does think of her mother – often – dressed in furs and silk, smelling of gin and lemon, tottering slightly on her high heels. She only exists welded to Bertie's side, so that they move awkwardly, like people in an endless three-legged race. Her mother's face turned into the shadows, offering only a vague backward wave of her hand. At the time, she herself had never questioned. But Ludo had seen.

Come on, she says. Time for bed. It's been a long day.

She takes the girl upstairs, goes back down again to make her a hot-water bottle. La-la-la-la-la she sings to herself but tears are forming in her eyes. Strangely it isn't Rufus who she thinks of now, in the silences which fall on the Guest House. Instead it's the other men. They come in layers, leaving their imprint and a jumbled collection of memories. Aftershave, starched shirts, unshaven chins, the leather seats of cars, hurried meetings in tea shops, the windows stained by rain. First, Ludo. Or was there a man before him? A man who danced with a woman in a crowded sitting room, while she, a tiny child, sat on someone's knee clapping her hands.

The gramophone starting with a hiss, as the record glides under the needle. *Paradise here, paradise close, just around this corner.* They dance as she and Rufus sometimes dance, pressed close together. The woman's hand moves on the man's back, feeling the muscle tightening as he turns. *The place where happiness is for me.* The carpet – patterned red and blue – flows under their feet. The sideboard, the bookcase, the mirror over the fireplace, all kaleidoscope into each other. The wall lights, shaped like swans' necks, blink, the line of silver tankards on the mantelpiece swirls past. The pink rosebuds on the wallpaper are bursting into bloom. Perhaps that was her mother dancing with Stanley Bunton, the father she never knew. Or maybe that memory is a fragment from some film. But Ludo – she can remember every detail. And maybe all the other men were only so many roads back to him.

La-la-la-la-la. She goes back upstairs, hands the hot-water bottle to Jemmy as she lies under the patchwork bedspread, her thin arm bent over the top, her hair spread on the pillow. That daisy-decorated album of photographs lies beside her on the chair. Mollie is frightened for herself and for the girl. She's too young, too uncompromising, too honest. Mollie knows what happens to girls like her.

## 24

## BEFORE

### Lara – Sheffield, June 1975

Lara sits at the kitchen table with her box of crayons and draws a picture of the place where they buried the baby. It wasn't a real baby, just a plastic box containing some bloody cotton wool and paper towels. The baby was in there somewhere, Mollie said, but only the size of a baked bean. They'd wrapped the box in tissue paper, tied a ribbon round it like a birthday present, then gone on the bus to a place outside Sheffield to bury it. On the bus they'd talked about how they'd walk through the fields, find a meadow, a shady spot under some trees, maybe even a river. But the rain had come, and they didn't have coats or proper shoes, and so they'd had to make do with a lay-by.

Lara always does a picture when a baby dies and Mollie puts them away in a special box so there's something to remember. Donny Samuel croons on the radio. *How can you ever understand how a young heart feels. How can you ever know?* Mollie has got the sewing machine out and she's about to alter a pair of checked flares for Lara which she bought in a second-hand shop. In her hand, she grips a glass of gin. Earlier in the day, when they were digging the hole in the rain, she'd been tearful but she's smiling now. She wears dark glasses to hide the bruise but, as she peers down at a copy of *The Stage*, the glasses travel down her nose.

Oh-la-la. Auditioning for *Seven Brides for Seven Brothers* at the Bristol Hippodrome, she says. That'll be good money. If Rufus doesn't get Iago then I'm going for that – and he'll just have to get whatever he can.

But Mum, you don't want to be in a musical.

Right now, love, I'd be in anything that pays, Mollie says, pushing her glasses back up her nose and taking a swig of gin.

Lara knows where the babies are. They're at a boarding school called Frencham Heights. Lara has a brochure about Frencham Heights in the drawer in her bedroom. It's all green lawns and white dresses and big old stone buildings with a sundial and wide stone steps with urns on the top of balustrades. In the dorms, tartan blankets are on the beds and laughing girls play tennis or peer through microscopes. Lara is glad that the babies have gone to Frencham Heights because they're certain to be happy there. Mollie says that isn't right. Children who go to boarding school are desperately unhappy. Of course they are. How could they be otherwise if they aren't with their mothers? Except the girls in those photos don't look unhappy. They look like angels. You can't quite see their wings but still they have that pale translucent angel look and doubtless their silk-slippered feet don't touch the floor. And they sing that anthem Lara has heard in church. *Oh for the wings, for the wings of a dove. In the wilderness build me, build me a nest.*

Spencer Talbot – off to LA. You know, I was going to go once. Just before I met your father. Had an audition with MGM, could have been in *The Night of the Iguana*. You know, the Tennessee Williams play with Richard Burton.

Lara looks impressed although she's heard this many times before.

Oh look, a photo of Jerry and Tabitha in *As You Like It*. You remember them, don't you? Mollie pushes *The Stage* towards Lara. Lara nods as though she does remember. She wonders about Jerry and Tabitha. Surely in the evenings, after the theatre, they don't go back to a flat in the top of someone else's house, have stale bread and spaghetti hoops for supper, and alter second-hand trousers? Or perhaps they do?

And Kerry Lovage getting married to Jason Spens – you'd have thought she'd know better. And Patrick Lougeville – can you believe it? Can't act for toffee.

Lara squirms in her chair. She herself can't act for toffee – or for fudge, banana bread or Black Forest gateau either. She goes to auditions nearly every week but she never gets a job – not even in a pantomime. *Oh no she doesn't.* At the auditions she lines up and her tap shoes stomp across the floor and her voice croaks. She's six inches taller than all the other girls, with fat knees and her smocked dress is too short and tight across the white skin of her chest. She can hear the crash-crash-crash of her feet on the parquet floor. *Stand aside, dear. Yes, sorry, darling. Yes, you with the red hair. Stand aside.* Mollie says, Don't get discouraged, you haven't reached your playing age yet. Lara suspects she might have to wait a long time before fat knees and frizzy red hair are what is required. She's heard her father tell Mollie to give up. *The girl is useless, you're wasting your time.* She's tried to hate her father for that but her true feeling may be closer to gratitude.

In her picture, she draws the spreading branches of the oak trees and the river that wasn't there. Mollie said they'd plant a tree for the baby. She says that every time but it never happens. Remembering the Frencham Heights brochure, Lara adds a sundial and wide stone steps with urns perched on the top of a stone balustrade. She leaves out the overflowing rubbish bins and the concrete block which contained the public loos. Mollie drains her gin and looks through the sewing tin, trying to find the right colour cotton for the trousers. The window is open because, despite the rain, it's been a hot day.

On the windowsill field daisies are arranged in a willow-pattern vase. Mollie had bought the vase the Sunday before, at a jumble sale in the car park of the church next door. She and Lara had chosen it together, deciding to take it despite the chip in the rim – or perhaps because of that. No one else seemed to want the vase so Mollie said it was down to them to give it a home. Outside the light is growing dusky over the allotments opposite and the church beyond. Lara hopes that Rufus will keep working at the Crucible for a while because then they'll stay in this flat. She likes the white walls, the blond wood and the view through the floor-to-ceiling window. And she likes the white box-shape of the building, the circular window like a porthole on the landing, the brown swirling wallpaper in the hall.

She likes her school as well. It's called Sutton Road Primary and her teacher is called Miss Sweet. If you put that in a story it would be silly but she really is called that. Lara helps her give out the books and keep the craft cupboard tidy. Miss Sweet says that Lara is an exceptionally clever little girl and that it's a great shame she misses so much school. The other children don't speak to Lara because they've been told she won't be staying long. Lara doesn't mind because that's the price of living creatively. She knows herself to be Mollie's only compensation, knows she alone has the power to make it all up to Mollie – but she can only do that by being a good actress. Any other kind of good isn't good enough.

What do you reckon? Mollie says. Is this about the same colour?

Lara moves around the table, looks at the thread which Mollie is holding against the checked trousers. A knock sounds at the door. Oh why don't you get stuffed? Mollie shouts, in the direction of the door. What does old Missy Misty want at this time of night? Hasn't she got anything better to do with her time than come bothering us? I've told her Monday.

The knock sounds again. Mollie turns the radio up so that it blares through the room. She props her glasses on the top of her head, bends down over the machine, tries to thread the needle. The bruise is turning green now at the edges.

Mollie used to like Missy Misty and Lara loved her. Now Mollie doesn't like her and so Lara tries to feel the same. With grown-ups it can be hard to keep up. Missy Misty is divorced and reads tarot cards. She also teaches psychology, which is to do with being mad, at the university, and she designed this house herself. The knocking at the door comes again but Mollie takes no notice. Lara wriggles and sits on her hands. Missy Misty allowed them to take this flat although they didn't have a deposit and, when they'd first arrived, Missy had asked them down into the house below, cooked them tagine for supper, read the cards for Mollie. Missy has twin Siamese cats with thin and mysterious faces who wound themselves around Lara's leg. While Mollie and Misty talked about Dutch Elm disease and the Greenpeace ships trying to stop the whalers, Lara sat in a basket-work swing chair which hung from the ceiling with a tangerine coloured cushion in it.

Missy Misty has photographs everywhere of her two grown-up daughters. One of them is in Paris, studying languages, and the other works for *Vogue*. Both of Missy Misty's daughters went to Frencham Heights, a very progressive school. Missy Misty had been there herself and she'd been determined that her daughters would go as well. Lara stared at long photographs with hundreds of girls all in the same uniform and the date underneath and a curly crest all in gold with a Latin motto. Missy Misty had said that Lara was clearly a clever girl, and maybe she could get a scholarship to Frencham Heights. She'd sent off for the brochure, which she'd then given to Lara. They did Assisted Places at Frencham Heights, the full fees. Wouldn't that be helpful, Missy Misty said, what with all the moving around?

Now Mollie turns the radio down and starts to work the sewing machine. Lara adds a few flowers into her pictures at the foot of the oak tree, on the banks of the river. She holds the picture out to her mother. Look, she says. What do you think? Mollie holds the picture under the light. Oh, darling. It's beautiful, she says. Absolutely beautiful. You've captured it all so perfectly. Oh thank you – that will be so lovely to go in the box. Mollie is suddenly tearful and catches hold of Lara, kisses her on one cheek and then the other, then she does it again and again. Lara pushes herself against Mollie, gets a handkerchief out of her pocket and wipes at her mother's tears.

A shuffling and banging sounds at the door.

Oh God, Mollie says. It's your father. What's he doing back? He was meant to be going out. The banging at the door comes again and Mollie hurries to open it.

Rufus falls into the flat. Lost the bloody key, he says. Come in, come in. He gestures towards Phoebe. Lara recognises her from the Crucible. She plays Ophelia in *Hamlet* but she wears a long blonde wig for that. Her real hair is short and coal-black.

Hello sweetheart, Rufus says to Lara, but she doesn't move from her chair near the window because she's seen the anger on her mother's face. For months now her dad has been promising to take her to see *The Towering Inferno* but it doesn't look like that'll happen tonight.

Can you believe it? Rufus says. We were going out to the Anchor and guess what? It's burnt down. So anyway, we didn't fancy anywhere else so we thought we'd come back here. Plenty of food in the house, I said. Come back and have supper with us.

Of course, Mollie says. Of course. You're very welcome. Sit down. Sit down. Her voice is friendly but Lara can hear the spite in it.

My, my, Phoebe says. Aren't you a big girl now? So big – growing all the time. She smiles widely, screws up her nose, giggles. Lara keeps the muscles of her face still. Mollie pulls out chairs, hurries the sewing machine and the trousers from the table, pushing them in through the door of Lara's bedroom. Lara clears her crayons away.

Have a drink, Rufus says, and pushes the gin bottle across the table and takes glasses from the cupboard. Phoebe hiccoughs and giggles, nearly misses the chair as she sits down. Rufus picks up the gin bottle, ready to pour, then notices that the bottle is nearly empty. Is this all we've got? he says, turning to Mollie.

Oh no, Mollie says. There's more. She takes a bottle out of the cupboard and passes it to Rufus.

That's my girl, he says. So what's for supper?

I'm just going to pop out, Mollie says. I'm out of eggs. But it won't take a moment. She picks up her bag from the sofa. Come on, Lara, she says.

Lara follows her mother out of the door. On the top landing Mollie hesitates, listening. The house below is silent – Missy must have gone out. Mollie and Lara hurry down the twilight stairs, past the wooden bead curtains at the kitchen door, and the curling cats, the hanging basket chair with its tangerine cushion, the wall of mirrors in the hall. Lara sees the whiteness of Mollie's hand as it clutches her bag. They cross the hall and step out of the front door.

How can he do this? Mollie says, wiping tears from her eyes. How can he turn up suddenly wanting supper? And bringing that tart with him. If she had any decency she'd know not to arrive at someone's house uninvited, particularly when – Mollie has taken her purse from her bag and she's sorting through the contents of it although she must know it's empty. I can't provide supper for people if I haven't got any money – what am I going to do?

Lara feels the evening melting, everything around them growing heavy, sagging. She hopes no one will walk down the street and see. Clinging to Mollie's hand, she stares up and down the dusky, summer-evening street, wondering what she can suggest. Next door is the church where they bought the vase. The people there were friendly – maybe they would help? But the church looks all closed up. Don't worry, Mummy. Don't worry. I'm here. I'm here. Mollie raises her dark glasses, wipes at her eyes.

Thank you, love. Thank you. What would I do without you? Come on, I've got an idea. There was a torch in the hall. Let's go in those allotments at the back. At least there we'll find something for a salad.

Lara doesn't like this idea – what good is salad? What if someone sees them? But together they set off down the garden. Missy Misty doesn't have time for the garden so the grass is long and brambles grow along the fence. Trees, shrubs and a fallen-down wooden fence divide Missy's garden from the allotments. Mollie and Lara push their way through the shrubs and step over the remains of the wooden fence. The grass on the far side is up to their knees, the ground soggy. Mollie switches on the torch and waves it across the allotments. In the distance, Lara can see the lights of other houses. She imagines the normal families in those lighted rooms. Just like a Ladybird book. Mummy, Daddy, Janet and John. Mummy does the cooking in a frilly apron, while Daddy, smoking a pipe, reads stories to the children next to the fire.

It's too early in the year for much to be growing. Runner-bean canes stand up naked in the wavering light. Planted rows are marked out but only a few shoots grow. Mollie walks further along, until her torch touches on flickers of green.

Come on, she says. Lettuces. They're a bit small but they'll taste good.

Lara stumbles after her. She watches her mother grubbing around in the damp earth. Turning, she looks back. She can see the church spire and the upper floor of Missy Misty's house. The lights are on, and she imagines shadows moving past the window. Her father will be up there, drinking and smoking, laughing, telling theatre stories to Phoebe. But there's no sign of him. Her mother passes half-grown lettuces to Lara, wipes her hands on her skirt. Her dark glasses sit askew amidst hair which is falling down over her face and she stumbles as the heels of her sandals sink into the earth.

Come on, Mollie says. As they climb back over the fence, the frill of Mollie's dress gets caught on a spike of wood and she nearly falls. Lara has to catch her and the lettuces fall from her hands. Mollie can't stop giggling and, as they pick up the lettuces, Lara starts to laugh as well. Stumbling back through the garden, Lara expects to hear Rufus's bellowing voice from above but the house is strangely silent. At the front door, Mollie takes the lettuces from Lara. Listen, she says. Old Missy Musty is bound to have some food in her fridge. You go and see what else you can find.

Lara watches her mother fade away up the helter-skelter stairs and hesitates. She knows where the kitchen is. Missy took her in there when they first arrived and gave her apple juice. Lara had never had apple juice before and she can still remember the taste. Now she creeps towards the kitchen and pushes the bead curtain aside. Behind her she hears noises, a shuffle, a squeak. She presses herself back against the fridge. The noise comes from a corridor which leads to Missy Misty's downstairs bathroom and the garage. Lara hesitates. She should just get the food and go back upstairs – but what if a burglar is in the house? Lara knows that if she goes along the corridor she'll see something she doesn't want to see – but she can't stop herself from moving towards the sound.

The bathroom is on the left and the sliding door of it isn't properly shut. A pool of light spreads onto the linoleum-tiled floor of the corridor. Through the crack in the door, pink tiles, a bubble-patterned shower curtain, a tiny window high up in the wall with a cracked extractor fan. Below the window a blonde head is pressed back against the wall. Rufus's back heaves and presses. What is he doing in Missy Misty's downstairs bathroom? A sound of shuffling and grunting muffles out from the door. Phoebe's glittering high-heeled shoe is swinging in the air, moving back and forwards. Lara turns, hurries back along the corridor.

In the kitchen she looks in the fridge – eggs, milk and butter. See what's in the bread bin. The fridge hums and when Lara opens the door its butter-yellow light makes a square on the floor like a slice of cheese. She takes the eggs and milk out, puts them on the kitchen table, lifts the lid from the bread bin. Her heart is trying to get out of her chest, her fingers fumble and the bread bin clanks. Three quarters of a loaf is wrapped in a paper packet. She reaches into the bin and lifts it out.

The light goes on and Lara jumps back, the tin lid of the bread bin crashes onto the floor. Missy Misty has pushed the bead curtain aside and is staring at her, her eyes wide under the fuzz of her hair. The kitchen light glares, Lara is suddenly conscious of her muddy shoes. Her hands, where she touched the loaf of bread, feel scalding hot.

What are you doing? Miss Misty says. She's wearing a lime-green kimono and she grips a roll-up cigarette between her fingers. Her eyes are lined with fierce black liner and her curly hair stands out in a halo around her head.

I was just— Lara says.

Stealing?

Lara feels that word like a slap in the face. No.

Then what?

Lara senses the world slipping away from her. Missy Misty shakes her head. Don't worry, love. I did try to come up and see you earlier – I was a bit worried about your mum. Should I be worried about your mum?

Lara says nothing, shuts her eyes, pleads for this to end.

Listen love, I don't need tarot cards to tell me – she should go to the police.

Lara feels herself starting to cry. She knows what Missy is saying because she's heard it before. Landladies, teachers, people at the theatre, nodding their heads and whispering. Lara knows what they think but they don't understand.

It's not like that, Lara says.

Silence crowds into the cramped space of the kitchen. An image flickers through her mind – the back of her father's jacket, that dangling glittery shoe.

Missy Misty shakes her head, draws on her cigarette. You're a good girl, aren't you, Lara? Far too good. But don't worry. I'll have a word with your mother.

Lara puts the food down on the table and wipes at her tears with her bare arm.

Not easy for you to be all of your mother's children, is it? Missy Misty says.

Lara stares at the shameful loaf of bread.

Come on now, Missy says. Don't you worry. You take these things. She takes a string bag off the door handle, opens it up and puts the eggs, milk and bread inside. What else do you need? Is there anything else?

No, Lara says. No. Thank you very much, thank you. She hurries away past Missy Misty, heads back upstairs, with the food gripped against her. Mollie has broken the lettuces up and arranged the leaves on a plate. Lara stares at their tender greenness, the torn leaves, the near-transparent stems, milk-white. She feels that the lettuces shouldn't be involved in this. And then she thinks of the dead baby, no bigger than a baked bean. Mollie has moved the field daisies in their green-patterned vase from the windowsill onto the table and lit a candle. She won't have people at the theatre thinking she lives like a slut. Lara hands her the eggs, milk and bread.

Rufus appears, followed by Phoebe. Just popped out for some cigarettes, he says. Phoebe has got lipstick smeared up her cheek and she's giggling, straightening her dress. Mollie shoots her a dirty look, slams the plates down onto the table. Rufus pours more gin.

Come on, Lara. Time for bed, Mollie says. You've got school in the morning.

Lara goes into her bedroom but leaves the door ajar. As she gets undressed, she hears the accusing clank of knives on plates. Rufus's voice is loud but she can't hear her mother or Phoebe. Lara finds her school maths book then gets into bed. She was meant to be doing the exercises at the end of chapter four for homework. She did those as soon as she got home from school and she did chapters five, six and seven. Now she starts on chapter eight. She hasn't done these kind of sums before but there's always an example so it's easy to work it out. *Eight plus eight, divided by four.*

Lara, switch that light out.

She gets out of bed and flicks the switch but then takes a torch out of the drawer. The music from the sitting room thumps in her ears. Rufus laughs, and from down the corridor the door slams, Phoebe must have left. The music shrieks, a crash comes from the sitting room, Lara hears Mollie shouting and then the sound of Rufus grunting in pain. *Nine plus seven plus three.* She knows that the first night when her parents met, her father pushed her mother off a roof. They tell that story often, laughing. Lara is glad that the floor-to-ceiling window in the sitting room doesn't open.

Fuck you, fuck you. Rufus voice is muffled by the music.

The music is making the walls of the flat vibrate. Mollie and Rufus are screaming with laughter. Lara longs to sleep. *Eighteen plus eight plus sixty-two.* A heaving crash comes from the sitting room, as though a piece of furniture has fallen and the music jerks to a halt. Lara hears her parents' waves of laughter. A moment later the music comes on again. *Nine divided by five. Add ten and carry five.* Lara's head is heavy with sleep and her mouth is dry. She wants to go to the kitchen to get some water but she daren't get up. She imagines her mother falling from a roof, her limbs spread, her hair swirling, dropping down and down. Lara's head lolls beside the maths book. That image from earlier in the evening comes again – the back of the jacket, the glittery shoe.

The green lawns, the white dresses, those shining angels with their arms linked, and their feet never touching the ground. She wishes that she could be there with them. She has filled the application form in carefully, writing all the words out on a piece of paper first, to check they will fit properly, before copying them onto the form. She would like to give the form to Missy Misty because then maybe she could visit that place – just once.

Lara is awoken by a sharp banging at the door of the flat. She knows that particular bang because she's heard it before. She swallows, gets out of bed, picks up her maths book and puts it away. From down the corridor she can hear voices and the crackling of a walkie-talkie. Footsteps advance towards the sitting room. Lara gets out of bed and moves towards the bedroom door. Through the crack she can see the back of a black wool jacket, black trousers, silver buttons at the shoulders and cuffs. She goes back to bed, pulls the covers up over her head. Her parents' voices sound like slammed doors. She knows that soon the police will go away because they don't understand. Lara curls herself up tight into a ball and waits. The voices die away, the front door bangs shut. Silence follows. Lara waits. Her head is foggy with tiredness but every muscle is tight.

The door opens and the bedroom light goes on. Lara feels the eiderdown pulled away from her. Have you been talking to her? Mollie says. Have you been telling her things? What lies have you been telling her?

I haven't, Lara says.

Yes, you have, Mollie shrieks. Yes, you have. How many times have I told you to mind your own business? Little Miss Busybody. Little Miss Do-Good.

Mollie, Mollie. Rufus catches hold of Mollie and starts to pull her away. Mollie fights back but Rufus is far stronger and has Mollie gripped tightly by both arms. Tomorrow Mollie's arms will be bruised, Lara thinks.

Come on, love, Rufus says. Come on.

He drags Mollie out of the bedroom. Lara jumps out of bed, slams the door, stands behind it shaking. Grabbing a chair, she wedges the back of it under the door handle. Then she switches out the light and gets into bed, hides her head under the covers. Of course, it's all her fault, she knows that. She shouldn't have told lies to Missy Misty, she shouldn't have said anything at all.

Next door the noises begin. Laughter first, and an occasional squeak, then a rhythmic banging. Then shrieks of pain, louder bangs, and crying. Lara pulls herself down further under the blankets, kicks her foot against the wall, smashing her toenail against the plaster again and again. What will happen tomorrow? Impossible to know. Mollie might stay in bed and cry for days – or she might wake up with a loving smile and say she's sorry, get some money from Rufus, take Lara out and buy her a new dress. With grown-ups it can be hard to keep up. Lara shuts her eyes tightly and dreams of angels.

# 25

# Now

## Jemmy – Brighton, March 2003

Good morning, Jemmy speaking, how may I help you? As Jemmy takes the call, she shifts in her seat, straightening her back, easing her weight onto one hip.

Her desk is far from any windows and the dry air-conditioned atmosphere of the office makes it impossible to tell what the weather might be. But when Jemmy went out to get a sandwich at lunch the sun had been suddenly alight – the first sun in months – so that now she wants to get outside again.

Her mobile phone beeps with a message from Bill. Since she moved out, he's called her every day, just as he always did. And last week they met for a drink after work, at a bar down at the seafront, then walked towards Hove and sat on a bench, doing nothing in particular. Meanwhile, she tried to decide whether to tell him about the pregnancy or not. When she went for the sixteen-week scan she took care not to look at the screen. Best to wear a loose cardigan and say nothing. She can cope with this for herself but not for him. Later Bill asked when she would come home. And she said, Soon probably. But then the evening grew darker and she said goodnight, kissed him on the cheek, went back to Mollie and the Guest House.

Last night she'd been going to take Mollie to the Spiritualist Church but then a cat had had kittens and so they'd stayed in to look after her, made a bed for her in the back kitchen. Later Mollie had listened to Robin Cook's resignation speech on the radio. *We cannot now pretend that getting a second resolution was of no importance. No support from NATO, the European Union or the Security Council.* When the speech was over Mollie had joined the cheering heard from the House of Commons. He's absolutely right. The only one that's got any principles. A clear and present danger, my foot. If Saddam's so weak he can be defeated in a few days then why is he such a threat? They can't have it both ways.

Jemmy agreed, started work on the new curtains. An absolute bargain that material, Mollie said. Five pounds a metre, can you believe it? The fabric is bright blue with red flowers – a bold sixties-type pattern on good-quality, heavyweight cotton which will hang well.

As she takes another call, Jemmy thinks of Mollie. There she is – so bold and brazen with her fishnet tights and her feather boas. And it doesn't matter that her car breaks down, that she owes the tax man thousands of pounds, that her husband has gone. Mollie always navigates the rapids with consummate skill, rides the levels. Once Jemmy asked her, *Why do you love the theatre so much?* And Mollie had replied, *Because it's real.*

Mollie is so very different from the people in Jemmy's childhood. There everything was about fear. Fear of the unexpected, of the unconventional, of the big uncontrollable world out there. So that Jemmy herself felt large and ungainly and uncontrollable – although she was really none of those things. Just a person who liked colour and light and wanted to study textiles. To her parents everything she might do was a waste of time. But it wasn't clear what time was being saved for – except to watch more television and check and double check the window locks, the padlock on the garden shed, the car doors.

Jemmy loves Mollie's lightness. The fact that she believes everything she reads in the newspapers, empathises with everyone's story, repeats the views of the last person she's been talking to with fervent conviction, believes in rubbish to do with the crucifixion and resurrection. When Jemmy is with Mollie she feels the great stretch of time and how it renders almost everything irrelevant. All will pass. And Jemmy loves the fact that for Mollie physical objects are human. She talks to sheets and blankets, the wobbly leg of a chair that she is screwing back into place. *Come on, love, we'll get you fixed up. Seen better days. Well, haven't we all. We are none of us what we once were.*

Jemmy does love Mollie – but she isn't entirely fooled. Mollie is frightened that her husband won't come back, although she does her best to hide it. And she's worried sick about Jay, as everyone is. And she's sad as well, despite all that forced cheerfulness. Late at night it all comes out, after they've finished watching the news. Or the lack of news. Mollie drinks too much then and talks in a confused way about her mother and the Blitz. The names seem to change all the time, so Jemmy can't help wondering if some of it is made up. Mollie says she remembers seeing burnt and blackened buildings in Coventry from her pram – but does anyone remember being in a pram? And then there's the lost birth certificate and a man called Ludo who she loved once.

Jemmy knows that Mollie wants to look after her but really it's Mollie who needs looking after and Jemmy has already started on that – not only the curtains but clearing up the kitchen, cooking, washing sheets. Mollie has shown her a copy of Jay's letter and Jemmy remembers his words – *can't keep on discussing whether we should have salmon or lamb for supper, whether we should go on holiday to Italy or Spain.* But in this period of waiting, this no-man's land, trivia is comforting. Pansies. When the weather is better they're going to plant some in those bizarre wellington boots, full of earth, which clog up the front steps. And at the weekend Jemmy is going to take down that torn and dirty rainbow flag and wash it. Perhaps she'll forget to put it back up. Jemmy has learnt at the Support Group that the line between the helper and the helped is sometimes so thin that it fades into nothing at all.

Hello, Jemmy speaking. How can I help you?

Jemmy deals with the call and then heads to the loo. And it's there that she finds blood. Not very much of it, only a drop or two. But it makes her head disappear down into her shoulders, her spine curve as though waiting for a further blow. Of course, many women bleed in pregnancy. It's a relatively common thing. And pains in your back don't mean anything much – except this isn't the dull ache of a strained muscle, instead it's a sharp stab of pain which comes every ten minutes or so. Only one or two drops. But that's how it begins. Then blood, pain, endless visits to the hospital and the days spent lying on the sofa, waiting. She knew, of course, she always knew that it would happen again.

Sixteen weeks. That's far too early. That's what they said at the hospital last time – *far too early*. She knows that nothing she does and nothing the hospital do will make any difference so she'll wait a few days before she goes to the hospital, she wants a few more days. While she doesn't go to the hospital, she can pretend that maybe there isn't a problem. She steps out of the loo, feeling blurred. Mrs Jarvis is sailing across the office towards her wearing an electric-blue suit. Her varicose-veined legs are contained in orange tights, her feet overflow from court shoes. Her bleached blonde hair is scraped back into a chignon and her face appears scraped back as well. Jemima, could I have a word with you, please?

As Jemmy follows Mrs Jarvis to her office, she spreads the loose material of her blouse over her tiny bump. Of course, she hasn't told anyone in the office she's pregnant again. Mrs Jarvis's office has a low ceiling and a large window which looks out onto a wall and a ventilation shaft. She talks about targets, numbers of calls, the department being under pressure. Jemmy prepares herself for being sacked. If she were still living with Bill, then it wouldn't matter too much. But now she's pregnant she needs to save money and she's got the rent to find. Mollie says, *Oh to hell with it, love, it's only money.* But Jemmy pushes the cash into the knife drawer when Mollie isn't around.

Jemima, I'm concerned about the time you're spending on certain calls.

Jemmy feels the muscles in the bottom of her back contract and shifts in her chair. Mrs Jarvis produces sheets of figures. This is what is expected of staff. A target of so many calls per hour, and the figures are affected if even one person fails to meet their target. Jemmy has heard all this many times before.

I'm not saying that your figures are bad, Mrs Jarvis says. They're not. But over the last two months you appear to have spent a total of nearly four hours talking to just one client – a Mrs Joyce Waldron.

No. Not Mrs Waldron.

Yes, Jemima. That's what the printout shows.

Yes, but Mrs Waldron is dead.

Oh. OK. Fine. So you're talking to the person who represents her estate?

Her husband. Mr George Waldron.

Yes, fine. Well, the point is—

Mr Waldron is elderly, Jemmy says. And he's had some difficulties getting the address right, and filling out the form, and he has arthritis in his fingers and so the form had to be sent back a number of times and I'm just trying to help him because he's a client and he does have a right to make a claim.

Jemmy has Laurie's power, she's invincible. If his death didn't kill her then nothing will. No matter what happens, it'll never be as bad as that. Fear has put an end to fear. Of course, what Mrs Jarvis is saying is true. Mr Waldron does say the same things again and again and it can get dull but Jemmy also knows that it's normal. It's how people grieve. They're like that at the Support Group as well, telling the same stories again and again, as though trying to make themselves believe. *Just to see is something. I don't know what good it does but it does do something.*

Yes, I'm aware of all of that, Mrs Jarvis says. But four hours?

Yes, but he's in a bad state. And he's all on his own.

That's not your business, dear. No need for you to become involved in his personal affairs. Just say you're sorry and move on.

But who, Jemmy wonders, will become involved? Everyone thinks it isn't their business.

Have you tried to sell him another policy, Jemima? He might have needs which you don't know about yet. I don't see any evidence that you've sent out any brochures or discussed a new policy with him.

But I don't think that's what he needs. I mean – why would he insure his own life when he's certain to be dead in a few years anyway?

Listen, Jemima, Mrs Jarvis says. We're all part of a team here. I know that things have been difficult for you recently.

Jemmy feels a sharp pain fire in the bottom of her back. Everything is beginning to break apart. She's spent too much time over the last five months being polite to people. Why isn't Mrs Jarvis listening to her? Why doesn't anyone care about Mr Waldron? There he is, struggling on his own, with the emptiness of the house all around him, and the silence, and no one to talk to him, or make him feel as though he's significant, as though what happened to him matters. Jemmy winces as pain strikes again in the small of her back.

Perhaps you should try and get out a bit more, Mrs Jarvis suggests. The girls in the office will look after you. They're a friendly group.

Mrs Jarvis has got targets to meet, a business to run.

Yes, Jemmy says. Yes. But what about Mr George Waldron? Who is going to take care of him?

Jemima, I've just said.

Yes, but who does look after the Mr and Mrs George Waldrons? Jemmy hears her voice shake as she speaks. And it isn't only him. Hundreds of people are like that. Like the lady I live with who is elderly, and her husband has left her, and her grandson is in Iraq, and her daughter will hardly speak to her because she blames her. That's what I don't understand. Who deals with all the soaked pillows, the damp handkerchiefs, the quiet desperation and the days when you just think you might chuck yourself under a train, or into the sea, and have done with it? It's none of your business, I know. But it doesn't seem to be anyone's business. If they can't keep up in the Great Race then leave them weeping beside the track. Jemmy gasps for breath.

Mrs Jarvis's face is solid as a brick wall. Jemmy knows that she wants to say, *Listen, my dear. Ideally we try not to employ people with strange ethnic clothes and degrees in textile design. So take your dead baby away and don't come bothering me with it. And don't involve me with the likes of Mr George Waldron with his arthritic fingers and unfinished cross-stitch. Just sell him a life-insurance policy and get him off the phone.*

Well, it's a question worth asking, isn't it? Jemmy says into the silence.

Jemima, I think we've said all there is to be said. Please ensure that you keep your calls short and meet your targets. Now please go back to your desk and get on with your work.

Jemmy keeps her eyes fixed on Mrs Jarvis but stands up to go. Another sharp pain rises up her spine as the muscles contract. She's aware that she's upset Mrs Jarvis and she's glad. She strides out of the office, and heads back to her desk. All eyes are turned on her. In some fantasy world she imagines Tiffany or Monica offering her a tissue or a cup of tea. But of course that isn't going to happen. They think she's been sacked. In a few days she probably will be sacked but what does it matter? All these insurance policies. All they do is feed on fear, try to persuade people that they have some control over their lives when they don't. No amount of life-insurance policies would have done anything for Laurie.

It's only quarter past five but enough is enough. Somewhere outside – through those distant plate-glass windows – the sun is out and Jemmy needs it now. She picks up her bag and heads out of the office, feeling those pitiless eyes following her. Why bother? Mrs Jarvis may have been momentarily unnerved but she didn't really listen. Jemmy feels punctured, despairing. She thought that if she spoke her mind to Mrs Jarvis then she would feel better and she did – for five minutes. But she's not going to give up on Mr George Waldron – or on Mollie. She's sure of that. She has Mr Waldron's number keyed into her phone so she can call him any time.

She walks back to the Windsor Guest House via the church. She's stopped there before to light a candle. She's not quite sure who she should light a candle for – Laurie, Mrs Joyce Waldron, this tiny nub of something which is growing inside her – whose days might be short? Or perhaps for Mollie? As Jemmy lights her candle she looks up and sees a man watching her. He's an ordinary sort of man – very tall and solid but strangely light on his feet. Has she seen him in the church before? He has greying hair combed straight back from his forehead and ordinary, old-man clothes. The way that he looks at her isn't unfriendly but there is something disconcerting in his gaze. It's as though he knows something that she doesn't, as though he sees some significance in this moment that she can't discern.

Jemmy picks up the candle she has just lit, lifting it from its spike. She looks at the man as she holds the candle up to her face, then she blows on it, enough to make the flame dance but not enough to blow it out. For a moment, the man nearly smiles, which is what she wants. She's trying to tell him that it isn't all as worrying as he thinks. Even though it is that worrying really. Bloody awful. As bad as it could possibly get. So bad she can't believe it's happening. She replaces the candle, stares into its dancing yellow flame for a few moments more, and then turns and leaves.

# 26

# Now

## Jay – Baghdad, March 2003

Hi Mum, Granmollie, Grandad, Friends,

Sorry I haven't been in touch. Everything is changing so fast and it's just so hard to find anyone with a phone or a computer connection but now I'm typing this from Greg Marsden's computer. He says I have to let you know what is going on. The situation is like this – yesterday morning these three journalists were arrested in the desert near the border and no one has any idea what's happened to them. Now it just isn't safe to drive through that area. Greg had a car on standby for days, waiting to leave.

I thought maybe that was a good idea because it's hard to find a place in a car unless you have a lot of money. Then yesterday morning Greg's editor phoned and ordered him out and we were just about to leave – but then there was the news about the journalists and now everyone says it's safer to stay. Yesterday when all this stuff came up I was pretty scared for a while but now I feel OK. This was what I wanted so in a way it's easy that the decision got taken for me.

But the thing is, Mum and Granmollie, I need your help and I just hope that even if you're angry with me you will try and do what you can. I know I should have kept in touch more. I'm doing some work here for people who run a website which posts up stories written by Iraqis. Ask Wilf to show it to you. They need someone to find the stories, get them translated and take some photographs, so that's what I'm going to do. It's a really good job for me as that's what I like doing anyway. This organisation can't pay so I need some money. I still have quite a bit but it's not going to last. Problem is there's no way of getting money into this country unless you carry it in by hand. Greg says I'm a bloody idiot and I should have gone but when he gets out he'll be in London and he can pick up some money there. Can you ask Wilf and the others if they can help? I know that's a really big lot to ask and they already need money for other things but I don't know who else to try. Even a really small amount of money could be a really big help and every time anyone does something to help the Iraqis they are just so full of gratitude that it is almost embarrassing. Might be worth asking Ahmed because he might know as well.

These fucking people going on and on, telling me that I'm putting my life at risk for no purpose, that there's nothing I can do here, and asking me whether my mother knows that I'm here and what she thinks. All these people are talking about is their own fear. This American woman who is meant to be a fucking Christian giving me a lecture about being self-centred and wanting to create some huge drama and not being able to understand that maybe I actually CARE about this place. But I don't give a toss what any of these people say. I'm not frightened and I know that what I'm doing is right. I know that I can help and that I'm going to do it.

This place is deadly quiet now and there's been this weird wind. They call it a turab and the light turns yellow and the air is thick with dust so you can't see the sky. The wind goes clammy and whips down the streets. All the shop signs rattle and the branches get torn off the date palms. Suddenly everyone is listless. All the shops are shut up and the windows are covered in tape, trenches are dug in the street. Thousands of Iraqis have packed up their stuff and moved out of the city. People are stockpiling food and fuel. Soldiers and security guards are all over the place.

I'm staying with this Iraqi family in the Mansour District. The peace protest people who are still here and Voices of Truth are in the Al Fanar Hotel and the guy who owns it said I can go there even though it's crammed full of his family as well, but I'd rather stay here. And also Patricia is staying here and Hans as well and they say I can always sleep on their floor. In order to stay here I'm meant to have a visa and I do have one because one of the Iraqis I know has connections in the Foreign Ministry but the visa could get taken away at any time. Greg and the few other journalists who are left are all moving from one hotel to another, trying to work out where they need to be in order not to be bombed. Everything is just rumour after rumour and everyone building up supplies of food and water and taping up windows. You should see the kit the journalists have got – special suits to wear for a gas attack, a generator, a kit to build a bomb shelter. At present they're betting on the Palestine Hotel although that may change again any time. In the basement there's a bomb shelter but it won't withstand a direct hit. The bombs may start tonight but no one knows. Mum, I know you'll be angry about the money and about a lot of other stuff. And I know you must be frightened but it will be OK. I promise you – it will be OK. Sorry, have to go right now. Greg needs the computer.

Love you all.

## 27

# Now

## Lara – Brighton, March 2003

The television screen shows the silhouette of city buildings illuminated by exploding balls of orange lights. It's thirty-six hours since the first bomb dropped and Lara has watched every minute on BBC News 24. She lies in bed now with the map spread out and tries to locate where the bombs are falling – but it's no good because no specific addresses are mentioned, just buildings. The Ministry of Defence, the Royal Palaces, the Al Rashid Airport. Lara can find the airport but nothing else. Are any of the Royal Palaces close to Mansour? It's impossible to know.

And now there is bombing everywhere.

Last night a few explosions hit the city at two in the morning, which was five o'clock in Baghdad, just as dawn was breaking. They came with a sound like the roll of thunder and then miniature mushroom clouds had bloomed, beautiful and deadly, in the early silver light. Lara had thought then that perhaps the Americans were going to keep their promises and that only specific military installations would be bombed. But now night has fallen in Baghdad again and the screen is crowded with a fireworks display, flashes of purple and orange light. Briefly a city – low rise and dust coloured – appears. Smoke pours out of the roof of a building. *Military targets only. A broad and concerted campaign.* Bush's various statements have always been contradictory. Is collateral damage anything more than a euphemism for murder?

Lara clambers out of bed and pulls on her jeans. She can't watch any more – but what else is there to do? She misses Alan, horrid little press-and-communications Alan. Truth, Justice and Peace Alan. The nerve centre, the clandestine operation. Librarian from Southend stands against the great tides of history. Oh how she hated him and his sanctimonious little emails but he had at least kept everyone informed. And she misses that. Who now will send her an email or call with news? For those other waiting relatives, it's over now. Their sons, daughters, brothers, fathers are all home safe and they'll avoid her as the cured avoid the terminally sick. A few peace protesters have stayed but Lara has no idea who or where they are.

Oliver, he is her only hope – if he's there. She puts on trainers, a jumper and coat. And if he isn't there then she'll have to go to her mother. Mollie is the only person who cares for Jay as much as she does. Almost certainly she'll be at home watching television and so at least they can watch together – and without Rufus. Lara picks up the folder where she keeps all her phone contacts. She wonders if Mollie might have been in touch with Greg Marsden again. He obviously has some ability to communicate with Jay. Perhaps they could ask him to persuade Jay to get to the Palestine Hotel. If it's full of foreign journalists then it must be the safest place.

Lara sets out through the dwindling light. For a moment, her mind swirls in confusion and she expects to hear that thunder-like rumble and see a ragged circle of light appear over the dull glitter of distant roofs – but then she remembers. It isn't Brighton that is being bombed. But still those images fill her mind as she walks – past the corner shop, the pub, the gate into the public gardens. It's a just a normal evening in Brighton so why does everything seem exaggerated, enlarged, laden with hidden significance?

As she nears the Guest House, she peers at the area railings, looking for the familiar glow of the forty-watt kitchen light. But it seems no one is home. Where can Mollie be? Does she even know the war has started? Lara lays a hand, briefly, against the railings. Looking up she notices that the ghastly flag which has always hung between the two third-floor balconies has gone. Thank God for that. Maybe the wind finally blew it away. Lara walks on, turns back at she comes to the church. A girl is approaching the door of the Guest House. A rope of dark hair hangs down to her waist and she wears voluminous trousers, a fitted coat stitched with flowers. Lara has seen this girl before but she can't remember where. The girl steps up to the front door, takes keys from her rainbow shoulder bag. Is she a new lodger? Another of Brighton's waifs and strays? Does Mollie have to take them all in? The girl dissolves, enveloped by the darkness of the house.

Lara turns away, heads down the road at the side of the church. She needs to find Oliver. The entrance hall at the Community Centre is thick with Zimmer frames and wheelchairs. Bingo night, or bridge. Lara threads her way through the ranks of pale cardigans, hearing aids and shuffling shoes. Oliver isn't in the office or the café and so Lara pushes open the door that leads to his stairs. The stairwell is dark and when she presses the light switch nothing happens. Her shoes echo on the bare boards as she climbs. She knows he isn't in, can feel his absence. She bangs on the door a couple of times then heads back down the stairs.

The only other place she can go is the peace protest office. They've raised money for Jay – a thousand pounds so far. That news made her feel ashamed because most of the people in the peace movement haven't enough money to buy a coffee. The door to the basement is open and a light shines. Lara hears the sound of a news reporter's voice but the office is empty except for Spike who sits with his wool socks and sandals up on a desk, eating a bag of prawn-cocktail crisps.

Good evening, she says.

Hi there, Ms Ravello. He nods at her vaguely, goes back to the television and the crisps. She wants to ask him if there is any news but what news could there be? Everyone is seeing the same.

So where is everyone?

Gone to London for the vigil. Had to go now because there's trouble on the trains.

Oh right. And Ahmed as well?

Oh no. Not Ahmed. Didn't anyone call you? He's gone to pick up your mother.

What? Where from?

She broke down on the motorway on the way back from London, couldn't get back. But fortunately it's Ahmed's night off at the hotel so he borrowed Wilf's car and went to get her but that was only half an hour ago so it'll be a while until he's back.

That was kind of him.

Spike's eyes are still fixed on the television.

And I wanted to say, Lara says. Thanks very much. The thousand pounds. I think that's great, really kind.

Spike shrugs. Yeah, well. A fair bit of it came from your mum. Anyway, not much good now, is it? Spike says, then his face brightens and his sandy hair appears to stand up a little straighter. Except maybe a couple of the photos will get picked up by the national press.

What photos?

You haven't seen.

What photos?

Uuum. Jay took some photos – maybe last night, maybe earlier this evening. And they've gone up on the website. I can show you if you want – but are you sure?

Nobody told me.

I was going to email but I just— Ms Ravello, I'm sorry.

Spike is standing up now, shrugging his shoulders, his palms raised. Lara is about to ask him why the hell he didn't call her – but then she sees that he's exhausted and despairing. He's worked night and day for three months in this grubby basement room and still Baghdad is being bombed. And now the look that he's giving her is touched with concern, kindness even. She wonders if he's never looked at her like this before, or whether she's never been fully aware of him until this moment.

Lara, she says. It's fine for you to call me Lara.

Spike's plump finger flicks the computer switch. While he waits for the connection, he pulls at the line of studs in his ear. Lara's eyes fix on the screen as it flashes from page to page. As Spike's forearm moves, his dragon tattoo ripples. He opens the home page of the Voices of Truth website which Lara has seen a hundred times before. Then he clicks again. A photograph fills the screen. It shows a stretcher being unloaded from the back of an ambulance. On the stretcher a prone and bleeding figure is half covered by a sheet. Four men are handling the stretcher and the edges of their bodies are blurred due to the speed at which they move. One of the men is shouting, his mouth a twisted blur of silent desperation. Another man stands by with his head gripped in his hands.

And this one, Spike says.

Another image appears. It's flame-filled, blazing. But in the foreground figures are running towards the camera. Three figures, silhouetted black against the burning building, their arms outstretched, their legs flailing as they run. Then further back, closer to the building two other figures drag a man along the ground, pulling him by the arms. Behind them the building is like a human face – the door a black gaping mouth, the eyes and nose dark yawning holes in the mass of orange flame. But it's the figures which Lara watches – and in particular the two at the back who pull the body along the ground. How close are they to the burning building?

And where is the person holding the camera?

Lara sits down, clasps her hand to her mouth. If Jay is holding the camera then he can't be more than twenty metres from the flames – and presumably, all around him, unseen, there are other burning buildings. These are the real pictures – not the whizz-bang-pop computer-game images on the television screen. And Jay is right there, just out of the scene. A boy who loses everything, who is too disorganised to do a university course, who misses every train, leaves his wallet on the counter in the corner shop. And yet somehow, just hours ago, he was standing in the midst of this burning city and taking photographs. Lara wants to put out her hand to the place where Jay must have stood. She wants to touch this young man who she doesn't know at all.

Fantastic, aren't they?

Spike puts a cup of coffee down on the desk beside her, then another plastic cup and a bottle of whisky. He pours a measure of whisky into the plastic cup, pushes that and the coffee towards her. Lara realises that tears are pouring down her cheeks. She wants to say – *he's very brave* – but feels she can't now. It comes too late. He's been brave now for the last six weeks, longer.

Of course, it's no good now, Spike says.

What do you mean? No good?

Well – because the website is being closed down.

What?

Sorry. I thought you knew. There's been an injunction. One of the big American news channels.

They can't do that.

Yeah, I know. Except they just have – taken out an injunction and threatened to sue us. We spoke to a human rights lawyer and he would help us but he needs a ten thousand pound fighting fund just to begin and the real costs would be far higher. Right now we don't have money for a new toner cartridge for the printer. That's why I said – hopefully the national papers might pick up those images. Everything else is embedded reporters.

Lara turns back to the screen and the place where Jay stands, just out of the photograph, somewhere in that burning street. So her son is risking his life for these photographs and they won't even be used. Rage moves through her as suddenly as the flames which engulfed that Baghdad building.

I'll get you the money, she says.

Thanks, Mrs Ravello, Spike says, shrugging.

Lara.

Yeah, sorry. Lara. But it's not even clear we'd win.

So you're going to give up?

Spike shakes his head, sighs. I thought you'd just given up your job?

Yes. I did. But there are other ways in which I can get money.

Lara's mobile phone rings, the sound loud and insistent. No number appears on the screen. She stares over at the television where a British general is being interviewed. She feels Spike watching her as she presses the green phone.

An American voice leaps at her. Is that Ms Ravello?

Yes. Lara closes her eyes, waits. So this is the moment.

So you're Jay's mother?

Yes. Lara can hardly force the word out. She sits down on a chair, feels fear smash against her like a wave. She wants to turn the phone off, not hear the words.

OK, right. Well, this is Greg Marsden and I need to talk about—

Where is he? Lara hears the suppressed scream in her voice.

The line makes a sound like someone kissing a microphone and then is silent. She remembers seeing Greg Marsden on television. A big man with a fleshy, sunburnt face, wearing combat clothes and loaded down by technology – cameras, headphones, a flak jacket. A rhinoceros-type man, loose in his leathery skin, with a thick neck and a large head. Dusty-looking with blank eyes, ready to charge. The phone line puckers again, the thread of sound snagging.

Where is he?

Well, here. Well, not right here. But downstairs in this hotel. But the point is that I've really tried to talk to him. He's doing things which really aren't helpful. There are agreements in place. You know about the Green Zone? And there are reasons of safety and security and I have tried to explain this.

Well, I—

A rustling and popping, overly intimate.

This is not an English tea party we're having here. You understand that? It's all very well, you meddling peace protesters with banners and what all. But your son should not be here and I don't think you have any idea of the danger.

Yes, but—

Don't get me wrong, Jay is a great young guy but this is no place for him.

Excuse me.

He's behaving like an idiot. I can't be held responsible and so you just need—

The phone crackles and Greg Marsden's voice fades, stutters, speaks again, loudly. Ms Ravello, for God's sake, your son is wearing pyjamas.

Mr Marsden, Lara says. I only want to know one thing – is your paper going to use the photographs he's taken?

The phone clicks and buzzes and Lara is talking into silence. With a vibrating hand, she presses the button to ring back. The phone buzzes and an American voice says that the number is unavailable. Lara is crying tears of rage. She picks up the whisky plastic cup and drinks from it, splutters, begins to recount what Greg Marsden said although she knows that Spike heard it all.

How dare he? How dare he assume—

Of course, Greg Marsden is only saying what she was saying three weeks ago. But that was three weeks ago and now things are different. She looks over at Spike. He was never even in favour of the human shields, thinks that they were – and are – irrelevant. But still the look in his eyes is strangely yielding.

So do you want the money? she says. Shall I try and get it?

Can you?

Yes. No. Well, I don't know. I can rent the flat out – or sell it. In the meantime, I can take out a loan. I think.

I don't know. It's up to you.

We can't just let this happen. Can we?

You're right. If there's any way.

I don't know. But we've got to fight.

Spike looks at her and suddenly his face lights with laughter.

OK. OK. You're right. Let's try. I'll call the lawyer.

He stops with his hand on the receiver, his eyes questioning.

I won't let anyone call my son an idiot, Lara says. That's all.

She wants to say something more – or she wants Spike to speak – but they are both silent, unnerved to find themselves suddenly in agreement.

Right, Lara says. I better go. I've got work to do. Goodnight.

She heads up the basement stairs and into the hall of the Community Centre. The bingo or bridge is still in progress. Lara feels weightless, unstable. She stops to take a tissue from her bag, to wipe her eyes and nose, passes the door of the café. It's closed now but Oliver is there, sitting on one of the canteen-style chairs, reading a book. She's struck again by his stillness, his ability to command the scene around him with no visible effort. She pushes open the glass swing door, prepares to explode in explanation of the photographs, the injunction, Greg Marsden's call, but something in Oliver's eyes stops her.

The globe lights which drop from the café ceiling attack her eyes. She sits down at the table, pushes her head down onto her folded arms, blocks out the screaming lights. She draws breath into a throat like sandpaper. Oliver feels like a stone quay, dark and unmoving, in a mass of seething, storm-tossed water. She would like to put her hand out and touch him, just to steady herself. She keeps her head pressed against her arm for a long time – five minutes, ten? She has no idea. Finally she looks up, her eyes firing with tiny stars in the now unaccustomed light.

I need to go home, she says. Could I ask you – would you mind walking back with me? It's only five minutes. Just coming in through the front door on my own, knowing he won't be there. I find it hard – would you?

Yes, he says. Of course.

She stands up and walks ahead of him, placing one foot in front of the other with care. He follows her out and she shudders suddenly in the night air. They do not speak but walk on together towards the road, Monmouth Street. Lara thinks briefly of Greg Marsden. She'll have to email and apologise, she can't afford to argue with him. Oliver's feet sound on the pavement beside her and she looks at him briefly. As they reach her front door, she rummages for the keys in her bag. Someone has parked a bike in the hallway, which isn't allowed but what does it matter now? Oliver follows her up the blue-carpeted stairs.

Together they enter the flat that she's decided to give up. The thought leaves her reduced but strengthened. For years this was all she wanted – a flat with spacious Georgian rooms, wrought-iron balconies, high ceilings with cornices. And she's made it just how she wants, everything white and clean and organised. She knows every inch of it, remembers each decision, where each light switch should be placed, how each bulb should be angled. And now she's going to sell it. Renting it will not bring in enough money. No more worries about the difficult neighbours, the glass of red wine tipping over onto the white sitting-room rug.

Oliver stands near the door, like a servant waiting to be dismissed.

I don't suppose you want a drink, do you? she says.

He looks at her as though she's speaking Chinese.

I mean, like – a normal drink, she says.

It's kind of you – but no.

You don't really do normal, do you?

He nearly laughs but won't allow himself that.

Ah well, Lara says. Maybe another time.

They stand on the pale oak boards, under the five-armed crystal light that she brought back from Italy years ago, insisting that she take it as hand luggage, much to the airline's annoyance. What will she do with that light now? Oliver knows nothing of the light, is not a part of that story. No point in telling him. They continue to linger, unable to speak or to part. Finally she turns away from him, leaves her bag on the hall table – bought in a Brighton antique shop, always just a little too big for the space. He moves to go.

Thank you, she says. You know I owe you a great deal.

He nods, raises his hand to acknowledge her thanks.

My war now, she says, nods, feels tears forming. She moves towards him, raises her arms, holds him briefly, stiff and unyielding in her arms.

I'm glad you're safe, he says. And then he's gone, his feet noiseless on the stairs.

## 28

## BEFORE

### Rose – Coventry, April 1941

Rose kneels by the unlit fire in the sitting room, folding washing. When Mrs Bostock got pneumonia for the second time, Mr Bostock took her away to stay with family in the Lake District and so the house is empty now. Rose is wearing three cardigans but still she shivers. Her hands are chapped, the skin raw and cracked so that it catches in the fluff of the material as she folds. Every few minutes she stops and does nothing, just stays where she is, staring at the wall above the sideboard. Beside her Mollie sits on a tartan rug, banging a spoon on a tin bucket. Rose folds one of Mollie's vests, laying it out flat on its front, turning the sleeves back, folding the vest in half from top to bottom.

If her hand slips, she might lose her nerve.

Mollie is standing up now and has pushed the empty metal bucket over. She bashes the metal spoon against it. The clattering noise vibrates inside Rose's aching head. She starts to fold another vest – lay it out flat, turn the sleeves back, fold it in half from top to bottom. Mollie is rolling the bucket across the dark red and blue patterned carpet but her tiny hand catches in the metal handle and she yells. Rose moves to pull the bucket away, takes a deep breath and pushes her own screams away inside her.

For a moment she looks up towards the sitting-room window. It should be spring by now but it isn't. Everywhere is strangely silent. So few people are left in the city now. She thinks of Frank, thin and shadowed standing in the hall, trying to smile. The last time he was home – lifting Mollie up, swinging her around. She wishes so much that she had been kind to him. It's blackout time and she hears a voice calling from the street. Stand up, switch off the hall light, put the blackout blinds in place, draw the curtains. Arthur's bags are stacked by the window but he stays over at Division B First Aid most of the time now.

Shelter. Shelter. Mollie waves her spoon, indicating the sound of the siren. They have to go to the shelter now. The shed in Broad Street where the bus was stored was blown up a month ago.

A knock sounds. Rose puts the light out, goes to the front door.

Miss Mayeford?

Rose would like to tell him that she's really Mrs Fainwell. But she never changed her name, never even put Frank's name on Mollie's birth certificate. She regrets that petty rebellion now, would at least like to hold onto his name. *Well, at least at the end of all this your conscience will be clear.* How could she have said that to him?

Sorry, she says. The blind must have slipped. I'll go and fix it.

Do you want a hand, love?

The warden follows her into the house. His eyes range over the bedding on the sofa, the unwashed plates, the cold grate. He goes to the window and adjusts the blind. Time to get to the shelter, he says. Come on love. I'll give you a hand. Have you got your mask? And a coat for the child?

No, Rose says. No. I'm not going.

I can't be responsible.

We'll be all right here, Rose says. I can't go.

Come on, love. You know the situation. It's not the bombs, it's the fires, the incendiaries. If the water goes off.

It doesn't matter, Rose says.

The siren starts to wail and the warden shakes his head, hurries away, shutting the door after him. Rose takes the torch from the table, catches hold of Mollie's hand, picks up Bobby the toy dog and heads to the cupboard under the stairs. Since the letter came, she hasn't inhabited her own skin. She still doesn't understand – the letter came from Portsmouth and Frank was in Stepney. She'd been sure there was some mistake but Fainwell isn't a common name. And the letter was signed by Edwin Harris, Secretary of the Portsmouth Peace Pledge Union. A man like that wouldn't make a mistake. Rose thinks of the neat, cramped handwriting. *Contracted pneumonia and despite the best of medical attention was taken from us.*

But no one dies of pneumonia, not with all these bombs coming down. Frank should at least have been allowed to die in an explosion or a burning building. When the letter came, Mr Bostock had gone to the post office to call for her because Rose wasn't sure she would be able to speak properly on the phone, even if she could get to the post office. It took four hours for Mr Bostock to get through to Portsmouth and, when he did, the contents of the letter were confirmed.

But Rose is still waiting for Frank to come home.

Now she tells Mollie they aren't going to the shelter and Mollie doesn't understand, but neither does she protest. Rose moves a mattress from behind the sofa, pushes it into the cupboard and then lays damp blankets on top of it. The kettle on the range in the kitchen has boiled now and she makes a hot-water bottle and a cup of tea. She tries to remember when the letter came – a week ago or two weeks? It's in her pocket and sometimes she hears the crackle of the paper as she moves.

It may be that she and Mollie have been dead for some time themselves but have failed to notice. Rose is glad to feel herself relieved of the responsibility of life. She guides Mollie into the cupboard and they lie down to sleep. She should read Mollie a story or play a game but she doesn't want to waste the battery of the torch. So she pulls the child to her, puts the hot-water bottle next to them and arranges the blankets. In the darkness, she can hear Mollie sucking on Bobby's ear. She has to keep her knees up because the cupboard is only four foot long. The darkness is absolute. The paper of the letter crinkles in her pocket.

She understands that Frank's death was her fault. If only she'd continued to believe in him, then he would still be alive. She remembers the feel of him. His thighs, the rise of his buttocks under her hands. They had thought, the two of them, that they could outwit the likes of Violet, that they could take their own road. They'd been children, they hadn't understood.

The bombs start, first a low crash, far away, then an explosion far closer. The force drives Rose's eardrums towards the centre of her head. She claps her hands over Mollie's ears. The floor of the cupboard shakes as another bomb comes down. Usually a few bombs come, and then there's quiet for a while before the next wave of planes come over, but tonight there seems to be no break. Rose remembers the big November raid – the night the cathedral went. The bombs went on all through that night. Rose can identify the different kinds of bombs from the sounds they make but the most dangerous are the ones that make no noise as they fall. The anti-aircraft guns, stationed around the city, provide an alto line, a dim rattle. Everyone knows that they only fire the guns to raise people's morale. They never actually hit a plane – in fact, the lights from the guns show the Germans where to bomb.

She should have gone to the shelter. This is November all over again, even though everyone had been sure it could never be that bad again. She weighs up in her mind what to do. The shelters are crowded out on a normal night. Probably the best bet would be the cellar under the college in Butt Street. That's only three streets away. It's dirty in that cellar and there will be nowhere to lie down but it might be safer. Is that smoke? Sitting up, she sniffs the air, then she leans over and pushes the door of the cupboard open.

Smoke. Definitely. Her stomach has turned to water. She opens the cupboard door, scrambles out, her legs stiff and numb. She feels for her shoes, pulls them on, fumbling with the laces. Then she reaches into the cupboard, wraps Mollie in a blanket and drags her out, propping the child's drowsy head on her shoulder.

Bobby, Bobby.

Rose kneels down again, shines the torch into the cupboard, pulls the toy dog from the blankets. As she stands up, the front door opens, a flash of light blooms in the hall, a voice shouts.

The warden gathers Mollie in his arms and carries her to the front door. He stretches out his hand and Rose takes hold of it. Outside it's light as the middle of day. The sky is littered with sparking balls of fire, and above the rooftops burns red. The street is alight with incendiary bombs which burn like Roman candles, flickering and hissing, throwing showers of sparks. Shadow men stand in the street with stirrup pumps, shovels, buckets of water. A parachute bomb, like a vast iron coffin, is suspended between the gable ends of two houses. Rose runs down the flame-dancing street.

Don't look back, the warden says.

The pub on the corner is alight and a crater has been punched into the road. At least she hears the bomb. *You never hear the one with your name on it.* The warden pulls her down an alleyway between two houses and into the entry at the back of Shackleton Street. Looking up at the sky, they see a ball of light ahead of them. The warden shoves Rose into the back gate of a house and forces her down onto the ground. Mollie is underneath him, wailing. They feel the bomb hit, the ground buckles, a flash of light breaks on their closed eyes.

God spare us, the warden says.

He gathers Mollie up and they head on towards Butt Street. At the gate to the college, the warden hands Mollie to Rose and sets off down the street towards the place where the bomb fell. Rose runs through the college gardens to the cellar entrance. When she gets there, they tell her that there is no room but they don't try to turn her away. In the darkness, Rose and Mollie are pushed into a mass of bodies, of beating hearts, of people struggling to draw breath in the black heat. Somewhere at the side of shelter a man is singing in a reedy voice. *Nearer and nearer draws the time, the time that shall surely be.*

Because Rose has a child, she's pushed towards the back. Pallets are propped on bricks and covered with mattresses, and children sleep, piled on top of each other like kittens. *When the earth shall be filled with the glory of God as the waters cover the sea.* Rose lays Mollie down on the edge of a pallet, pushing her up next to a sleeping boy. She puts Bobby the stuffed dog into her pocket to make sure he doesn't get lost. A man stands aside so that Rose can position herself near Mollie. Rose steadies herself against a tiled wall that's running with condensation. Occasionally the light of a torch flashes in an arc across the low ceiling.

Rose is sweating but she's packed in so close that it'd be hard for her to get her coat off. She hasn't the energy anyway. The air around her buzzes. She tries not to think, not to feel. Don't look back. An echo sounds – like someone far away tapping on a pipe, a secret message, a coded warning. People in the shelters usually stand in silence but now a woman starts to talk, and then another. Their voices rise to a shrill pitch. And then one of the women is screaming.

Stop it. Stop it now. Rose hears the sound of a slap, then sobbing. Time has ceased to pass. Morning must be ahead of them somewhere but it never seems to come and Rose stops believing in it. She feels that she has been in that cellar all of her life, even before her life began. And they will all of them remain in this cellar for all the centuries to come. Rose stares down at Mollie, as she shivers fitfully on the edge of the wooden pallet. She's wondered sometimes if she should kill Mollie, if that might be the bravest course of action. That's what the Japanese do, they kill themselves and their families rather than be captured.

Don't look back. But she did look back and she saw. A great wall of fire advancing up the street, a solid mass of flame ripping through the fronts of houses, swallowing walls and chimneys, blazing into the night sky. The Bostocks' house will be gone. She knows that – but her mind can't encompass that information. Frank's cufflinks were there, in a box in her suitcase. Silver and in the shape of a four-leafed clover. She'd bought them for him as a wedding present. Will they melt or turn to dust? Could some fragment of them be left in the ashes? Don't look back. Rose feels panic rising in her throat. She leans her head against the wall.

Water, a voice shouts. Water coming in. Bodies press against Rose. Panic vibrates through the shelter. Like being on the inside of a drum. Water seeps through the leather of Rose's shoes.

It's coming in from here. Bodies heave and Rose's head spins.

We're going to drown, a woman screams. *Nearer and nearer draws the time, the time that will surely be.* Rose feels the water break in through the tops of her shoes. The shelter is filled with moans and wails. Rose's head is bashed against the wall as people lift their splashing feet. A slopping sound and then a splash. Drowning is probably worse than being bombed or burnt. Overall, she would prefer a bomb. That way you probably know nothing. Like poor Mrs Watson. A sudden flash of light? A dull thud?

Blocked it up. All right. Blocked it up.

The shelter sags and breathes again. Rose drops her head against the wall again. Perhaps she sleeps standing up. Hours, days, weeks pass. *When the earth shall be filled with the glory of God, as the waters cover the sea.*

Rose dreams of Violet. Violet with her white skin and bulging eyes, her thick blonde hair and white dresses. Violet – tiny and neat. As unchanging as the sun and not a question in her head. Even the Luftwaffe will know better than to bomb Violet. As soon as she gets out of the shelter, that's where she'll go – to Violet. That's what she should have done before. Rose is on her way to the house now, hurrying across the Green, carrying Mollie with her. Soon she'll be there, folded into the generous shadows of that house. Maybe she misses Violet more than Frank.

She reaches the gate, passes the stone lions, hurries up the front steps. The door is open ready for her. And Violet comes running down the stairs into the sun-speckled hall. A brand new cardigan, soft as a cloud. *You will kill yourself with all this, Rose Mayeford.* Arthur's voice rises up through the house, singing. *Paradise here, paradise close.* And Frank is there, with his tight collar and his hair pressed down, standing next to Violet, the mirror image of each other. Siamese twins, indivisible. *Violet, Rose, Rose, Violet. A few flowers more and we'll have a bouquet.* And behind them is the dining room, and beyond, the garden, where wisteria still grows across the once-white wrought-iron arch with its Moorish twisting spike and pineapple-shaped knob.

## 29

# Now

### Oliver – Brighton, March 2003

Spring is here and even now, at seven o'clock in the evening, the sunlight soaks the streets and people sit out on balconies or doorsteps. Oliver opens his window, keeps his eyes away from the roofs of the building opposite, worries that he might see a man balancing there, close to the edge, trying to decide whether to jump, waiting for Oliver to dash up onto the roof, and supply the voice of comfort and reason that'll bring him back from the brink. But tonight no lives are at risk and so he enjoys the last warmth of the sun as it sinks amidst satellite dishes, chimneys and treetops.

When he hears footsteps on the stairs, he knows it'll be Lara. She tends to come and see him around this time. He never expected to like her but now, as he opens the door to her, he realises he's pleased to see her. She looks so different – not in an obvious way – but something has changed. She is lighter, looser, more vital. She begins to tell him about websites and injunctions, clearing out her flat, getting ready to move. He knows that she's at the peace protest office most days now, is fervent in her commitment to the cause. She's surviving as best she can. Oliver enjoys her normality, her enthusiasm. She's at ease with the surfaces of the world as he's never been.

So I don't suppose you want to go for a drink – a normal drink? That mocking question again. It's become a joke between them. You don't really do normal, do you? she says.

Actually, he says. I've spent the last few years trying to be normal.

Oh right. You and I obviously have a different idea of normal.

She laughs and he's surprised to hear himself laughing as well.

So – what about dinner? We could get the car. Drive out of town somewhere.

I don't go in cars.

What? What do you mean?

Just that.

Oh for God's sake. You can't live in the modern world and not go in cars. But anyway – why don't we just go down to the seafront? I'll pay.

He can't explain why he finds her suggestion difficult. Money, yes, and the fear that there might be a death and that he'll be responsible for it. But there's something more. For a long time he's never allowed himself to think that he could be part of that normal world out there. Perhaps he's always considered himself above it. He doesn't want to find out that he also might be capable of a bit of trivial pleasure. And beyond anything else, he fears other people's kindness.

Come on, she says. Please.

Sometimes he does walk down to the seafront so it wouldn't make any difference to have dinner there. If he's with Lara, he won't worry about a wave coming in off the sea and sucking people away, or the big wheel on the pier spinning out of control and cartwheeling down into the waves. He'll take her up on the offer, he's bored by the cliché of the faith healer who can't heal himself. Doubtless he should put on some smarter clothes but he doesn't have any. So he combs his hair and puts on the one good jacket he has. It's oddly intimate, doing those things with her in the next room, catching sight of her face in the mirror as he combs his hair.

The American military killed fourteen people today – unarmed civilians, she says. People in a shopping centre with no military targets anywhere close. And I haven't heard anything from Jay but I'm not worrying about him – or not really.

He turns to look at her, nodding vaguely, uncertain whether he should support her in her optimism. Of course, Lara doesn't look anything like Grace. There's no similarity at all – and yet, just in that moment, there was something. He's seen it in others as well, people with cancer or heart disease, people stuck in some liminal world between life and death. People who can hear the distant rustlings of mortality. People who have absolute power because they have no power at all.

Together they wander down to the seafront. People are sitting out on terraces, music plays and the streets smell of fried food and beer. Lara talks to him all the way, telling him about what she's been doing – helping out at the Stop The War office, going to London to meet the lawyer who is trying to save the website. He enjoys the pulse of the streets, the brackish smell of the sea, everything around him flat, one-dimensional, like a picture postcard. Everything only what it is. She takes him to a restaurant on the seafront, with windows that look out over the beach. He allows himself to be seduced by ease and abundance. On the beach people are still hovering at the water's edge, or sitting on steps, eating cones of chips or kebabs. The sea is grey-green and rolls in gently, with a long suck, a shy splash.

They order drinks and food. Oliver considers with contempt the resilience of the human body, remembers eating a full English breakfast the morning after Grace's death. But still he's captured by this experience, starts to remember how to behave – sitting across the table from Lara, he drinks a glass of wine, asks her occasional questions. Her fingers fiddle with the stem of her wine glass. She spreads butter onto small pieces of bread, eats hungrily. Occasionally she raises a hand – a wax-smooth hand – to push her straggling red hair back from her face. The waiter brings wine and food. Oliver experiences the relief of eating a meal he hasn't cooked himself and the knowledge that there'll be no dishes to wash up afterwards. Lara has a talent for talking about herself. He's glad that he doesn't need to say anything much. It would hardly matter if he weren't even here, he thinks, without bitterness.

He asks her about her mother. He envies Mollie, a person of simple faith.

Lara shakes her head, sighs, pours more wine. I don't know. She's so kind and good and funny. And she's amazing for her age. Virtually brought Jay up for me and never asked for anything in return. So then why is it that I've only got to be in her company for two minutes before I'm seething with anger?

She stares out over the sea, tells him yet again that she's being punished.

What have you done that's so terrible? he asks. When he was a vicar he heard spontaneous confessions all the time. Adultery, minor financial swindles, thoughts of murder or suicide. All of them confessed with hand-wringing as though they were great evils, when really they were nothing more than paragraphs from the ancient ledger of human weaknesses.

Well. I had an affair, for a long time, with my married boss.

She's hoping that he will chastise her, express shock or condemnation, but he will not allow her that.

Consenting adults, he says.

Yes, I know but once I got someone sacked. She was a secretary and we lost a job because a fax wasn't sent out. And I claimed she should have sent it when really it was me.

He's finding it increasingly difficult not to laugh. Lara looks at him and for a moment she's offended but then the sides of her mouth begin to twitch.

The worst of it was – the secretary's name was Innocent.

They are both of them laughing now. He registers how much he's enjoying himself, senses danger. The food is finished and the second bottle of wine arrives. The light on the beach is dimming. The lamps from the restaurant window flicker, reflecting back and forth, spreading patches of light onto the beach. She starts to ask him again about the faith healing, as he knew she would. When she's asked before, he's headed her off, but here, where everything is so normal and straightforward, it suddenly seems a conversation that he can have quite dispassionately. It's no different from what the other people around them are discussing – house prices, schools, the chances of getting a flight to Australia at short notice.

So how did you start? she asks. And why?

I liked the power, he said. I liked the sense of being in control. It's like a drug. If you can heal people, you make yourself enormously important. And I'd been indulging that for a long time. I did it first when I was child. I was in this garden with these other children. He throat tightens as he speaks. And there was this one little girl and we were in the garden of my parents' house in Falmouth and she—

Lara is distracted by paying the bill.

Sorry – you were saying.

No. Nothing.

They leave the restaurant, walk down onto the beach.

So the idea is that some external force really does the healing? Like – God. She says the word uncomfortably.

Well, some people would think that. I'm not sure. Everyone is a healer, everyone has that power. And one should never underestimate the influence one human can have on another. After all, people are infinitely powerful – far more than they know.

But lots of people do believe?

Oh yes, of course. People are always determined to see agency where none exists. That's a basic human trait. We all tend to think that something happened for a reason, or to connect things up to make a pattern. But coincidence may be a more honest explanation. People don't want to believe that. As a healer, you can make people believe anything if they're desperate. It's incredible how gullible some people are.

They walk down towards the sea, feeling the pebbles shift and grind under their feet. Oliver thinks about the conversation they've just had. He feels a contempt for himself. He shouldn't have played the cynic. She deserves something better than that. He thought before that it didn't matter what he said to her, that she wasn't really capable of understanding. But either he was wrong or she has changed.

So you gave it up?

Yes. A few years ago.

But why?

Because – well, I stopped believing. I didn't stop believing in God – not at all. For me, it isn't even a question of belief. It's about experience. I see and feel God everywhere, always have. But I don't believe now in a Good God.

I don't believe in God at all – or I certainly didn't. But now – what you said about meaning. I do believe in that. And if I really think that, then I must believe in some great external forces, organising the whole thing. Or at least – I have to believe some of that now.

She had turned away from him, looking back towards the town, but now she moves back. And what made you stop believing? she says.

He looks out to sea, feels the depths of it, the pull and suck of the waves.

Grace?

Yes.

His feet shift on the pebbles. A small wave bubbles and breaks, close to his feet. He can hardly see Lara's face in the darkness. Memory ambushes him – another beach, a time long past. That Weston-super-Mare day, the baggy black swimming costume, her damp, crumpled hair, water running down from her shoulders and forming rivulets down her thin white arms. Her teeth chattering on the metal edge of the cup as she sipped tea, shivering. He would like to forgive Grace but he can't. He pulls his eyes back to the safety of the seafront, tries to join his heartbeat to the beat of the nightclub music. But behind him the sea waits and he knows that however hard he looks he will not see the place where sea and sky meet, only an unending blackness.

Grace suffered from a rare medical condition, he says. People who have it are perfectly healthy but they can suffer a violent allergic reaction at any time which stops them breathing.

He doesn't want to talk about her. If he does then Lara will say she's sorry. And she may say it with kindness and sincerity but in doing so she will turn Grace into someone who can be dealt with by a mere word. Grace can't be betrayed in that way. Since words can't encompass her loss, he prefers that nothing is said. And he doesn't want comfort. If anyone can comfort him then Grace can't have been worth much. He can't hold onto her but must hold onto the idea of himself as the grieving husband. How can he begin to get over what happened when he doesn't yet believe it?

Because of this illness, he says, she was always meant to have medication with her and breathing equipment.

Lara moves towards him across the shifting pebbles, lays her hand on his arm. He finds himself holding her, dropping his head so that his cheek is close to hers. His body is wracked by some strange spasm as he feels her against him. He hadn't touched anyone since Grace died – not properly. Lara turns her head and her lips touch against his. He wants to kiss her, to feel the warmth of her lips, to pull her tighter to him – but doesn't.

Says instead, I think this is rather too easy, isn't it?

Her lips are an inch from his and her eyes are fixed on him, questioning.

Yes – perhaps.

You have more important things.

Yes.

But you're lonely? he says.

I suppose so. She steps back from him, purses her lips, looks away. I didn't realise. I used to think I had friends, a lover, but now I realise it was nothing. And that's how it's always been, I suppose.

Since?

Well, Liam.

Liam is Jay's father?

Yes.

And he abandoned you when you were newly pregnant?

She nods, turns away from him, embarrassed, but then stretches out her hand as though to draw him back up the beach.

A very old story, she says. One of those endless young women who fall for the myth that you can create an identity for yourself by having a child. But for you – there was a great love affair?

261

He doesn't speak but feels the breeze blowing through him as though he has no flesh, only bones.

Sorry, I shouldn't have asked. Come on, let's go back. We've come too far.

As they walk, her hand remains in his and this knot of their hands feels disjointed, swollen. He feels suddenly exhausted and is uncertain whether this is drink or genuine tiredness. On the seafront skateboarders and cyclists still glide along the bike lane.

I'm sorry, she says. I shouldn't have asked. It's just— I owe you so much. So I wish I could think of something that would make you happy.

You don't owe me anything. And I'm quite happy not being happy.

He feels embarrassed by having revealed himself. A feeling of betrayal as well, the sense of an agreement broken. As they wait to cross the promenade, she stands too close to the kerb. Her foot moves forward. That car is close to them, too close. Can she not see that? He takes hold of her arm, pulls her back. She's his responsibility now, whether he wants that or not. As they reach the other side of the road, he should let go of her arm but it's better to hold her. That way no harm can come to her. And yet his arm feels stiff around her and he can't match his step to hers, so starts to let her go.

Don't, she says. Don't. I know that we're not going to. But still if we're friends then we can? She lays her arm back on his, he catches hold of it and they step out through the waning streets, heading towards the church. He settles against her, walks in time to her steps, enjoys the feeling of her leaning in close to him.

I don't know what I should say, she says. About Grace. I could say – time will heal, or isn't it time for you to move on? Or she wouldn't want you to grieve for too long. I usually do say the wrong thing. Better not to say anything?

Yes, he says. Better not.

Mind you. I don't think it helps you living in that horrid place.

They come to the end of Monmouth Street.

You know what you said earlier, Lara says. About being gullible? Sorry. I shouldn't have.

No. You shouldn't because you don't even believe that.

He's surprised that she's read him accurately. It sometimes happens in circumstances like this that people who appeared entirely one-dimensional are suddenly found to have insights you never could have imagined. This is one of the gifts of pain. The best things about people arise from the places where they are most broken.

Before you said that everything has a purpose to it, she says.

Yes, well. Maybe. But, you see, comfort is what I used to do for a job. Meaning may only be a game people play in their heads but that doesn't mean they should stop playing it.

Don't, she says. Please don't tell me it's all a trick. It made everything possible for me. Whatever strange thing you did, it worked for me.

I didn't do anything.

Yes. You did. Why do you mind me saying that?

I find it difficult. Other people's expectations. I could never really cope.

You're coping with mine.

You were an accident, he says. I didn't intend anything.

When they get back to the church he doesn't want to say goodnight to her – but both of them admit to being suddenly, overwhelmingly tired. So he kisses her chastely on the cheek, watches her as she heads off down the street. As he walks up the bare wooden stairs, no bodies appear dangling from the rails. In his flat, he expects the vases to speak, to taunt or accuse him, but they're silent. He walks to the window and looks out for a moment at the haloes of city light spreading outwards into the starless night. In his bedroom he pulls off his clothes and falls immediately into that long and deep sleep which has eluded him for so long.

# 30

# BEFORE

## Lara – Brighton, June 1984

Outside the Stepping Stones Employment Agency, Lara takes a piece of gum out of her mouth, sticks it under a railing and hitches her bra down. After eighteen months it still doesn't fit properly. It was Mollie who'd suggested this particular agency. *You know, that one in Queen's Road. With pink striped chairs and flowers in the window.* A bell tinkles as Lara pushes the door open. Before she came out, she had a bath and washed her hair but still she worries that the smell of bottled baby food hangs about her. She weighs the leaden burden of her own exhaustion, feels hysteria bubbling below it.

You'll need to speak to Ms Carver. The lady at reception shows Lara through to an office at the back. Just wait until she's off the phone.

Lara smooths down her skirt. She'd found it difficult to decide on the right clothes and even now she isn't confident that she's got the look right. A black Lycra pencil skirt, a black roll-neck jumper, sheer tights, plenty of make-up, a gold necklace and large gold earrings shaped like hearts. She's scraped her hair back off her face to make sure she looks tidy but perhaps she's wearing too much make-up? She needs it to hide the bags under her eyes. Through the door of the office, Lara can hear a voice, low and smooth, confidential and flirtatious.

No, you didn't. Well, you really shouldn't. What, on the washing machine?

Lara isn't certain. Should she close the door? She steps back, clears her throat.

Sorry. Someone's here. I'll call back. I definitely need a few more details.

Lara hears the phone go down, knocks on the half-open door.

Come in.

Ms Carver is in her thirties and wears red-rimmed glasses, a black suit with Channel-swimmer shoulder pads. She looks Lara up and down carefully, taking in every detail, then gives her a coercive smile, asks her to sit down, offers a coffee. As Lara sits, her skirt feels sleek across her thighs. She hasn't worn a skirt, or high heels, or make-up, for months. Pushing the pram around the park annihilates the need for image, or fashion. She must remember to keep her hands behind her back so Ms Carver can't see the raw marks on her knuckles. The doctor says they'll go but they're getting worse. Lara sometimes wonders if she caught the infection – or whatever it is – from Liam. His parting gift to her, something to keep forever. That – and Jay.

Ms Carver opens her desk drawer and takes out a form. The office is warm and drowsy, the carpet thick beneath her feet. Everything feels padded and safe. Lara looks around her, enjoying the pink candy-striped armchairs, the grey carpet, the walls stippled with pink paint. A vase of carnations perches on a glass side table. Surely they're too perfect to be real? Outside the window is a bare brick wall, frosted glass windows, the metal steps of a fire escape – but even this manages to suggest New York-style urban grit rather than Brighton squalor.

Name? Ms Carver asks.

The lady from reception appears with a cup of coffee in a white china cup, a mini biscuit perched on the saucer. She places the cup on a low table and gives Lara an encouraging smile. Although she's sick with nerves, Lara is worried that she might fall asleep because she's been up since four thirty. She reaches for the coffee and drinks it down hurriedly although it's too hot. For a moment she's seized by panic. Something is missing. Jay? Where is Jay? Then she remembers. And the bag with the nappies, the sterilised bottle, the bag of rusks? Mungo, the felt dog? She left those with Mollie too.

Well, Lara, you're a good-looking girl, Ms Carver says.

Lara is surprised by how much pleasure this compliment gives her. No one has said anything kind to her for a long time, no one has even noticed her existence. She feels herself begin to unfold. Settling back into her chair, she crosses her legs, fiddles with her hair. She'd almost forgotten that she's a good-looking young woman – or not bad anyway.

You're not what I usually have here, Ms Carver says.

I was at Frencham Heights, Lara says. She knows that Ms Carver will have heard of the school. Lara mentions her A levels – one A and two Bs.

Wonderful.

I had a place at university, Lara says. I was going to Exeter to read law but then I decided against it – I thought I'd rather get straight down to work.

Well, you're very well placed, Ms Carver says. I don't have many people with your qualifications.

Lara is amazed by how easy this is. She's back in a world she understands, the world of the good girl with high grades and a promising future. She remembers how to display herself, how to charm.

Well, just let me write down a few more details. Address?

Block 2, 13B Brunt's Court.

Ms Carver raises her eyebrows. She knows Brunt's Court because everyone in Brighton knows it. A man was stabbed there two weeks ago and last year Social Services found a baby with maggots in its nappy. Ms Carver nods but, behind that purposeful smile, her eyes are doubtful.

Ms Carver is looking at the form again. Marital status? Single?

Yes, Lara says.

Definitely and completely single. The coffee has made her stomach churn.

Children?

Lara hesitates. Ms Carver has asked this question because she's looking for the missing piece in the puzzle but Lara is reluctant to oblige. The promising young woman ruined by the early pregnancy is such a cliché – and yet she's become that cliché. Perhaps Ms Carver won't find her a job if she says she's got a child? And she does want a job – or at least a reason to get out of the flat, just for an hour or two. If she can't do something other than push the pram around the park, then she'll kill herself. She remembers Mollie's voice – *Well, I don't know, love. But you can't go on like this.*

No, she says. No children.

Ms Carver nods, pushes the form aside. Well, as it happens, Lara, I think you're in luck. She begins to explain about a job that is available straight away. The boss is a friend of mine, she says. Craig Riven. In fact, I was on the phone to him just as you arrived.

Oh really.

Yes. Odd coincidence, isn't it? Fate, you could say. Craig and I go back a long way. Charming man. He runs a highly successful interior design business. Craig Riven Designs. Anyway, he was explaining the type of person he wants and I just wasn't sure who I could find – but now... Ms Carver shrugs and smiles.

Lara likes the idea of interior design. She's always loved looking at design magazines and sometimes she designs rooms in her head, planning the curtains, the furniture, the colour of the walls.

It's a stylish place, Ms Carver says. Creative. They need someone temporary right away, but between you and me, they'll make the job permanent if they get the right person. And they've plans to open a London office.

Lara begins to imagine. The offices are like this room, minimal, barely more than the meeting of a few carefully designed lines. Cups of coffee are served with little biscuits on the side. The men wear square-shouldered Italian suits and they ask her out for drinks after work. She'll get herself a suit like Ms Carver's and perhaps some red-rimmed glasses. Move to London maybe.

And he's prepared to offer up to eight thousand, Ms Carver says.

She's taken out another form and is talking about skills. Lara's head is full of striped wallpaper. If she took this job then she might be able to have a flat of her own, move out of Brunt's Court, buy some new clothes, make a lovely nursery for Jay with a wooden toy box and a bunk bed.

Shorthand? Ms Carver says. Filing?

Lara claims to have worked as a receptionist before and to be competent at shorthand, although she isn't quite sure what it is.

Typing speed? Lara has no idea what this means.

Forty perhaps? Ms Carver says.

Yes, Lara says. That would be about right.

The hours are eight thirty until six.

Oh. Oh.

Is that a problem?

Well.

I did assume you want full time?

Sorry. Yes. No. I don't think I could really do full time. Perhaps a couple of days a week maybe? Or three – possibly.

Oh, Ms Carver says. Oh. Well, that's a pity. A great pity. Because we never really have much part-time. In fact, we haven't got any at all at the moment. Lara senses that Ms Carver enjoys giving her this last piece of information.

Oh, Lara says. Yes, I see. She reaches her hand up to rub her eye. Ms Carver has noticed her scalded knuckles but Lara doesn't care now. She's no longer the bright girl from Frencham Heights with the university place. She's forgotten her lines, stepped out of character. The curtain has come down, the show is over. She's so tired she wants to lie down on the floor. She shouldn't have come, can't possibly do this. She's a single mother living in council accommodation with a baby son who never sleeps. How could she have been so stupid as to hope for something more?

Childcare problems? Ms Carver says.

Lara nods because, in her sleep-deprived state, she doesn't remember what she said before. Ms Carver considers her over the distance of the pine desk. Lara knows she needs to get up and leave but she hasn't the strength.

You know, love, if you want a job, then you've got a perfect right. I've four at home and there's no way I'd spend the day there.

Lara stares at Ms Carver in disbelief.

Yes. I set this agency up myself but all the money goes on the au pair. I don't care. People say how difficult it is running a business, going out to work. But jobs aren't work. In fact, nothing which doesn't involve looking after small children is work.

Lara finds tears running down her cheeks and looks in her bag for a tissue.

It's up to you, love. You decide what you want. If I was you, I'd take that job. I'll tell Craig you can only stay until five. But I'm not pressing you. Something part-time might come up. The tax office or vehicle licensing – anyway, you give me a call about it later. See what you want.

Lara promises she'll call later, says goodbye to Ms Carver and leaves, her stomach still churning. Outside the weather is indecisive. In the distance a weak sun shines but overhead the sky is ash grey and rain dribbles down. Briefly a segment of rainbow appears above the roof of a building and then is gone. Lara longs to spend some time wandering through the town, sitting in a café, window shopping, but her father will be back around four and she wants to pick Jay up before then. Of course, she can't take the job, she knows that. She fought to keep Jay and she's not going to give him up. Still she's grateful to Ms Carver who at least told the truth. Why do women always lie to each other? Why do they so diligently promote the myths that deprive them of their freedom?

Across the street, she sees two girls who might have been at school with her. She doesn't actually recognise them but she knows the type – good teeth and pink lip gloss, only the slightest hint of make-up, smooth blonde hair held back by Alice bands. Navy and white spotted ra-ra skirts, round-neck lambswool jumpers, hanging long. Scruffier than everyone else in the street but also more stylish. Perhaps they're home from university for the holidays? Just back from skiing in the Alps or on their way to Jamaica or Lanzarote for some early summer sun? When she was at school she'd been invited a couple of times – a villa in the

South of France, a chalet in Méribel. For a moment, Lara feels a sting of jealousy. She's exiled from all that – permanently. Teenage pregnancy is not a language they speak in that country.

Turning away, she finds herself staring into the window of a toyshop. She wants to buy something for Jay, although she hasn't really got any money for toys. She looks at a Duplo train and a toy tool set but both are too expensive. So she chooses a jigsaw with a farmyard scene on it – brightly coloured pictures of cows, chickens, sheep. She imagines his tiny, smiling face, his hands clapping together. Reaching his arms up towards her so that his T-shirt rides up and his tummy sticks out.

When she gets back to the Guest House, she hears the hoover, and the radio playing. Mollie and Jay are in room three on the second floor. Jay isn't wearing any trousers and he's got a lollipop stuck in his mouth. Mollie is hoovering and Jay is helping her, holding the pipe and running it back and forwards across the floor. Jay laughs so much he falls over.

Hi, Lara calls, over the noise, but neither Mollie nor Jay hear.

Mollie chases Jay with the hoover, then pretends to hoover up his trousers, which are lying on the floor. As they stick to the end of the pipe, she whoops in horror, and then snatches them away, as though saving them from the jaws of death. Jay waves his hands above his head, screams with laughter.

Hi, Lara calls again, but still they don't hear so she moves further into the room, waves at them.

Darling. Hello. How are you? Mollie yells and waves. Jay's got hold of the hoover and is manoeuvring it up and down the floor.

Jay, Lara calls. Jay. She bends down to his level but still he doesn't see her. She waves at him and he looks up. We could do a jigsaw, she says. I've got you a new jigsaw. Do you want to come and see? But Jay continues to wave the pipe of the hoover.

Don't worry, dear, Mollie says. We're just finishing off up here. We'll come down to the kitchen. You go on down and get us a cup of tea.

Mum, we've got to go.

Oh no, dear. Don't worry. Your father rang, he's not back until six. Stay for tea. Coffee cake and doughnuts.

Lara stands up, conscious again of her tight skirt, her heels. She stands at the bedroom door and watches as Jay swings on the pipe, Mollie making zooming and whooping noises, pretending to suck up the side of the bedspread

Heading downstairs, she puts the kettle on, sits down at the kitchen table. Looking up through the area railings, Lara sees that the weather has now decided on rain and is throwing spears of water down with vigour, as though making up for earlier indecision. She wants Jay to come down, to do the jigsaw with her. She minds about the fact that he isn't wearing any trousers. She always insists he's properly dressed. But, of course, she won't say that to Mollie because it isn't fair to criticise someone who's just done two hours' childcare for you. Mollie and Jay bump downstairs with the hoover, Jay still laughing and shouting. Lara pours out tea.

Mum, thanks so much, she says. Thank you. It's really kind of you to look after him. It's always like this. She's always thanking Mollie and it's only right that she should because Mollie does so much to help. She wouldn't have got through the last eighteen months if Mollie hadn't come around every day. But what Lara can't understand is why, no matter how many times she thanks Mollie, it never feels enough. She wishes she could understand. Was it the pimp who seduced Mollie when she was fourteen? Or the fact that Rufus pushed her off a roof? Lara isn't sure if these stories are true.

You do look better, Mollie says. Much better. It's what I said. You need to get out a bit more.

Lara tells Mollie about the job.

Darling, how wonderful. I told you there'd be hundreds of jobs for you.

So Mollie has proved right again. She's always right about everything. It's never worth going against her advice because she'll always turn out to be right. And Lara's success is never her own, always Mollie's. Lara hates her mother for this, and she hates her for her goodness, and her simplicity and her ability to bear everything with a defiant smile.

Interior design, Mollie says. Right up your street.

Yes, but Mum – it's full-time and I can't.

Why not? You could do. If you want to.

Mum, you can't look after Jay all the time. It isn't fair. You've got enough to do already, with Dad and the guests.

Yes, dear, but *I* don't find Jay a trouble. In fact, he keeps me company. He can just play around the place while I'm working. Really he's no bother.

No, Mum. It's too much.

Really, dear. I don't mind in the least. And you've got to do something.

But what about Dad?

Well, he'll just have to get used to it, dear. I mean, Jay is his grandson and he does enjoy having him around, no matter how much he pretends he doesn't. All that's the past. Your father has a lot of faults but he doesn't bear a grudge.

Lara doesn't bother to contradict this – even though Brunt's Court is the result of Rufus's grudge. She could have had Jay at home if it hadn't been for Rufus. How strange that he has the power to ban her from the Guest House when he doesn't own it. He must have heard from Mollie about Brunt's Court. The armies of woodlice crossing the kitchen floor, the snail tracks on the sofa, the axe holes in the front door, the tape over the letter box so that people don't piss through it – but he's never suggested that perhaps she should move back home. No, Rufus doesn't bear a grudge. He just dispenses with anyone who doesn't fit into his plan.

Anyway, Lara says, I said I'd ring back if I want it.

Well, why don't you ring now?

No. I need to wait for something part-time.

Well, do they have much part-time?

Mollie flicks the radio on. Lara rattles the jigsaw box at Jay and he comes to her, takes the box from her hand. Pig, he says, dropping the box. Lara clears a space on the table and sits Jay down opposite her so they can do the jigsaw together but Jay throws the pieces at her.

No, she says. No. Don't throw. Come on.

She picks the pieces up and lays them out on the table.

Help me find the bits with the sun. Look here – bright yellow sun.

Jay picks up a puzzle piece and hurls it at Lara. It hits her in the eye and he laughs. Lara wipes her eye, picks the piece up from the floor.

No, Jay. No throwing. Come on. Come and sit here with me. Have you seen this picture of the dog? Can you see his tail?

Jay runs his hand across the table, sweeping all the jigsaw pieces to the floor. Then he jumps down from the chair, runs to Mollie and throws himself against her leg. Really, Jay, you shouldn't do that, Mollie says. Don't do that to Mummy. But she picks Jay up, holds him against her, makes him laugh by rubbing her nose against his. Lara fixes the bits of the black and white cow together and looks over at the picture on the front of the box – the farm, the pigs and cows, the cockerel, the bicycle-wheel sun. She's never seen anything so mournful in her life.

Have a break, dear, Mollie says. You must be worn out. Take no notice.

Lara looks at Jay, at his defenceless perfection. His startling blue eyes, unmarked white skin, bright red lips, shock of hair, tiny, damp hands. He's meant to compensate her for everything. For not having a job, for being exhausted all day every day. She's not meant to complain because she has the miraculous gift of a child. Some women can't have children at all. Mollie herself lost four after Lara was born. So she's lucky, really lucky. But everything they tell you – it's just not true. When you have a child, you lose so much – and the fact of the child just doesn't compensate you for all of that. How come everyone else can do it but she can't? Don't other women find it desperately boring building a tower of bricks again and again just so a child can knock them down?

Don't other women feel that they must have been intended for something more?

Mollie takes Jay upstairs with her. Lara listens to laughter from above. She knows Mollie wants Jay, has wanted him from the beginning. Jay is the living second child she never had. So why not let her have him? Mollie doesn't mind the sick, the exploding nappies, the spaghetti bolognaise rubbed into Jay's hair. In fact, she loves it all because she's a good person. And I am not, Lara thinks. She goes to the telephone and dials Ms Carver's number.

## 31

# Now

## Mollie – Brighton, April 2003

So this is it then? The Spiritualist Church – Mollie must have walked past it hundreds of times but she's never noticed. It's a windowless building with curving sandstone walls, a spaceship parked halfway up George Street. Mollie wishes she'd worn comfortable shoes. But it's good to get out of the house. On television all they talk about is that wretched Jessica Lynch whom the Americans rescued – nothing about those who are working for peace, nothing about the Iraqi people and their suffering, nothing about Jay.

The people crowding into the Spiritualist Church don't look anything special – Women's Institute types mainly. Grey hair held back by little-girl clips, drab waterproofs, support tights and orthopaedic shoes. A few alternative types with trailing rainbow skirts, earrings in the shape of ancient runes, grey plaits. Mollie wriggles her toes, lifts one foot, then the other – perhaps she should get a pair of those orthopaedic shoes herself. She follows Jemmy into the reception area and then into an oval-shaped room with a domed roof and no windows.

Jemmy sits down, her face stretched tight, watching and waiting. She wears loose Turkish-style trousers, a singlet and an orange cardigan. Her collarbones stick out beneath a necklace of Liquorice Allsorts beads and her long hair catches on her gypsy earrings. Mollie thinks of those strange books she brings back from the library. Ancestor worship and appeasing the souls of the dead. Not healthy really – in a young girl of her age. She's an odd girl. Charms the words, the souls, out of people's mouths as a snake charmer draws out a snake. Often makes Mollie think of Jay. Not surprising that they were friends. Only friends? Surely more. The young people educate the old, not the other way around.

Mollie knows how much Jemmy longs for a message from Laurie. Mad, of course. Or probably, anyway. She herself doesn't discount the possibility. Who can know? If it provides people with some comfort then why argue? But if Jemmy receives a message, Mollie hopes very much that it will say – *Leave that poor dead baby in peace and make some space for the living*. But perhaps spirits don't say that kind of thing?

Mollie has told Jemmy again and again that she needs to go to the hospital, find out about this bleeding, but Jemmy doesn't want to go. Poor girl, what can anyone do? Of course, the truth is that for all anyone knows the baby might have already died inside her. She won't tell that poor young husband of hers anything either.

Mollie never said anything to Jemmy but Bill came around to the Guest House once when she was out at work. Lovely young man. The girl doesn't know when she's well off. A bit dull perhaps but there's a lot to be said for dull, as Mollie has reason to know. Doesn't want to know anything about the baby boy, of course, but who can blame him. Life may be long but not long enough to forget that.

In the oval-shaped room, chairs are arranged in a circle. Vases of flowers perch on stands. The room is built of curving stones and the tiled floor is divided into segments of white and black which meet at a central point. Lights on the walls form the points of illuminated triangles. A piano stands against one wall covered by a sheet. Mollie only came along because she thought it might provide Jemmy with a bit of comfort. And because Mr Lambert's weeping is getting on her nerves. Jilted again. Bless him, all he wants is a little love but that can be hard to find. Mollie focuses on the point where those black and white tiles meet. Can there really be messages from the dead? Mollie wouldn't mind getting a message from Ludo – since he's been in her thoughts so much recently. And maybe someone in the nether world could tell her where her birth certificate is? Mind you, she wouldn't get into Iraq anyway.

Everyone is seated now. One of the rainbow-skirt ladies announces that the meeting will begin with a meditation. Imagine a fountain of light, she says, bursting up towards the ceiling. A bright sparkling fountain of light. Her voice is self-consciously breathy, calming. Mollie wriggles her toes and wonders if she should take off her shoes. She thinks about Rufus. She knows he's alive and well because Baggers tells her so but then why doesn't he call? How dare he do this to her at a time like this? Once she gets the car fixed she'll drive up to London again, see if she can track him down. Her nose is beginning to run but she mustn't disturb everyone by opening her bag to look for her handkerchief.

Now imagine the light breaking up into a thousand particles, the woman says. Imagine it flowing down onto all of us. Mollie's throat is starting to tickle and she tries not to cough. That flat in Roma Street, she must tell the agents to advertise it again. Looking over at Jemmy, she sees her face, calm and attentive, her eyes turned slightly upwards, feeling the particles of light falling onto her. The room is silent now. Mollie's nose tickles and the back of her throat is like chalk dust. She wonders if she turned the oven off before she came out.

Has anyone got a message? the rainbow woman asks.

Eyes turn towards a young woman with carefully arranged dark hair and thick make-up covering blemished skin. She's unhealthily thin and wears tight jeans and stiletto heels. Yes, she says. Yes. She stares at a point far up the wall, concentrating. I've got a message from a woman. She's an elderly lady with grey hair and she's wearing an apron. She's someone who always fries her sausages. And she says that the message is for a person who always grills their sausages.

Oh yes, a large woman on the other side of the circle says. That's my mother. Definitely. She was always telling me I ought to fry my sausages rather than grill them. We spoke about that often.

The thin young woman nods her head. She's saying – you've got to look beyond the problem. She's very insistent, almost angry. She keeps saying that. You've got to raise your eyes and look beyond the problem. And something about a ring which was lost. She can help you find it.

Everyone in the circle nods, their faces serious, appreciative. Mollie will have to get her handkerchief. She bends down and tries to do it without making any noise but she can't find the handkerchief and so she has to rummage in the bag, and pull things out. Her powder case drops to the floor with a crack and, in trying to pick it up, she also drops her hairbrush. The thin woman is delivering another message. I've got an elderly woman who is tall with snow-white hair and she's got a message for someone here who's got a problem with their plumbing. Who would that be?

A woman with a gypsy-type scarf in her hair half raises her hand, her face suddenly alive. Yes, yes. That's my sister. Definitely and there is a problem.

No, no, the thin woman says. Don't lead me. Just let me try to see. She closes her eyes and her face is screwed up with concentration. You're looking in the wrong place. There's no point in taking up the tiled floor. There's a leak in the loo but it's not to do with the pipework under the floor.

The gypsy-scarf woman is animated. Yes, she says. Yes. The leak, yes. The builders are coming tomorrow to take up the floor.

The people around the circle smile and nod. A lady next to the gypsy woman clasps her hand. Mollie is busy wiping her nose. In her mind, she's always had a clear image of the dead. *Then like stars, His children crowned, all in white shall wait around.* But perhaps that isn't right. The realms of the dead may be more banal than one supposes. Even there people may be largely concerned with culinary tips and plumbing problems.

The room is hot and something moves across the wall, a shadow, a dancing beam of light. The room doesn't contain more than thirty people but now it feels crowded. Mollie has the sense of people pushing forward from behind her. She hears voices and the shuffle of feet. She wishes that she could leave now but the messages continue.

A message about a baby – a child who didn't live long. Can anyone take that message? Mollie feels Jemmy stiffen beside her.

The message is about photographs which are pinned on a board.

Jemmy moves, her hand starting to rise.

This baby. No, a child – a girl.

Mollie looks over at Jemmy, her hunched shoulders and clenched hands. The shadows on the wall are forming into shapes. Mollie can't understand why the room feels so hot. Would it be acceptable for her to get up and walk out? Really this is a thoroughly unchristian activity. A load of hocus-pocus. Dead people should stay in their graves and people who are living shouldn't bother them. It's sinful, and dangerous. All it does is give false comfort. Make some space for the living. But the knowledge comes to her now that there is no space. The ranks of the dead are so numerous they crowd out all else. She longs for Rufus. If only he would come home then they could go out dancing together. She needs him now, misses him fiercely. Even his shouting and raging, debts and drinking – she misses even that, now that he's gone. He promised her, he promised.

I have a message from Arthur, the thin woman says.

Eyes dart from face to face, someone stifles a cough.

Can anyone take that message?

Mollie twiddles her fingers, sighs. How much longer?

The message is for the lady sitting there, the thin woman says, nodding in Mollie's direction. Staring down at the floor, Mollie holds on to her bag. Of course, it wouldn't be that Arthur. She never knew him, he only came to the house that one day. As an actress she should be able to manage this situation, defuse it, say something funny or clever. But her voice is fragile and plaintive, the voice of an old woman.

I'm afraid I don't know anyone called Arthur.

Although it's a common enough name, of course. Perhaps in

the realms of the dead they also make administrative mistakes? Like the mess with her birth certificate. Blood rises to her cheeks. She feels the guilt of a liar although she isn't lying. The room is filled with a roaring silence. Mollie is breathing in glue. Sausages and plumbing. Is it not possible to go back to that?

He knew you as a child and he met you once later. But the message isn't about him. It's about Rose, your mother.

No. No. My mother was called Violet.

But he's insisting. A woman called Rose. She's your mother.

No.

He says that you must be careful of this woman. He offers this message in kindness because he loves Rose – but he wants you to be careful.

Mollie's mind slips backwards, a slow yielding, like the beginning of a landslide. And she sees a white house with many chimneys and curling iron balconies. Not the house of her childhood in Worcester but a house standing beside a green space, a city park perhaps. And she's inside the house, a small child, a peg doll in a doll's house, sitting on a red velvet chair in a hall with a curling staircase and an eagle in a glass dome. The floor is scattered with pieces of plaster and broken glass. A picture has dropped from a wall and lies face down on the floor. Peg doll Mollie climbs down from the chair and steps up the green-carpeted stairs, stands on a landing which stretches far in every direction, then walks forward towards an open door. Yards of satin, salmon-pink walls, a cream Chinese carpet, a huge bed with a seashell headboard.

Rose, Violet. Mollie. Mollie. Rose. Violet.

The thin lady in the spaceship room is still talking. He's a man who smiles a lot, and he's bringing music with him – jazz or dance music. He can sing and his voice is – he has an accent – French or Italian.

Mollie tries to bring her mind back into the oval room. Sausages and plumbing. She doesn't know anyone called Rose. But the bedroom is still there, the salmon-pink bedroom with the seashell bed and the dressing table. And a woman is standing on the far side of the room, near the long bow window where the dressing table stands. One of the drawers of the dressing table is open. A window is shattered, the glass glitters on the carpet. A blackbird crouches on the end of the curtain rail, its clawed feet slipping. Peg doll Mollie raises her hand to her mouth to stop herself screaming but is lifted by strong arms. And when she turns back her mother has disappeared, dissolved like a pantomime villain, into a cloud of dust.

And Mollie – back in the oval room – stands up, grabs her bag, stumbles against a chair, hurries towards the door. Sausages and plumbing. But there is no door and she'll be here for ever now, walking round and round the oval walls, without ever finding her way out. And those shadows endlessly moving on the walls. She falls into the hall, fumbles down the steps, out into the honesty of the night.

## 32

## BEFORE

### Oliver – Weston-super-Mare, May 1986

Although it is barely dawn, Grace is waiting for Oliver outside her flat with a basket of food, a rug, her swimming things, a rubber ring in the shape of a yellow duck and a multicoloured seaside windmill, its wings spinning, stuck in the top of her bag. She wants to drive and so Oliver agrees. He is happy to agree to anything, just to have the day with her.

She is a mass of excitement. For her, a trip to the seaside is the best possible day out. The normal is always exotic. As they get into the car she tells him about all the things she loves at the sea. The white stucco buildings, the spidery piers, the tea shops, sticks of rock, candyfloss and fish and chips. She likes to walk on a pier with the pitching and tossing sea visible through the cracks in the boards under her feet and the seagulls circling overhead.

The Bristol back streets are still sleeping as they set off, heading towards Weston-super-Mare. She drives as she always does – a little too fast, taking too many risks. And he resists the temptation to tell her to be careful. It is two weeks since he last saw her and he'd worried then that he'd never see her again. He'd called several times after she'd come out of hospital but she hadn't rung back. For days he's been in agony. Then finally she'd called, making no reference to what had happened, suggesting a day at the sea.

He'd borrowed the car from the churchwarden. The exhaust rattles and it smelt of dog, elderly and moulting Jack Russell, to be exact. They laugh about that smell. He watches as her foot goes down onto the accelerator, pulling away fast from a junction. She hasn't retained the beauty she had in that Falmouth garden. Her red hair is often messy, her teeth cross over at the front and her skin is sometimes blemished. Her hands have become coarse and red from making pots and glass-blowing. But her eyes still have that same coolness and her face the same smooth oval shape. He is responsible for her but it is like being responsible for the weather, or for ensuring that the earth keeps on turning.

They come to the open fields, cross the motorway into the endless roundabouts and housing estates around the town. It is May but the weather is chill and blustery. Grace talks about the exhibition that has just finished. It was on the first night of that exhibition that she'd stopped breathing, and been taken into hospital but she doesn't mention that. Instead she is excited about the work – she sold everything and several people asked about commissions. She looks over at him, wanting him to share her excitement. She must have a good day out, and he must do the same.

Sorry I didn't call, she says.

That's OK. I understood.

Kiss me, she says. So I know you forgive me.

Oliver wants to kiss her but not while she is driving. And yet he can't say no so he leans across and kisses her on the cheek. She laughs at him and turns her head to kiss him properly. He keeps his eyes on the road, puts his hand out to steady the steering wheel.

Be careful.

She laughs again, wobbles the wheel a few times, mocking him.

I love you, she says. And he knows that in that moment she does – but there is no guarantee it will be the same tomorrow, because there is no guarantee that there will be a tomorrow. He begins to wonder why he had wanted to see her so much, when he will worry all day. Can he ask her what the hospital said? Is the situation getting worse? She doesn't want to discuss any of that.

When they arrive in Weston it is still only eight o'clock and hardly anyone is about. The streets are littered with bottles and paper from partying the night before. A greengrocer is opening up his shop and a café owner places an A board on the pavement advertising bacon sandwiches. They walk together down to the deserted beach. The donkeys haven't yet arrived and the pier is silent. The small train which usually rolls along the seafront has not yet started its journeys for the day.

The sea is in – Grace checked the tides to make sure it would be. They put their towels down and sit on the damp sand in the stinging morning air. Around them the once-grand Victorian buildings were both garish and grey, a line sweeping out towards Birnbeck Pier. Seaside hotels, cheap restaurants, old people's homes. They drink a cup of tea. He thinks of the map he looked at, the distance to the hospital. And he can't help but ask her then, Have you got your blower here?

Yes, yes. I've got it. Her voice is patient.

Well, I just ask because obviously you didn't have it.

Yes, I know. I know. And that's my decision, Oliver. I refuse to have my life ruled by this. You know that. Anyway, blower or no blower, there's risk.

They have had this same argument so many times and Grace always says the same thing. *This is how I live.* Oliver always wants to say, *Yes, but I can't live like that.* But it feels wrong to do that, when it is so much harder for her than for him. She always leaves him, always comes back. They even lived together for a while but then one day she was gone. He knew he was at fault. He should've been able to live as she lived, thinking of nothing but the day. He longs for a cure but knows that she is the illness, the illness her. A doctor said to him once that Grace was allergic to the unknown but it seems to him that she has fallen in love with it. She frequently fails to turn up for medical tests which might help to make the attacks more predictable.

I'm just saying, you don't have to make it worse than it is.

Oliver, can you shut up? I've come to the sea for the day. I want to enjoy it. She leans over and kisses him. Let's swim, she says. Come on.

So where actually is it?

In this bag, she says, pointing, making an effort to be reassuring.

Everything is the same to her, nothing is permanent. Life with her is continually the last day of term. The confusion, the hurried farewells, the dizzying sense of liberation. She drives too fast, walks too far, sleeps too long in the mornings, and always asks, What shall we do today? Go to Alaska, buy a hot-air balloon, ride on a camel? She likes cake – particularly cake with colours and cream, the cheaper the better.

Come on, she says. Let's swim while there's no one else in the water.

Maybe.

OK. Well, if you don't want to swim, let's walk along to the West Pier.

No. No. You swim. I'm fine here.

She yanks her swimming things out of her bag.

I know you're waiting for me to say thank you. But I'm not going to. OK?

That's fine. I don't expect any thanks.

Good. Because you didn't do anything.

It made him angry that an intelligent woman could deny the facts. He watches her as she pulls off all her clothes, not bothering to hide herself with a towel. He likes the white stretch of her limbs, the curve of her waist, the triangle of hair at the meeting of her thighs which is the same pale red as the hair on her head.

I just started breathing again because that's what sometimes happens.

Oliver watches her, saying nothing.

It didn't have anything to do with healing, or God, or any of that stuff.

You're sure about that?

Yes, I'm sure.

The hospital didn't seem able to give any explanation.

They never have any explanation.

So nothing happened?

No. I'm not saying that. Something happened. I know that. But it didn't have anything to do with you or with God. It's random, Oliver. It's just the toss of a coin, the turn of a dice. That's all it is. You can't control it. You're not responsible.

Yes but—

Yes, I know. I know there are loads of people out there who honestly believe that you have special powers and that you can call on the power of God and make the blind see and the lame walk. But those people are just gullible.

No, Grace. No. That isn't fair and you know it. You've seen. Through the grace of God many of those people find that.

Shut up, Oliver. Shut up. You're ruining my day.

The worst crime, ruining her day.

Listen, she says. Listen. Just because, when we were children, you might – or might not – have saved my life doesn't mean you have to be responsible for me forever. I don't want to have a relationship with God, just with you. I just want to enjoy the day – and preferably I'd like to enjoy it with you. But it seems like I can't do that.

She turns away from him in anger, marches away down the beach. Her bathing costume is baggy and black with a crossover back – like something left over from school. And she has a ridiculous swimming hat into which she has shoved her hair. It is green rubber with flapping flowers, like something from the fifties. The kind of jokey kitsch which Grace loves. Now she pulls it down further over her ears as she starts to run. Oliver watches her go. She is gangly and angular as a coat hanger. Grace-less really. But somehow she seems to fill the whole beach as she splashes at the water's edge, gasping at the cold, running backwards and forwards, into the waves and out, a pantomime performance, unable to find the courage to plunge into the freezing water.

Oliver is glad to sit on the beach watching her. In the parish where he works he is always busy. He hadn't known before he became a vicar just how much illness and death there is in the world. Now his whole day seems to be spent at sickbeds or conducting funerals. And then there's his faith healer training as well. Lying back on the sand, he watches the seagulls overhead. They glide and swoop and sway on the wind, moving with joy and ease through the air. They are in their medium, he thinks, as we humans never are. On the road along the front, traffic is building up and he hears the buzz of engines. He hopes that the weather might get a little hotter and then he'll go down and swim. But there seems no chance of it. The day wears a determined scowl.

He has tried to form relationships with other women and he finds that easy. In the community of believers, competition is limited and women like him. Young women who help out at the church, and believe in God, and talk to him fervently of their faith. Doubtless these women would make excellent vicars' wives. And there is no reason to think they will die young. Oliver occasionally goes out with these women, likes them, tries desperately to talk himself into making a decision to spend his life with one of them. But it never works. There is always Grace. He can't escape her and he loves her – has done ever since the first day they'd met.

He looks out towards where she is swimming. The air is still fuzzy with spray and morning mist. His eyes are dazzled by the seaside light. He sees the pier, spikes of black against the headland beyond. But where is Grace? His vision becomes clearer but he can't see her. He jumps to his feet. Something black is washing at the end of the water. He starts to run. In his mind he goes through it. Should he go back for the blower now? Will he remember which button to push? Could the battery have gone flat? She could just be lying down at the water's edge but no, no.

Grace, he yells. He is still wondering whether he should have brought the blower with him straight away. Should he check first whether she is breathing and then run back and fetch it? He keeps running as he tries to decide. Should he go back? The moments are gasping by. She lies just above the tide line in her black costume, wet and slippery as a seal, her hat gripped in her hand, with her hair spread out. He kneels down beside her, calls her name. Above him the seagulls are screeching and the frilled edge of the water rolls up towards her. He stares down into her face.

Then her lips move. She opens her eyes and laughs. Jumping up, she runs away from him back into the sea. Shaking, he stands up and starts to shout. Then he keeps on shouting, the salt air tearing at his lungs. Standing at the edge of the sea he yells abuse at her, but his voice is lost in the sound of the sea and she seems not to hear, ducks in and out of the water, waving back at him happily. But still he keeps on shouting until he is exhausted.

He stamps back up the beach, sits on the towel again, puts his head in his hand. He can't stop remembering the fear he felt as he saw her lying there. It runs through him again and again and he watches her with hatred as she swims, her green hat bobbing in and out of the waves. Images come into his mind of violent acts. He imagines hacking her up, here, in the sand and throwing her bleeding limbs into the sea. Smashing her head with a large rock, or strangling her.

He pours himself a cup of tea and takes deep breaths, tries to stop shaking, to banish those images. She comes running up the beach, stops to shake herself, like a dog, her hair whipping around her head, then she sits down beside him and pleads for tea. He pours her a cup but is so angry he can't look at her. She lays a hand on his arm. When he glances across at her, he knows she has seen his anger.

You're so arrogant, she says.

She is right. It is arrogance. He should be able to live as she lives.

For God's sake, Oliver. Get a sense of humour.

He is conscious of her watching him. She doesn't often do that, she lives too fast to look at anything for long. But her eyes are now fixed on him. She reaches out her hand, touches his arm again, takes hold of his hand, interlaces her fingers with his.

Sorry, she says. I'm sorry.

He knows that he should apologise as well but he can't. Sadness has fallen on him and he can't shake it off. He is frightened, still frightened, by the image of her lying at the water's edge, by the image from two weeks ago of her on the pavement, and the people crowded around and the ambulance arriving. And he is there, pleading with God not to let her die.

Oliver, she says, putting her arms around him. I do love you, you know. I really do. And I know I shouldn't say those things. I know it's important to you, God and stuff. But I just can't. He feels her kisses, her cold body shivering in the towel, close to him. She faces him with her luminous green eyes, damp and flattened hair.

Listen, she says. Listen. I've got an idea. Let's get married.

He laughs at her, knowing she is only saying this to try to make him feel better, to make sure that this turns out to be a good day.

No. Don't laugh. I'm serious. Let's get married. I love you, you love me. So let's just do it – now.

Now?

He spills tea down the front of his jumper.

Yes, now.

But we would have to wait a while because—

Oh for God's sake, Oliver. You're a vicar, aren't you?

He watches her sipping the tea. She is blue with cold and shaking convulsively, so that the metal cup rattles against her chattering teeth. That makes her laugh, and she pulls off the green plastic hat. Underneath her hair is damp and crumpled. Water runs down from her shoulders and forms rivulets down her thin white arms. She will make the worst possible vicar's wife.

You never think, do you? she says. Never consider that maybe I try to look after you, that I try not to let you love me too much, that I don't want you to be hurt. Sometimes I think I should leave you with God – at least he might be more reliable.

Should he believe her? Is her distance a kindness? He leans across, kisses her salty mouth, says, Of course, we should get married.

Now, right now, she says. She is always like that. Everything has to be now, she doesn't have time to wait.

I know it's for real, she says. But I want to pretend it isn't and I want you to pretend as well.

I'm not making a choice between you and God, he says.

Oh I think you will.

She kisses him then, lying on top of him, freezing and slippery, making his clothes wet. She pushes her mouth against his too hard, so that their teeth bang together, and when finally she moves away from him, he sees that she's got his blood on those unnaturally white teeth. And as he kisses her he feels sure that he could enter her world, that he could stop worrying, enjoy the time they have.

Now, she says. Now. And he agrees to her plan willingly because he knows that there is no escape. For her, marriage is just a good day out. It has no significance beyond that. She can't allow him to take the risk of love. And he has to accept that, because there is no choice. But still those images fill his mind – axes, stones, blood, strangling. He knows that he is trying to take possession of something that can't be possessed. Like getting married to a cloud.

# 33

## BEFORE

### Mollie – Worcester, July 1953

The visitor is in the drawing room. Mollie puts her satchel down and watches him through the crack at the hinge of the door. Usually nobody ever comes to the house. Her mother and stepfather go out but people don't come in. Cook said that the visitor is a friend of Mollie's mother – or perhaps a cousin – but her mother doesn't have any cousins, or any relatives at all, and this man is foreign-looking, grubby. He wears no hat and his overcoat is stained. The bottom half of his face is the colour of dried blood and one of his trouser legs is strangely crumpled. He might only have one leg. But still he's a visitor and dreams might be hidden within the folds of that dirty coat, or concealed inside that crumpled trouser leg.

Mollie is the princess in the tower on top of the hill, the beauty who's been asleep for one hundred years, waiting for her lover's kiss. But just at the moment, she doesn't look like a princess. Instead she's limp and shiny after a shimmering-hot school day. If only she had time to change. She has black patent-leather shoes and several pink and white silk dresses which Bertie, her stepfather, bought for her. They hang in a white wood wardrobe in her bedroom. The wardrobe has heart shapes cut out of the door and the same shapes are on the white headboard of her bed – like Little Red Riding Hood.

The pink and white dress – but there is no time. A visitor is here. Cocktail parties, bridge evenings, dinners, golf. Mollie hears about such things but she has no experience of them.

She never goes anywhere except to school and back. Perhaps if she's charming to this man he'll invite her – although she can't imagine going to a party with a man in a stained overcoat. But still she'll behave as her mother would expect. Cook must be asked to provide tea and biscuits, if she hasn't already done so. Mollie will make amusing conversation, offer the stranger a cigarette. She glides through the door of the sitting room, the perfect hostess.

The man turns, stands awkwardly, then stares and stares, his eyes wide and deep as tunnels. Mollie twists her arms behind her back, swings herself from side to side, looks down at the floor. Why is he staring? She wonders if her school dress is tucked into her knickers, runs her hands down the gingham cotton to check. The man is examining every detail of her, as though trying to convince himself of her existence.

You're Mollie, he says.

The man's voice has a strange lilt, the sound rising at the end of each word.

Yes.

And there's another Mollie?

No.

Ah, I see, the stranger says, although he clearly doesn't.

Mollie feels as though she has been caught out in a lie. Perhaps there is another Mollie and this stranger knows that? It's always seemed as though there might be some other Mollie, a girl who would fit into the pink and white painted bedroom, a girl with pale red hair perhaps, who would go out to parties with her mother and stepfather.

And your mother has – remarried?

Mollie doubts this man is a friend of her mother's. My stepfather is Bertie Fawcett, she says. He's General Manager of Roxwell Engineering, which is one of the biggest companies in Worcester. Mollie is aware that this sounds boastful but just the sound of Bertie's name might anchor this situation, might untangle the conversation.

I am Arthur Bonacci, the man says.

Mollie stretches out her hand and the stranger takes it. His grip is warm and dry, his hand enfolds all of hers, his fingers hold hers tenderly.

Warwick Road. Coventry. The house was cordoned off when I got there. I was told the back of it had been blown off, the stranger says. ,

Yes, Mollie says. Yes. We've had a lot of problems with the house. The roof has been redone and they had to dig out the foundations as well.

So this stranger must know her mother well or how would he know about the foundations? Now the stranger is looking around him, taking in the dimensions of the room, the mirror over the mantelpiece, the velvet-covered sofa with its tasselled and sequinned cushions. Perhaps this stranger also knows that soon the house will fall down? Mollie's mother has told her so many times about the structural problems which no builder can solve. Despite the fact that the roof has been redone, and the wiring and the plumbing, despite the fact that the timbers in the cellar have been replaced and the foundation underpinned, cracks will move like spiders down the wall. The glass in the windows is so fragile that it might blow in at any minute, the foundations are too shallow and no matter how many fires you light you'll never get warm. It's a house on the edge of a cliff and at any moment the land may shift. Mollie begins to forgive the stranger for his dirty coat, his foreign voice, his missing leg. He understands and Mollie is less alone.

I was looking for Violet, the stranger says. She's my cousin. I've been away for ten years – more. In Italy. Violet used to live in Coventry before the war. But now I'm not sure. There is some confusion.

Mollie begins to understand. This man has been injured in the war, has been wandering on the Continent for several years, uncertain even of his own identity. Mollie knows about people injured in the war. Her friend at school's father has got one side of his face crushed and an eye missing. Down in the city, near the cathedral, men sit around on benches, babbling and drinking beer from bottles. One has a leg which finishes at the ankle and is wrapped in a bloody sock.

Arthur Bonacci isn't so badly injured but the war has sent his mind upside down. Now that Mollie understands, she knows she must help. A clean overcoat must be found. Perhaps he needs a hot bath. Mollie imagines herself as a nurse, turning a hospital corner, pressing a cold flannel against the man's forehead. She may even need to clean the bleeding, gristly stump of his leg, but she'll do that heroically if that's what needs to be done.

This is my mother, Mollie says, and points at a photograph in a silver frame on the mantelpiece. Surely once the stranger sees a picture of her mother and Bertie then he'll be able to sort it out? But the plan isn't working. The stranger is staring at the photograph, holding it up close to his face, eating it up with those gaping eyes.

I don't understand, he says. Rose Mayeford. Alive. Still alive. I don't understand. Then his face changes. Perhaps I should go. It was not a good idea for me to come. I wouldn't want to offend Rose, to make difficulties. I always had the greatest respect for her.

No, don't go. Please don't go. There's no need at all.

Again the stranger is staring. Then he puts his hand out and touches her cheek. Mollie Mayeford, he says. Alive. I saw you with your mother that morning but then you were listed as dead and I could never understand – Mollie Mayeford.

So that is the name of the other Mollie, the one with the pale red hair who would look just right in the pink and white bedroom. Such a lovely name. Mollie Mayeford. A name for a film star or a singer. Mollie can see the name glittering in neon lights outside a London theatre as long black cars roll along the raining streets, crammed with the furs and cigars of all the people who are coming to see the show. Mollie Mayeford. So much better than Mollie Fawcett, which sounds like plumbing.

Red Rose, that's what they called your mother. She sang beautifully.

I can sing as well, Mollie says.

But of course you can. What do you like to sing?

'Salley Gardens.' Mollie doesn't know why she suggests this song but it's always been one of her favourites and she's never usually allowed to sing it as her mother doesn't like it.

I shall sing with you, the stranger says.

Immediately he starts – and from his dirty overcoat and wobbly leg an extraordinary sound rises – a clear, pure sound, gently piercing, like a ray of early spring sun. *Down by the Salley Gardens my love and I did meet.* Mollie had expected to be nervous about joining him but she finds her voice drawn into his. Together their voices swoop and glide, dancing over the notes. *She bid me take love easy as the leaves grow on the trees.* He is the prince who has come to rescue the princess from the castle.

When they have finished, the stranger says, We must open the windows, it's far too hot in here. Then we'll sing again.

Oh but you can't open the window, Mollie says. But this man *can* open the window. In his hands, it will simply sweep open. The frame will not break, the lock will not stick, the glass will not shatter. And sure enough he goes over and sweeps the French windows open, steps out onto the terrace. Mollie follows him, stooping to unbolt the second door, copying his confident gesture. Below violets cascade down the lawn. And beyond trees hide the allotments, the stained red brick of the city of Worcester. The railway station, full of people who are going somewhere.

Mollie is amazed. She knows the garden, of course, because she's spent hours playing there, alone, making dens out of swept-up leaves. But she's never been aware of the frontiers between the garden and the house. For her, the only access to the garden has always been by the back door, which is around the other side. No windows are ever opened, and certainly not the French windows. But now it seems that one can simply fling the French windows open and step out onto the terrace – and nothing happens, nothing at all. Except that the fresh air flows into the house and the sun and the smell of the garden. Mollie is so thrilled that she turns on the spot with her hands stretched wide.

You know I'm going to be a dancer when I'm older and a singer and an actress, she says. At the end of this year I'm going to go to London – there are far more opportunities there. I've got an audition here next week – at the Swan Theatre.

Mollie's mind drifts away to the Swan and its deep red and gold interior and the glass boxes in the foyer full of photographs of past programmes and productions. And she thinks of actors and actresses emerging from the stage door, laughing down the steep steps and into the street. When Bertie takes her to the theatre, which he does often, he always allows her to wait at the stage door to see them coming out. And he buys a programme for her and she keeps them in a drawer in her room.

Oh so you're old enough to leave school already?

Oh yes, of course, Mollie says. Usually when she talks about her stage career, grown-ups tell her off for making things up. She's glad Arthur is wise enough to know the truth.

I'm sure you'll be a huge success, the stranger says.

Mollie feels her face turning bright with excitement and shame.

Let me put the record player on, she says. She isn't allowed to touch the record player but it must be all right when a visitor is here. She steps through the French windows, leans into the cabinet, lowers the needle onto the record which lies on the turntable. *Paradise here, paradise close, just around this corner. The place where happiness is for me.* The room begins to dance – the crystal lights beside the mantelpiece sway to the tune, the pattern on the carpet swirls, even the metal fireguard loosens its grip. When Mollie looks up at the stranger, she knows she's done the right thing because he smiles at her suddenly, a broad smile. And he steps forward and takes her hand, drawing her out again through the French windows onto the terrace.

But Cook – face like the head of a hammer – appears at the French windows.

Mollie, you were told not to. And opening the window – you were told on no account – now you go upstairs and stay upstairs.

Mollie starts to argue but Cook is vicious and Mollie doesn't want anything to spoil the sun and the music and the touch of the stranger's finger against her cheek. Mollie's mother will be back soon and she will be impressed by the way in which Mollie has dealt with this situation. Together they will be able to help this man. And maybe it won't even matter about the French windows waving open in the breeze and the record player singing.

Goodbye, she says. I'll be back in just a moment. Briefly she lays a hand on the stranger's arm. For a moment, he looks down at her and something in his look surprises her. He may be injured, confused and grubby but there's a strange solidity and grandeur to him. The house will fall – she knows that and he knows it. But even after it has all come tumbling down, he will still be standing here, quite unmoved, amidst the broken beams and crumbled walls. And her name will be up in lights. Mollie Mayeford. A star. Mollie feels Cook's cold gaze and hurries out of the room, her feet still dancing to the music.

As she crosses the landing, she hears the rattle of coat hangers. So her mother is already home. Then why hasn't she gone downstairs to see the visitor? Mollie hesitates. Something in the air has shifted and the evening heat now feels like a wall of resentment but still Mollie enters the room. Her mother, thin and brittle, is in her slip, searching through the wardrobe for an evening dress. On the dressing table, bubbles rise up through a glass of gin and tonic. The slip is made of black satin and above it the bones of her mother's back stick out, and her black hair, touched with grey now, falls in waves. On her shoulder that claret mark burns, a circular dent which puckers the skin. Mollie's mother has heard her enter but doesn't turn.

Sorry, darling, but I'm late back and your father will be here to pick me up in five minutes. Bridge with the Brakesons. She turns from the wardrobe and smiles. How was your day at school?

Mummy, there's a man in the sitting room. He's waiting to see you.

Yes, darling. I know. I've asked Cook to show him out. He's made a mistake. He must have been given the wrong address.

Mollie watches as her mother takes a sip of gin, then steps into the black evening dress with its tight bodice and full skirt. Her mother is so proud of that dress but Mollie knows that she herself would look much better in it. And in a dress like that she could go out to bridge – but no, not that. She wants to dance and she could have gone with the visitor. Or at least she wanted to say goodbye to him. If only she could fall gravely ill. She imagines herself lying in bed pale and shivering, wrapped in eiderdowns, warmed by hot-water bottles while solicitous adults hover, whispering.

That man knew about the house, she says.

The room smells of lemon and gin. Everything in it – the silver hairbrushes, the sheets and towels, the dressing gown on the back of the door – is monogrammed with her mother's initials. V.F. Violet Fawcett. Mollie thinks monograms are silly. After all, who forgets their own name? Her mother is applying eyeshadow, leaning down towards her mirror. Her hand draws back, her eyes open wider, she stares at Mollie in the mirror, turns. Her face is blank but patches of red have appeared on her cheeks. Mollie's fingers wander over an evening bag which lies on the bed – it is oblong and black with a golden snake clasp. Her fingers click the catch open and shut.

You talked to him? she says.

Yes. You weren't here so I thought someone should talk to him.

Well, you shouldn't have done. What were you thinking of? How could you behave in such a cheap way?

I thought he was a friend.

What house? her mother says. What did he say about the house?

Mollie doesn't answer, lays the black evening bag back on the bed. She had wanted her mother to be impressed. Surely she'd done the right thing? She'd entertained their guest. She imagines him now, in the sitting room, as the house comes tumbling down.

Sorry, darling. I don't mean to be grumpy. It's just that I'm in a hurry. You know Bertie doesn't like to be kept waiting. Do tell me – what did that man say about the house?

He just said – that there had been problems with it.

Oh yes – only that?

He was looking for his cousin who is called—

Mollie's mother jerks her hand, knocks the eyeshadow case to the floor. Then reaches for her glass, gulps, looks around the room as though it's a prison, a place where she has been incarcerated for many years, but still continues to search every day for a chink in the stonework, a loose bar at the window. Mollie, that man was ill in his head – mad. You understand that, don't you?

Yes, he was injured in the war.

He is mad, of course, but still Mollie must take his part, bear witness to whatever it was that he'd wanted to say. Her mother picks up the eyeshadow case off the floor, wiping the tiny spray of sparkling silver from her fingers. Then she spins around the bedroom, gathering cigarettes and a lighter into her evening bag, clipping on pearl earrings and a necklace, stopping by the mirror to put on another layer of powder. So what else did he say?

He said he knew my father.

Rubbish. Total rubbish. And what else?

He was looking for someone called Rose.

Rose?

Mollie's mother stops by the glass of gin, stares at it for a minute, then drains it down. Mollie, listen to me. I've just said, haven't I? I've just explained – that man is mad and so what possible interest could it be to either you or me what he says?

None, Mollie says. None whatsoever.

Good. Right. Well, I'm glad we've got that sorted out. Now please make sure to do your homework and be in bed before nine. And be sure to bolt the door as soon as I've gone. Cook has got a corned-beef sandwich for you when you want it.

This is how it always is. Her mother is always leaving, always going out somewhere. Her stepfather doesn't want to go out every night. Mollie knows that because she hears the arguments. Her stepfather fights for her but he never wins and never will. And so every night he comes straight from the office, picks up Mollie's mother and then they set out to a dinner, or drinks or bridge. Now Mollie wanders to the window at the back and stares down onto the drive. Her stepfather stands in his shirtsleeves and tie next to the curving arc of the wheel guards at the front of the car. It is already turned around, ready to leave. He looks up and waves at her. She waves back, blows him a kiss. His face is kindly, confused, and he keeps on waving for too long. She wants to call down to him, to warn him, to tell him that she's holding a stick of dynamite, has a match to the fuse.

Mollie's mother picks up her fur from the back of a chair and swings out of the room, her heeled shoes thudding on the landing carpet. Mollie follows her and the house shudders. Her mother reaches the top of the stairs, starts to descend.

But how did that man know my name?

Mollie's mother turns and looks up, her face white as the moon in the shadows of the stairs, suspended there, shocked and staring. Listen, Mollie. Listen. I am alive. We are alive. Do you know how incredibly lucky we are? Just to be alive – today. Even just this one day. Mollie's mother hurries on down the stairs, into the shadows of the hall. Mollie has heard her mother say this before – *I am alive* – but is it true? Is being alive rationed? Perhaps there isn't enough alive-ness to go around. If one person has it, then others can't.

Fairy tales are silly. Why do princesses always wait? Mollie follows her mother down the stairs, opens the front door and steps out onto the drive. She feels herself glowing like a lamp, knows herself to be dangerous. Mollie's mother is stepping across the drive, departing, endlessly departing. Wearing a fur coat now, despite the July heat. Tottering slightly on her high heels, drawn to Bertie as though by a magnet. And he moves to meet her, enfolding her, shielding her, the two of them moving together in an awkward shuffle, a three-legged race. Her mother's face turned into the shadows, offering only a vague backward wave of her hand.

She gets into the front seat of the car, folding the skirt of her dress in carefully. Bertie is about to shut the door when he hears Mollie's footstep. His face shines as it always does when he sees her and for a moment Mollie thinks he might step forward and kiss her but he doesn't dare.

Mollie, what are you doing? Her mother's voice has the same sharp metallic snap as the catch on her evening bag.

I just—

Something has changed. Mollie isn't frightened of her mother any more because she only has to say those words – *how did that man know my name?* She's spent all her life trying to please her mother. What a relief now to know that she'll never succeed, that perhaps there are other people she could please. In the far distance, she hears the whistle of a train coming into the station, full of people who are going somewhere.

I just might go for a walk.

Behind her, Mollie feels the house shudder. It's falling. If she goes upstairs she will open a door and find that the wall at the front of the house has gone missing. She'll stand in her mother's bedroom and stare straight down into the garden. And then the floor will tip and she'll drop forward, slipping and falling, down and down, through the clear air.

What?

I walk to school and back.

Yes, but you can't walk now. Not in the evening. Not on your own.

Mollie knows she will walk and that she'll fail to bolt the door when she returns.

Well, why not? Bertie says. Why ever not? It's a fine evening. It won't hurt for her to go up and down our street.

Cook has been given instructions.

Well, I shall change the instructions, Bertie says and strides towards the house.

Mollie and her mother stand in silence, avoiding each other's eyes. Mollie might like to smile in triumph but instead feels pity for her mother, who stares about her, adjusts her hair, feigns indifference. Bertie's voice is heard in the hall and he returns, smiling.

All settled, he says.

Bertie. We're due there at seven. We really must go.

Smoke will pour out of the roof, the foundations will give, the timbers will shatter, windows will drop out of their frames and the whole thing will crash down in a cloud of plaster dust, splitting open, spilling tables, chairs, glass, record players, theatre programmes, white painted furniture with holes cut out into the shape of hearts. Down and down towards the allotments, the railway line, the canal.

Bertie. We really must.

Her mother slams the car door. Bertie smiles at Mollie, tips his head towards her – saluting their joint victory. Watching him as he gets into the car, Mollie feels the knowledge that stretches between them like a gossamer thread. And the love. It'll always be there – no matter how often he goes out for the evening, no matter that her walks will soon take her far beyond his street. She smiles at him and rocks gently back and forward from the toes of her school shoes to the heels, testing out the idea of walking, of heading out through the gates of the house and into whatever lies beyond. The engine splutters, roars and the car slides away, low and glistening, the rattle of its engine growing as it pulls away through the gates.

Mollie walks down to the end of the drive and out through the gates but there is no sign of Arthur. She walks up and down the street a couple of times, beside the wisteria-clad walls, garage doors and gates leading to other houses. And she wonders about being alive. Then she heads back to the house and walks in through the front door, leaving it open so that it can blow in the wind, so the glass in the panels can smash. Let the house fall, pull it down, plant a bomb in it, blow it to bits.

The sitting room will never be the same again. It's been stretched into the shape of the stranger, continues to carry his imprint. She goes to the cocktail cabinet, pours herself a gin and tonic, switches the gramophone on and steps out onto the terrace. She imagines the stranger is still there, holding her against him, her feet moving in time with his, as he turns her across the cracked paving stones. Below her the fading red-brick city, the cathedral, the River Severn, the Malvern Hills are replaced by the glow of floodlights, the glitter of sequins as the music from the gramophone quicksteps her away into beckoning and brilliant uncertainty.

## 34

# Now

### Lara – Brighton, April 2003

Lara is keeping her side of the bargain. God – or whoever else – will look after Jay. Everything happens for a reason. This is the story she tells herself and it must be true because she got a buyer for the flat immediately. Six people came to see it the first day and now a couple moving down from London want to proceed. Lara isn't surprised, she takes this as tribute to her talent for design – even though that concept has come to seem irrelevant. And this is part of the plan, this is how it's meant to be. She hasn't heard yet when the sale might happen but she's got to be ready.

It's eleven in the morning and she hasn't put the radio on, or the television. She knows that Jay will be all right. He's doing what he wants to do. The days are unfolding as they should. American troops have reached the outskirts of Baghdad so maybe they'll take control of the city soon and then Jay will be safe. She surveys her bedroom and plans the next stage of the packing – her wardrobe first and then the chest of drawers. Everything must go, she knows that. The flat has been a drug, an addiction. Flats should be harmless but this one has eaten her. She offers it up as a penance, gladly. The only problem is Jay's room. How can she begin to unstick his posters from the wall or put his greasy bike bits into a box?

As she sorts through shoes in her wardrobe, she thinks of Oliver, of that strange moment on the seafront. She *had* wanted to kiss him – and more – but it was right that she didn't. She wouldn't want to take second place after Grace. And if she'd started to kiss him, they would have finished up in bed, but after two weeks it would have come to an ugly end. She can't afford that, she needs Oliver, he's her friend. Even inside her head, she uses that word with care because she knows now that she's never properly understood what it means. That must be the case because otherwise why is she alone here with no one to help her? No one to drive a defunct CD player to the tip or offer a home to a shabby houseplant?

When Jay first left people did ring up but she never returned the calls and now they don't ring any more. When she told her friend Annabel – and others – that she'd left her job they'd behaved as though someone had died, which was odd because for years those same people had nagged her to give up her job, or cut down her hours. But now she's done it, they seem curiously unnerved. And then Annabel came around a few days ago and burst into tears. *Oh Lara, I've been such a bad friend to you. I haven't given you what you need.* Lara had made tea and dispensed comfort while thinking – isn't this the wrong way round?

But she'd quelled that thought because she's trying to be good now, although it's hard to know where to begin. If God wants people to be good He should make it easier.

She finds the jacket at the bottom of a box on the top shelf of the wardrobe. It's green suede, with a leather collar and cuffs. The elbows are shiny and creases suggest the bend of her arms. She remembers that stain down near the pocket – was it red wine or coffee in that London café? The stain is shaped like an upside-down horseshoe. Perhaps that should have served as a warning? She pulls the coat out of the box. It feels powdery, smells of dust. A green leather button dangles from a thread. She slides an arm into the jacket and it settles around her as though it's arriving home, as though the last twenty years or so have suddenly evaporated.

She'd worn the jacket in the short period of her youth. She must have bought it in a second-hand shop when she was in the sixth form at Frencham Heights. Everyone there could afford as many new clothes as they wanted and consequently bought all their clothes second-hand. At that time Lara had been expecting to go to university and become a lawyer. The world a luxurious department store displaying exotic possibilities.

She wore the jacket later as well – after Jay was born.

In the park she would count the laps – ten, twenty, thirty, forty. Through rain and sleet, through puddles which crackled with ice, watching the other people who still had their lives. Jay wouldn't even allow her to go to the loo on her own. He followed her in and held onto her knee, trying to help her with the loo paper but dropping it so that it unravelled all over the place, and she had to ravel it up again. She remembers once weeping uncontrollably because it was so very hard to wind the paper back onto the roll.

The jacket feels slightly damp and stiff but it fits her. Over the last two months that extra stone which she's spent twenty years trying to shift has fallen away of its own accord. So now she's the size she was when she was eighteen. And looking in the mirror now, she sees that she's become the kind of woman she's always despised. No make-up, ragged hair, wearing jeans, trainers and a stained old jacket. She runs her hands down the powdery material of the jacket, leans down to examine the stain.

Strangely, at times over the last two weeks she's enjoyed being in the peace protest office. The people there may be the walking wounded but at least they are still walking. One evening Wilf put music on and they shared a bottle of cheap vodka. Martha had got tipsy and danced with the dog until everyone cried with laughter. Lara had wondered whether she might be starting to have the teenage years she'd missed. And even the morning after the vodka, she'd found herself sparkling with energy. For the first time in her life, she's on the side of right. Moral rectitude is clearly good for your health.

Looking in the mirror again, she imagines her life unravelling backwards. Like one of those old-fashioned cine machines, the tape unspooling and spilling onto the floor. There she is as she was two months ago, wearing her suit for work, going to London every day, backwards and backwards to the moment when she bought this flat ten years ago. And there she is, moving in the furniture, and then on again, backwards, to her first day working for Craig, in the original Brighton office, putting on a black Lycra pencil skirt and a black roll-neck jumper, sheer tights, plenty of make-up, a gold necklace and large gold earrings shaped like hearts. Leaving Jay with Mollie. Was it wrong? At the time she'd felt that, once again, she was leaving behind all the mess of her childhood and turning into the person she was always meant to be. So why has everything started going in reverse? It's a surprise to find that she's not unhappy – now that she's become the kind of person she never wanted to be. She realises that, all of her life, she has made the fundamental mistake of believing herself, and the events of her life, to be significant.

Still wearing the coat, she heads down to the kitchen to make herself a coffee. The kitchen table is spread with envelopes sent by letting agents. She rang five of them last week, in a sudden panic, knowing that she would need to find somewhere else to live. She's seen the envelopes arrive but hasn't opened them. She needs to take a brutal approach to this business. She will not be seduced by a wrought iron balcony, a Scandinavian light fitting, Eames-style kitchen chairs. When she opens one of those envelopes and takes out the list which will doubtless be inside, she's going to look at the flat which is second up from the bottom, and she's going to work from right to left, and the first two-bedroom flat she comes to which costs less than eight hundred pounds a month, and is reasonably central, is the one she's going to rent.

The place has to be basic, perhaps even a little squalid. Like the recovering alcoholic with the one sniff of whisky, the promise of Farrow & Ball paint, or Fired Earth tiles, could prove her undoing. She eases open an envelope, pulls out the rental list, thumbs through the expensive family properties at the beginning until she comes to the one- and two-bedroom flats at the back. Second row up from the bottom. Preston Park – too far away. Woodingdean – also too far. The next one is marked Central. It's in a Georgian-style town house but the paint on the window frame is peeling and the walls are stained.

But that isn't the only problem. Something else about the flat unsettles her. She looks at the address – 42B Roma Street. The flat is owned by Mollie. She has to take the first one she sees – she promised herself that. But no, she can't go and live in a flat owned by Mollie. Of course, Mollie needs tenants and particularly ones who might pay the rent. And the flat is certain to be squalid enough for her requirements. But no, she'll have to try again.

She opens another envelope. This time she'll take whichever property is in the top column, furthest to right, on the second page of two-bedroom flats. She finds that page, looks in the top right-hand corner. The property is 42B Roma Street. She crumples the magazine closed and drops it back on the pile. She feels like the victim of a practical joke. She opens another envelope. This time she'll give herself two choices – either the first flat listed on page two or the first one listed on page three. The first one listed on page two is in Heron Street. It's central and has two bedrooms. A photo is included. The flat has swirling carpets and even in the photograph Lara can almost see them crackling with static. A picture of the kitchen shows shiny pine and brown tiles. The woman with the frizzy red hair, no make-up and a stained jacket will fit in there just fine. Right, I'll ring the agent first thing to tomorrow, she thinks and pours herself a coffee. Then she decides that she'll look at which one was on the third page – just to check. 42B Roma Street.

The phone rings and she stops at the kitchen door, hesitates. Then she walks slowly into the sitting room. No need to panic, everything will be fine. But as she tries to put her coffee cup down she misses the shelf and the cup falls, the black stain of it spreads across the boards. For a moment, Lara worries about the stain and then she remembers. Soon these boards will not be hers any more so what does it matter? She hears Spike's voice – We've had a message. Apparently they hit the Palestine Hotel but we can't find out. The news is on one of the Arab websites.

I'm coming, Lara says. I'm coming. She steps over the spilt coffee and grabs her bag. As far as she knows, Jay isn't in the Palestine Hotel but loads of journalists are and he knows those people, they invite him to go there. The streets reel past her – the pub, the corner shop, the entrance to the park gates.

In the peace protest office, Spike and Wilf are crowded around the television. As always, Ahmed is fixed to the computer screen. Martha is on the telephone. We've seen a report. Are you able to confirm? No, the report is on an Arab website. The Palestine Hotel. Yes, yes. We've heard that there has been an explosion to the east of the centre. Yes, we've heard that. So you haven't heard anything more?

On the television screen smoke is rising from a building but Lara knows immediately that it isn't the Palestine. It must be that other bomb to the east. She picks up the remote control and switches to another channel. Wait a minute, Spike says. Wait a minute. We need to see this.

That isn't the Palestine Hotel.

Yeah, I know.

What did they say? Lara says to Martha, who has put the phone down.

They don't know. They haven't heard.

We've got to find out, Lara says. Jay could be there. He goes there.

Lara, please, Spike says.

The dog in the box starts to shuffle and whine.

Now come on, please, Martha says. Everyone keep calm. You know he's a rescue dog and his nerves are bad.

She bends to pet the dog, her plaits swinging.

Where is this website? Let me see.

Lara, can you just please switch back to the channel we were on?

Show me the website. Lara leans over Ahmed's shoulder, looks at what is on his screen but he's reading a report about that other bomb.

Listen, can you just show me where you saw it?

He'll do it in a minute. If you could just wait.

You don't understand.

Ahmed turns and silence rises across the room like the pulling up of a drawbridge. Lara has only seen Ahmed's face once before, months ago, at the Guest House when he was explaining about the nineteen pence he owed for the second-class stamp. Now his black marble eyes are fixed on her and his mouth is set in a tight line. Can you shut up? Can you just shut up because I'm trying to read this?

Well, I'm sorry. But I'm just asking.

I know what you're asking.

Listen. I just want to see that website.

No, Miss Ravello. No. You just listen to me. This is my country here. This is my country that is dying here. And this is not about some journalists who may be staying at a hotel. This is about the whole of my country. And a bomb has gone into a residential area and this is what we need to know about. We need to know what is happening to my country, to the people there.

OK. OK. I'm sorry.

No. You are not sorry at all. You care for nothing except yourself and your son. But your son went to this country through his own choice.

Yes but—

No. You listen to me now. This is not about you and your son. This is about my country. Because people have died in this building and each of those people who have died is somebody's son. And over the last ten years hundreds and thousands have died. And they were all somebody's son. But you, you can't understand that.

I do – I'm trying to help. I got a loan to pay for the lawyer, I'm selling my flat. Lara hears her voice like the jangling of a triangle in a force ten gale.

You don't care, Ahmed says. You don't care at all. Let me show you. Let me explain. Let me make you understand. You want to know what is happening in my country then I'm going to show you. Ahmed reaches into the drawer of the desk. His fingers rip at an envelope and he pulls out photographs. You come here. You come with me. I will show you what is happening in my country. And in my family. I will show you my brother. You will see.

Ahmed is spreading the photographs out on the desk behind him. Lara's eyes stray to the television. Still there is no mention of the Palestine Hotel.

Look please, Miss Ravello. See. See what is here.

Lara looks down at the table. A photograph of a charred body. Next to it a photograph of a corpse with both of the hands amputated. Lara raises her hands to her mouth, feels her stomach rise. She looks away but he shouts. Look. Look. Will you look at this? In this place – they found a meat grinder there.

The images jumble in her mind. Legs without bodies, bodies without legs. A man's torso with puncture wounds all across it, a man with his face beaten to a pulp – is he alive or dead? Lara tastes acid in her throat. This is like something you see in a film but this isn't a film.

This is what is happening in my country. These are somebody's sons. Somebody's daughter. This here. This here. He points at a photograph of a corpse. My brother. You understand. Ahmed is gulping as he speaks. This my brother. He went for me. He went to complain after I lost my job. He did that for me and I should never have let him do it. Or I should have gone with him. And so it was my fault.

Ahmed turns, wipes his hand across his eyes, walks out of the room, the rhythm of his feet sure and slow on the stairs. Lara sits down beside the photographs, feels herself starting to cry. The room is silent. No one looks at anyone else and no one looks at the photographs spread on the desk. The phone rings and Martha goes to answer it.

I'm sorry, Lara says. I'm sorry. But she knows that sorry isn't going to be enough. No words are of any relevance now. Her eyes stray back to the photographs. She thinks of these people now, of their suffering, of the people that mourn them. She thinks of Ahmed and his dignified silence, the neatness of his clothes, the long hours spent washing up at the hotel, followed by the unending hours in this office. Briefly she longs for her mother but knows that Mollie would side with Ahmed, not with her. Everyone will always side with him.

She heads to the door, wondering where he might have gone. She walks upstairs and looks through the door of the café and into the Community Centre. Then she goes to the door of the church but he isn't there. She heads out into the street, and stops, uncertain which way to turn. She sees him, sitting on the seat of the bus stop at the end of the road, his head bent down, staring at his clasped hands.

She crosses the road towards him, then stops. It won't do any good to say she's sorry. As she watches him, she sees the size of the gulf that separates them, a gulf which can't be crossed. Her world and his will never meet. Even if it turns out that Jay has died in a bomb attack, the divide will still be there. She can pay for a lawyer, she can even sell her flat but she can never begin to understand. She'd been told, of course, that he'd lost some of his family in Iraq but, if she'd thought about it at all, she'd assumed they'd been shot. She hadn't thought of torture, or mutilation. Her mind convulses again at the thought of those images. Ahmed looks up, sees her standing there. He sits up straighter, moves his hand to the knot of his tie, then rubs his hands together.

I am sorry, he says. I am sorry that I was angry with you.

She stares at him, searches for words. No. No. You mustn't be sorry. I'm sorry. I'm very sorry. I didn't understand. I didn't think. I'm sorry.

He nods his head, gets up.

Please, she says. I am trying. I will do anything. You just have to tell me.

He nods his head, considers this question. Right now what we need is an extra power point, he says. An electrician. This would be most helpful.

Lara knows about the three computers and printer all loaded onto one plug, the regular power cuts. Every day there are discussions about what can be done. But she'd wanted to offer something more, to participate in some grand plan. She longs to be forgiven for being white, affluent, safe and previously interested in interior design.

Of course, she says. Of course. You're right. I know. That is quite a problem, of course. I'll find an electrician, I should have done that before. I'll do it straight away.

Thank you, he says. Thank you very much. He walks away from her, crosses the road but then turns back.

And Miss Ravello. If you don't mind me saying as well. I think you should visit your mother. You have a mother and this is very lucky and your mother is very worried. She has been to the church and received a message from your father who is speaking to her from the dead. She needs you.

My father? Dead?

No. Sorry. Very sorry. Not your father. Somebody important but I don't know.

He nods his head, then heads back towards the church. Lara watches him go and then sinks down onto the bench. Her head is full of those photographs. She shuts her eyes but they're still there. Suddenly her body is shaken by sobs. Martha comes out and sits beside her.

We've telephoned. It wasn't true. It can't be because the BBC have been in touch with someone at the Palestine.

This news doesn't matter any more. The exact details of who's been killed aren't important. Lara stands up, wipes her eyes. A power point, an electrician. Then she sits down again. The great warm bubble of certainty which has enveloped her for the last two weeks has burst. She was so sure she had found her purpose, her mission. She'd thought she'd found a way of relating to Jay, a way of pleasing God so that Jay would come home safe. But now it's all gone. Ahmed is right. She doesn't understand and she can't understand. This war has arrived in her life and she's part of it but it isn't her war, her world.

Instead it's all about power points – and Mollie. 42B Roma Street. And now Ahmed criticising her for being a bad daughter. She looks back on the last few weeks – all the activity, that sudden moment of certainty when she'd offered to pay for a lawyer. Maybe all of it had just been a distraction, a way of getting through the day, a way of avoiding the small mess of her own life.

Come inside and I'll make you a coffee, Martha says. Or a tea.

No, no. Thanks very much. You go back. I'm all right.

Sure?

Lara nods, wipes at her eyes, crosses the road to where the Guest House is. It's silent and ghostly, like an unlit grate. She takes the key from her bag and heads up the front steps. Standing in the reception area she calls up the stairs but no one answers. Where would Mollie be? Has she gone up to London again to try to find Rufus? Lara can feel that he's gone, not gone in the usual way, not a mere ceasefire before the continuation of hostilities. But gone in some more final sense which has affected the structure of the house itself, so that the damp which has always infected the basement is now in every timber, and the pools of light from the low-hanging yellow bulbs are weaker than ever.

The cubbyhole which Mollie used as an office still remains from the time when the Guest House was operational. The brass bell sits on the desk waiting for some new arrival to ding it. Beside it, a board of photographs, which Lara stares at briefly. Rufus, Rufus, Rufus. He is everywhere, occupying every inch of space, occupying all the space. But you can never know him. He needs so much effort to hold himself together that he has no time for anyone else. Lara peers more closely at a faded photograph. Rufus with Liam. Strange, she's walked past this board of photographs hundreds of times but she's never really noticed that photograph before. A wilful unseeing. Odd how Liam disappeared from their lives so entirely. Even in the photograph only half of his face appears, the rest of the space being occupied by Rufus. *Your mother has received a message from your father who is speaking to her from the dead.* Lara shakes her head as she thinks of Ahmed's mistake. It's certainly possible to believe that not even death would silence Rufus.

Lara peers in through the door of the sitting room. Mollie never uses this room because it's meant to be reserved for the guests, but they never use it either. The décor is all heart-shaped cushions, pictures of fluffy cats, ovals of lace marooned on polished table tops. Lara backs away, wanders down to the kitchen. A sewing machine is out on the table – not Mollie's old Singer but a large and modern machine. On a rail by the radiator a rack of clothes are drying, among them several small white thongs decorated with pink hearts. Presumably they belong to the girl who Lara saw entering the Guest House the other day. Lara imagines her and Mollie together in the evening, cooking supper, chatting, drinking tea. Something about the pants – hanging there so innocently – causes a gush of sadness. It should be so simple – all she has to do is love her mother. Lara sits down at the kitchen table, longs for the day when she helped with the sewing, when her pants dried next to the radiator, when she was a contented and good daughter, longs for a world in which that day really existed.

# 35

# Now

## Oliver – Brighton, April 2003

Oliver works with a bucket and mop, soaking up rainwater that has come in through the roof. He knew the rain would come in – it was heavy and vertical. Rain blown at an angle doesn't come in but vertical rain does. It's happened several times over the last few weeks. April weather – bright sun and then a sudden deluge which leaves the city steamy. Oliver half expects rickshaws in the streets and houses with tin roofs.

Occasionally the vicar, who has two other churches to care for as well, tells Oliver of his worries about the surveyor's report which revealed ten years ago that the roof needs stripping off, totally rebuilding. Oliver offers words of encouragement but isn't worried himself. This church, along with most others, is an abandoned building and so it's appropriate that rain should come in through the roof.

Oliver looks at his watch, finds that the day has already slipped away. He finishes the mopping and tips the water down the sink in the kitchen behind the parish office. Then he sits down in one of the pews with the intention of doing nothing for a while, except enjoying the half darkness and the rustles and tickings of the church. Up at the front two elderly ladies in felt hats are knelt in prayer. They have been deceived, he's sure of that. And yet he understands them, and their desire for deception. He's glad that they are comforted although he can no longer participate in such comfort himself. Briefly he thinks of Lara. Now that the war is ending her son will come home and she'll return to the spacious, shiny world of normality. She'll be a little embarrassed by their friendship, deny its intensity. It'll all turn out to be one of those good news stories about how, through adversity, a woman finds her son. She keeps her bargain with God, and God keeps His with her. Such stories do exist. She'll be lost to him then and He'll miss her when she's gone. But the danger will have passed. In the world of sadness, memory, he is safe.

Behind him he hears a noise, sees a shadow slide across a wall at the back of the church. Oliver is always pleased to see people in the church, even if they're only getting out of the rain, or using the church to shelter a match that would otherwise blow out. The shadow moves, is defined as a young woman. Oliver's seen her before. She's come to the church often over the last few weeks but never as late as this. She's wavering and vivid as the candles she occasionally lights. She walks on the edge of a cliff but is sure-footed, fearless, despite the abyss below. Her hair is as long and dark as a night-time river, her ears heavy with a line of gold rings, her coat decorated with felt flowers.

Often she just sits in a pew, waiting. For what? But today she is different, purposeful, nervous. Excuse me.

Yes.

Sorry to disturb you but – as I was walking up the front steps I heard something. It was in the alleyway, to the right of the main door. It was—

Oliver waits, finds himself drawn into the panic filling her eyes.

I think there's a baby. It's crying. In the alleyway. Sorry – it was dark so I couldn't see. I know you're probably trying to lock up but we must—

Oliver knows the dank alleyway which runs along the side of the church. To one side of it an iron railing, and a locked gate, closed off steps down to a storeroom under the church which hasn't been used in years. Beyond the gate, the alley curves muddily away between black wood fences and overhanging laurels before emerging into the next street. It's seldom used except by drug addicts, fly tippers and rent boys.

Oliver has to go there sometimes because people dump rubbish bags in the alleyway or even heave them over the railing. So then he takes the key to the gate, pulls out the rubbish bags, unearths the various paraphernalia of modern pleasure – condoms, needles, cans and bottles. Discussions have taken place with the council about closing the alleyway but no money is available for gates. He's quite sure the girl is wrong. No one would dump a baby there. But there could well be some old tramp there – an old man whimpering his last breath – and Oliver will arrive too late, be powerless to save him.

He fetches the key for the gate, his hand fumbling as he takes it from the hook. He should have a torch but the last one broke and the vicar has not yet provided another. When he returns to the church, the girl is waiting for him, follows him down the aisle. She wants to run, to rescue the crying infant in the alleyway, but her movements are slow and deliberate, each step is significant. Although her coat is loose and hides the shape of her body, the knowledge comes to him that she's pregnant. He can almost feel the baby lying there, like a lump of molten metal inside her. Someone has told him a story about this girl-mother but he can't remember now.

He wants to hurry but feels that he must move in time with her, even though the imagined tramp is struggling for breath, the light suddenly passing from his stunned eyes. And still they move together down the aisle, an unlikely bride and groom, with the empty pews on either side of them and the air a vacuum, empty of music. He feels some strange desire to take her arm, to stop her from falling. But there is no danger that she will stumble. Her ability to control fear is complete.

Then he remembers – not what he was told but only that she's living with Mad Mollie Ravello. What can she be doing there? She's too unstained for such a place. Mollie had been at the service on Sunday and she'd talked to him briefly afterwards but he was in the middle of dealing with a weeping drunk. He'd thought she was talking about Jay but instead she was talking about – Ludo, was it? A man who taught her to sing. He can't remember now.

No news? he asks the girl. Of Jay?

No. But they took the airport today so that surely means something?

Oliver takes care never to see a television screen, never to hear the radio, but nevertheless this news had already drifted up to him from the peace protest office. So many people who need to be saved – a whole city, a whole country.

I knew him, the girl says. At college. It's very hard for Mollie.

Outside the darkness is shallow, the road deserted.

I've been longing so much for him to come home, the girl says.

Across the street bikes are chained to railings, and lights shine through thin curtains, televisions flicker. Oliver comes to the entrance of the alleyway and listens.

The cry, the girl says. Like someone in pain.

At first he can hear nothing because of the splutter of a passing motorbike. But then a thin, anguished cry spills towards them. The girls stretches her arms forward but he moves first, stepping into the alley. Behind the railings, a tiny flash of red light. It's either the eye of an animal or some piece of red material shimmering in the dark. It could even be the reflector of a bicycle – but who would lift their bicycle over the railings? The alley smells of urine, engine oil, rubbish bags and rotting leaves. The flash of light comes again, wavers in the darkness, disappears and then flashes again closer to the railings. He looks up at the exterior wall of the church and the narrow strip of sky above, dark grey against black. Fear flutters inside him, leaps in his throat.

It is a baby, she says. It must be.

No. No. A fox or a cat. Perhaps you should go home.

No. Not yet. I must go soon because of Mollie. But first we have to check.

A snuffling noise, the hint of a whimper. Again a flash of red in the dark. And also shapes – boxes, bins, the metal lines of the railing. The noise stops and Oliver waits. Then it comes again. Almost certainly a fox has slipped in through the railings and is going through the rubbish. The red light doesn't appear again but a crackle sounds, then a ruffling and snuffling. Short, brutal sounds. Oliver imagines a pig, a wild boar. An animal with bristles, a snout and red eyes, crouching amidst the bins and the damp cardboard boxes.

You must go, he says to the girl. You must go now.

No. No. I'd rather stay with you.

Please. You don't understand. Please.

No.

Oliver clenches his teeth in anger. Why doesn't she see? Why doesn't she go? He can't protect her from the animal behind the railings but he must try. He advances a little further. Again he sees the red eye, hears that grunting snuffle. The smell of rot and urine fills his nostrils. He knows this animal, has seen it before. It brings violence and destruction. It's come to claim someone – but who?

The girl, it must be the girl. Sweat is running down his face. Once he would have had the power to grasp the animal, choke the breath from it. Once it would have whimpered in terror, fled away. But now he's alone, entirely alone. As he was on the A23 dual carriageway, crossing the South Downs. Nothing at all between earth and infinite sky and it won't matter how long he shouts into the night for help, none will come, no one is there. So who now will defeat the animal and drive it away?

The girl steps forward, steady and certain. He wonders at her. It isn't the case that she's simply not frightened. He knows that. So why is she doing this? How does she dare? She knows as well as he does that the dog has come to take her. But she's resolute, standing staring ahead. Again he is conscious of the baby inside her. She carries it ahead of her like a flaming torch.

It's all right, she says. You're right. It was a fox – or perhaps a cat. I didn't know they could make a noise like that. But I think it's gone.

A glimmer of sound echoes from further down the alleyway. The night is settling back into itself. Oliver realises that one of his hands is pressed against the wall of the church, that he's sucking breath in. He pulls himself upright, rubs his hands together, tries to match her expression of blank ignorance.

Just a fox, she says.

Yes. Or a cat.

He sees her long, sharp face in the grainy shadows. She pulls her flower-stitched coat more tightly around her, moves her hand to adjust a swinging gold earring.

Yes, she says. One or the other. It must have got in down there where the railing is bent – see? Her face is still organised into a look of bright stupidity. Of course, she knows but she wishes to save him from this. And he's grateful for her kindness.

Stupid of me, she says.

They turn to go, reach the front steps of the church. She pushes open the door and light floods out on them. She will not allow herself to ask for anything. She might say goodnight, or thank you, or express some hope that the imagined cat will come to no harm, but instead she turns and runs lightly down the steps, is swallowed by the night.

Oliver hurries into the church and pulls the door shut behind him. He checks that the two old ladies have gone, then draws the heavy iron bolts, rushes through the church, checks that the glass doors which lead to the Community Centre at the back are secure. This is ridiculous and he knows it. Nothing more than a fox or a stray dog. But his face is still wet with sweat. And the red eyes stay in his head. He won't sleep. Even if he'd dared to go into the alleyway, it would'nt have done any good. All this is his fault. He set the animal loose. Nonsense. He tries to tame his mind, but his breath grinds as he walks up the stairs to his flat. The fox-dog will be back, of course. And Oliver knows now who it will claim.

# 36

## BEFORE

### Mollie – Worcester, October 1953

Mollie is running through the cramped and raining streets near the canal. She's going to an audition, a real audition. Her school shoes slap out that word, rainwater gathers in the gutter of her school hat, her blazer is soaked, her satchel bangs against her hip. The streets smell of canal water. But none of that matters. She's going to an audition. At a bus stop a fat woman wrestles with a bucking umbrella and men grip their hats. A voice trills – *the Severn will soon be over its banks.* Mollie slows, passes the Hop Works and a corner shop, turns into a street of red-brick terraced houses, hunched and secretive.

Mr Brandt's shop is at the end, attached to the other terraced houses, but larger. A sign on the front says The Arcade Music Emporium. The wide window is set back and edged by shiny brown tiles. Velvet-covered boxes display clarinets, flutes in their cases, and sheet music pinned up in the shape of a fan. A violin is propped forward and surrounded by triangles, castanets and recorders. Mollie can hear those instruments in her head, imagines how their sounds would mix together. The instruments are arranged in front of a velvet curtain that comes halfway up the window. A notice announces that Thorens record players are available inside.

Moving closer to the window, Mollie sees Mr Brandt, outlined against the cavernous shadows above the velvet curtain. Small and precise, he has a bald head and a small moustache. He wears a neat pinstriped suit over a small potbelly and a red handkerchief is arranged to spout from the breast pocket. The cuffs of his shirt are a delicate shade of mauve and held together by heavy gold cufflinks. And wrapped tightly around his neck is a green wool scarf which comes right up to his chin. Mollie has seen him many times before at the theatre but never spoken to him.

Audition, audition. The word is still drumming in her head, giving her courage. She's borrowed a pair of her mother's stockings and snakeskin shoes with square toes. The stockings she put on in the loo before leaving school. Now she pulls the shoes out of her satchel, pushes her wet feet into them and shoves her sodden school shoes into their place. She hesitates. In the Folies Bergère romances, the plucky, raven-haired heroine always strides into the theatre, sings like an angel, and is immediately given the main part in a musical.

She steps towards the door. The disembodied face of an old lady appears in the window of the next house, framed beside a heavy damask curtain. The lady wears a hairnet and is all white – white hair, white face, white blouse – so that Mollie wonders if she's really there at all. It seems, in the dim light, that she has no eyes, only hollows dug into her face. Mollie finds herself drawn into those hollows, unable to look away. But then the door of the shop opens and Mr Brandt is there. Mollie steps back, in her too-big shoes, and is about to turn away.

Come, come, he says. And ushers her into the velvet interior of the shop with a wave of his hand, as though he's the doorman at an elegant hotel.

You are interested in music?

Mollie is embarrassed for him because he has a foreign accent. She hopes he isn't German. Opening her mouth, she tries to ask about an audition but no words arrive. Her school satchel bulges with her school shoes and socks. It's difficult to play the part of a theatre star with that on her shoulder so she puts it down, pushes it close up against a shelf of sheet music but that only makes it more obvious. Mr Brandt is looking her up and down. He might take her between his thumb and fingers, feel the quality of her warp and weft, decide to buy a yard or not.

Yes, Mollie said, clearing her throat. Yes, I'm interested in music. She stares around at the instruments and racks of sheet music in an attempt to validate this statement. Her throat is dry and she coughs, worries that she might sneeze. Her school blazer feels soggy on her shoulders, rainwater drips from her hat. Around her the shop is strangely dark, illuminated only by a lamp on a distant desk.

I've come – I want – an audition.

An audition? Mr Brandt's black eyebrows travel up into the ridges of his forehead. He raises his finger to his lips, still considering her. His eyes seem suddenly to have too much white to them and they roll more than they should. His thick black hair lies in neat furrows as though recently combed with hair oil. The sleeve of his suit moves up his arm revealing more of the mauve shirt, the glittering gold cufflink.

Yes. I spoke to Stan, at the theatre, the doorman. And he said—

Mr Brandt laughs, moves his hand in a circular motion, as though welcoming her again. Well, good old Stan. Would you like a cigarette? He reaches into the inside pocket of his jacket, takes out a silver case, snaps it open, holds it out towards her. Ludo, he says. He twirls a cigarette in his fingers. Do call me Ludo. Mollie has never been offered a cigarette before. She worries that she won't know how to smoke it, so shakes her head. She'd felt so sure that Stan's advice must be right because Ludo does look rather like Arthur, that stranger who came to the house, who she'd loved for that brief, singing afternoon. The same dark hair and pitted olive skin but – Mollie feels disloyal to even think it – fortunately no wooden leg.

The door opens with a bang, a bell rings and three girls, followed by two much younger girls, come giggling into the shop, followed by umbrellas which they flap shut so that water sprays across the maroon carpet. The older girls have raincoats with belts pulled in at the waists and dainty, flat shoes. Their smooth hair is held in place by bands around their heads. Mollie recognises them as actresses from the theatre.

My dears, how lovely to see you. Ludo's voice has a rolling lilt to it, like a man with a limp. He grabs each of the girls and holds them against him while kissing them loudly on the lips, then he disappears to the back of the shop and returns with a glass jar of sweets. The two little girls push their hands into the jar eagerly. The prettiest of the older girls is called Donna and, as she talks to Ludo, she twists her fingers in between his. Under her mauve raincoat, her dress is low cut. The lids of her eyes glint with a line of blue shadow and her eyebrows are drawn in a high, brown arch. Behind that thick band, her dark hair is looped up into an elaborate chignon like a picture in a magazine.

Mr Dabricci sent us, Donna says. Can you play the piano for a rehearsal tonight because Mrs McClintock can't get in with the flooding at Kempsey?

Yes, yes. Of course, I'll play.

And you owe me some money? Donna says, twisting his hand in hers.

Oh do I?

Yes, for the dinner. Tuesday night.

Yes, you owe my sister money, one of the little girls says. For the dinner.

Ludo takes a tobacco tin from a drawer, pulls out a thick wad of notes, counts out a few and hands them to Donna, who puts them in her pocket, smiling.

Please, Ludo, Donna says. A drink? Please.

No, my dears. Not now – another day. Can't you see, I have a visitor. A young lady who has come for an audition. He gestures to Mollie who stands uncertainly by the harpsichord.

An audition? Donna says. She laughs, rolls her eyes, and one of the other girls digs her finger jokingly into the silk of Ludo's waistcoat, then they are gone, laughing out of the door, leaving behind a smell of rain, hairspray and boiled sweets.

I sing in the school choir, Mollie says, into the silence left by the girls. And I sing songs by Kay Starr, Jo Stafford and Billie Holiday. These are names she's read about in magazines.

Ludo continues to measure her with his eyes, calculate, estimate. Outside the light has dimmed so that now the shop is even darker than when she first entered. The glow from the desk lamp spreads a circular fuzz of yellow across the back of the shop but everything else is shadowed. The cabinets around her might contain bottles of poison, skulls or shrunken heads rather than sheet music and instruments. The door to the street seems suddenly distant. She swallows and raises her chin.

I sing in the school choir.

Of course, Ludo says. Of course, I'm sure you sing beautifully. But what about your mother? Will she not be expecting you home?

No, Mollie said. She's busy – very busy.

Oh really. I see. I s-e-e-e. Well, in that case I can audition you now.

Now?

Why not? I'm just about to shut up the shop.

Ludo produces a ring of keys from the desk drawer. Mollie swallows several times as she hears the rattle and click of the key in the lock. Ludo opens a door at the back of the shop and she follows him into a dark hallway, up narrow stairs, hearing her too-big shoes clanking on the wooden boards. In the Folies Bergère romances the plucky, raven-haired heroine is often drugged by the evil pirates and shipped to Marrakech but a prince always comes to rescue her.

Mollie had expected the upstairs of the house to contain several narrow and cramped rooms but the whole of the upstairs is just one room, with heavy curtains shutting off the back section. The walls are painted blood red and a sofa is upholstered in zebra stripes. Ludo pulls thick velvet curtains across the front window, shutting out the lights from the street. The walls are covered with theatre photographs and publicity shots of breathless young women and girls with pigtails and endless smiling teeth. Mollie keeps her eyes away from the photographs at the top that show women in their underwear, their breasts heaving above the top of laced corsets. A piano is piled high with sheet music and a camera perches on a tripod. African masks glower down from above the fireplace. A vase of white lilies stands on the mantelpiece, the water pale green, petals edged with brown, and drooping, ready to fall. In one corner a hatstand is hung with crowds of shirts – pale blue, white, lilac, striped and checked – and bunches of silk ties. Shoes and shoe trees are piled around it. Everything is thick with dust and crumbs. Mollie can't see any cobwebs but the ceiling is surely festooned with them.

Ludo motions to Mollie to sit down and so, sliding off her snakeskin shoes, she organises herself on the zebra sofa in a film-star-type pose. She should have accepted that cigarette. Tomorrow she'll buy some blue eyeshadow like Donna had. Beside her is a tiny gramophone, hardly bigger than a thick book, in a green crackled case, with a carrying handle. Mollie has seen a gramophone like this before somewhere.

What shall we play?

Ludo waves at a pile of records on the table in front of her and she looks through them. She doesn't know most of the song titles but then she comes to one she does know, that same record that she played when the stranger came to visit. She passes the record to Ludo who takes it from its sleeve, balances it neatly in his hand, then places it on the turntable. He slides the arm across the record. It clicks and the record begins to turn. He drops the needle down onto it and, with a hiss, music washes through the room. *Paradise here, paradise close, just around this corner. The place where happiness is for me.*

I don't know your name, Ludo says.

His voice jerks her out of that shadowy remembered world.

Mollie – Mollie Mayeford.

A beautiful name, Ludo says.

Mollie had known before she spoke that Ludo would enjoy that name. She'd decided to use that as her stage name as soon as the stranger Arthur had said it. It was his gift to her. Mollie Mayeford. A name for a film star or a singer. Mollie can see the name glittering in neon lights outside a London theatre, as the big black cars roll along the glistening streets, crammed with the furs and cigars of the people who are coming to see the show.

Would you like a drink? Ludo asks.

Mollie knows her mother always asks for gin and tonic but her nerve fails her.

Martini? Ludo says. Why don't you have Martini?

Oh yes please. Why not?

As Ludo's takes hold of the lid, twists, the neck of the tonic bottle appears perilously small in his engulfing hands. The bottle moves up from the glass with a flourish and then down again as he pours. His cigarette burns on an ashtray, filling the room with a blur of smoke. His black hair is combed back from his forehead, so that Mollie can see the furrows left by the comb. In the slanting light his face is long, the shadows under his cheekbones deep. She likes the way that he wears that scarf, tied up close to his neck, like a gangster or the Mafia.

The sound of banging leaps from the wall. Mollie holds onto the edge of the sofa, feeling for a moment that the house might shiver, rock, collapse. The banging comes again, making the dust on the bookcases jump, the African masks quiver. A petal falls from a white lily. Ludo shrugs, smiles grimly, turns the gramophone down. Mollie remembers the hollow eyes of the old lady next door and feels sure that those eyes can see right through the wall.

So difficult, Ludo says. To live among such Philistines – but it's better not to upset them. No one can tell where that might lead. Although apparently it's quite unfair to say Philistines – in reality they made exquisite pots, or so I'm told.

He hands her the Martini in a tall red glass and it tastes so bitter that Mollie can hardly force it down. Of course, Ludo is right. It's often been hard for her as well, living among Philistines, pots or not. She looks up again at the board of photographs. No doubt those are all the girls who Ludo has worked with in the theatre. She wants her photograph up on that board. Ludo asks her about her singing and she talks grandly, reeling off more of the names she's seen in the record shop. Ludo goes to the piano and she stands up, trips on the snakeskin shoes. When she looks up, she has the sense he might be laughing at her.

They discuss what she would like to sing and she longs to be able to offer some of those record-shop songs but she doesn't know them. Ludo suggests various possibilities. The names mean nothing to her. How disappointing that he should make things so complicated. He was meant to know immediately the right song for her to sing.

'Greensleeves'?

Mollie knows that's not the right song for a real audition but she has to agree.

So very English, he says. Mollie has always thought that being English was something to be proud of but now she feels ashamed. Ludo plays a few bars and she wonders whether she should start. His fingers are tapered and pale, the nails long, immaculately manicured. She opens her mouth, but no sound comes out.

Relax, my dear. R-e-lax. Ludo lays his hand on the bottom of her spine and a spark of lightning travels up through her body and into the nape of her neck. She tries to breathe deeply, but when she starts again her voice comes out thin and squeaky. She keeps on going and soon even she's surprised by the graceful flourish of the sound. Closing her eyes, she imagines herself in a theatre, under the glaring lights, faces in the shadows turned up towards her. After that she sings 'The Ash Grove' and knows she's impressed him.

When she's finished, he turns to her, claps his hands together, then reaches around her waist and pulls her to him. You sing beautifully, he says. Beautifully. He takes hold of her face in his impeccable fingers and examines it closely. And you're very beautiful – altogether.

So I could get a job in the theatre?

He looks at her, laughs, tinkles a few notes on the piano. How old are you?

Seventeen.

Fourteen perhaps?

Fifteen, Mollie says, although his guess is accurate.

You have the most exquisite voice, he says. And you could certainly have a big career in a music hall or theatre. No doubt about it. But let me give you some advice – don't bother with the local theatre here. Do some preparation and then go to London. I know all the people in the best theatres in London and I can get you an audition – when the moment comes. But first we have work to do. You must learn how to focus your voice, how to present yourself. I can show you all that. Will you be able to come here for lessons? Would your mother allow it?

As I said, she's very busy.

And your father?

Stepfather. Busy as well.

Oh, I see.

So I can come any evening.

Oh, Ludo says. Oh. His fingers move in an arpeggio up the keys.

His words – and the Martini – have made Mollie feel dizzy so she asks if she can go to the bathroom. He points her to the velvet curtains at the end of the room. Is that really the bathroom? With no proper door? Mollie blushes at the thought of it. Taking her glass, she pushes through the curtain into a room of glass wall tiles, oval mirrors, and dark green linoleum on the floor. A pot of face cream stands open on the windowsill and, next to it, a string of pearls in a white china dish. Mollie stares at her flushed face in the cracked mirror, then sits down on the loo, swaying a little because of the drink. She's embarrassed to pee because she's scared that Ludo might hear so she tries to be quiet but still the sound echoes all around her. Beside her a brassière – peppermint green and edged with black lace – hangs from the end of the towel rail. The intimacy of its small, neat cups makes Mollie shiver. The brassière must belong to Donna but Mollie knows herself to be a match for a cheap girl like that. Screwed up by the sink taps is a pair of wet, peppermint-coloured knickers.

She picks up her glass and takes two large gulps of the Martini. Soon she'll be ruined and she doesn't care. She'll go to his bedroom and together they'll do what married people do. The thought makes her hot inside and she wonders if she might be sick. But he works in the theatre and is going to teach her to sing. Feeling too hot, she undoes the catch on the window. It opens narrowly onto fenced back yards and the dipping darkness of the canal. From somewhere a dog whines, desperately.

Twisting her head up, Mollie can see a silver shower of lights above. One of those lights might be from 48 Langley Crescent. It's only a half a mile away, across the canal, beyond the allotments and the railway line, up the hill. For an aching moment, she longs to hurry up the hill to 48 Langley Crescent. Tea with sugar, a hot-water bottle, a cool hand laid on her feverish brow. But it won't be like that. The house will be empty and fragile, her stepfather away on business so there won't even be his laughter to fill the gap between floor and ceiling. And Mollie will lie awake at night, waiting for the moment when it will come tumbling down. She slams the window shut, turns back to face the nauseous green linoleum, the velvet curtains, the swaying light above her head.

Won't your mother be worrying about you? he asks again.

No, she never worries about me.

But that uniform is the Alice Ottley school, he says. And you a young lady? Why doesn't your mother worry? She should.

Mollie wonders why he's asking so much about her mother. He should see her power, understand that she can do whatever she likes, go out when she likes, borrow her mother's clothes, come in at eleven o'clock. The only reason why she doesn't do those things all the time, every night, is because of her stepfather. For a moment, she thinks of his laughter and his presents and the arguments she hears behind the bedroom door as she comes home at eleven wearing her mother's fur coat. Of course, she could make her mother worry if she wanted. She only has to say those words – *why did that man know my name?* And there are other words as well. She can't make their shape on her lips but she can feel them inside her. Dark words, spells and curses, mysterious in their power. And so her mother will never ask. Instead she pours a gin and tonic, goes out. Leaving, leaving. Climbing into the long black car next to her yearning, laughing stepfather.

Perhaps I'll have another drink, Mollie says.

He turns to pour it. Can you dance?

Oh yes, of course.

Mollie has only ever done the Dashing White Sergeant in the assembly hall at school but surely it can't be difficult? He pushes back the rugs revealing a parquet floor. Mollie's head is swimming from the Martini and when she shuts her eyes everything rolls backwards. The needle drops down onto the gramophone. That music again which comes from another time, another place. Ludo catches hold of her and spins her around and strangely she does know how to dance. It must have been there in her limbs all the time.

Take off your stockings, he says. Or you'll slip on this floor.

He watches as she unclips her mother's stockings. His eyes are on the flesh of her thighs. As they dance, her chest presses against the beat of his heart and she feels his legs against hers, and a lump of something that presses against her. He smells of lavender or is it roses? A heavy, sweet smell that thickens her throat. Surely she has heard this song before? That lump presses against her again and she feels tears brimming in her eyes.

As he turns her against him, an image comes to her of some other room where a man and woman danced. To this same song – surely? And another man with Arthur's lilting accent laughed and she, a tiny child, sat on his knee clapping her hands. The scent of wood smoke and pork chops, furniture all stacked up. The gramophone starting with a hiss, as the record glides under the needle. The woman's hand pressed firmly against the man's back as they dance. *The place where happiness is for me.* The carpet – patterned red and blue – flows under their feet. The sideboard, the bookcase, the mirror over the fireplace, all kaleidoscope into each other. The wall lights, shaped like swans' necks, blink, the line of silver tankards on the mantelpiece swirls past. On the wallpaper pink rosebuds burst into bloom. And Mollie's hands are no longer clapping but stretched out, motionless, as though ready to gather the dancers into her arms. Twisting and turning, the man and woman melt together. Floating away into the sky, the stars. Until the man stumbles and the image fades away. A fragment, lost.

Mollie closes her eyes, feels the music lull away that loss, sinks into its cadences, as she twists and turns, her bare feet gliding over the parquet floor. She knows that soon he will drug her with laudanum and they will do something so disgusting that she can't let her mind think about it. The peppermint brassière with the black lace is printed into her mind, and the spectral eyes of the old woman in the house next door. Ludo swings her away from him and back, away and back. And then as he turns away again, the scarf at his neck unravels.

A splash of red appears – a patch of skin, vivid and raw. A wound, a scar which covers the side of his neck. The skin is bright red, thin and furrowed, the edges jagged. Ludo sees her staring and, trying to laugh, raises his hand to cover the scar in a mock exclamation of horror. This moment must pass, the scar must not be significant, the dance must go on. But Mollie pulls away from him. The drink, the twists and turns of the dance have made her stomach clench. A rush of saliva fills her mouth. The redness of the scar waves like a flag in front of her eyes. She imagines herself touching it, blood breaking through the thin, damaged skin and pouring down his chest.

His hands gather up the scarf, bunch it up against the scar. She knows that he wants to retie the scarf but if he does so then he'll reveal it further. And so he steps away from her, back into the shadows of the room.

You must go, he says. Your mother will be worried about you.

Mollie's head floats and spins as she grabs her stockings, pulls them on, picks up her school bag. She must go and never come back. When she looks up, Ludo has retied the scarf, pulling it up tight to his chin. She moves towards him, stares into his eyes, which glint like warning lights.

Please, he says. Go.

For a moment, she wonders if he might be about to weep. She steps forward, lays a finger on the green scarf, raises her other hand to touch the place where the hidden scar lies. Ludo is like Arthur. He's been injured in the war and it's her job to nurse him back to health. She wasn't able to do that for Arthur but she'll do it for Ludo. Bottles of disinfectant, beds made with hospital corners, night lamps burning low, her hand holding his, soothing away the pain.

No, please, he says. Please go.

She moves her hand away but his eyes still grip hers. Of course, she should go. She can do that now because her tenderness has trapped him. As she pulls on her coat, the floor rises up to meet her and she steadies herself against the arm of a chair. Stumbling down the stairs, she trips over an umbrella stand. Ludo has followed her but doesn't come close. She feels the distance between them, knows he's measuring it as well. He moves past her in the narrow hallway, pushes himself in against the wall so as not to touch her, unlocks the door, stands aside so that she can step out into the street, which sleeps in red-brick righteousness, unaware.

## 37

# Now

### Jay – Baghdad, April 2003

Hi Mum, Granmollie, Grandad and all peace protesters,
I'm sorry I didn't write sooner. Just not enough time and didn't
know what to say. Thanks so much for the money and can
you thank everyone else as well. You are amazing. Everyone
here is really grateful. I'm at the Palestine right now on Greg's
computer. The thing is everyone thought this was just about
a war, and then the war would stop and the problem would
be solved, but maybe it was never going to be that simple. I
suppose what I realise right now is the things that matter you
can't film and you can't even explain to anyone. Like what
happened earlier today which does need to be written down
but not in some human rights report, written down in blood
or carved in stone, or I don't know what.

I don't think I quite believed in this war until today. Just
a great big fireworks display with things jumping off tables
and windows shaking in their frames and nobody getting any
sleep. Anyway, I went with these journalists to see a place
which was hit this morning because there are still bombs
going off but no one knows why or who is responsible. It's
hard to get anywhere because the streets are crowded with
cars and lorries and people are just emptying out buildings –
carrying washing machines out of launderettes, rolls of fabric
out of shops, monkeys out of the zoo, boilers, doors and
boxes of shoes – with no one to stop them. But eventually
we arrive and everyone is arguing about whether this was an

American bomb or an Iraqi shell. People are standing around shouting and crying. And three buildings have just gone missing from this street, like teeth punched out.

And all these people come up to the journalists, wanting to tell their story. A man, who thinks I'm a journalist, explains the whole thing to me, except I don't really understand. It's hot and this sweaty wind blowing yellow dust into your eyes. And the journalists want to head back because they've got their story but I don't want to go. I know enough Arabic to say I'm sorry, so I say it again and again. Because somebody needs to say – I'm from England and the vast majority of people in England never wanted this war. And you know they do understand. In fact, they know it even before I say it, clap me on the shoulder, thank me. They really don't have any bitterness much. There is a fatalism here that is both heroic and depressing.

Anyway, I stay there for quite a while and by the time I'm going it's cooler and I don't really know how I'm going to get home. So I just start walking and I've only gone a couple of streets when I see this woman sitting on a doorstep and she's gesturing at me desperately. So I walk over and then – well, there's all this blood on her but very dark, like almost black. And it's then that I see the child. Or maybe it's a baby. Small anyway and I can't really see because there's lot of black blood so I just want to run away because I feel like I'm going to throw up. But I understand she's telling me she needs to get to a hospital.

This woman is really calm and demure and she's got this cloth arranged very neatly and tactfully over whatever it is that she's holding in her lap. But I'm sure – Christ I really can't write this – but this child – has almost certainly been dead for some while. I mean, like before I didn't really know about what's inside people – like ripped flesh and sinew – I can't write about it – like something really nasty you've seen in a butcher's shop window. Except this thing – must have been dead for some while – oh God I really can't write this, it's making me want to throw up. There's flies and still the woman is asking me if I can help her get to a hospital.

So I tell her yes, help her to her feet. And we walk to the end of the street, turn into the main road. And this part of Baghdad is really quite lovely – palms, buildings with patterns of tiles on the front, the river yellow and full of silt but flowing by – and she and I are just walking along, with the evening sun shining down and the wind has dropped for a while. I take hold of her arm to steady her. And I've no idea whether I should say to her that maybe it's a bit late for the hospital.

Then we're lucky because this jeep goes past with an EU flag flying and when I wave it down the men stop because I look Western and harmless. So I start to try and explain, only the guys in the jeep are Italian so they don't understand but they open the door to let us in. And so we drive off with these guys singing and swigging down arak. In the back of this jeep there are three of us and so I'm pushed up really close to this woman and I'm keeping my hand on her arm because I want to comfort her. But there's this really bad smell and probably it's just the smell of people in the heat who need a shower but I have the idea that something is rotting and covered in flies.

Then we get to the hospital and it's like hell. Bleeding people everywhere and if there were huge fires and people being roasted on spits it really wouldn't be that much worse. Then on top of that some kind of minor war is taking place at the entrance to the hospital with a machine gun and guys hurling rocks. Also this man standing shaking a chair with only three legs, like you can stop machine gun fire with a chair. All this is because the hospital is in danger of being looted and people are trying to defend it. Already all the other hospitals in Baghdad have had all the equipment taken out of them. I mean, can you believe that? Can you believe it?

Now jeeps pull up with big yellow TV notices taped up in the windows and a couple of journalists start filming some of this. I can tell that they're kind of frustrated because although

337

stuff is being chucked none of this is really quite dramatic enough for the evening news. But still they keep on filming instead of actually trying to defend the hospital. And by now this woman is really in despair so she leans down against a wall and then, under the cloth, I see this hairy leg. And there is no child or baby, instead a dog. The whole thing is just so gross and I can't understand because the Iraqis don't even like dogs. There are hundreds of strays here and no one cares.

So I find myself collapsed against the wall, kind of laughing. I don't know what this story is but it isn't a story about a woman whose dog has died. But then a young guy I know, a medical student, comes up to me, and he's pleading with me to try and find some American marines to save the hospital. And a rock gets thrown which narrowly misses his head. Both he and I know that all this is entirely hopeless because there are no Americans anywhere. No one can find them. Just shut up behind their roadblocks and locked up in their vehicles and letting this happen. This medical student says they'll have to get another Saddam if they want to keep the peace.

Anyway, I'm writing all this like you don't know but I'm sure you do. I just don't understand. I really, really don't understand. We all campaigned against this war but still I did think it could actually work, like it could achieve its short-term aims. But now I just don't understand. And right now I long to be home – not where I'm staying. Home, home. You and Granmollie and skateboarding on the Brighton seafront. I really long for that. Except this is permanent now, I think.

Anyway, this medical student and me did actually find some American soldiers who were quite helpful, even though they're the same age as me, drinking beer and thinking that Iraq is in Africa. They took us to see some more senior guy who says yeah sure and we can't let equipment be taken from a hospital. No siree, we certainly can't and action will be taken. And maybe it was and maybe it wasn't.

Anyway, when I got away from the hospital I realised that I should have taken photographs and written things down. No one would use the photographs anyway but still I found a pen and paper but I'd lost the ability to write and it just isn't possible to turn what's happened into a statistic. Now I have to go because I'm in Greg's way. I don't know what else to say. I love you.

Jay.

# 38

## BEFORE

### Mollie – Worcester, March 1954

Mollie is wearing a pair of Ludo's socks. He's lent them to her because the streets are awash with March slush and so her feet were soaked as she walked from school. Her singing lesson is finished now and Ludo has lit the fire. Mollie lies on her stomach on the zebra sofa, swinging her socked feet, writing in the purple leather notebook which Ludo bought for her which has a pencil attached as well. On the front page it says – Mollie Mayeford. A name which should be written in neon italics outside a London theatre. A name for a girl with huge mascara-lined eyes, a dazzling white smile, a dress pinched in at the waist and square-toed court shoes.

Gin and tonic? Ludo asks.

Oooh. Yes please.

Outside the rain smashes against the windows, thumps down on the roof. It's been raining for three days now and the levels of the Severn are rising. Everyone says that when the water comes down from Wales, the city will flood once again, maybe as badly as in 1947. Mollie imagines cars, park benches, whole houses swept away by the black waters. Meanwhile, she and Ludo step out of his bedroom window onto their own private Noah's Ark.

Mrs Griffiths bangs on the wall and Ludo turns the music down. Mollie goes back to her purple notebook to make plans for when she and Ludo go to London. She notes down the addresses of theatres, draws designs for dresses, writes lists of plays she wants to see. When Ludo takes photographs of her she often sticks them into the back of the book – evidence of something, she can't quite say what.

Would we live right in the centre of London? Or Kensington?

The centre, Ludo says, passing the gin and tonic and a plate of hot buttered toast sprinkled with cinnamon. Mollie sits up, makes room for him on the sofa, and they share the toast. Mollie shows him the map of tube stations in Central London which she's copied out of a book belonging to her stepfather. The music which she sung earlier still echoes in her head. After five months of Ludo's lessons, she knows how much she's improved. She's almost ready for a real audition now. She lays her head against Ludo's shoulder and he wraps an arm around her.

Can we look at the photos? she asks.

He smiles at her but doesn't answer. She gets up, pads across the floor in his socks, reaches down to pull the albums from the bottom shelf. They're scuffed brown leather with a border of gold, much of which has rubbed away. Mollie carries them back to the low table by the sofa, spreads them out, feels the crumbly dust of their leather, imagines the crackle of the tissue paper inside. To her they speak of concert halls, dusty attics, foreign places, grief. Now they're like a theatre before the curtain has gone up, hushed and expectant.

Mollie knows that Ludo never looks at these albums with anyone else. Not Donna or any of the other theatre girls. No one except her. And she remembers when he first showed them to her, lifting them from the bottom shelf with infinite care. And then speaking slowly and precisely, as though the words themselves were precious, fragile. These are photographs of my home, where I lived when I was young in Austria. And then a pause, a snatch of breath. Photographs of my family, the people I thought of as my family.

And then they had sat on the sofa together, looking at the photographs, as they will do now. Mollie reaches for an album, opens the first page, waits for the world inside to appear. A house by a lake like a miniature fairy-tale castle, the roof heavy with conical towers and dormer windows. Around it a geometrical garden of box hedges, fountains, stone steps, terraces. The photographs are shades of grey and brown, the edges furry. Beside it another photo shows people lined up formally in front of a fountain, the men dressed in boaters and bow ties, the women in white dresses. At the front of the photographs, two boys are dressed in sailor suits and three girls stand grouped together, their thin legs sticking out from beneath summer dresses, their dark hair held back by ribbons. Whippets with heavy, jewelled collars sit beside them. In the background, standard rose bushes are lined up like lollipops and statues of lions play beside the fountain.

Tell me, Mollie says.

And so Ludo tells it again. Here are the cousins, Elsa, Liesl and Freida – who played in a string quartet with their brother Max. Ludo was older and was studying music at the university in Vienna. He used to go and see them at the weekends. And here are their parents – wearing fur and velvet and standing amidst potted palms beside long glazed doors with brass handles. Ludo's fingers move through the pages of the album with the same fluidity that they move over the keys of the piano. Here are the girls standing in a line, wearing white lace. And here in their bathing costumes, sitting on a jetty, with their long legs hanging down and their arms linked around each other's waists.

In many of the photographs the lake is frozen, the landscape bulging white, the turreted house laden with snow. A photograph shows two of the girls skating, gliding across the ice, with their hands pushed into fur muffs. Mollie can feel the smoothness of their movements as theyr sail through their ice-enclosed world. The pages turn and turn, everyone in the photographs has the same shadowed eyes, the same smile – certain, eternal, invincible.

Mollie longs for the day when she will go with Ludo to that house. They'll go to Paris first, then take a night train across the Alps. And then she'll walk by the lake with Viennese dance music playing. And she'll attend those elaborate picnics with tea urns and china cups and sandwiches organised on three-tiered plates.

Run her fingers over the skinny ribs of the whippets, take hold of their thick, jewelled collars. For this is the place where she was always intended to be – not the cardboard, balsa wood and glue of Langley Crescent but the eternal world of the house by the lake in Austria. Where she will be married to Ludo, and wake every morning in his arms, in a turret room with a view over the dark waters of the lake.

Ludo lays the album down and Mollie moves closer to him, snuggling her head against his shoulder. He takes hold of a strand of her hair and twists it around his finger. Such beautiful hair, he says. Liesl had hair like yours. As he speaks, his voice falters. Mollie turns her head towards him. She feels the weight of the past lying heavy on him and some part of her wants to weep with him. But she's also aware that now – at this moment – she may be able to control him. Surely now he will kiss her? Kiss her properly – not on her cheek or hand but her lips. She's waited so long for him to do that. Months now, nearly six months.

You know the thing is, Ludo said. They weren't even really Jews.

Mollie doesn't know what it means to be a Jew. She turns her face towards his, moves her lips closer. But Ludo moves away, stands up, takes out a handkerchief, blows his nose. He begins to gather up the albums. She wants him to sit down with her again and so she stretches out her hand. He comes back to her and she settles against him but the moment when he might have kissed her has passed.

And this is how it always is. Mollie waits endlessly for something more to happen. Now she lays her hand on his knee and moves it up and down uncertainly. This doesn't feel right. She's stroking Ludo as one might stroke a dog. But how is one meant to do this? Obviously she's got the technique wrong. Donna must know how and so do some of the other theatre girls. So why doesn't she know? And why doesn't Ludo offer any help? Instead his hand stretches out and he takes hold of her fingers, pulls them gently away from his leg. Then he raises her fingers to his mouth and kisses them, as he has often done before.

And, of course, she likes him to kiss her fingers. The gesture is kind, respectful. But Mollie doesn't want kindness or respect. She doesn't want to wait for London, or Paris or Austria. She wants what goes on in the bedroom upstairs now. She wants him to stick his thing up her, as she's seen in well-thumbed books in the school library. She doesn't know quite how this would happen but it certainly isn't going to happen on this sofa. Apparently there are women that men marry and women with whom they make love. Somehow Mollie has found herself in the wrong category.

Of course, she does want to marry Ludo sometime and she knows she will. But in the meantime – what holds him back? The phone rings and Ludo stands up to answer it. Why can't he just let it ring? She drops her head down against the arm of the sofa, waits. Why are there always so many interruptions? Mrs Griffiths. Calls about the shop or music lessons. The girls from the theatre ringing up or coming around. Ludo's voice is low but she hears the name Donna. Mollie imagines the bedroom upstairs, that room she's never seen. If she went up there what would she see? Donna with her foot up on a chair, peeling a peach-coloured stocking down her leg. And Ludo like the heroes of the Folies Bergère romances, tall, dark and dangerous, standing by the window, watching.

Ludo's voice is low, anxious. Mollie remembers all the times Donna has come around. *Have you got our money for us?* Ludo opens a tin, pushes rolled-up notes into her hand. These girls never have any money, he says to Mollie. You know working in the theatre isn't well paid. But I try to help them out when I can.

Mollie hears the word police and enjoys the surge of fear it brings. So Ludo is in trouble. She's always known it. He's been trapped by Donna. She controls him, forces him to let her stay in his flat, insists on leaving her clothes in his bathroom. That's what the money is really about. Ludo doesn't love Donna as he loves her but Donna is powerful – a witch, a devil, an enchantress. She's taking money from him, blackmailing him, cursing him with evil spells, controlling his mind. Men are so often entrapped. It's the same for her stepfather and probably the same for Arthur as well. Mollie knows that she must save Ludo, take him away, marry him. The time is coming soon. They can't stay here much longer. The floodwaters are rising and soon the whole city will be swept away.

Ludo puts down the phone. I'm sorry, my dear, but I must make some calls from upstairs so I think you must go.

No. No. Don't worry. I can wait.

Won't your mother be worrying about you?

He knows that this question annoys her so why does he ask? She presses her head into a sofa cushion, waits until she hears the tread of his shoes on the uncarpeted stairs. He's done this once or twice before – gone to use a phone up in the bedroom. Mollie fetches a blanket from a nearby chair, pulls Ludo's socks up and lies down on the sofa again, waiting. *Won't your mother be worrying?* She remembers a night in January – two months ago – when she had come back so late that her mother was already home. When Mollie, stepping across the hall, realised this, she felt glad. Now there would be a showdown. She'd come up the stairs, in her mother's shoes, waiting for that moment. Strangely, longing for it. She'd reached the landing, the door of her mother's bedroom was open. She couldn't see her mother so she coughed twice.

Her mother came to the door, dressed in a long Chinese robe, with a cigarette in her hand. The brown shadows of the bedroom behind her, the light glittering dully from the mirror on the wardrobe door. Her mother had looked at her, taking in every detail. She looked as though she might speak but then didn't. A conversation happened without actually happening. Her mother had stepped back and slowly and deliberately shut the bedroom door. And Mollie stood there wanting victory. But there was no victory. What point is there in having power unless you can hold that power over someone else?

But Violet has refused to play the game. And Mollie has been denied the opportunity to lie, which is unfair, as she likes lying and knows herself to be good at it. Violet shuts the door. So that now Mollie's power and freedom hang around her shoulders like the too-big fur coat. She wonders what she would have to do to make her mother care. Perhaps she should try and find out? Hidden deep is the fear that nothing will be enough.

She longs to hear voices from behind that door, her stepfather saying – *Really, Violet, I do think. Dangerous. Irresponsible.* She waits for him to come, to tell her that she's in danger, to lecture her about coming back too late, to forbid her from going out again, to promise that he will stay in every evening to check on her. But her mother has always stood in front of her stepfather, obscuring him from view. Mollie drifts towards sleep, dreams of the station, less than half a mile away. The road out, the long lines of silver stretching away across England, Europe, through the night. Dreams of the stranger who came to the house, except that man now has Ludo's face. Mollie stands with him outside on the terrace, looking down the violet-covered lawn. And Arthur-Ludo doesn't have a limp and he's dancing with her mother on the terrace. And Mollie is watching them, standing on a brocade armchair which – bizarrely – has appeared on the terrace. And now she is small – tiny – hardly bigger than a doll and standing on the armchair listening to the music and watching the figures twist and turn and she knows that soon Arthur-Ludo will walk over, pick her up, swing her around.

She wakes, the real Ludo stands beside the sofa.

Mollie, I have to go out. You must go.

No. No.

Yes, I must.

No, Ludo. No. You don't have to.

Yes, I do. Donna is in some difficulties.

Mollie flings herself at him.

Please, she says. I want you to marry me.

He holds her back, shakes his head. Mollie, I'm already married.

Mollie hears the words like a punch in the chest. How can Ludo be married? Where is his wife? She looks around the flat as though a woman with an apron might suddenly appear from the kitchen carrying a leg of lamb on a silver dish. Some part of her mind has been left behind on the terrace at Langley Crescent.

My wife has gone to live in Paris with a painter friend of mine.

Mollie is glad to find that Ludo's wife is far away but still she doesn't understand. Her mother and stepfather don't allow anyone who is divorced into the house. People who are divorced live in shame and poverty. They don't have friends and run art galleries in Paris.

Ludo, please. I don't mind that you're married. Please.

She wants him to take her up to the bedroom and take advantage of her innocence. In the Folies Bergère romances, the man is always tall and he bears down upon the woman and she raises her mouth to his and is overwhelmed. But she raises her mouth towards his and nothing happens.

Ludo, why not? she says.

Because. He moves away from her gently. Mollie, really, you must go.

Mollie turns away from him, furious. Why does he want Donna and not her? He's like her mother. He doesn't care.

I'm sorry, my dear. I must go. I'll leave the key. Put it under the stone.

He puts on his coat and hat.

I will see you tomorrow? he says. She doesn't answer although she knows that she will come back tomorrow. She hears him go and feels the temperature drop. Without him the room is dirty and dislocated, meaningless. Cardboard, balsa wood and glue. Of course the money, the phone calls, the police are not to do with blackmail. Something else happens, something she doesn't understand. Maybe it's Ludo who is evil. She hopes he is because then she must be the victim, the innocent young girl shamelessly seduced by the wicked older man. That's what happened the first night she came here and it's been happening again and again. He rips her clothes, forces himself upon her, holds her cheeks so tightly between his vice-like fingers that she has no choice but to kiss him. And now he has left her, cast her aside, abandoned her.

She stands up unsteadily now, the damaged and bewildered victim. She peels off his socks, straightens her clothes, stifles a sob. She finds her scarf, coat and shoes. Reaching the stairs she takes hold of the stair rail, supports herself as she staggers down. He's injured her so badly that she can barely walk. Another wail rises in her throat. The distance from stairs to front door seems infinitely long. Will she get out alive? Finally she emerges into the starless night, looks around her at the black faces of the houses, all curtains closed, all light extinguished. She stops for a moment to button her coat, tie her scarf.

And Mrs Griffiths is there, watching from the window next door. Hair net, white hair, white face, hollow eyes. It's gone eleven so why isn't Mrs Griffiths in bed? She must have been waiting up to see Mollie leave. Mollie feels a moment of tenderness towards this ghostly old woman who perhaps does care. And so she turns back and faces the window, stretches out her hand beseechingly, looks the old lady in her non-existent eyes, puts her head in her hands, gives a pantomime sob. The black holes where Mrs Griffiths' eyes should be watch. She cares for me, Mollie thinks. She cares.

# 39

# Now

## Lara – Brighton, April 2003

Lara puts her suitcase down on the green nylon carpet in the sitting room of the Roma Street flat. She's been in London for the last eight days. Keeping her side of the bargain. The flat is stale and overheated, smells of new paint. Dead flies are spread on a windowsill, a house plant wilts on a brown wood coffee table. Lara kicks off her shoes, puts on the kettle. This flat requires less walking at least, nothing is more than ten feet from anything else. She considers putting the radio on to listen to the news but thinks of Sharifa's words yesterday. A young lawyer, half Iraqi and half English, Sharifa is working to defend the Voices of Truth website and Lara has spent the week helping her.

News? Sharifa had said. There is no news in Iraq any more. News requires a story – an ordering of events, a sequence of cause and effect. But Iraq has no story now, only a vacuum, drift, random events. Mobs roaming the streets, anti-American demonstrations in Fardous Square. People shouting – Islam, Islam, no America, no Saddam. But the point is that Saddam was a tyrant and even he had problems with the different sects and ethnicities in Iraq. So what chance do the Americans have with no plan, only vague talk of liberty and human rights?

Those words frightened Lara but still she likes and respects Sharifa and her legal colleagues. They occupy a corporate world which Lara can understand and yet still they organise Wilf, Spike, all the motley and prickly peace protesters, with kindness and humour. They manage not to offend Ahmed, not to reveal their selfishness, if indeed they have any. Lara wishes she had their skills. Perhaps if she'd trained to be a lawyer herself, as she had once planned, then she would be more able to move between different worlds gracefully. She makes herself tea, sits down on the upright foam sofa with its fake tweed cover. Two extra power points have now been installed in the peace protest office. Small victories.

On the kitchen noticeboard she's pinned up a copy of Jay's most recent email. *Written down in blood or carved in stone.* On the news that evening she'd seen images of a hospital being looted but she never knew if it was the same one. Above her, Jay's globe, still draped in its bicycle chain, hangs from the ceiling, dangles over the coffee table with its wilting pot plant. When she was moving, she worried that if she put the globe away in a box it would smash and so she'd hung it up. Temporarily, she'd thought. Something of its cheap drama brings Jay into the room. *It symbolises the world in chains, doesn't it?*

Briefly she remembers one of the few occasions when he'd talked about the war. It must have been a week or two before he left. And she'd agreed with him then that there was no case for war – hadn't she? She tries to remember. This is another thing she's learnt from the younger lawyers, the peace protesters. The details matter, you must remember things exactly as they are, you must not slip into convenient confusion or exaggeration, you mustn't be coerced into telling someone else's story instead of your own. Yes, yes. She's sure. She did listen to him.

But that isn't what matters now. Instead she remembers that she hadn't let him finish that conversation before asking him about university. He was meant to be taking time off, thinking things over. Had he contacted the university, had he made any decisions? And then – in one of his sudden gusts of temper – he'd thrown down the papers he was reading, scattering them, shouting at her. But his temper had blown out as suddenly as it had flared and they'd got on fine again and she'd said, It's just that you do need some qualifications. And he'd said I don't and she'd said you do. I don't, you do, I don't, you do. Before he went out, he'd come to her in the kitchen, where she was sitting on a chair, and he'd knelt down in front of her, and kissed her stocking-clad knees. I'm just Troubled Youf, Mum, don't worry about it.

The email, the globe, these fragments of memory. Lara is trying to recreate him, to piece him together, to assemble him into a pattern which she can understand. But he remains fragile, slippery, fading. When he'd knelt down and kissed her knees had she run her hands through his hair, kissed his cheek? Probably not but she had laughed with him. One of his books lies on the windowsill. Published by the Peace Pledge Union, it's about conscientious objectors in the Second World War. Lara doesn't know why she kept that book out when she packed everything else away. One sleepless night she'd started reading it. She'd never really known that so many people had campaigned against that earlier war and paid the price.

Her mobile phone rings and every bone in Lara's body leaps. She grabs it, draws air into her lungs, presses the green phone icon. She hears Wilf's voice. Oh, she says. Yes. Oh. Well, why didn't she ring me?

Keep calm, she tells herself. Remember to breathe. Typical Mollie. Of course she would break her wrist at a time like this. A tape starts to play in her mind, unspooling a litany of ancient grudges, but she halts it, tries to be positive. I'll go straight around there, she says.

She feels almost grateful for the news. She's known for some time that she needs to tackle Mollie and it's better to do it without thinking too much, without making mental preparations, rehearsing speeches. She takes her bag, sets out, walks without noticing anything.

At the door of the Guest House she gathers her resolve around her like a cloak. Think positive. And the truth? That's doubtless too much to expect but she must at least ensure that she doesn't collude in any more lies.

She calls out, steps down the narrow stairs to the kitchen. Mollie is standing at the sink, unaware. Lara realises that the reason why she hasn't been to see Mollie is that, as long as she and Mollie don't meet, they don't have to know what is happening. Meetings and vigils, letters and tea making. But now – seeing Mollie's dark hair wrapped onto her head in a loose bun, seeing her unbent spine, the white collar of her blouse – there's no avoiding the reality of their situation.

Mollie turns, offers a greeting, and Lara sees that she too knows that a moment of reckoning has arrived – although it remains unclear what exactly is to be weighed and measured here. Mollie's arm is in a sling but she's gripping a dishcloth in her other hand. The television is on with the sound turned down. A chat-show host introduces a glittering guest, the roar of applause is imagined in the silence. Lara sees Mollie manoeuvring a saucer with one hand. She has to admire Mollie's ability to carry on as though all is well. Mollie can do anything – except finish with Rufus.

Mum, are you OK? Sorry I didn't come sooner. I was up in London. You know, the lawyers. Sorry. I only just found out.

That's OK, dear. Wilf took me to the hospital. So kind. It's a clean break. Shouldn't take long to heal. Lovely young doctor. Cup of tea?

No. No, thanks. I came to help. What can I do? Some shopping? No, no.

At least let me wash up.

No, no. I'm fine.

I insist. Come on. Please, sit down.

Lara pulls a chair out from the table and manages to steer Mollie into it. Standing at the sink, Lara understands herself anew. She's no longer the feckless, materialistic daughter, who is always busy with a job which everyone else considers pointless. Instead she's in charge, purposeful, on the side of right. Kindness has always been Mollie's most lethal weapon. But now Lara can make some small claim to kindness – to goodness – as well.

After all, it is inevitable in all families that the baton is passed on, that the power shifts, the new generation takes the wheel. Lara puts down her bag, fills the kettle, continues with the washing up. The water is lukewarm and globules of congealed grease float on the surface. She feels Mollie beside her, restless, perched like a pecking bird on the kitchen chair.

No news? Mollie says.

No. Nothing more. Wilf gave you the email, didn't he?

Darling, really there's no need. Leave the washing up. My arm is fine. You know, it's just— Your father hasn't been in touch.

Lara finds mugs for tea. As she places them on the table, she looks at her mother. Mollie seems to have grown smaller, become thinner. But she's still charged by the same buzzing energy, although her eyes have fallen further back, into the depths of her face.

Hasn't been in touch. Not for weeks now. The voice is plaintive, a hand-wringing, eyes-pleading voice. Lara hates that voice.

But he's with Baggers, isn't he?

Well, yes. I suppose so. I don't know. I ring Baggers and he says he'll pass a message on but he doesn't say anything much else. So I just don't know. Leave that washing up. Sit down, love, sit down. Particularly at a time like this, you'd think he'd keep in touch. You know, he always calls. I don't think there's been a day of my married life when he hasn't called.

Briefly Lara remembers a game she used to play with Jay when he was a child. Cards showed the head, the middle section, the legs of different characters – a policewoman, a tennis player, a nurse. The game involved putting the different cards together to make a whole person but it began with the legs of a tennis player, the middle section of a policeman, the head of a nurse. Difficult sometimes to fit a whole person together but you've got to try. No lies, no delusions. But, as ever, Mollie is more difficult to deal with in the flesh than in the imagination. Lara picks up dirty sheets, heads to the washing machine, wonders if there'll be any washing powder. Now, with Jay in such danger, shouldn't they all just be kind to each other?

Please, Lara. Those sheets have already been washed.

Oh. OK. Sorry. I was just.

Lara lays the sheets back down in the basket, feels air drain from the room. Look for biscuits, put them on a plate. The biscuits can surely be relied upon.

You know I just keep thinking and thinking, Mollie says.

I know. So do I.

Things back in the past. You know I've got this girl staying – such a lovely girl. But she asks all these questions – about Ludo.

Oh yes.

Yes. And looking back. It was my fault, of course.

We were talking about Dad.

Yes. Yes, of course. No, dear. No. Don't touch that cupboard door. The handle keeps dropping off and then I can't get it open. Let me. There's a knack to it. What are you trying to find?

Biscuits.

Oh, do you want one?

No.

Neither do I.

OK. All right. Sorry. I'm just trying to help. Lara can't keep the petulant note out of her voice.

Mollie sighs, stands with her hands pressed down onto the kitchen table. What I need is for you to drive me to London. I just don't trust the car. I could go on the train but it isn't easy – all the way to Hampstead, to Baggers. But I do need to get there because if I could talk to him—

Biscuits and sheets. The truth. The truth.

Mum, I'm sorry. Really. But don't you think? Maybe it's time?

Well, it's been time for you for years.

No. No. Listen, you know I've given up my job. And all this waiting. And waiting. If we're going to help Jay, we've got to be honest.

About what?

Well, everything.

Lara makes herself very tall, feels the weight of the room behind her.

Since we're on the subject – Dad, she says.

Mollie is theatrical, waves a hand in a grand gesture. Oh yes, Dad. Dad.

Silence appears for a moment, solid as a wall. Lara takes a shivering breath.

Well, go on then, Mollie says. What particular truth is it that you want to tell me? Do you honestly think there is anything you can tell me about your father that I don't know? What do you want? To repeat some cheap bit of gossip about a girl?

Mum. It isn't cheap gossip. You know it isn't.

Of course, I know. Of course.

Mollie is tossing her head, flashing her pride.

What do you think I am? Entirely blind and stupid? I know all of that. But I love your father and he loves me. And he's a very talented man, a man with an artistic vision, someone who stays true to what he knows, at least in the artistic sense.

Yes, Mum, but he's also—

Mollie's head drops and her moment of courage is ended. Tears wash into her eyes. Lara wants to feel triumph but all she feels is pity. She'd been so sure that she felt able to deal with Mollie but she's being defeated once again. Mollie is right. What truth is there to be told? They both of them know all that there is to know about Rufus. Lara considers all that she doesn't know about her mother, all that she will never understand. She has spent so long endlessly trying to heal the wound, except she doesn't know what the wound is. The dog in the Coventry Blitz with the child's arm in its mouth? The pimp who seduced her when she was fourteen? Rufus pushing her off a roof? Those stories probably aren't even true.

And now finding Rufus will be like pouring acid on the wound – but Mollie wants that acid and why is Lara trying to stop her? This is meant to be an epiphany. She's meant to be taking charge of Mollie, caring for her, guiding her towards some better path. Opening her up to the truth, liberating them all. But there is no great truth to reveal, no subsequent moment of light and liberation. Instead they are both of them falling deeper and deeper, further and further. But still Lara's promised herself not to lie and so she picks up the acid bottle, pours.

Mum, he'll be with some other woman. You know he will.

Of course, I know.

Mum, I'm sorry. I'm just trying to do what's right for Jay, that's all.

What would you know about what's right for Jay?

Mum, please.

If you want to help – drive me to London.

No. You've broken your wrist. You should be trying to rest.

Mollie has pulled a chair out from the table now and sits down, collapsed, head in hands. Lara knows that she should move towards her now, lay a hand on her heaving back, but she doesn't want to touch her. Mollie gets up suddenly, walks to the draining board, grabs a bottle of whisky and pours some into a mug, drinks it down.

The past, she says. The past. Her hand grips her chest in a moment of manufactured drama. I think so often about Ludo. You know he never did. It was all my fault, my imagination. He was a good man.

Lara swallows down a surge of anger. She knows Mollie's repertoire so well. The evasions and exaggerations, the distractions and dramas. Somewhere, deep in the middle of Mollie's skeletal frame a real person must exist and briefly Lara imagines seizing Mollie, digging her hands right into her flesh, groping around inside, pulling out the essence of Mollie, the person who has evaded her all these years. But all she can do is try to stick to the facts.

I thought we were talking about Dad.

Mollie pours more whisky, sobs. The kitchen seems crowded by all the words that can't be said. Lara longs to reach up and pull them down, one by one, string them into sentences, make them into some structure of sense which will turn all the random junk of Mollie's kitchen into a book which can be easily read. Mollie grips the side of the sink, shakes her head as though it's come loose on her neck.

I'm frightened, Mollie says. I'm frightened Jay's going to die.

I know. I know. I just feel sick all day every day – but he's doing what he wants to do. And what he's doing is right. We need to remember that. You read that email. What he did to stop the hospital being looted.

She knows that isn't quite what the email said, but it should have said that.

I know but I'm frightened, Mollie says.

Stop it, Mum. Stop it. What – you think I'm not? You think I don't care? You think that just because when he was young I was working—

Lara feels the air collapse. The possibility of building some new structure has gone. They're back where they always were, always have been. All these years. And, of course, it isn't about the job. She always knew that. It's about the appointment in London, the piece of paper with no name, only an address, the green looping writing. Mollie never even knew of the existence of that possibility yet still it lies between them. *What particular truth is it that you want to tell me?* Lara wonders now why she ever felt that she could change anything. She has no choice except to agree to what Mollie wants.

Look, I'm sorry, Mum. I'm sorry. I've got to go. I promised Wilf I'd help him. If you really want to go to London I can probably do it. Is that what you want?

I think very often about the past, you know. Very often.

Yes, I'm sure you do. Now look. Are you sure there's nothing else you need? Will you be OK now? Are you sure?

Yes, dear. Yes. I'm so sorry. You and I. We must try not to argue, when we love each other so much.

I'll sort it out – London.

Lara hugs her mother stiffly, hates herself for crying. Why must she always be defeated? She gathers up her bag and leaves, walks out into the listening street. A Sunday-evening quiet has settled, the evening is supple, a warm breeze faintly stirring. What can she do now? The only option is to walk back to Roma Street. All her life she's been trying to carve out a little space on which to stand. Her flat had once been that space and now it's gone. Now there seems to be no space at all, just an exposed headland on which she stands, buffeted and battered from all sides. She always wanted to be different from her mother, but a person established only in opposition to another person isn't real.

She finds herself taking the road along the side of the church. It's unlikely that Oliver will be at home because Sunday is a busy day for him. She pushes open the glass doors, wanders towards the closed door of the café, peers briefly into its abandoned spaces – chairs up on the tables, light shining listlessly onto the stainless-steel counter, the clock continuing its motionless crawl. Around her she hears the spaces where music usually plays, where wheelchairs or bags or dance kit are usually stacked. She opens the door marked Private, starts to climb. The light from above has been sifted through endless unwashed windows. She knocks on Oliver's door without hope but he opens it immediately, his face preparing itself for bad news.

It's OK, she says. Nothing happened.

Oh, he says. Oh good.

Can I come in?

She wants him to be that place where she can stand. She wants him to have that certainty that he had when they first met.

Are you all right? he says.

No.

He comes towards her, wraps his arms around her. Her face is against the scratchy ribs of his jumper. She holds him as though holding the core of the earth.

It's my mother, she says. I can't.

He sits her down, moves to the kitchen, switches the kettle on. Those words taped to the wall – *He who saves the life of one man, saves the whole world.* It all sounds so simple. She gets up, unable to keep still, moves through to the kitchen, switches the kettle off and takes hold of a bottle of wine that stands beside the toaster. As he finds glasses, she notes how carefully he balances, sees that he's determined to steady her, even though he isn't steady himself. As they move back to the sitting room, those sea water vases – splashes of green and blue, the twisting shapes of waves – watch them from their shelf, their lips tightly closed. Lara moves to take the bottle from him. Wine blurs her lips, warms her throat. She might live, after all.

My mother, she says. She's always been this good woman, oppressed by this monstrous husband. The endless victim. But you know, despite all of that she always gets what she wants – always.

Oliver nods, pours himself wine.

And you know what? You know what I'm going to have to do now?

She pauses for effect, raises a hand in a gesture of surrender, insists that Oliver should understand the weight of this decision.

I'm going to have to. I've got no choice.

What? he says, happy to play the game. What?

I'm going to have to ring my father and ask him to come home. Can you believe it? When I've spent all my life waiting for him to leave?

Oliver nods and Lara sees him bend his will towards understanding the gravity of this situation. But he fails to convince either her or himself and so slowly, creaking and gasping, Lara starts to laugh. His lips twitch but he will not let himself laugh until she lays a hand on his shoulder, leans against him, allows herself to be washed away by a sudden burst of mirth. Then he holds her, laughs against her hair.

Fuck, she says. Fuck. I don't believe it.

She steps away from him, drinks.

I ask a lot of you, she says. When you don't even like me.

I do, actually. I didn't expect to but I do. Very much.

He puts out his hand and she takes hold of his fingers, tightly.

You saw Jay's email? she asks. I left a copy for you.

Yes, of course.

She sinks into a chair, pours herself more wine.

I read it like I don't know him, she says. I never knew he could be that person. Someone so... amazing.

He has an amazing mother, Oliver says, and moves towards her, slides his fingers into the tumble of her hair. She leans against his hip, snorts with laughter. Oh shut up, she says. Shut up. But she's touched by the compliment, wonders if it contains an element of truth.

Later, as the evening flows on, washed forward by wine and a determination not to sink, not to drown, she finds herself lying next to him on his narrow, short, single bed. They cling together like children, seeking warmth. Their closeness is devoid of desire but the comfort of him brings a similar oblivion. Three pairs of his shoes stand crooked against the wall, pigeon-toed, duck-footed, light from the kitchen touches on the pale blue cotton of a shirt hung on the back of a chair. Her hand lies on his chest and she feels the rise and fall of his breath. He asks her then about Liam.

You haven't told him where Jay is?

No. I've never told him anything.

You said he was an actor, that he went to America.

Yes. A glittering career.

Would I have heard of him?

I don't think so. I did see him once on an advert for a cordless hoover.

She feels laughter shudder inside him. The room is surely darker now. It must be night in that distant world of the street, the city. She twists a button on his shirt, is grateful for the half light.

I always say that Liam abandoned me. I don't know. I would never have known him if it hadn't been for my father, my parents. I was trying to make it up to them. It's complicated. But that's what it's all about. All this.

She knows that he doubts that there is any – *all this*. Doubts that there is a key somewhere that will suddenly fit into a certain lock, explain Jay's decision and all that has happened since. She's said to him before that *all this* must be about the fact that Jay didn't have a father. But he was doubtful, quoted Freud. *Sometimes a cigar is just a cigar.* Now he takes hold of her hand, spreads her fingers one by one. In his touch she feels him accept that she will not talk more now. Sometime. Sometime.

You know when we first met, she says. Jay – before he went to Iraq?

The bed creaks as his weight shifts.

What I said was true, Oliver says. We never talked about Iraq. Only – he wanted to know about healing. About who can heal and how. And he wanted to know about prayer as well, about whether it ever works.

And what did you say?

I said that God is beyond anyone's influence. One should not rely on him. But then I talked about people. About how you should never underestimate what effect one human being can have on another. That might be prayer.

Oliver's voice is so quiet that she struggles to hear him.

This whole thing he had about healing, she says. I never took it seriously because he had been ill himself.

Yes, but people do heal from the places where they are most broken.

Maybe, she says. Maybe. But still I don't understand.

Sometimes people endlessly give out what they are actually hoping to receive. But have no capacity to receive.

His voice fades out and she reaches up to touch his face, feels the bluntness of his chin, the prickle of stubble. She's glad that Jay talked to Oliver before he left, not for the details of the words which were said, but simply because Jay must surely have taken some part of Oliver with him. Some courage, some calm. A talisman to put in his bag and keep with him in that distant country where story has broken down into strings of meaningless events, a cacophony of senseless babble.

## 40

## BEFORE

### Lara – Brighton, August 1982

Lara stands at the door of the Guest House kitchen, feels the floorboards shift beneath her, a gentle roll, as though the tide is coming in. Her stomach heaves and blood throbs in her head. She steps into the room uncertainly, positions her suitcase against the radiator, swallows, licks her sandpaper lips. Pulling off her jacket, she notices that the stain from the pub is still there, a shape like an upside-down horseshoe on her green suede jacket. So Liam has told Mollie and Rufus. He must have done. How very like him, poor stupid fool. And he didn't even warn her. Lara knows she should blame Liam, blame him for so many things.

There's no question – he *must* have told them because Mollie has tidied the kitchen, and a bottle of champagne sits on the table in a bucket of ice. Lara feels fear squeezing her throat. She should never have come back here, she must leave – but where can she go? Not back to Liam. She takes hold of her suitcase again, steadies herself against the radiator as the floor shifts. From a basket in the corner three cats stare at her, forming their judgements.

She thinks of school friends, of that world of houses with drives and double garages, skiing chalets, flats in London. Thank-you letters, boxes of chocolates, slender calf muscles, compliments which appear so sincere that you believe them. If she told any of those people her dirty little secret, it would only confirm what they've always thought – that she doesn't belong. Her cover would be finally and totally blown. But she has two months still until university and nowhere to live. She turns back towards the stairs, gripping the suitcase. But she's too late. Rufus is upon her, wearing a blazer, rubbing his hands. He has made an unsuccessful attempt to flatten his hair with a wet comb.

So, he says. Congratulations.

Lara opens and shuts her mouth in the hope that the right words might appear. How can Liam have been such a fool? But she doesn't find it hard to imagine how he told Rufus, in some London pub after the show. *An Inspector Calls.* Liam – nervous, impetuous, dangerously trusting. That rubbery, weak lower lip wobbling as he blabs out the news. From above, Mollie's shoes clatter on the stairs. The stage is set for her, every prop in place. Lara imagines her in floating pink, her hair piled on her head, a feather boa twirling. In fact, Mollie wears a plain black wool dress but that doesn't erase the previous image.

Darling, she says. We're thrilled, absolutely thrilled.

No, Lara says. No.

Mollie steers her towards a chair.

It's a shock, of course, Mollie says. But how lovely, absolutely lovely. A baby. Your father and I are thrilled, absolutely thrilled.

Rufus laughs as he tears the foil from the champagne. Liam? That naughty boy. Oh my dear, do stop crying. It really isn't the end of the world. It would have happened sometime anyway and Liam loves you to death. He'll see that everything is all right.

Lara stares at her father. Isn't he meant to threaten to shoot Liam?

Liam has got a big career ahead of him, Rufus says.

Perhaps you should get married at the Grand Hotel? Mollie says. A baby, how lovely, just imagine. I always hoped to be a grandmother.

Mollie gets glasses out of the cupboard, wipes dust from them, talks about how much she loves weddings – particularly white weddings. There's always the church next door. Perhaps they could even have the reception at the Guest House if they get the place mucked out.

Lara wipes her eyes, slumps exhausted at the kitchen table. She'd been determined that Mollie and Rufus would never know but, now that they do, she feels a certain relief. If nothing else, the problem belongs to someone else, just for this moment. She thinks of Liam, blabbering in the pub, Liam as he was when she first met him.

The Easter holidays and she was back from school. And there he was sitting at the kitchen table with Rufus. Liam Langton – who had been on the front page of *The Sunday Times* supplement only a few weeks ago. Liam Langton who'd won an award for *Henry V* at the Whitehall. She'd known that Rufus would be working with him, had boasted about that at school, but she hadn't expected to meet him.

But there he was – younger than he looked in the photographs, only two years older than her, and less interesting in the flesh than he had appeared on the magazine cover. A head shot only – it's apparent why. And even his face is not a particularly fine face, but still. What was it? He seemed to gather the room to him, to fill the air with a discreet sparkle. Mollie and Rufus have already fallen for him so entirely that it's hard for her not to like him too. Rufus always loved the Irish and now his voice started to take on Liam's lilt. He often pretended to be Irish, when he wasn't pretending to be Italian. One of the first things Liam had told her, in his heather-and-peat Irish brogue, was that he was an orphan. Lara had been flushed with envy, found herself barely able to imagine such luxury.

But Mollie had said, Oh what a tragedy. But, of course, we will adopt you.

Now Rufus places a glass of champagne on the table. The bubbles race upwards, gasping for air. Lara looks over at her suitcase. Is it really too late just to get up and leave? But what point would there be? She would only have to come back later.

It's the shock, of course, Mollie says. It's all come sooner than you really wanted. But Liam and you seem so happy together. Perhaps the wedding will be in the papers?

Quite an opportunity – going to America. I always fancied that, Rufus says.

He wants her to be married so that he can silence her, as he has silenced Mollie.

Oh yes, Los Angeles, Mollie says. You know, I was going to go once. Just before I met your father. Had an audition with MGM, could have been in *The Night of the Iguana*. You know, the Tennessee Williams play with Richard Burton.

I'm going to university, Lara says. I'm going to be a lawyer.

Mollie and Rufus know about Exeter University but they've never believed in it. They feel a contempt for the stupid people who don't work in the theatre, who go to offices in suits and have four weeks' holiday a year. People who have been conned out of their lives, fooled. Close to death, pale and shadowy, with the blood drained out of them as they make their weary little journeys on the train with their thermos flasks, type their memos and letters, die quietly of too much comfort.

Maybe you could go to university in America? Mollie says.

I'm not going to marry Liam.

Silence descends loudly. The clock ticks. The cats have decided to withhold judgement and have retired to the sides of the room. Perhaps they feel the storm coming. Now that she's started, she must go on.

Actually, Liam and I have split up.

Oh darling. Don't be silly. It'll be lovely, Mollie says. He's a wonderful man and he'll make a great father. Don't you think so?

It had certainly seemed like that – obvious, inevitable. And who could deny that there was much to like about Liam? Tall, nearly as tall as her father. Kind and considerate. Not at all like an actor, no drinking or smoking, his rented flat so clean that you could see the lines where the hoover has recently gone across the shag-pile carpet. And everyone had been terribly impressed. On her birthday he'd sent a vast vulgar bouquet of flowers to the school and Lara had walked back from the school office, past crowds of girls heading to lunch, trying to look as though this happened every day. And just for a while the skiing holidays and Range Rovers didn't count for so much.

And Rufus had been thrilled, of course. When Liam had asked her to go to a film premiere with him, Rufus had taken her out and spent more than one hundred pounds on a dark green dress, covered in sequins and high-heeled shoes with tiny straps, which later proved to be too tight. And for a brief moment she had been the girl caught in the flash of a camera, teeth gleaming, eyes emphasised by rings of mascara. A star in orbit around Liam's planet. She might not be an actor herself but she could be the girlfriend of a famous actor.

You know this Broadway contract is only the beginning of things for him? Rufus says. He's on his way now. Already been offered a film audition.

I don't want to marry him, Lara says.

But darling, why not?

I just—

How can she begin to explain when she doesn't know herself? The eczema on his face, the bow legs, the unfortunate cowboy boots, the leather jacket which is too short, the narrow squinty eyes. All of that does matter, of course, but not enough to damn him. Because she likes Liam and many people marry for less than that. There are leagues in love and Lara knows she isn't due anyone better than Liam. So then what's the problem? Hard to say. It isn't even the fact that he's Rufus's man, even though the need to defy Rufus is always there, an inch below the surface.

Ridiculous, Rufus said. Of course you should marry him.

Lara, darling, really.

But her mind will not bend.

I don't want to marry him.

She thinks back to her conversation with him two nights ago, late at night in a smoky pub. Something sticky had been spilt over the side of the table and she didn't see it soaking into her jacket. It was then that she'd decided, that she'd told him that he must go to America without her. And he'd pleaded with her, but only, she was sure, because that was the decent thing to do. And perhaps that was the problem, finally. His decency. The fact that when she'd got pregnant he had – with his awful Irish Catholic forbearance – offered to marry her. The pain of that, the fact that he was prepared to lay down so much of his life for her. She'd liked him more than ever then, and known with greater certainty that she mustn't marry him. She herself could never be free but he could. One of them might walk out of this whole. It couldn't be her and so it must be him. That's what she'd thought – watching him through the smoke of the pub. Dear God preserve him – naïve, hopeful, ignorant, concerned about her stained jacket. Even that bad skin must be preserved in all its touching, raw longing.

Why did you sleep with him if you don't want to get married? Rufus shouts.

Lara wants to say, *How many women have you slept with and not married?* But that wouldn't be fair on Mollie.

I only went out with him because you wanted me to.

Lara is amazed at her own courage but she has to say that because it's true. When Liam had first asked her out, Rufus had insisted she must go. He'd bought her the train ticket to London, walked with her to the station, something he'd never done before.

Oh it was all my fault, was it? If that's the case then how come you're pregnant?

Lara doesn't want to think about that question. She knows, deep down, that this is her fault, that it can't really be anybody else's fault. To begin with she had insisted that Liam used condoms but after a while he'd said, *Darlin, I don't want to suck a sweet with the wrapper still on.* And he'd convinced her that he'd pull out, that all they had to do was count the days. *S-sure darlin. Everything will be just fine, you'll see.* And Lara had known that she was falling for the oldest lie in the book but still she agreed, certain that somehow the general laws of nature would not apply to her.

Lara, darling, I really think you should think this over, Mollie says. Because it isn't fair on Liam, is it? A man wants to be with his child, doesn't he? And it won't be any fun for you on your own.

I'm not going to marry him.

Do you have any idea what it means to be a single mother? Do you realise what hard work it is, and how lonely? There'll be no point in you going to law school. You'll be tied hand and foot.

I'm not going to marry him.

Then there's only one other choice, Rufus says.

Lara knows her father is right. She's known that all along and she's even booked the appointment. She has the piece of paper in her pocket. Thick and white, the lettering of the address green and looping. No name or organisation, just an address.

It isn't really a baby, after all, only a few cells. At least her father understands this.

Yes, she says. That's what I'll have to do.

Mollie turns away.

Yes, Rufus says. If you're really not going to get married then you're a fool. But if you aren't then you need to put a stop to all this.

Lara nods, feels her blood settle heavy in her veins.

I'll even organise it for you if that's what you want.

Mollie starts to weep loudly. Lara keeps her eyes fixed on her father. Although she hates him, he's the one who can pull her through. Lara tries not to listen to Mollie's weeping, not to think about Tupperware boxes filled with bleeding rags.

Rufus, I won't have that kind of talk in this house, Mollie says.

You leave her alone.

And so Mollie and Rufus start to argue, back and forwards, finding their rhythm, swords crossed, a jab, a thrust. Lara stares at the tablecloth, realises that she has already become mere scenery. If she picked up her suitcase, slid out of the room, they wouldn't even notice. Act Two. The great kitchen-sink drama. Mollie grips her hand to her chest, sobs. Rufus rages. Together they are magnificent. Lara provides their audience, bleakly aware that the pregnancy is not a drama that will be resolved by the end of the third act. She wonders how it can be that her parents know, in theory, so much about life. And yet when real life arrives at their doorstep they have no way of coping with it. They can organise life into grand scenes – a wedding, an abortion, a row. But the long days of pregnancy and motherhood, this is a pain they will not bear.

Mollie stretches out her hands to Lara, clings to her, paws at her. Abortion is the same as murder. I won't let you do it. I won't. I won't.

Lara tries to disentangle herself from Mollie's clinging hands. Her parents have always been victims of too much vocabulary. At the Guest House, words are a smokescreen rather than a means of communication. Cliché is used as a defence against meaning.

Shut up, shut up, Rufus shouts.

I won't have it. I won't.

Mollie wails about the miscarriages, about how much she longed for another child. The life of a child should never be taken.

Briefly Lara imagines blood, cold pieces of metal poked up inside her, a formless bloody lump lying in a white kidney-shaped dish. No box to be buried in a field under the spreading branches of an oak tree by the banks of a river – or even in a lay-by with a concrete toilet block and an overflowing rubbish bin. Mollie and Rufus, through the shouting, have made the baby real so that Lara lays a hand, fingers spread, on the flat of her belly. She and the baby are real. They aren't an intellectual discussion about timing and cadence.

Don't listen to her, Rufus says. If you're not going to marry Liam then you know what you need to do.

No, Mollie says.

Well, it's your choice, Rufus says to Lara. It depends whether you want to ruin your life or not. Make your decision. But let me be clear – I'm not having some unmarried slut living in this house.

And so Rufus makes his exit. Lara hears the front door slam, listens to the strangled sound of her mother weeping. Move stage left, comfort mother, as she has done so many times before. But she doesn't want to do that. She wants to go to that appointment and walk out of this situation in one piece. Go to Exeter to study law, move to London, buy her own flat and guard it like a castle.

But the stain will never come off the jacket. She has already scrubbed it several times. What is she to do with her mother? With that poor broken life, wasted talent, hands raw, roots of her hair grey where she hasn't had them tinted.

Don't worry, Mum. I'm not going to have an abortion.

The words taste bitter.

I knew you'd never do such a terrible, terrible thing.

But I'm not going to marry Liam, she says.

Whatever you decide I'll support you, Mollie says. I'll be with you – whatever.

Lara knows how she's been trapped, knows that she'll never be free of her mother now. *No one ever betrays us as thoroughly as we betray ourselves.* Already she can feel the years unfolding and she knows how it will be. This baby will be her and Mollie's plot against Rufus, their cheap little shred of defiance. And Mollie will be needed, she will be a grandmother.

Lara considers herself to have run a good race, to have come close. After all, she won the boarding school battle. And she'd managed to impress those shiny girls – just about – with her theatre boasting and her bouquet of flowers. And she'd won her place at university without even trying. And the road had been ahead of her, smooth and straight. The way out. But in the marrow of her bones she'd always known that she'd never escape. That the Guest House would pull her back into its smeary embrace, its crowded, dusty grasp.

# 41

# Now

## Jay – Baghdad, April 2003

Hi Mum, Granmollie, Grandad, peace protesters etc.

I just have to write to you because I'm so angry. I mean, I'm so so so so so angry. Because some of the Western people in this country are so appallingly stupid and arrogant and they turn up here with their textbooks about development or the economy and they start telling everyone how this should be done when there clearly isn't any right or wrong and all anyone is doing is staying alive from one moment to the next.

This woman came up to me – she works for some aid agency which has turned up here with shiny new computers which don't even work in this country, and jeeps and plenty of survival equipment – for themselves, of course. And she came to talk to me and she told me not to give Iraqi people money. She's sure my intentions are good but I need to understand that there's no point in just giving money. But the point is that I was here in this country right through the whole fucking invasion and I've spent every day since I've been here talking to people and seeing what's happening and she arrives out of nowhere and lectures me.

If you just give people money, she tells me, then it encourages dependency. Have you ever heard such a pile of total shit? Have you ever heard anything so fucking patronising in your life? This Iraqi woman has got five children, and her husband has been killed, and his family have refused to help her due to some row about an inheritance or some shit like that, and she's got nothing to eat so what the fuck is she meant to be except dependent?

And I say this to this aid woman – I mean, not in these exact words you'll be glad to know – but I explain to her what this looks like from where I'm sitting. And this stupid woman with her survival equipment and her notepads and her computer which doesn't even work here, says that money is better spent on helping people to look after themselves. Like, for example, this woman with the five hungry children would do better to go to college and get herself some qualifications because that would be more sustainable and enable her to look after herself in the long run.

And this aid woman says – It's very important to have an overall strategy and draw up a plan. You must make a Needs Fucking Assessment and then estimate what the costs will be and what the exit strategy is and check that the assistance you give is going to be sustainable.

And I say – what fucking college? They've all been blown up and looted and closed down because no one can get to them and there's no electricity in any of these places which makes it a bit complicated for anyone to teach any classes there. And this shitty woman from the aid agency tells me that obviously I'm harbouring a lot of anger and that maybe I need to take more rest and look after myself.

And then I tell her that if this woman with the five children waits until she's got a college qualification then her children will be dead. And then the final card – I turn to this Iraqi woman with the five children and ask her if she has any qualifications and it turns out that she's got a fucking PhD. And by this time even this brain-dead aid agency woman is beginning to realise that the particular example that she picked here is a really bad one – but that's part of the problem with these people. Everyone is a case study, or a statistic, or an example of a particular problem. Well, actually, they are none of those things. They are people and they should be listened to as people.

And the truth is that this aid agency lady is getting really nasty with me because she hates to be made a fool of and also because this is really all about something else. It's about the fact that there have been articles in the paper about me and she doesn't like that. Because she wants there to be articles in the paper about her instead. It's just like Patricia says – everything here is about who got their fucking photograph in the newspaper. And yes, Greg did write that article about me and he showed it to me, and yes, I'm glad but only because it will bring in more funds and it will tell people about what it's like here, and how much money is needed and that it's needed for people who are in really bad trouble right now.

And that's what I told this woman and I was yelling at her until she just started reversing out of the room. And I was so fucking angry that I just wished that she would die and then I was angry with her for making me feel like that. And I kept on being angry and shouting at people for the whole of the day and I hated myself for being like that because it doesn't help and actually this aid agency woman isn't a bad person really. She's just a person like the rest of us. And it took me so long to calm down and even now I'm not calm. Partly it's just because it's too hot here and not enough water. I know that what I'm doing is right but I get exhausted. It's so weird here. Sometimes it is just like normal life. People sit around in the bar and drink and they even swim in the pool like it's a holiday. And they watch CNN on the TV and the stuff they're showing is happening a mile away but you can't believe it.

Then one day you're walking through a street and everything is on fire and people are dead. Hans found a part of someone's leg in the road. And everything is so confused because no one knows really what they want, or what should happen. And people half hate the Americans and half love them. I suppose that all I know with certainty is that every day you make the choice – to be kind or not to be kind. And all anyone can do is to keep choosing kindness. Again and again. That's all there is. God I could kill for cornflakes or tea with proper milk. Mum, it's a big thing to do, giving up your job, because I know it was important to you. And it's funny but I even wondered if it is the right thing for you to do – can you believe it after all I've said? But you are right. I have to go because some person here wants to talk to me and I can't understand what he's saying and he seems to want me to eat some bread. Shit I hope this message is going to send now that I've typed it all out.

Love, Jay

## 42

# BEFORE

## Mollie – Worcester, March 1954

Mollie hears his name whispering in the pipework, echoing in high-ceilinged corridors. *Ludo Brandt. 54 Canal Walk. Oh. Him.* The walls of the police station are painted dark green at the bottom and a lighter green above. Rooms have been created from partition walls which do not reach the ceiling and panels of frosted glass. Strip lighting bathes everything in a dull, cold glow. Cigarette smoke swirls and shadows are the colour of weak tea. People cough and shuffle their shoes, a typewriter stutters. Somewhere a man cries out, his voice half muffled.

Below them, floodwater laps through the lower streets of the city. The river, black and sticky, is still rising. Most of the police are out stacking sandbags, helping people move to drier ground. *Up ten foot in the last twenty-four hours*, a voice says. A metal bucket stands in the corridor, catching drops of water which fall from the ceiling with a regular tick, tick, tick. Mollie is led past the ticking bucket to a narrow room, asked to sit in a beige armchair that is crammed in next to a desk with a typewriter and a filing cabinet. *Caught a pike in the Rose and Crown apparently.* Laughter ignites then falters. A fat elderly officer appears with a cup of tea and a blanket. Mollie cries because the situation seems to require tears.

Don't worry, love. Got through to your mother now. She's on her way.

Mollie tells herself she doesn't understand what's happened. She was at Ludo's house, she was showing him some dress designs in her purple notebook. The doorbell rang and he went downstairs to answer it. And then she was in the back of a police car, being driven through the raining city. Playing too loud. Mrs Griffiths complaining. But where is Ludo? Mollie is sure he's somewhere near. She can hear the beating of his heart, behind one of the many half-glazed doors. He left the house without a coat. Mollie hopes that at least his scarf is tightly wrapped around his neck.

High heels rattle in the corridor. Mollie's mother enters with a swish of fur coat and black evening dress. She grips a tiny, diamond-clustered bag in her bird-claw hands. Mollie darling. Are you all right? She places stiff arms around Mollie. Her smell is fur, smoke, gin. Mollie remembers that feeling from long ago, those thin arms stiffly pulling against her.

Just let me speak to the officer in charge.

The policeman raises his eyebrows, gestures to Mollie's mother who follows him out of the door. Together they move along the corridor into another room. Mollie follows them, listens. I quite understand your concern, Inspector, but I'm sure there's nothing like that. Mollie's a very sensible girl. Her mother's voice is clear and concise, confident. All of this is a misunderstanding.

With all due respect, Mrs Fawcett, I'm afraid I can't agree. Mr Brandt is known to us. He's a German and divorced. There have been complaints.

I must take Mollie home. It's late and she's obviously most upset.

Yes, Mrs Fawcett. Of course. But it is necessary.

At the end of the corridor, a brown shadow moves, crossing from one office to another. Tick, tick, tick as water drips into the bucket. Mollie steps back, worried that she'll be seen. *Complaints.* She always knew, of course. No one is arrested for playing music too loud. This is all her fault. Mrs Griffiths saw her crying just a few days ago. Mollie wonders now how she could have been so stupid, how she could have put Ludo at risk. Mrs Griffiths would be capable of any lie. Mollie needs to speak to Ludo immediately, to apologise, to explain.

Mollie hears her mother's voice. Of course, I had no idea she'd gone out of the house. She's never done such a thing in her life. Never.

A murmur, the scraping of a chair.

I don't know what you're suggesting. Yes, I was out for the evening.

The shadow moves again. Mollie slips back into the room with the beige armchair. She pulls her purple notebook out of her bag, grips it tightly. Shadows on the frosted glass reveal people entering the next room. *Brandt? No. They can't keep anyone in. That's the instructions. No staff. Emergency situation, isn't it?* A moment later her mother returns, holds the teacup out to Mollie, who drinks. Their eyes meet for a moment over the rim of the cup. The stick of dynamite, the fuse. She isn't the only person who must work out what story she will tell.

A young policeman comes in and sits down. He is followed by a stiff-backed lady who seats herself at the typewriter. The policeman considers her over the table, notes the quality of her shoes and coat, raises his eyebrows at her, without smiling.

Good evening. Just need to write down a few details. Name? Mollie Fawcett.

The typewriter slides and pings at the end of each line.

He turns to Mollie's mother. Name?

You know my name and my husband's name.

Yes, Mrs Fawcett – but I still have to put it on the forms.

Once my husband returns from his business trip, he will speak to the Chief Inspector.

The young policeman is undeterred. Miss Fawcett – if you could just explain to me how you happened to go to Mr Brandt's house?

Mollie is on stage and this is her moment. A spectacular performance is needed. Just like in the theatre reviews – controlled, emotional, convincing. Step forward into the light, make everyone believe in you. She is the young girl seduced by the monstrous Ludo with the bleeding gash on his neck. Perhaps not the theatre but film. Cameras, action, roll.

And so Mollie tells it all as it happened when she first went to see Ludo, five months ago. Having played the role of innocent victim so often in her head, she is fluent, convincing. She cares for Ludo's safety, of course, but more for her own. I didn't want to drink anything but he gave me this strange red drink and I thought it was only fruit cocktail but it made me feel strange.

The policeman's eyes are stakes pinning Mollie down.

And then?

Well.

Did Mr Brandt behave improperly to you?

Really, I must protest, Mollie's mother says.

Mollie feels the pressure in the room. The lady at the typewriter turns, gives Mollie a look which would sour milk. The policeman clears his throat and Mollie watches his fat hand spread on the desk. Mollie feels the waters of the Severn, moving up the banks towards the cathedral, the High Street. The policeman isn't convinced. How dare he doubt her?

Miss Fawcett. You don't have to be specific but if you could just say.

Of course, Violet says. Of course. Can't you see?

He tried to kiss me, Mollie says, then bursts into tears.

I see. And this was the first time that you had been to Mr Brandt's flat?

Of course this was the first time, Violet says.

The policeman says that Mollie will need to make a statement, if she feels able to do that. If not, she can go home and come back tomorrow. Violet says that Mollie will make the statement now. All this is most upsetting. It will be best for Mollie just to go home and forget about it. Mollie can feel Ludo somewhere close by and she longs for him. The floodwater is lifting the lids of the drains, filling cellars, moving up steps towards sandbagged doors. Where is their Noah's Ark?

Will he go to prison? she asks.

He certainly could.

Perhaps he just made a mistake.

The policeman narrows his eyes and flexes his fat hands. Miss Fawcett, you should be quite clear what kind of man Mr Brandt is. A neighbour has told us she often sees girls as young as ten going into that house. It's full of photographs of young women.

Who work in the theatre.

His house has been searched, there are other photographs.

But those photographs are of—

The sound of the typewriter stops.

Could you repeat that? The policeman says. Mollie thinks of the house by the lake. She thinks of Else, Liesl, Frieda, the snow weighing heavily on the branches of trees, the whippets with their fur collars, shivering. She imagines the hands of the policemen sorting through those photographs, seeing the girls in their swimsuits sitting on the jetty. She moves her hands to her throat, struggles to breathe. No, no, no. Mollie doesn't care what the policeman says or does but he mustn't touch the photographs. He mustn't smear that ice-perfect past, that future which lies so near that Mollie can hear the sound of the waltz music as she walks down the stone steps towards the lake.

Could you repeat that?

No, Mollie's mother says. No. It's time for us to go home. Mollie is upset and overwrought. She's been given alcohol. She needs to sit quietly for a while.

Mollie understands that she's no longer the innocent victim, the nice little girl tricked by the evil monster. Instead she's on the side of the monster, on the side of darkness and bedrooms with drawn curtains and pairs of wet knickers screwed up beside sink taps. She's dirty and cheap – like Donna – but she doesn't care.

The policeman leaves and the typewriter woman follows. Mollie is alone with her mother. She tries to think, to plan, but her mind dashes from place to place. She used to ask that question all the time. What would I have to do to make my mother care? Finally now she's gone far enough. The hot-water bottle will be filled, spoons of sugar will be added to the tea. Except that now it's too late for tea and hot-water bottles. She's crossed the line, is on the other side.

Will he go to prison?

Come along, dear. It's time to go home.

It isn't right that he should go to prison.

Come along, Mollie.

I'm in love with him.

The partitioned walls, the frosted glass, draw in a sharp but stifled breath. Mollie feels her mother's muscles tighten. Soon they will both be engulfed. Usually the floodwaters never come anywhere near the white house high up on the hill. But floods cause landslides and they rot foundations, bring disease.

Mollie, just follow me. Now.

Mollie spreads her thin frame spaciously in the beige armchair.

I won't make a statement tomorrow. I won't say anything.

Her mother's voice hisses. Don't be silly, Mollie. Why waste your life on a lost cause? Believe you me, I did that once and I paid for it – as you will. Come along now.

Mollie knows she holds all the power. If she doesn't want to make a statement tomorrow then she won't. Time to scare the grown-ups, time to light the fuse. Mollie Mayeford would never betray the man she loves. The strip lighting above has no mercy. It shows Mollie every detail of this ordinary little kingdom which she now rules – the brown filing cabinet, the crouching typewriter, the heavy glass ashtray with its hundred angles. But just for now she might as well go home. She doesn't want to cause any more trouble for Ludo, doesn't want him to worry about her. So she shrugs, picks up her notebook, reaches for her school bag.

But something odd is happening in the room. It's as though the lights have suddenly dimmed and the temperature has dropped. Violet's face has become grey and rigid. She's staring at the notebook in Mollie's hands, at the name on the cover. Mollie Mayeford. Her hands are convulsing as she tries to pull a handkerchief from her evening bag. Mollie watches those bird-claw hands wrestling, fears that her mother might fall on the floor or start to foam at the mouth. She takes hold of the evening bag, pulls out the handkerchief, passes it to her mother.

That slick black water that lies all across the lower streets of the city has soaked through the roots of Langley Hill and the white house up above is finally disintegrating, as it was always certain to do. The beams creak and crack, the glass in the windows splinters, sections of the staircase fall and then everything starts to slide as cracks move like spiders up the white façade of the house. Fear suddenly hits Mollie because her mother has shrunk up to nothing, is no more than a little child – powerless, bewildered, her tiny hand clinging to the handle of the door. Mollie knows that she must get her mother home, even if the house has fallen down, and then after that she must run, otherwise Mollie Mayeford will be washed away by the black, seeping Severn, or buried under the falling rubble.

Later that night Mollie stands outside Ludo's house, stares up at the needle-thin line of light that pierces the gap in the curtains above. The rain has stopped but water still drips from gutters and lies in lakes across pavements and streets. Mollie has packed her bag and is ready to leave. Hopefully Ludo will be ready as well, then they can take the last train to London. Mollie's suitcase pulls her shoulder down, weighs heavily on her aching hand even though she didn't pack much. Just a few dresses of her mother's and Alfie the teddy bear and her purple notebook. In her pocket she has twenty pounds which she took from the desk in her stepfather's study. Leafing through the notes, she had thought of him briefly. He had tried so very hard. It had felt wrong to take his money but surely she was owed something and what else was there to take?

She moves towards the door. For a moment she expects to see Mrs Griffiths' white face at the window next door but the damask curtain is drawn. Mollie rings the doorbell, hears the sound above, dull but insistent. She puts down her suitcase, waits. Her mind starts to wander back to that moment in the police station, her mother suddenly tearful and childish. But she mustn't think of that. She expects to hear Ludo's feet on the stairs, the hall light to click on and shine through the glass door, but nothing happens and so she rings the bell again, holding her finger against it for longer this time. And now there is movement inside, feet whispering, a flicker of shadow at the door but no light. A chain rattles, the door eases open a few inches.

Mollie, for God's sake.

I need to talk to you.

No. You must go – don't you understand?

Please.

No.

Ludo. Please.

Go to the canal bridge. I'll be there in five minutes.

Ludo shuts the door and Mollie turns away, heading for the bridge. She knows it well, has walked that way many times but in the darkness everything is different. Her suitcase gnaws at her hand. The water in the canal has risen so high that the bank is no longer visible, just a line of dark water an inch below the tow path. One more drop and the water will be over, sliding down into the street below. Mollie turns right along the tow path. She thinks briefly of her stepfather. He often warns her about walking beside the canal, tells her that he's happy to drive her anywhere she wants to go. Would all of this have been different if he'd been at home this evening? Mollie doubts that it would but still she yearns for him, for sunlight, for the times when he's driven her in the car, her bare legs sliding on the sticky leather of the black seats, her tongue running up the side of an ice-cream cone to catch a stray drip.

Mollie enters the mouth of the tunnel, stops. She doesn't dare go further. At least from here she can still see the yellow haze of street lamps, the black outlines of the roofs of terraced houses. She sits down on her suitcase, grips her hands together. This is wasting time. She and Ludo need to go and get the train. One way or another they must be out of the city by the morning. The station is only half a mile away, full of people who are going somewhere. And soon she and Ludo will be there as well. Around her drops of water fall from the brickwork above and a boom of sound from further up the canal echoes dimly across the dank blackness before. Eventually she sees him, the square shoulders of his overcoat moving uncertainly, sliding through the shadows. His hands are pressed into his pockets, his head down. He enters the mouth of the tunnel, turns towards her, waits.

Ludo, I'm sorry, she says. I'm so sorry. It was my fault.

No, Mollie. No. My type of person is always accused of something.

Their voices echo back at them, disturbing the dripping bricks, the water below.

We need to go, she says. You need to pack. If we don't hurry the train will go.

She hears the smallness of her voice, listens as it is absorbed into dampness.

Mollie, please. You need to go home now. And then tomorrow you must say to the police whatever you need to say, whatever it takes to make everything right.

No. No. I won't do that. You need to pack. We planned it all.

Mollie, please. You can't go to London. You need to go home.

No. No. I'm not going back – ever.

He moves towards her, stares down at her through the liquid grey light.

Why not?

Mollie stares back at his varying shades of darkness. She wants to find the words but there aren't any. In their place is just unease, discomfort, stifled horror. How can she explain? In that house, something struggles unseen, something terrifying which is tied up in a black bag but whimpers and struggles and tries to get out. But it's silenced, pushed back into the cellar, stuffed under sacks of coal. She longs to say this to Ludo and make him understand. But even trying to find the words makes her feel the ground slide away below her feet, makes her step back against the slimy wall so that she can take hold of it and stop herself from sliding into the canal water. Ludo would save her if she could speak but she can't.

This situation, Ludo says. Your mother. She's allowed you to do this. For five months she's asked you no questions, made no enquiries. Anything could have happened to you. Any man could have—

Including you.

Yes. Including me. But why?

The creature inside the bag struggles and whimpers, is pushed back into the cellar.

We need to go, Mollie says.

No.

I'll go to London alone then.

No. You're too young.

I'll have to – because otherwise they'll make me say something and then you will go to prison. And I won't allow that.

Ludo nods his head and she feels the air between them soften, grow mellow. They both know that this story of sacrifice is fiction but Ludo will allow her this because otherwise they'll need to speak again of Langley Crescent, and he'll ask about her mother and her stepfather, and the black struggling thing in the sack will be with them again. The narrative of sacrifice is more exciting, less dangerous, necessary.

If you're really going then I should give you some money, he says.

No.

But he takes his wallet out of the inside pocket of his coat and pulls out notes. She's seen him do this often before but now he pushes them towards her. She takes several five pound notes but divides them and pushes half back at him. She wants him to insist, to push all the money on her, to tell her that he's worried about her safety, to make some payment for the sacrifice that she's making. But he surrenders easily, puts some of the money back in his wallet. Her mind decides not to understand this as a measure of her worth.

But you will come and see me in London?

She feels him take a breath, harden his jaw, prepare himself for brutality.

No. No. You must understand. We must never see each other again.

But I need a job. You have theatre contacts.

Mollie, you have a beautiful voice.

Again that booming sound echoes along the canal, disappears into the blunt silence. Everything is evaporating. She should love him less now but loves him more. She raises her hands to her face. A thousand glasses are shattering inside her head. She thinks briefly of the house up above them. It's made of sheets and flaps in the wind. It has no stability at all. It isn't even there. And neither is the solid, red-brick city below, or the school. All of it is untethered, drifted from its mooring, carried away by the River Severn. With its floods and rages.

We will still go to Austria?

There his brutality fails. He raises his hands uncertainly, pushes his hair back from his eyes, shakes his head. The world of the house by the lake is so close, they need only pull the veil aside and they'll be there. His hands twitch again and he looks away along the canal, sighs.

Mollie, there's no one there for me to visit now.

No.

Yes. No one.

There is. I know there is.

No.

She wants to touch him, to take hold of his hand but if she does he might crumble. Mollie knows now what happened to the house in Austria because she's read about it in books. The crystal smashed, the pictures slashed, the wardrobes pulled open, fur and silk held in grasping hands, the down from feather bolsters spread like snow, other people's boots tramping across the parquet floors. Those images sting but in a way that's half pleasurable. She prefers them to some simpler loss – getting married and moving away, bankruptcy, the passage of time.

I know what happened, she says.

No. You don't. Ludo is brutal again now. Don't make me a victim, Mollie. Don't allow me that excuse. It insults those who really were.

She's breathless now, fighting tears. But still she must know the worst.

Ludo – why did you never?

He considers this question, shrugs wearily.

I always knew that sometime I'd have to do something good.

Mollie watches him, shakes her head. So she has inspired goodness? The improbability of this touches a nerve of laughter. Oh what a fool Ludo is. Why did he have to be good? He clearly has no talent for it. And yet she can't help feeling glad because she knows that he feels satisfied, occupies a position of moral superiority just for once. The air between them has lightened and she should leave it like that. But still she must poke her finger into the wound.

You never loved me?

He steps back from her as though she's smashed her fist into his face. Silence holds them both hostage. But then the air expands, the night releases its grip. He moves forward, touches her cheek, leans down to look into her eyes.

Yes. I did. Far more than you can know.

She stands shocked. His smallness is almost worse than his cruelty.

And that is why you must leave, he says.

Then he moves forward, takes hold of her and kisses her as he never has before. She moves close to him, slides her hands inside his coat, his jacket, wraps her arms around him, feeling the starch of his shirt, the warmth of his skin beneath. But his mouth is cold and tastes of cigars, his teeth snag against her lip. The kiss is finished and still she clings to him, although she doesn't want him to kiss her again. He moves her aside, picks up her suitcase and carries it out of the mouth of the tunnel, places it on the tow path. She has no choice but to move towards it. Inside she's pulled tight, ready to break.

She looks at him blindly – the furrows in his carefully combed black hair, the worn collar of the velvet jacket, the scarf wound tightly around his neck. Already he's become a mere smudge in the blue-grey air. The kiss should turn the toad to the prince, not the other way around. Some part of her is glad to be leaving. There will be plenty of others. He was only a small man, after all. With his beautiful shirts, his handkerchiefs, his fine cigars. A flower in his buttonhole and presents for the girls – stockings, exotic notebooks and powder cases. She'll survive this but he will not – or she certainly hopes he won't. The great occasion has come and he's failed to step forward to meet it. Beside them the black waters of the flooded canal reflect the dull lights of the night.

# 43

# Now

## Lara – Brighton, May 2003

Lara is crying like a waterfall, tears spouting from between her fingers, dripping from her chin, soaking into her shirt. She snorts and sobs, pulls a hand back from her eyes so that she can wipe her cheek with her sleeve. Martha pulls a tissue from a box while Wilf eases the telephone from her hand. Lara tries to speak but is engulfed in another bubbling sob. She takes a tissue from Martha, shudders.

I just didn't know what to say, she says. So little time and I didn't know.

I'm sure you said the right thing, Martha says.

He misses the rain, Lara says. And you probably heard – I said something stupid about how I could put some in a flask, send it to him.

Lara sobs and half laughs, takes another tissue.

That was a lovely thing to say, Martha says. Lovely.

I just had no idea he would call.

No, of course.

Most of the time he was just saying – are you still there? Because he couldn't hear properly.

And she had wanted to say, *I'm here forever now. Here all the time. By your side.* But he'd had to get off the phone before she could speak. Now she looks up and sees a shadow moving on the stairs beyond the door. Something about the shadow, the slow weight of it, its particular blackness, is familiar. Critics have always said that his timing is faultless. The shadow forms into feet in battered brogues, crumpled suit trousers, a rounded belly held together by the button of a jacket. Red hair, sprouting eyebrows. Rufus moves into the room. His hangover-eyes consume the scene in one gulp. Bad moment?

Jay called, Lara tells him.

Oh. For a moment his cynicism cracks. Is he OK?

Yes. For now. Yes. The line was bad. We both kept speaking at the same time. But I said— I didn't say—

Right, Rufus says. I see. He's looking around now at the spider plants, the cardboard box containing the skinny dog with bad nerves, the thick pipes across the ceiling, the high window framing snapshots of feet that pass in the street. He nods briefly now to Martha and Wilf, puts his hands in his pockets, assumes an air of one who has popped in while passing, is merely browsing. But his bull head swivels back to Lara. Perhaps for once I don't need an audience. Maybe you and I should walk?

Yes, Lara says. Yes. She hurries to pick up her coat and bag, wondering why she still jumps to attention for her father. At the door, she turns back. Thank you, she says to Martha and Wilf. Thanks very much. Both of them have been silenced by Rufus's presence. Even the back of Ahmed's head – white collar stiff and clean – seems to have shrunk to half its normal size. Lara takes another tissue, wipes at her eyes, follows Rufus out of the office. The hall above is empty except for a shrivelled lady in a wheelchair, parked in a corner, babbling desperately, a purple fleece rug sliding from her knees. Lara wonders briefly if she should rescue this old lady, offer to push her somewhere. If she fails to do that will Jay die?

But Rufus has gone, out through the glass doors and into the lane. For a moment Lara hesitates but then turns and follows. Even when she's caught up with him, in the lane that runs along the side of the church, he doesn't slow his pace. This is what he always does, stalks on ahead as though he's in a furious hurry, leaving Mollie, or Lara, or whoever else, to trail behind. She waits to see whether he will turn towards the Guest House but instead he heads towards the seafront. Above the chimneys and television aerials of the houses opposite, the clouds are stacked up, in a pearl-grey sky. A persistent wind pulls at Lara's coat, catches in her hair, stings against her damp cheeks.

So, he says, turning back to her. You called me?

Lara buttons her coat against the wind.

Yes. You heard my message.

You want me to come back?

Please, Dad. Don't play games.

He waves his hand with a theatrical flourish, a gesture from a Molière play.

Well, I'm just saying.

They've stopped now in the street and Lara stands close to the railings, feels herself backed against them, trapped. Yes. It's what I said in the message. It's Mum. I can just about do all this – with Jay and everything – but I can't cope with Mum as well. She's just – going mad. Talking all the time about the past. I don't understand.

Rufus shrugs, walks on. They come to the seafront and he stops to cross the road, nearly puts out an arm to usher her across. It seems that he needs to reach the beach, the sea, despite the ripping wind and the occasional drops of rain flung down from the glowering clouds. Lara feels the pebbles of the beach sliding under her feet. Rufus comes to a stop in the shelter of a closed-up deckchair shed. He takes cigarettes and a lighter from his pocket, holds the packet out to Lara who refuses only because she doesn't wish to suggest that companionship might be possible.

So what was it that you didn't say to Jay on the phone?

Well, I didn't say—

The wind comes in a sudden gust, blows Rufus's lighter out, flips Lara's coat collar and hair into her mouth. She turns to shield herself from the blast and manages to force the words out.

I didn't say that I love him.

That was the one thing you needed to say?

Dad, please.

Well, was it, for God's sake?

Rufus pushes himself in closer to the peeling orange paint of the deckchair shed, succeeds in lighting his cigarette, stares along the beach past Lara, his face as forbidding as the sky above. When he speaks he makes each word separate, like the sound of gunfire. So you didn't tell him to come home?

No.

Rufus laughs bluntly, lays the palm of his hand on his forehead, sighs.

Dad. Please. Look. You need to understand. I'm trying to do things differently. I'm trying to listen to him. I'm trying to be honest because I've thought a lot and there's always been this thing between him and me. Look, you know what I'm talking about, don't you? When I was first pregnant. You remember?

No.

Yes, you do. You were trying to help me and I've always treated you like someone who wanted to murder my child.

What?

You remember.

No, Lara listen to me. Actually I really don't remember. Strange as this may seem, large parts of my brain have gone. That's what alcohol does. And as you well know, I don't do the past.

Lara stares at him, looks straight into his clouded, shallow eyes, realises that he genuinely doesn't remember. So much of their lives have been about that night, and much of what is happening now. It's taken her so long to work that out. And he doesn't remember.

Listen, Lara. Listen. Please. We're in the wrong play here, the wrong film, the wrong bloody television miniseries. This is not the scene where we all face up to our mistakes in the past and then that paves the way for a happier future. For Christ's sake, girl. Wake up. Use your brain. You've at least always had a good brain. What's happening here is that your son – who you love and who I love – is in a country which is blowing itself to pieces. And so there's only one thing you need to say, which is – come home. Get the fuck out of there. Now. Right now. And yet you didn't say it. What in God's name are you doing? Getting involved with all this anti-war rubbish, turning into some flakey-loony-liberal wittering on about the past and inner peace and reconciliation. That's what your mother does. Do we need another bleeding heart in this family?

Lara feels as though he has hit her but in another part of her mind she's starting to laugh. Looking at her father, she sees that he's similarly struggling to remain entirely serious. Do you want a drink? he says. I didn't – but I do now.

Lara nods, feeling the salt wind washing tears down her face. Rufus turns and strides along the beach. He's heading for the King's Arms in Rack Street, one of his regular haunts. As they walk the rain thickens, moves in a grey curtain across the seafront. Somewhere in the distance a siren blares. As they cross the road, a drunk sitting on the pavement waves a bottle and shouts, Fucking cunts. Rufus and Lara turn into Rack Street, walk up past the Chinese takeaway and the bookies, past a pink painted sex shop. Feather dusters bloom in the window and pots of wax are piled high in order *to shine your stick.*

The pub is on the corner, ancient and grimy with smoked-glass windows, a revolving door, patterned carpets. Lara sits down in a window seat of green velour while Rufus goes to get the drinks. In the corner a slot machine flashes and somewhere in the sepia distance men lean over a pool table. The air smells of sweat, bacon crisps, spilt beer. Lara considers Rufus's spacious back, wonders whether his absence might have been about something more than Sarah on box office, or Lisa in make-up. She'll never know. Rufus has always made her feel cramped, a person desperately trying to have an existence but constantly crowded out, swamped, silenced. But despite the fact that he's always occupied all the space with his ceaseless me-me-me, it's impossible ever to know him. Now he returns with a pint of beer and a glass of white wine as big as a goldfish bowl. He sits down, drinks from his pint. A line of white froth appears along his red moustache.

I'm sorry, love, he says. But I mean what I said. We just need to get him back.

Lara looks at him across the table. He's aged since she last saw him – the skin of his face sags, his neck is fleshy, the whites of his eyes are yellow, veined with red. Usually he makes an effort with his clothes – bow ties, cravats, a check tweed suit, gold cufflinks – but now he looks like a bookie who's spent several nights on a park bench. She feels herself turning to liquid, fears that she might cry again. How quickly Rufus can demolish whole worlds. But the worst of it is that he's right.

Must say, the lad's got guts. I would never have thought it of him.

Rufus drinks again.

Look, I'll deal with Mollie and you get Jay back. Is that a deal?

Dad, I'm not sure there is any way.

Try. Do everything you can. Insist.

There is this Spanish journalist, Patricia.

OK. Good. Well, that's a start. You've got to do all you can. And I'll deal with your mother. Not right now. I've stuff in London to finish with first. But I'll definitely come home by the time Jay is back.

I'm just not sure.

You can do it. Of course you can.

Rufus doesn't need to say that Jay will never need to know what's happened in his absence. Jay will need to feel that the home front has been united – perhaps for the first time ever.

And after that we'll do the reconciliation scene – all right? Rufus says.

The distant pool players blur in a sudden rush of tears. Lara sees a whole world before her, a world which she has never known. Happy Families. Mrs Bun the Baker's Wife and Miss Bones the Butcher's Daughter. Or that Ladybird book world of Janet and John where father sits by the fire smoking a pipe. The loss strangles her, every bone feels broken. How she hates him. But as she leans forward and sobs, she allows him to lay his hand above hers on the sticky, dark wood table. Lara longs for one person in the family to be whole, able-bodied. The jukebox plays.

Dad, why do you always come back?

Oh, socks, shirts, car insurance, he says, stares away from her, into the pool-table gloom, but then looks back. Because I made her a promise, he says. A long, long time ago. And I've broken a lot of promises in my life but I won't break that one.

She can't allow his sincerity. The old habit can't be broken.

So was that before or after you pushed her off the roof?

Rufus eyes her narrowly. She expects him to shout but his voice is smoke and gravel. Oh yes, of course. Monstrous Rufus pushes poor weak defenceless Mollie off the roof. What a bastard, what a scandal. Come on, Lara. You spent eighteen years living with us – or at least eleven. I think you know.

Lara wonders what she's ever known. The fault line. That's what she's always tried to identify but every time she comes close, it shifts. The push and pull of need and sufficiency, of tenderness and brutality, their strange dance of hate and desire. Movements so swift that only Mollie and Rufus, with their surprising neat feet, their carefully aligned movements of hips and arms, can ever hope to follow. And there she is, her feet always dragging behind, endlessly out of step.

Maybe it was the war? Lara says.

Rufus shakes his head, sighs. You know your mother was actually too young to remember any of that. And as for the pimp who seduced her when she was only fourteen. I don't know. But sometimes things do happen in life, things so bad that all you can do is just get up, walk on, take care not to look back. The present isn't determined by the past. Not unless you let it be.

But Dad.

Listen, love, you will never understand. You can't. There may actually be no Mollie to understand. Now come on. For Christ's sake. Get on with the present day. Allow that boy to be something other than an argument between you and your mother.

Behind them the music swirls again and balls on the pool table click. And she thinks then of Jay. Where is he now? He made the call from the Palestine Hotel so he might still be there.

Maybe he's in the lobby and perhaps it's not so very different from this Brighton pub. The same sky overhead, the same foggy air – hotter there perhaps and laced with sand, but still the same. Blonde marble there instead of dark wood. And more light but still the feeling that everyone is passing through, purposeful but lost, caught as though by a camera in this particular moment, spectacular and insignificant.

Rufus has finished his beer and stands up, ready to leave. Again she sees how the years have accumulated in him, leaving him stiff, heavy, marooned. He puts on his coat, squares his shoulders. Lara thinks of what Mollie says about him. She does have a point, finally. What must it be like to spend your whole life working towards something and never having the success you feel you deserve? Underneath all the layers of pretence, there's a kind of purity to him, a courage. Oliver once told her that people can die for lack of praise. We all of us live in the belief that hard work and determination will be rewarded – but sometimes it just isn't like that. Lara could feel some pity for her father but she knows that, beyond all else, he would hate that.

# 44

# Now

## Jay – Baghdad, May 2003

Hi Mum, Granmollie, Grandad, all you guys back home,
It was great to speak to Mum a few days ago. I guess you'll
have heard what happened. This Spanish journalist called
Jordi just got killed – shot in the back of the head at point
blank range and he wasn't down some dark alleyway in
a dodgy area. He was in the Green Zone on his way to a
meeting in the middle of the day and someone just shot him
in the back of the head. I didn't know him properly but he
was someone I'd said hello to plenty of times and there are
loads of people here who did know him well. Everyone is just
in shock – people not even crying, just sitting around with
these flat expressions on their face, not saying anything at all.
Hans was in the next street when it happened. And my friend
Patricia is broken up in one hundred pieces because although
he's not the same news channel she knew him pretty well.
And everyone knows hundreds, maybe thousands of Iraqis
got killed, certainly many more than the media are saying,
and probably a load more are going to be killed before too
long and no one thinks that matters less but it's just really
scary because it means that foreigners are actively being
targeted. Also it just shows that this place is breaking down,
which is anyway clear as you'll have seen on the news.

It was always so obvious that this was going to happen,
which is why the peace movement asked all those questions
about reconstruction plans but no one listened and now

things are really out of control and now it's a sad time here. Except that I don't feel it so actually. A few weeks ago I was really low and fed up and hopeless but that passed and I feel really fine. I'm glad to be alive, and here in this city that I love, and I feel you all very close to me, right here. In the evenings I just sit around in this house where I'm staying. It's not great there because the electricity is off and the daughter of the family had a miscarriage, probably caused by the stress of the bombings. But still people cook food and play music and they light candles and talk. I go up on the roof and from there you can see quite a lot of the city. It's really beautiful sometimes when the sun is going down and from below I can hear people chatting and laughing. It's really strange the way people's lives just go on. Sometimes one of the women down below sings to her kids. It's like a lullaby to get them off to sleep. She has this really beautiful, quiet, echo-like voice and it's just such an amazing sound travelling over the roofs. I can't really understand much of what is going on although I get more and more.

There's an old guy here who is the great uncle of the family and he has a kidney problem which isn't going to get proper treatment and so being entirely realistic I should think he doesn't have too long to live. He speaks really good English so we talk a bit together and he's really happy. Just really, really happy. It's hard to know why except we both agree that maybe it's easier to be happy when you don't have anything much to be happy about. Anyway I have to go now because Greg needs the computer. Thanks so much for all that you guys are doing in England. I love you.

Jay

# 45

## BEFORE

### Mollie – London, March 1963

The show is over. Mollie sits in front of the lighted mirror in her dressing room and waits. She's taken off her make-up, changed her clothes, applied cream to her face, neck, hands. She pinned her hair up in a high ponytail but still she waits. The room is windowless, the ceiling low. Costumes – silk and lace, itchy and stiff – hang from a rail. They carry the imprint of other bodies, the material worn thin at shoulders and cuffs, stitching stretched across the bust.

Behind her, vases of white lilies, red roses, carnations, violets are crammed onto a narrow table. Some of the flowers are wilting now and their petals, brown at the edges, have floated down onto the table. The dank smell of their water lies heavy in the overheated room. Mollie stares at her hand – small and vividly white under the harsh lights. If she looks hard enough, she'll see straight through her fingers to the white Formica of the table below.

Usually a driver takes her home but tonight she's cancelled him. Although perhaps in some shadow life a woman who looks just like her has walked out through the stage door, wearing a mink stole and an acetate satin shift dress, signing autographs, sliding into the car, giving a queenly wave as it pulls away. Mollie wishes she could do that now, as she has done so many nights before, but her white hand is the same colour as the white table below and it's hard to see the difference between hand and table.

A rattling noise sounds in the corridor outside. Footsteps shuffle. The other dressing rooms are being locked up now. The show is over, has been over for more than an hour. People must have come in earlier to enquire as to her needs, to offer assistance. What did she say – if anything? Standing up, she reaches for her mink stole, then leans down to pull her two-tone shoes with tapered toes from under the dressing table. Her hands seem able to position her shoes, fasten the clip on her stole, but still they're transparent. She reaches to pick up her black evening bag, even though it's full of acid that might spill onto her hands or clothes, burn through her flesh. Her fingers close on the slim silk, feel through to the document within, the birth certificate that can't be hers because the date is wrong.

Her mind flicks back to Somerset House – the high windows looking out onto the street, the pale brown light, the radiators sighing, secretaries in clicking shoes passing along the endless corridors. Cavernous ceilings, a smell of cooking cabbage, desks behind glass, queues. She had thought it would be so simple. Just a copy of her birth certificate so then she can apply for a passport. She needs one because she's got auditions with Seven Arts and MGM. They're making a film of Tennessee Williams's play *The Night of the Iguana*. Only one of the minor roles – but still.

And so she sets out mid-morning, with a mild headache from the night before, walking along the Strand through aching sun, towards Waterloo Bridge, Somerset House. And amidst the muffled echoes of the reception area, she fills out a form. Name? She writes Mollie Bunton, of course, the name of the father she never knew, who was killed near Dunkirk. It feels strange to write it down, she never has before.

Mollie Fawcett, Bertie's stepdaughter, that's who she really is. Bertie always said, *Of course you're really my daughter, the best daughter a man could have.* Briefly tears crowd to her eyes as she thinks of him. Date of birth? 28 February 1940. Coventry. All done. She hands the form in, collects a number, sits down on a bench seat under one of the long windows. Other people eat sandwiches, pour tea from flasks, comfort whining children. The minutes stretch into hours, lunchtime arrives. Many people who arrived after her have gone. Finally she is called to the counter. The man behind the glass can't be more than thirty-five but is entirely bald.

I'm sorry. There must be some mistake. No one of that name, on that date.

But there must be.

No. We have checked several times.

28 February 1940.

Are you sure? Because that really can't be the case.

A light, round like the moon, shines down onto the man's smooth head.

The register must be wrong.

That's impossible, the man says. It is never wrong.

She feels a slight jolt, an unsettling of the pale brown light.

Mollie Bunton. She says the name loudly. 28 February.

The man's hands, gripping a piece of paper, are small and sinister. So very hairless, but with red spots, as though recently shaved. His glasses are square and thick, his eyes behind them red and watering. On his chin, a shaving cut has a piece of tissue paper stuck to it. Inside the stiff cuffs of his shirt, his wrists are horribly thin, the blue veins standing up against shivering white skin.

Are you sure? Because that really can't be the case.

Please will you check. 1940. It must have been 1940.

Again she waits, wishes she had brought sandwiches with her. The sunlight at the long windows has gone. Occasionally she hears the distinctive growl of a taxi's engine or the upper level of a red bus appears at the high windows next to her. Men read newspapers, a woman knits, her needles gently clicking. Occasionally Mollie looks up at the row of moon lights which hang behind the glass partitions, their weak light softening the brown shadows. She is called up to the same counter again.

Yes, we did find that name. 4 November 1940. Would you like a copy?

Mollie swallows, looks back briefly at the bench where she was sitting, those high windows. She shuts her eyes, takes a grip on her mind. That speck of tissue paper has gone from the man's chin revealing a smear of blood. What difference does that date make? She just needs a piece of paper that will enable her to get a passport. And that's what she's being offered. Clearly there has been some mistake but what is the point in asking questions? In arguing?

Yes, she says. Yes.

The man gives instructions about how to get a copy of the certificate that clearly isn't hers. Those hairless white hands gesture, his cuffs move up revealing more of those stick-thin wrists.

Shouldn't take more than twenty minutes.

She nods and smiles but when she sits down again she's shaking. She's always known, of course. Something has always been out of place, dislocated, fractured. Now she wants to know. What happened in Coventry? Is she not her mother's child? Images appear of her mother lifting a baby from a burning house – some other person's baby? An illegal adoption, an arrangement made between friends that was never formalised? The only person who would know is her mother and she's never spoken to Mollie since that night when she left, after the police station, after Ludo.

Her name is called. The copy is available now. A secretary at a different counter passes it to her and she puts the brown envelope in her bag. Good. All done. Time to get back now. She was up late last night, wants a rest before the theatre at six. But she doesn't leave, walks up and down the reception area, sits down, stands up again. She has to know. She takes another ticket, waits. The queues are less now. In half an hour – *just sit with your hands in your lap, do not think about anything* – she's back in front of the man with the bald head.

I need you to check. I need you to find if there was any other child called Mollie born on 28 February 1940 in Coventry?

Sorry but we can only deal with a known surname. Otherwise you have to write.

The man is wringing those fragile hands.

No. I need to know now. Please.

His fearful red eyes bulge behind the square spectacles.

I can't. There's still a queue. You can see.

Please.

Look, miss. I might be able to but you'd have to wait. Until we're closing up, until I've dealt with all the other numbers.

His thin lips are pursed, his eyes watering.

Thank you. I'll wait.

And so she waits. Walks up and down the corridors, tries not to clench her jaw. Occasionally Mollie looks over towards the bald man but his head is always bent down over papers. He knows she there but refuses to meet her eye. The clock ticks on until five o'clock. Shutters are being pulled down on the glass screens at some of the counters. Everyone is leaving. A cleaner appears with a bucket and mop, another starts to empty the bins. Doors slam, keys are turned in locks. Voices are heard calling. *Got through another one. See you tomorrow. Have a good evening.* The bald man looks up, raises a finger, nods. She steps out across the polished floorboards.

I did find another. Name of Mollie Mayeford.

Mollie's hand grips the edge of the counter.

But that was only a name I made up.

Even as she says the words, she knows this isn't true. Someone else said that name? Who? Arthur. That day when he came to the house. He said he was a cousin of her mother's. And later there was that moment, the night she left, the name Mollie Mayeford written on the notebook. The police station, the frosted glass partitions, the light suddenly dim. Her mother's bird-claw hands wrestling with the handkerchief, her face grey and rigid, her eyes fixed on that notebook, that name.

A period of time goes missing. Mollie finds herself sat on the bench under the high windows again.

Would you like a glass of water, miss?

The bald man clasps his hands together as though scared that he might drop them. Mollie stares at him, unable to speak. But the air is clearing. For a moment, everything had seemed tangled, cracked, ruined. But now the world is pure and healed. She always knew that she was Mollie Mayeford. When Arthur said the name she knew and that's why she chose that as her stage name. And, of course, there is no blood relationship between her and her mother. That's why they were never close, could never communicate. That's why her mother never liked her.

She looks up at the bald man, flashes him her most magnetic smile.

It's quite all right. It was a shock but now I understand. There always was confusion. You know, Coventry, the war. And then my mother remarried. I did always know that really my name is Mayeford.

Oh no, my dear. No.

Those plucked hands twist together.

Yes.

No.

Why not? Why not?

Because. Well, I'm sorry. But Mollie Mayeford is dead. Died in Coventry in April 1941, aged fourteen months.

Mollie stares up at him, focuses on the rims of his thick glasses, then the red lids of his eyes. Surely they contain the answer to her questions? Briefly his small hand flutters towards her, then crumples, like something dying. She has to stop herself reaching out for those childish fingers, grasping the thinness of that wrist. His lips crease open into a confused smile, then relax into blank bemusement. Mollie turns and walks out into a glimmering, grey evening. Waterloo Bridge, a boy on a delivery bike dashing past. She recoils from normality as though from a slap. She is dead, has always been dead.

She steps out of her dressing room, into the red-brick corridor. Flats and stage lights are stacked along it, and cardboard boxes containing old programmes. Behind her she hears again the rattle of keys. It's important that she doesn't meet the key person for he might offer kindness and she'll not survive that. So she slides away hurriedly, her shoes clattering down dimly lit steps.

Arriving outside the green room, she turns right, heading for the stage door. She needs the darkness, the night, for there it will be less obvious that she is losing her shape. The door opens with a clatter and she steps out into a dash of sharp night air, a splatter of rain. She turns her head away from the lights that glare from the bar opposite. Shadows move in the narrow street, a woman laughs raucously. Mollie pushes her head down into the folds of her stole, hurries on and so bowls into the front of his jacket before she's even seen him. She doesn't need to raise her eyes to identify him. Stepping back, she tries to dodge past but he moves fast.

Why did you cancel the car?

She doesn't look at him.

Excuse me, please. I'm in a hurry.

But I want you to have dinner with me.

Now she looks up, sees the blunt face high above her, the crest of red hair.

I'm sorry but I think I've made clear—

He mimics her words in a silly, squeaky voice. Then says, Come on. And lays his hand on her arm, steering her on towards the end of the street. He's never dared to touch her before and she feels the grip of his fingers as an act of violence. But she doesn't pull away, allows him to push her on down the street. Her heart starts to beat again, blood washes through her veins. If she has dinner with him then she'll remain distinct from the night, her hands will return to their normal colour, she'll become the woman who gets into the car that waits at the stage door. Even as she makes this decision, she smells disaster, sees a flare of flame, hears the scream of braking tyres, breathes in the smell of singed hair.

But still they walk on. London dances past them, liberated after months of snow. There were icicles a yard long, a car driven across the frozen Thames. Now that warmth has finally come people feel it like an electric current, swing their arms, smile for no reason.

Lights and traffic, pubs swelling out onto the pavements, shop models blank-faced in the lighted windows of passing stores. A newspaper headline reads – *Profumo denies affair with model.* Another announces – *Closure of more than 2,000 railway stations.*

A homeless woman sits on the street cuddling a dog and drinking a bottle of beer. A black girl smiles from a doorway, her hair standing out in a perfect circle around her head, fluffy as a dandelion clock. Mollie is conscious of the height and weight of the man beside her. He's holding up the buildings that line the street, keeping the traffic off the pavements. His head even supports the sky as it bristles with neon below a low, slim moon.

The restaurant is in a basement room, the air thick with the smell of marijuana. The wallpaper swirls and rubber plants crowd close to the table. *Paper doll, dressing up, so many clothes, so many colours, so many ways to be.* Rufus orders champagne and oysters. He wears a dark suit with narrowed lapels, a narrow tie. Is he Irish or an Italian with red hair? Rumour has it that he's Nigel Dalking from Dudley. Now that he's opposite her, she's reminded of all that she doesn't like about him. His size, his bulk, that ghastly red hair which he should wear short but doesn't. And his face – blunt and heavy, with thick lips, wild eyebrows, mean eyes. Mollie likes her men slim and sleek, sophisticated, genteel. She's had plenty of them, but has always managed things discreetly. Mollie Mayeford is a classical actress, not a chorus girl slut.

Rufus Ravello is only an understudy and would never have performed at all if Mervin Ratch hadn't lost his front teeth in an incident involving a fast-moving pavement. Rufus can do nothing to further her career – and she wants to do nothing to further his. Now she worries that he might use the wrong cutlery or be rude to the waiter but he plays his part with exaggerated style. They speak about something – the lead actor and his bad breath, the offer she's received to go to America. MGM, Seven Arts. Rufus knows all that, of course. It's all the gossip at the theatre. And she may get a Broadway audition as well. New York, city of dreams. Yes, she longs to see King Kong hanging over the Empire State Building.

It would be so easy just to say – because I'm going to Los Angeles, New York, I need a copy of my birth certificate. And then she could describe it to him – making it all sound rather funny, a jolly jape – the rows of desks behind glass. And the way that man kept saying, *Are you sure? But that really can't be the case.* And the birth certificate with the wrong date. What a joke. Can you believe it? But she can't say any of those words. Instead she sees the bald man's hands, like something small and dead. They sway and fragment in her head, as though reflected in water.

So exciting to see King Kong hanging over the Empire State Building. New York, city of dreams. Of course, it won't really be like that. She'll never get there, not now. Breath sticks in her mouth, refuses to travel down her throat. She smiles determinedly, laughs a little, drains a glass of champagne. Do not let him see the truth, the fear. She clings tightly to her knife and fork, the stem of her glass. I have drunk too much, she thinks, but knows that's the least of her problems. The coffee is poured, the slim mint chocolates eaten, the restaurant is growing quieter. Mollie is frightened by the spaces around her. Things may slip through the gaps, be lost for ever. People even. *Are you sure? Because that really can't be the case.*

You must take me home, she says to Rufus.

No, not yet. I want you in my car. I want to drive you – somewhere.

He allows no opposition, asks the restaurant to find a cab and sweeps Mollie into it. His hand is once again locked onto her arm and Mollie has to make an effort not to place her hand over his, just to feel the solidity of it. The garage where he keeps his car is near St Paul's, he tells her. The cab swoops down towards the river that is garlanded with strings of glittering lights. Across the water the slab-façades of County Hall and the power station crouch in the darkness. All of London is laid out just for them. Rufus takes Mollie in his arms and kisses her. He's surprisingly gentle, runs his tongue along the top of her lip.

The cab stops in a back street and they get out. Rufus takes keys from his pocket and unlocks the doors of the garage. Mollie waits as he heads into the darkness, hears the car door click open and then the engine start. The car glides out – it's ivory with a red soft top. Brand new, a Daimler Dart. Rufus winds down the window. Knobs and dials wink on the dashboard, the interior is all red leather.

Come on. Get in.

As soon as the door is shut, he slams the car backwards, then pushes his foot onto the accelerator, speeding out of the mews and into the main street. London spins dizzyingly past – Holborn, Tottenham Court Road, Oxford Circus, Piccadilly. Mollie slides across the red leather seats until Rufus puts his arm around her, turning the wheel with only one hand. The engine roars beneath them and the car moves without the slightest jolt. Trafalgar Square, the Mall, Hyde Park. Mollie laughs, clings onto his arm, as he takes a tight corner at Victoria. In Sloane Square, he jumps the lights and the windscreen of another car is suddenly close, enclosing a hollow-mouthed face. Mollie screams, Rufus brakes and tugs at the wheel. Mollie is flung forward and then back again, but as Rufus howls with laughter, she joins her voice with his. Behind them a car horn is blaring again and again.

Mollie thinks of Mervin Ratch and the fast-moving pavement. Rufus was there that night. You've got to put two and two together. But Mollie had never believed the gossip. Rufus slams his foot down again and shops, buildings, parked cars, lighted bars, merge together in a clash of colour. Tyres squeal, faces turn in shock, somewhere a siren sounds. Finally Rufus jerks the car into Chelsea Wharf, close to the river. And there they sit, shocked by the sudden stillness and silence, watching the river and the strip of dull yellow light which burns above the rooftops, bleeding into the blackness above.

You know I'm in love with you, Rufus says.

And I'm not in love with you.

Yes. I know. But I think you will be soon.

He kisses her again, slides his hand up her silk-stockinged leg. She's seized by panic. She doesn't want him, repeats this over and over again to herself. *I do not want this man, I do not want him.* But she's made out of cloud, or rain, or river water and so can do nothing to resist. She needs oblivion and Rufus's desire may prove enough to wipe her out entirely, erase her like a faint pencil line smoothed from the page.

Come on, he says. Let me take you home.

But he doesn't take her home. Instead the car idles up the King's Road, comes to a halt outside a mansion block near the Chelsea Hospital.

Is this where you live?

Where my friend lives but he's away. I can't afford a garage and a flat.

She follows him through a half glazed door into a marble and chandelier hall, up discreetly carpeted blue stairs. The steps narrow as they climb. The flat is right at the top with a cramped door but inside the sitting room is spacious with patio doors leading on to a terrace. White sofas surround a vast glass-topped table which stands on a zebra rug. Mollie thinks suddenly, achingly, of Ludo. Rufus is so much bolder but only because he has no kindness in him and has failed to see the danger. Now he goes to a drawer and produces a tiny white paper packet and a mirror.

You're a fake, Mollie says.

Of course, he says. Aren't we all? If you can't pretend, you die.

As Mollie bends over the white powder her face appears for a moment in the mirror – her nose huge, her eyes distorted, her mouth crooked. She breathes in and a wave breaks inside her head. She splutters, coughs and sniffs again. The wave rushes at her once more, causes such a surge of elation that her feet leave the ground. Like a child's balloon, she's floating away across the city, past the church spires and office blocks, the bridges over the Thames, all across the hop fields of Kent, out towards the open sea.

What's that door? she asks.

It goes out onto the roof.

Can we go out? I want to see the river. The sea. I must.

Later.

He leads her through to the bedroom, which is lined by endless cupboards with mirrored doors. Fragments of herself and Rufus flicker all around her. A camera is mounted on a tripod and a black leather chair is pushed into a corner. The bed is six foot wide and spotlights are positioned above so that their circular lights illuminate the crumpled satin sheets.

Take off your clothes, he says, and so she does, feeling the cool air of the bedroom touching against every corner of her flesh. What does it matter now? She had anyway grown bored of perfect little Mollie Mayeford and her pretty ways. Without clothes, Rufus is less than she expected. His body is too long, his legs short and bowed. He carries the marks of a man who drinks and eats too much. In her mind, she weighs revulsion and desire although finally what she feels is of no importance. All that matters is that his desire should be enough to wipe her out entirely. He moves towards her and eases her down onto the bed. For a while he kisses her gently but then he stands her up, turns the black leather chair around and positions her over the back of it, does something which she'd always thought to be illegal. She feels the thrill of humiliation, tries not to cry out as her hips are pushed against the back of the chair, again and again. She knows he's driven by hate, by the desire to damage her. In her mind, she pleads with him to stop but her lips remain tight shut.

Afterwards, collapsed on the bed, she can't keep back her tears. Oblivion can only erase her for a while. He comes to her, holds her, wraps her in the satin sheets. But she can't settle, feels herself set alight, possessed. Pulling away from him, she stands up and looks at herself in the many mirrors. And there it is, as she had expected. A seven-armed beast, or perhaps a black devil, or a serpent, clinging to her back, crawling up her leg. See what she and Rufus have released. A line has been crossed, they've entered into forbidden knowledge. Mollie finds Rufus beside her, shuts her eyes, presses herself into his arms. He knows that he's seen the beast as well, even though he might deny it. And so now she's bound to him forever. This will never be discussed but is printed into the marrow of the bone.

Please, she says. Please. Let's go out onto the roof.

Why?

Please. I need air. The sky.

She does not say – even now, the possibility of escape.

The river. I want to see the river. The sea.

Rufus pulls on a shirt, jacket, trousers, finds a bathrobe for Mollie. She follows him through the narrow door into the sitting room and out into the night. Ahead of them, steps lead up into a corridor along a gutter, onto a section of flat roof. The night air is shivering, wet with dew, buffeted by a shaggy wind. Mollie feels the damp wooden steps under her bare feet, the sandpaper scrape of roofing felt. Every sensation is gloriously magnified. Her skin is thin as tissue. Around her a jungle of chimneys rises, a hieroglyphic alphabet of TV aerials. The stars hang low enough that she might catch hold of one and pull it down, pluck it like an apple from a tree. Here Mollie is connected to nothing at all. Balloon. Park. Floating.

Where is the river? I want to see.

She leans against the sloping tiled roof to steady herself. Above her hangs a frosted glass window. Rufus appears with a bottle of champagne, the cork explodes across the sky. So much better to be out in the air, Mollie thinks, shuts her eyes, feels her body sway and dip. She hears Rufus speak to her, sees him offer a glass – but behind him the devil is there again, black and clinging. She seizes the champagne, pours it down.

And then the words break from her, jabbering, running away from her across the roofs like scurrying ants. That's not my birthday, not my birth certificate. In Coventry a dog was running down the street with a child's arm in its mouth.

Rufus grips her arm, shakes her.

The man at Somerset House, his hands. And then I asked about Mollie Mayeford, and she's dead. Dead all this time.

But we're all dead, Rufus says. Of course we are.

No, no. You don't understand.

Mollie pulls away from him, runs back down the wooden steps, into the sitting room where the zebra rug drifts high above the floor, ready to depart through a window like the Arabian Nights. And Ludo calls to her, warns her, offers to take her back home with him, back to Canal Street in Worcester and the photograph albums, the ice-perfect world of that Austrian lake. *So kind of you to offer, my darling, but it's too late.* In the bedroom, Mollie finds her acid evening bag, pulls out the birth certificate, hurries back up onto the roof.

Look, she says. Look.

Rufus will not take the paper from her but still the words keep running away from her. They multiply everywhere – by tens, by hundreds – running across the roof like spiders. It will be impossible ever to stamp them out. I need to ask my mother but she never wrote. I tried again and again to get in touch.

Mollie. Shut up.

I wrote again and again.

Shut up.

Not known at this address, Mollie thinks. But my mother was still there. With my stepfather, laughing, leaving. Violets on the lawn. I never minded much about her but he was different. You're really my daughter, of course you are, the best daughter a man could have.

Never stopped missing him.

Shut up. Shut up. Rufus is shrinking as fast as she is. All the pretending is falling away. Nigel Dalking from Dudley and a pencil mark on a piece of paper, easily erased, are entirely alone, together on the roof of this borrowed flat. Do not let the balloons float away. She looks at him and the layers are all peeled back, fear meets fear in yearning eyes. And Mollie knows that she'll remember this moment forever, just as she'll remember the black clinging beast. The turning in the road, all that might have been but will not be. Because Rufus is recovering himself, will never admit to any of this, will never allow it again, is searching now for the way to bring them back to themselves – or away – forever.

She feeds him the line, speaking in a squeaking, hysterical voice. And the house sliding down the lawn, collapsing slowly.

Shut up, he says. What does it matter? It's a piece of paper. Give it to me.

I can still use it to get a passport.

But when he snatches the paper from her, she doesn't resist. The passport doesn't matter any more and Rufus knows that. All that matters is that the evidence of that long ago lie should be destroyed. The paper rips in Rufus's blunt fingers, each piece is torn again and again. Fragments of white float into the night, caught in the twisting breeze. All gone now but still Rufus bends down, picks up a fragment caught on a roof tile, tears it into halves, quarters. Mollie stares into the damp greyness, watches the pieces drift away. Rufus is right. What does it matter? The clerk at Somerset House made a mistake. If she wants a passport she can simply borrow one from someone who looks like her. She knows plenty of people who've done that. Exile will become home, pretence the only reality on which she can depend.

Gone. Gone. She shouts, turns back to Rufus, kisses him. Dead, she says. And so now we can do anything, anything. I want to see the river. Where is the river?

She clings to his hand, pulls at it. So this is the way it will be, this is the byway they've taken. And now she needs to know just how far he'll go. Pretence can only grow, expand, accumulate. Truth and dare. Or a dare which covers the truth. Together they'll perform their lives. Make the gestures big, the emotions grandiose. Enunciate the lines clearly. Spell it out for the audience or they will not understand.

I'll see the river if I climb up.

No, you won't.

You think I can't.

I know you can do anything.

He's right. She can do anything. And so she starts to climb.

The tiles are slippery and her hands grip at nothing. But she's determined. She feels Rufus watching her, steadies her bare feet on the slope. The wind catches at the bathrobe. Soon she is up, her bare legs straddling the ridge of the roof.

I still can't see the river. I need to get up on the chimney.

A light comes on at the frosted glass window, the outline of a figure appears. The window rattles as the figure tries to pull it open. An arm appears and the edge of a sink, with a toothbrush standing up in a tooth mug. Mollie begins to stand, fluttering, taking care not to look down. Beyond the buildings on the other side of the square, that's where the river must be, but still she isn't high enough. She knows that she will not fall because he's there. She sees his face below – grey, suspended, featureless.

Mollie, for God's sake.

Under her feet, something moves, stones grate and crack. Her hands scrabble on the red-brick chimney, her cheek smashes against it. The world somersaults – roofs, chimneys, aerials, sky, stars. Everything spirals together. Bricks crumble and drop. A woman screams. Mollie's bones roll, banging and slapping over the roof tiles. Stop, stop, but she can't catch hold, folds like a rag over the edge. And now she will fall forever, into the square below.

But instead she lands immediately with a dull thud which presses itself into her bones. Her face is wet and she can taste blood in her mouth. She's lying on a sheet of black tar, next to a wall. A terracotta pot is inhabited by dead twigs, a mop propped against the wall. A light flicks on and she's bathed in its dull fuzz. Doors bang. She tries to move her twisted leg but pain dashes down her arm, across her back, into her hand. It's starting to rain now and so the stars will go out and she'll be washed away, washed off the roof like an autumn leaf, down into the streets, swept away down a gutter. A scraping sound and something is yanked open. A man's voice mumbles. Then Rufus is beside her. She can hear his breathing but she's turned the wrong way and can't see him. She wants to move but she's frightened of the pain.

Mollie. For Christ's sake.

He takes hold of her hand and she expects him to hold it gently. But instead he seizes hold of her and twists her around. Her whole body is blazing red with pain. It lights up the tips of her teeth. She's facing him now and his eyes, cheeks, lips are clenched tight. She tightens her grip on him, pressing his fingers together. Behind him she sees patio doors, the illuminated stillness of an antique-filled sitting room. In a corner of the room, an elderly man is speaking on a telephone. Mollie shuts her eyes and a woman's voice says, He pushed her, I heard them, I saw him, I was at the bathroom window.

Mollie tries to move again, feels that flame of pain flare across her back. Rufus is kneeling beside her, his face white and shapeless as a potato, flattened by shock. And now, as he holds her hand, he's crying. That pleases her. She'll forgive him for pushing her off the roof, of course. She needs his hatred, his loathing. Together they'll convince, together they will entertain the clinging devil and defy the power of pieces of paper, together they will be invincible.

Promise me, she says. Promise.

# 46

# Now

## Patricia – Baghdad, May 2003

Dear Mother of Jay,

Here is Patricia who is Spanish journalist and friend of Jay and of Greg. Greg gives me your email and so I am getting in touch. We know here that you are very worried about Jay and so I give you now the latest news. Everyone has told Jay that he has to go home for a while now. And we have told him as well that this is what you want with all your heart. He has been in this country where there is war and death now for three months and this is no good to stay so long. All of the journalists here and the Peace Corps come for a few weeks and then they go home and back again. This is very necessary and everybody here has said this several times to Jay. The adrenalin of war is a drug, an addiction. You come to the time when the normal life of every day will kill you. This is no good. Jay has been seen this morning in Saddam City. This place was never a good place and now is very bad with much violence and journalists and people from Europe are very dangerous there. I went there this morning with other journalists and an Iraqi driver and two armed guards. Also we have a TV sign in the van. But Jay is there without any guard and he may be safe because he is known and people see him. They understand that he is not like anyone else. But still it is dangerous. And I have not the English to tell you how it is really – but it is like he is on fire, with his camera, photographing and laughing and his clothes now in pieces and he is like an angel. Really like someone from another world with no fear and great happiness but also great sadness. I cannot explain but I wish you could see. Now Hans is going to fetch him back and Greg will book a flight for him as you asked. This is better than to drive through the desert but may take a few days because the earliest flight now is Tuesday next week. When all is organised again I will call you or Greg maybe. He says not to worry about money as he will sort this out when all is ended. I send you my love and I hope you can understand well my English. I know that Jay will come back to this country after he has rested because this is his home now but I am glad that you will see him and take care of him a little. He tells me often about Brighton and how good it is there and invite me to come and see him when all is done which I hope is soon now.

God Bless You.

Patricia

# 47

# Now

## Jemmy – Brighton, May 2003

Twenty-two weeks and three days – so nine more days until the baby might be safe, or eight and a half now. But twenty-four weeks isn't good enough. Jemmy asked at the hospital and at twenty-eight weeks a baby has a ninety per cent chance of surviving with no problems. But that's thirty-nine days still to wait. As the bus ambles back through Kemp Town, Jemmy does the calculations again and again, sure that somehow it must be possible to come up with an equation which equals safety. At the hospital they say that the situation isn't worse but it isn't better. As the pregnancy progresses, the placenta is sometimes pulled up, but that isn't happening in her case, or not yet.

At the hospital they are brisk with her. Once that would have hurt her but she understands now that the doctors are powerless, frustrated. A detached placenta isn't meant to happen once, and it certainly shouldn't be happening again. Although strangely, for her, it's easier the second time around. Last time she didn't ever believe that Laurie might die. Now she knows that it can happen and there's strength in that knowledge.

She'd waited so long for the appointment and now that it's gone all she can do is to wait for the next appointment in two weeks' time. When she lost her job she hadn't minded at all, had even felt relieved. But now perversely she misses the office.

She arrives back at the Guest House, climbs the front steps. At the hospital they say that the bleeding has made her anaemic and that's why she's out of breath. She uses the handrail to pull herself up, opens the front door. Inside the hall is silent – Mollie and the Stans are out. Mr Lambert might be around but it's hard to know. Jemmy sees him sometimes early in the morning, wearing a pink net skirt over his jeans and a neat pale blue cardigan with mother-of-pearl buttons. His make-up smeary, his eyes sore. All that love, all that passion and no place for it to go. Perhaps when they drain his ulcerated foot love will come pouring out, a poison. Jemmy's too tired to climb the stairs, sinks down on the bottom step, pulls her phone from her bag.

Mr Waldron answers immediately.

Who? Who?

Jemmy. You remember? We spoke before.

Oh yes, Jemmy. Yes, of course. How lovely to hear from you, my dear. How are you? Getting out to lots of parties, I hope. That's what you want to be doing at your age. Make the best of it while you can.

Mr Waldron sounds different. His voice bounces in a way it's never done before. Jemmy would like to tell Mr Waldron about the baby and about Bill but she knows that isn't part of the deal. She dispenses comfort, never asks for it.

And how you are? Jemmy asks.

Oh better, my dear. Really much better. There's a friend of Joyce's – lives in the next street. Wallis. Widowed five years ago and been a great comfort to me.

Oh good. That's nice.

Jemmy feels jealous of Wallis. Mr Waldron is her project. How dare Wallis barge in? She may have offered some comfort but she doesn't understand, not really, not as Jemmy does.

Yes, Mr Waldron says. A great help. Hope you don't mind, my dear, must be getting on. You see, Wallis and I are going away tomorrow, heading to Basingstoke to see her sister so we've a lot to prepare. Getting the coach, change at Reading.

Oh yes, I see. Of course.

Not at all. I always like to hear from you. And I'll be back from Basingstoke in a week so we could speak then?

Jemmy agrees to that and clicks the phone off. Tears rise to her eyes. She worries about Joyce's unfinished cross-stitch of the coach and horses. Will Wallis put it away in a cupboard? Or even throw it in the bin? Jemmy doesn't like to admit that she's angry with Mr Waldron but she is. It's too early for him to be going off on a trip to Basingstoke with some other woman. But she knows this is unreasonable. Mr Waldron has reached an age when he probably goes to a funeral most weeks. It's impossible for him to feel so deeply about everyone, impossible perhaps for him even to feel so deeply about Joyce. Instead he dusts himself down, gets on to the next thing.

Jemmy wonders if she's simply too young, too inexperienced in matters of death. For her, Laurie was the first. Death, like anything else, is probably something you get better at with practice. Perhaps she just needs a thicker skin. Put that cross-stitch away in the cupboard and organise a trip to Basingstoke. Jemmy knows that she shouldn't be too hard on Mr Waldron. He's only surviving as everyone is.

She stands up, heads on up the stairs, thinks of Jay. He's been gone so long now, so very long. But his mother has spoken to him on the phone and he'll be home soon. The situation in Iraq is more and more dangerous and he has no reason to stay. She thinks now of that evening – two years ago – when he came back to the room she lived in then, in the days of the many black cardigans and fingerless gloves. Usually she never let anyone into that room. Can it really only be two years? An evening as hot as an oven and Jay sitting on the cushions, his long legs bent up awkwardly, talking some meaning-of-life rubbish. That's what she thought, until she knew better. Such love. She remembers Jay's hands – white and thin but surprisingly strong and certain. She owes everything to him. And she longs now for his return because he will understand.

She gets into bed, curls up under the duvet, pulls Mollie's patchwork blanket up to her chin. The room is large around her, the towering walls decorated at the top with elaborate mouldings. A section of plaster is missing from the ceiling revealing brown slats of wood. The paint on the frame of the long sash window has bubbled and is flaking away.

Jemmy drifts into sleep. (Jay, we think that life is the normal state. We think we've got a right to it and so when someone dies we're shocked, outraged. Their life has been unfairly snatched from them. But it's life that is shocking, outrageous. A miracle. Just this day is enough – might have to be enough.) The front door opens downstairs, pulls her out of sleep.

Mollie must be back but she probably won't come upstairs. She's busy now, putting clean sheets on the beds, clearing up the cat mess, baking fruitcake. For other people things move on, problems get solved. Whereas she's like a record stuck in a groove, playing the same sad thread of melody again and again.

She thinks of Bill and considers calling him but she can't do that because he'll want a solution. More doctors. More tests. More rest. He's someone who just never accepts that there are problems to which there is no solution. When was it she last saw him? Two weeks ago? She'd worn a loose coat. He'd pushed her bike, as they'd walked along the seafront, and briefly she'd felt like a young person again. Like she felt when they first met. Perhaps they could be happy like that again sometime, as long as they just walk along the seafront and talk about nothing at all.

From downstairs, she hears Mollie singing. A surprising voice which swells up through the house, a voice which should come from a woman fleshy as a sofa, not from Mollie's skeleton bones. Rufus isn't back yet but Mollie says he'll be here soon. Dancing at the Grand Hotel in Eastbourne. Of course, the only reason why he's been away so long is because of projects in London, pains in his back. The image of a Happy Family is busily being created ready for Jay's return.

Sometimes Mollie does still bring cake and soup up to Jemmy's room but delivers them now with a certain impatience, makes Jemmy feel like a hypochondriac. This is the brutality of the survivor. Mollie has got away, now wants nothing to do with those left behind. Jemmy's seen it at the Support Group. The women who get pregnant again, who have a living baby, suddenly brisk and impatient with the grieving. She doesn't go to the Support Group any more because she's become everyone's worst nightmare. No one wants to know that lightning can strike twice in the same place. Where can she go? Nowhere, but mysteriously, she is still stubbornly occupying the planet.

Jemmy cradles the fragile weight of the baby in her arms. From deep inside her, she feels a flicker of movement, a dull touch against her flesh, a joyous fluttering. It helps to feel the baby kick because at least she knows that he or she is alive. She tries to make the most of every minute and doesn't think about the future.

The journey to and from the hospital has made the pains in her back worse. She turns over and picks up a piece of paper which lies on her bedside table, a copy of the email which Jay sent from Iraq. She reads it through although she already knows what it says. She likes the end, the description of the sunset city and the woman singing the lullaby and the old man who speaks such excellent English. Laying the letter down, she runs her fingers over the scars on her wrists. Falling in barbed wire on the Downs. And she remembers Jay's hands – so calm and precise with the bandages. She longs for him now, longs for him with every cell in her body.

(Jay, what was it that you did that night? Even now I'm not sure. Perhaps you just saw the ugly as beautiful. Your particular talent and you passed some part of it on to me. So that sometimes my mind can remain still, can reserve all judgement. So that there are no good days or bad days, only days where good and bad are so inextricably mixed that the one can't be sorted from the other.) Even at the time of Laurie's death, there had been moments when she'd been able to see the world like that. And it's there again in his letter. Do other people see it? Or is she the only one?

Below Mollie's voice floats to the end of the song, the hoover starts. Jemmy would like to see Rufus, after all she's heard about him. Allow Mollie her happiness, there's little enough of it around that one shouldn't judge the quality of it.

The lace curtain at the window is dirty but the sunlight shining through produces an interesting spider's web image on the wall. The duvet is warm and she's here with her baby – her baby who is alive today. *Maybe it's easier to be happy when you don't have anything much to be happy about.* Despair and happiness are not opposite ends of a spectrum. Instead they lie on a circle, close together, the one making the other possible. She has nothing left to lose. And so no choice. All she can do is enjoy the afternoon with her baby and that spider's web light shivering on the wall.

# 48

## BEFORE

### Rose – Worcester, March 1963

Rose, Violet, Mrs Bertie Fawcett. She is all three. And the Worcester morning – pale and devoid of questions – welcomes all comers. She stands at the French windows in the sitting room, looks down over the brick city. Canal, railway station, allotment, cathedral and the distant heather-coloured Malvern Hills. The day shakes itself awake, still tired and bleary-eyed. Traffic flickers on a silver ribbon of distant road.

Increasingly she feels marooned, up here, in the stately white house in Langley Crescent. The city has sailed on into record shops, night clubs, girls wearing tiny shift dresses and smoking in the streets. She shudders, puts on her sunglasses, lights a cigarette. Sitting down to drink her morning coffee, she leafs through the newspaper.

Towards the back, she sees the photograph, adjusts her glasses, moves the page closer. The face staring out at her is Mollie – but also the face which was hers, all those years ago. White teeth, a haze of black hair, playful eyes, skin flawless as fresh snow. For a moment, she pushes the paper away, turns her face as though to defend herself against assault. But then gradually she breathes again, opens the paper. She's Violet Fawcett and has nothing to fear. She runs her eyes over the article.

*Rising West End star. An accident falling from the roof of a mansion block in Chelsea. Comfortable in hospital but will not be completing the run of A Man For All Seasons at the Ambassadors Theatre. Mr Rufus Ravello arrested and then released.*

So. So. Rose feels her heart thumping, presses her hand to her chest for a moment. After all this time of not knowing. All that childish talk about the theatre. Rose is impressed but not, finally, surprised. Mollie inherited her talent, after all. But it isn't the story that holds her attention, it's the photograph. Her own face. And suddenly it all rushes at her – Coventry, the Peace Pledge Union, Frank. But as soon as the memories begin she cuts them off. One must not be sentimental.

What will she say to Bertie? Of course, he would love some news of Mollie. He's never stopped talking about her, never stopped asking. And it hasn't always been easy to head him off, to manage things. He's suggested endlessly that they contact the police, hire a private detective, put a notice in the newspaper. Out of kindness, she's resisted these ideas. Now that Bertie is ill, it's particularly important not to upset him, not to raise unrealistic expectations. She's always been in charge of the post and so intercepted those occasional letters. Not Known At This Address. Mollie might have turned up at the house one day, except she would know better than to do that.

Of course, it's all very stupid. When she first met Bertie, that Blitz night in the bar of the Feathers Hotel, straight off the train from the smouldering coals of Coventry, she could have told him. Or she could have told him at any time afterwards. *I am not really Violet Bunton, I am Rose Mayeford. I was confused, I made a mistake.* Bertie wouldn't have minded, he might anyway have suspected something. That night he might have seen the identity cards. But the moment to tell had never been right. It'd always been simpler to leave things as they were.

And initially Rose had been sure that Mollie remembered nothing. But then as a teenager Mollie became wild, uncontrollable. Perhaps the child did remember something? She'd always been a jealous child, always been determined to ruin herself. Mentally unstable, having sex with older men. It'd all been too upsetting. Beyond what anyone could understand. Rose had judged it best to let her go. Now she shakes herself back into the present, stands in front of the mirror above the mantelpiece to adjust her hair, finishes her coffee. Do nothing, say nothing. Except that the newspaper article presents an opportunity. She imagines a figure slipping from a roof, head and knees banging against the tiles and then the clean drop, unbroken.

She sets off up the stairs. Bertie is still in bed. The pain in his back is such that he often doesn't settle well, and so sleeps late. She opens the door, watches him. The room smells of trapped air, sickness. Bertie is collapsed against a pillow in striped pyjamas which might make him look ten years old, if it weren't for the wisps of grey hair, the bald patch, the rise of his paunch under the bedclothes. She hears his breath whistle and stutter. When they married she'd never thought that by sixty-five he'd be immobile. She finds his illness boring. He does still go to parties with her but he always wants to come home early.

Darling, she says. I'm so sorry. There's been some awful news. It's in the newspaper. About Mollie.

Mollie? Mollie?

Oh Bertie, I'm so sorry. How can I say it? Dead. In an accident, on a roof.

What? What?

She feels herself to be in a scene from an amateur theatre production – but then her conversations with Bertie often feel like this. As yet, she's not playing her part with conviction but her confidence will build as she presses on. Bertie is struggling to sit up, waves a weak arm. Phlegm rattles in his chest as he stutters endless questions. Where is her body? What about the funeral? Can they not go? Should they not ring the police? On this point he's insistent. She must call the police, she must get more information.

His opposition increases her conviction. She resists him with gentle certainty, with words of comfort. But he's stubborn, continues to insist on the police. For a moment, she wonders if she's made a mistake. Why does he have to keep asking so many questions? Why does it matter now that she's gone? But finally

Violet knows that she'll be victorious. He's immobile, in her power, will soon yield to her. It's important that he doesn't become agitated as that increases the pain. She goes to the bathroom to fetch painkillers and a glass of water. Two is the maximum dose but she gives him three. Sitting beside him, she holds his hand, kisses his forehead. It's so hard for him. He loved Mollie so much, perhaps more than he's ever loved her, and she's always been such a disappointment to him.

She leaves him then, goes back down to the sitting room, feels suddenly weightless, energetic. Could this be happiness? How would she know? Moving to the window, she stares out over the garden. The world may be slipping away from them but they are securely moored. Finally, after all these years, stable, stationary. The roof tiles are secure, the beams will not bend or buckle. She considers the future, sees it as a corridor, a vista, stretching out before her. She and Bertie travelling through light, happiness. They have always been contented but now they're safe as well. Their moment has come.

Of course, Bertie may not live much longer, she knows that. But he will leave her the house and she'll be free to do as she chooses. She could easily find another man, has always had many admirers. The merry widow. She could finally move out of this house, go abroad. She imagines the joy of packing up, selling the furniture, escaping. The future is all there – bright and spacious, bursting with bougainvillea, hotel rooms high above foreign ports, dinners eaten on vine-clad terraces, walks through narrow streets of ancient houses.

Soon. Soon. But even today contains new possibilities. Once Bertie has had a rest, she will suggest lunch out somewhere. And in the meantime find some flowers for his room, tidy things up while he sleeps. She goes back upstairs, hesitates for a moment at the door. A sound comes from inside – a splutter and a groan. She sighs, thinks for a moment of that other man who cried. She wonders why her life has been spent protecting men who are weaker than she is.

She walks up to the floor above, stands outside the room that once belonged to Mollie, hesitates, comes back down. It's so silly of Bertie. She feels too tired now to think of tidying, lunch. Her mind moves back to Coventry, the war. All that political passion. And now, living in this house, she has embraced the world she once wanted to destroy. How expectations lower with the passing years.

The house in Coventry, that morning. She had suffered several different deaths there. Is that excuse enough? Perhaps – but the world is not interested in excuses. She never found the road back. She could have continued to be Rose Mayeford and merely used Violet's name. Instead she had become stuck in a performance of the life that Violet might have had. And now she might weep for Rose Mayeford, for the person she lost, but if she starts she'll never stop.

Memories – Frank and the real Violet, as they were, together. That's how they should have stayed, undivided. She wonders now which of them she loved more, if she had ever loved either of them. She had done, surely. But she had been so young, unaware of the feelings she might provoke. It's dangerous not to be able to love but worse perhaps not to notice the love you have inspired. Then the business of mere survival had intervened and she had won that game. Except the victory soon revealed itself to be a diamond made of paste. For they – Frank and Violet – went out in splendour, in their different loves. And she is left to grow old, to remember. One cannot mourn for those who are dead but are not buried.

The brilliant vista of the future has narrowed, dimmed. She can never take what Violet is not able to have. What was it that killed her? Stanley's death? Or a bomb blast? Or had she died sometime before? At the moment when she lost Frank, her best friend Rose? *Violet, darling, rest easy, do not worry. You know I am beside you in that salmon satin bed and I'll stay with you as you sleep. Stay with you for all the long journey, always.*

In truth, there will be no new man, no foreign travel. She'll never leave this house. For although she's never loved Bertie, yet when he goes, she'll follow him. In the lobby of the Feathers Hotel, the bargain was brokered and can never be renegotiated. She feels certain of that, considers it without bitterness or fear. Her life has already been long, very long. But still she's glad that things are sorted out, that she is safe. A straight run for home now. Not long to go.

# 49

# Now

## Oliver – Brighton, May 2003

The noise is quiet at first. Tap, tap, tap. It could be water dripping or a twig touching against a window. Oliver sits at the desk in his room, listening. Another sound follows, a whisper, no louder than the sweeping of a broom. He stands up and turns out the lights. There's no logic to this action but he wants to make himself invisible, to hide. The tapping continues, grows a little louder. Occasionally it's accompanied by that soft sweep. Oliver stands up, moves to the side of the window, tries to look out without making himself visible to whoever might be outside. Although the two noises are faint, he knows they have significance. The Dying are close, looking for him.

The tapping grows louder. He pins himself against the wall. A rustling sweep. The noises are coming from below, possibly at the back of the church itself, or in the corridor near the Community Centre. He draws in a deep breath and waits. He wonders if someone has broken into the church. This has happened often enough before. The door to the Community Centre is made of security glass and has a strong lock but it would be possible for someone to force one of the windows in the women's loos. He'll have to go down and look. The tapping is growing louder again, the sweep, sweep, sweep is continuous now. He feels the weight of those who rely on him. The vicar, the peace protesters, members of the congregation, all of the hundreds of people who use the hall, who visit the café. And Lara, of course. Lara and Jay.

He can't let these people down. The webs which hold the world together are infinitely fragile. If even one strand breaks, then all may go. Still pressed against the wall, he knows himself to be entirely alone. The tapping has changed to a banging, the sweeping has become the swish of a scythe. He puts his hands over his ears, crumples into himself. But this will not do. He must go down, he has no choice. So instead he steps forward boldly, walks to the door of his room, pulls it open, switches on the light. He stamps down the stairs, trampling out his own fear. But as he reaches the bottom step the light goes out. This has happened so many times but surely it's not mere coincidence that it should happen now?

He stands on the bottom step and listens. Bang, bang, bang. He swallows and steps towards the door that leads into the hall, tugs it open. He sees a glitter of red light, knows the dog is there, hears its hiss and growl. His knees turn to liquid, his head dives like vertigo and he crumples against the wall, hears a door crash, a shout. The dog. The dog. He can't see it but feels its hair rise in a ridge along its back. He presses his hands into his eyes, the images start.

A sand-coloured country, low rise, blurred in the heat. A market crowded with people – some in black robes, some in football shirts, trainers or formal suits. Stalls sell piles of fruit and electronic equipment – cameras, radios, clocks. Rolls of cloth are propped against a wall and chickens squawk in baskets. A stall of meat buzzes with flies. Women poke at vegetables, dig into their purses to pay for purchases, gold bangles rattling on their arms. Old men sit at a table, chatting and drinking tea from glasses. Exhaust fumes pump from passing cars and trucks. The carcass of an animal turns on a smoking spit. Shadows are short, the air is thirsty, the sun murderous.

The boy is in the market, dusty and dirty, his curls sagging against his head. He wears trainers and no socks, pyjama trousers, a black baggy T-shirt with a picture of the Empire State Building and the words – New York, New York. A camera hangs around his neck and a canvas bag is looped over his shoulder. His arms and face are burnt red. He stares around him, his face innocent as a full moon. Two small boys kick a football between the crowded stalls.

A grey van is being parked outside a café – windows thick with dust, rear bumper hanging down crookedly. Two men turn to watch the van, gesticulate. A shout comes – slashing through the fabric of the air. Everyone looks around. A man runs, tripping over a stall, sending melons cascading down. Someone is keening like an injured animal, their screams writhing in the enclosing heat. People point – here, there. A woman's head swivels as she gathers her children. The boy stops still, watches, wide open, raw as an undressed wound. The earth jolts, white light rolls in, breaks like a wave.

Oliver forces his eyes open, topples back against the wall, slides down it until he is crouched on the floor. Pain hits him in the chest and his mouth snatches for breath. Then quietness comes. The air soothes, the dim lights of the hall are kindly. The dog has gone. Oliver peers through the darkness but can see nothing. The boy is somewhere close. Oliver could reach out and touch him, guide him into the café, put the lights on, make him a cup of coffee. And they could sit and talk, as they had done once before. *But it doesn't matter, actually, does it? Any of it, I mean.* The boy lived at the extremes, at the edges, where there is only hope or despair. Where can he find the middle ground?

## 50

# Now

## Lara – Brighton, May 2003

Where will Jay stay when he comes home? Lara has done her best to organise the flat but maybe he'll want to go to the Guest House instead? She still hasn't had a firm confirmation from Greg that Jay will be on the flight tomorrow yet she's sure he will be home by the weekend. Surely. Surely. Although no one can be certain until he's actually on the plane, as the road to the airport is one of the most dangerous places in Baghdad. Is Rufus back? Has Mollie organised a room for Jay? Lara has tried to ring but as usual no one answers so she decides to walk round and see. She's only worrying about these details as a way of keeping calm and passing the time – why not?

She turns the key in the lock and steps into the yellow hall. The usual smell of cat is overlaid now by the sharp tang of disinfectant. The stairs have been hoovered, a pile of boxes has been replaced by a potted palm. Lara has heard that Rufus isn't back yet although still she feels his presence like a question mark at the end of a sentence. She heads down to the kitchen. Something has been spilt on the floor. It lies in pools near the sink and then leads in splatters towards the table. Blood? Lara's never seen blood like this before, never seen so much in one place. Parts of it are still bright red but some has turned to the colour of wine. In her mind, two worlds begin to clash. In Iraq there's blood, not here.

Mum! she shouts. What's happened? Are you all right?

As she heads out of the kitchen, up the stairs, a figure appears, outlined against the yellow light above. Oh, yes. The girl. The pregnant girl, the curtain maker, the owner of the thongs drying on the rack. She's moving down the stairs like an old woman, holding on to the stair rail, wearing a white cotton skirt with a pattern of large red roses – material which must surely have been cut from a curtain. And because of the dim evening light, and the red-rose pattern, it takes Lara a moment to understand that part of the skirt is soaked in blood. Her feet and jewelled sandals are stained as well.

Are you all right? Lara says. What happened?

The girl shrugs. Sorry. I was just in the kitchen and it started.

You need to sit down, Lara says. I'm going to call an ambulance.

She pulls a chair out from the table, grabs the phone but thinks, I don't have time for this. This girl's problems don't have anything to do with me. I'll wait for the ambulance and they'll deal with the rest. After all, what can I actually do to help?

I don't think you need to call, Jemmy says. They said at the hospital there's no point unless the bleeding gets bad.

It is bad, Lara says.

Do you think so?

Lara picks up the phone and dials 999. Police, fire or ambulance? Hold the line. A voice asks what's happened and she explains. There will be a twenty-minute wait for an ambulance. The voice suggests that it might be better for Lara to bring the patient to the hospital herself. Lara swears, slams the phone down, calls a cab company which she's used often before. The *William Tell Overture* thumps while she waits.

Thanking you very much for your call, madam. No, madam. No. All cars fully air-conditioned and driver most highly trained. Yes. No. Not for one half an hour.

Lara puts the phone down carefully, making an effort not to panic. It isn't fair of this girl to start losing buckets of blood right now. She wonders if she might pick up a cab on the main street. Jemmy is at the sink, wringing out a dishcloth.

No, Lara says. No. You sit down.

The girl turns, her black hair falls down over her shoulder, and she pushes it out of the way. And suddenly Lara is back on that

January morning, a world away, when she was waiting for a taxi and the doorbell rang. This is the girl, the same girl. Lara remembers her feet – tanned, bony and bare. That long, mournful face. She wore square glasses then and a purple wool coat stitched with flowers. Lara's mobile rings and she pulls it out of her bag. The line crackles and she waits. Greg. She recognises the strange wind-howling moan that the satellite phone makes. His voice is faint.

Look, I can't find him. Right now I can't find him. And I need to speak to him because we may have to leave very early. We have to go when there's a military convoy. Again that strange moaning noise. Lara imagines the wind rising, the sand swirling. The phone line goes dead. She presses the button to ring back but she knows it's hopeless. Placing a hand on the table, she takes a grip on herself. Whatever happens is what is meant to happen. Lara thinks of Rufus, on the beach, shouting at her to get Jay home.

Jay? the girl asks.

Yes.

The girl is watching her with dark eyes which suck her in. Lara attempts a smile. She understands it all now. Back in January, she didn't help this girl, she was brusque, judgemental. Now she's being offered the opportunity to put that right. That's the reason why she's stepped over the threshold of this small tragedy. And if she puts things right then Jay will get on that plane and come home safely. She tries the phone one more time but it only beeps flatly.

Yes, he's coming home tomorrow.

The girl nods, smiles. Lara tries to clear her mind. She mustn't think about Jay, she must concentrate on this girl, in this kitchen, now. The girl is carrying a baby and the baby is probably dying, or dead. That's the situation. She spots Mollie's car keys lying in the fruit bowl.

I'm going to take you in the car. But first you need some clean clothes.

Jemmy picks up a clean skirt from the back of a chair. The blood-stained roses fall to the ground and she steps out of their circle. Then she stands on one leg to step into the clean skirt. Lara is uncertain whether she should try to help her but Jemmy seems quite stable. The metallic smell of blood surrounds them. How much is there? Two pints perhaps? It's impossible to know. Surely the baby must be dead? Lara tries to remember the things one should do in a crisis.

Don't worry. We'll get you to hospital straight away. Try not to be frightened.

Her words sound hollow and when she looks at Jemmy's face she finds no fear there. She herself is fluttering in some unseen breeze, fumbling, her fingers tying together in knots. The baby could be dying now. This minute. She pulls one of Mollie's cardigans from the back of a chair and wraps it around the girl.

We need to clear up the blood, Jemmy says.

No, it doesn't matter.

Yes it does. Otherwise your mum will be upset.

It's clear that Jemmy isn't going to leave the house until the blood has been wiped up and so Lara runs the tap, mops hurriedly, spreads far too much water on the floor, then grabs her keys and bags. Why hasn't Greg called back? Don't think of it. Don't think at all. She feels as though she should help Jemmy up the stairs but the girl seems perfectly capable of walking on her own.

The best thing to do is to count backwards, Jemmy says. Start at four hundred, breathe deeply, count.

They cross the road together. 400. 399. 398. Lara helps Jemmy into the car. 397. 396. Shuts the door. 395. Straightens the cat-hair-covered blanket on the driver's seat which hides the sticking-out springs and gets into the car. 394. 393. Turns the key and the engine splutters and roars. All the way to the hospital, they count. Past the houses, and the streets, and the people having normal lives, where nobody is about to die. At the hospital Lara helps Jemmy out of the car. She's pleased to see there's no further evidence of blood.

It's possible to lose a lot of blood and the baby doesn't necessarily die, Jemmy says. I lost a lot of blood last time. And of course Laurie did die. But it doesn't necessarily work like that.

Sorry?

Laurie. He was my first baby.

Lara coughs, chokes, watches a bird which is sitting on a signpost.

Sorry. I didn't know. I'm very sorry.

It's all right. It's easier, the second time.

In the Casualty Department, Lara expects alarms to ring, stretchers to appear, nurses to rush forward. But instead there's just a woman behind a desk and forms to fill in. Jemmy is told to sit down. Lara wants to shout, *Get a doctor, a stretcher, a baby is about to die*. Lara and Jemmy sit on plastic chairs and wait. Through glass windows, Lara can see nurses and doctors writing at desks, putting papers in files. She decides she'll give it five more minutes before she goes and complains, wonders if she should hold Jemmy's hand.

I'm twenty-three weeks pregnant, Jemmy says. That means they could try to deliver him but he wouldn't have much chance of staying alive.

Lara is shocked by the girl's matter-of-fact tone.

I have a feeling the baby is a boy, the first says. If I'm right then I'll call him Sebastian.

A man appears with a gash in his hand, surrounded by friends. He moans, cries out. The friends steer him to an empty seat and he lies down with his head on one of the plastic chairs. A woman with a whining child is complaining that the coffee machine doesn't work. Jemmy sits still, hands folded in her lap. Lara shuts her eyes and counts again. 400. 399. A plaque on the wall explains that the chairs in the waiting room were provided by the Rotary Club. Jemmy sits up straighter and Lara sees her decide to make an effort at normality.

Sorry, she says. I've heard all about you. I wish we hadn't met like this.

That's all right. Quite all right. I know that you're a friend of Jay's.

Well, not much. Not really. But he was very important to me.

Lara thinks, A romance? That seems improbable. But something else. What?

He helped me, Jemmy says. You know how he could do that, of course. How good he is at helping people. Like he used to come here, didn't he? To the hospital. The Camera Boy. But for me, it wasn't like that. It was — I don't usually explain. It's rather difficult. I used to be a person who always wore thick, black cardigans.

The words are dry, difficult. Lara takes care not to look at her as she tells her story. The boy she's describing is someone that Lara has never known. After Jemmy has finished speaking a silence settles over the two of them, a private, intense silence, despite the moaning man and the coffee-machine complainer.

Then Jemmy says, I always thought if he came back, if he was here—

Do you think that's why he went to Iraq? Lara asks. To help people?

I don't know. We'd sort of lost touch before then. But I always thought so. And I don't know what it was that night – not religion, or magic, or any of that. Love is a silly word. Too big. Kindness perhaps. It was hard for him to make people understand.

A young male doctor appears through swishing double doors. He asks some questions and then Jemmy is sat in a wheelchair and pushed through those doors. Lara follows her as they travel along corridor after corridor, passing people being wheeled in hospital beds, old men shuffling along pushing drip stands. Eventually they come to a place where there are tiny baby beds, posters of breastfeeding mothers, nurses carrying bottles of milk. Again they wait.

Is there anyone you should call? Lara asks.

I don't know, the girl says. My husband, really.

Husband?

We split up but still. His child.

Shall I call him? Lara says.

No. No. He doesn't know.

Doesn't know?

No. And I can't face telling him.

OK. Give me the number and I'll send him a text. Just telling him to come to the hospital, nothing more.

I don't know.

Come on.

The girl gets out her phone, reads the number out. Lara types it into her mobile. A nurse appears and Jemmy is wheeled into a room full of equipment and lifted onto a bed. Pale blue jelly is rubbed onto her swollen belly. Lara sits behind the doctor as he does the scan. The baby appears, a cluster of grey in a black and grey wilderness, surrounded by a mass of white flecks. Like seeing film of the moon, or deep under the ocean. The curve of the baby's skull is perfectly spherical, his tiny spine and the spread of his ribs, like a fish bone. She's shocked by how complete the baby is, a whole person, every detail in place. Briefly he turns and it seems that he's waving a tiny gloved hand, a message from another world. This is a first day at school, an eighteenth birthday, a wedding, a grandchild. This is a dream, a hope, a possibility. This is a place to accumulate love.

Lara looks at the doctor, trying to read his face. Jemmy keeps her hands locked over her eyes. Then a sound comes, a microphone thump, a sound like someone clearing their throat, a rush and a gurgle and then thump, thump, thump.

Got a heartbeat, the doctor says.

Lara feels a ball of relief rise up into her throat. The doctor continues to move the sensor over Jemmy's belly. He plots dotted lines on the screen, consults his notes, shakes his head.

I need the consultant. She isn't in the hospital now but she'll be here soon.

Lara can't listen any more. In the distance she hears Jemmy asking questions, the doctor explaining that they may have to deliver the baby but it's too early. He won't survive. Or they may be able to wait. Lara erects a barrier in her mind to block out the words. What did Greg mean when he said he couldn't find Jay? Lara is swallowing again and again. For a moment, she raises her hands, as though to hide her eyes but then knows that she mustn't do that, mustn't let Jemmy see her panic. As she lowers her hands, her eyes fix on their blue-veined backs, the short, dirty nails, the silver hairs, the clear expanse of skin. And she knows then what she needs to do. A nurse is fixing a drip into Jemmy's arm.

I've got to go, Lara says. But I'm going to come back. I know someone who can help. Will you be all right until I get back? I sent that text.

Yes, Jemmy says. Yes. I'll be all right. Thank you very much.

# 51

## BEFORE

### Jemmy – Brighton, July 2001

Jemmy never usually lets anyone into her room, least of all a man. So now she wonders why she's let the Camera Boy in. Drink, that's the only answer. He's propped on her cushion, his long legs folded awkwardly, drinking coffee. She met him down on the seafront earlier, been at a party there, met a guy she liked called Bill, then her head started swaying and she headed home. And then she'd met the Camera Boy. He'd followed her home, talking all the way, and on the doorstep he'd pleaded – *Just a coffee.* And she'd said – *All right, all right but really just a coffee.* And now he's annoying her with his meaning-of-life talk. She sits with her back propped against her bed. Her window is pulled wide open and outside a feverish night is settling on the city.

So why are you so miserable? he asks.

I'm not miserable. Why would you think I'm miserable?

He sits up straighter, crosses his legs, watches her. He's wearing an old-fashioned dinner jacket, ripped at the elbows and hem, and a collarless shirt which must have come from some vintage shop. His hair doesn't look as though it has been brushed for a week and she suspects that he might smell – of peanuts or burgers or something.

I haven't got anything to be miserable about, Jemmy says. Nothing at all. I mean, I'm young and in good health and I've got career plans and enough money to live on – just about. So I wouldn't have reason to be miserable, would I?

The light from her bedside light falls in a circle, touching his knees but leaving his face shadowed – but still she can feel his eyes on her.

But do those things make people happy? he asks.

She shivers and drinks more red wine. Over the last three years she's had as many of these boring student meaning-of-life conversations as she ever needs to have. She wishes she'd stayed down by the pier, with her friends – or gone somewhere with that guy Bill.

Look, she says. The point is that when I was growing up my parents had quite a bit of money. I mean, I didn't really get on with them but I never had to worry about having clothes, or meals, or stuff like that. And so I was lucky really. I mean, people who don't have enough to live on – those people would be miserable, wouldn't they?

That's what I used to think, he says. But now I'm not so sure. Because it wouldn't matter if you had all the meals and clothes that money could buy – if you didn't have people you could really be close to.

*Money can't buy you happiness, can't buy you love.* How tedious. But she feels the room shift around her and wonders if she might cry. She drinks more red wine, stubs out her cigarette. Although the sun has finally burnt itself out, the room seems to be getting hotter and her cardigan sticks to her, the cotton itching at her neck. The boy shuffles himself closer to the bed, rests his back against it. She knows he wants to get her into bed. She doesn't want to talk but the red wine speaks for her.

It was all right, she says. While I was at school and at college because I knew what I had to do. This is the course material, these are the assignments you have to complete, this is the date of the exam. But now. Since I finished the course, I don't know what I'm meant to be doing because, well, it's not clear what success is now. There are too many choices. I mean, if I get a job with one of the London design houses then is that success or is it selling out to commercialism? And if I start my own business is that success?

But why ask yourself that question? Why not just ask what you want to do?

That, she thinks, is the kind of thing he would say.

I mean, what do you want to do? he says.

Again she feels herself close to tears. Because this is the question she asks herself all day, as she sits in the shop. Place your bets. And the ball spins round the roulette wheel again and again but never drops into place. And she can't understand why she doesn't know the answer because it can't be that complicated, can it?

I did have a job interview, she says. It was in London. Junior Knitwear Technologist. And it was for Angelic Threads who are like a new, really exciting fashion design company. And actually it wasn't like I applied to them. I didn't – but they asked me to go for an interview because they'd seen some of my garment work. So it should have been pretty likely that I'd get the job and I did everything right. I'd done lots of research into the company and I managed to say it all in just the right way – but then—

She stops and pulls at her sleeve, wishes she hadn't drunk so much.

Then. Well, I didn't really like the people but they wrote and offered me a job and well – I never replied to the letter. And they left three messages on my mobile.

She cries, sobs shaking her shoulders. She feels so ashamed. Why did she ever let this boy into her room? Why is she telling him these things? She wipes at her eyes, digs in her cardigan pocket for a tissue. It was only a job interview, only a decision she failed to make. She's still a person who won the second year prize for textiles for the whole university, a person with enough money and friends. She tries to shut the tears up inside her and shades her face with her hand. Feeling him close to her, she draws back. His hands touch her cardigan.

Get off me, you creep. I'm not interested. I told you.

But his hands undo the buttons of her cardigan.

I'm not trying to do *that*, he says. I'm just trying to say I'm sorry. That's all.

His hands keep working on the buttons and then he eases the cardigan off her shoulders. Underneath she wears a white sleeveless camisole. She winces as his eyes fall on the skin of her chest, her sticking-out collarbones. As he takes hold of her wrist, she pulls back, feeling the shock of his touch. He apologises, and with infinite care, peels off one fingerless glove. A piece of white material is revealed, wrapped around her wrist. She waits for him to draw back but instead he peels off the other glove. Now the bandages which cover both of her forearms are there for him to see. She's always imagined a moment like this, a moment when someone finds out. Now the Camera Boy is going to feel sick, start shouting, talk about doctors and drugs. But he doesn't – instead, taking great care not to hurt her, he gently pulls her cardigan down and edges the sleeves over the bandages.

No, no. She says. No, no, no. She keeps her eyes tight shut and her head down. Once he knows then everyone will know – and then they will hate her. She won't be able to pretend any more. But when the cardigan is off, and the bandages and plasters and cuts are all revealed, the Camera Boy registers no shock at all. All he does is stare at her arms. She can feel the hot night air on her skin and she shivers. The plasters don't cover all the cuts and scratches. She can never do the dressings properly because she always has to do them with one hand. All she does is cut slabs of lint and stick them to her arm with pieces of plaster. That usually stops the blood from getting on her cardigan.

The boy is kneeling now, holding her wrist across his knee. Gently he begins to remove the dressings, easing the plasters off, lifting the pieces of lint. Then he takes the safety pins from the bandages and undoes those as well. One of the cuts is deeper than the others and it oozes blood.

Jemmy remembers how it felt to make that cut. The sense of power and control, the excitement and immediacy, the sudden exquisite stab of pain. The cuts are never as deep as she wants them to be. It's always her intention to cut into an artery but she hasn't the courage and her sewing scissors aren't sharp enough.

The boy is staring down at her arm but he isn't disgusted or shocked. She's always taken such care never to let anyone see because she knows she won't be able to bear their looks of horror, and the judgements and questions and doctor's appointments which will automatically follow.

The boy examines the cuts more closely.

Beautiful, he says.

Yes, she says. They are.

He stays still, watching them. His finger moves above them, as though mapping the pattern they make.

It's clear to her now that the boy is mad. But she feels strangely comfortable sitting with him while he stares at her cuts. Without her cardigan, her skin can breathe and she's stopped sweating. Beautiful. He's right. When she cuts herself, she does it with care. No wild and desperate slashing. Instead a deliberate positioning of the blade, measuring the angle of this new cut against the one before. And then pushing the sewing scissors down into her skin hard and watching the flesh split and the blood appear in a sudden swathe of crimson. You have to push down hard. Human flesh is surprisingly resilient.

That moment of exhilaration. The knowledge that she's here, that this is her arm. That she's in Brighton, that this is the year 2001. And then the slow sawing, cutting into muscle and vein, pushing down and down despite the pain and the running blood – just to be absolutely sure, to know for certain, that she is here, that this is her arm. And now this boy can see the pattern, and how carefully it's been done. So that he too knows that she's here.

He asks her if he can take a picture of the cuts and he makes her lay her arms out on the bed, on the white sheet. And he gets his camera and spends long minutes adjusting the lens, lining up the shot. First he positions himself high above her and takes pictures from there, but then he comes down to her level, on the opposite side of the bed, and photographs her arms from the side. While he works, she cries – slowly, quietly, happily.

The strange thing is that now that he's looked so carefully at the cuts, they've ceased to matter. For so long they've been a dark and hidden thing, a deep and terrible shame. Because of the cuts she's never gone swimming, never sunbathed, never gone to the doctor's, never gone clothes shopping with friends. She's never been able to have a proper boyfriend because she can only have sex in an alleyway, or a car, where she won't have to take off her clothes. Always wore a black cardigan and fingerless gloves in case the blood seeps through.

And all the time she'd imagined the moment when someone finds out. The doctors, the shrinks, the psychiatric ward – the disgust. She's always stayed with the people she knows well. Those people never dare to ask why she doesn't ever take off her cardigan and gloves. The cardigan is part of her oddness, it's attributed to excessive modesty, considered rather charming.

The boy is putting his camera away. She looks down at her lacerated arms on the bed. Only a few cuts. Most people probably do that kind of thing sometime. They could just be scratches she got while trying to climb over a barbed-wire fence, or falling on some sharp stones. The boy comes back and kneels beside her, on the opposite side of the bed, watching her intently. One of the cuts has opened up and is starting to bleed. Slowly he lowers his head and kisses it. When he raises his head, his lips are stained red. Despite her tears, she can't help laughing at his clown-red mouth.

The Camera Boy laughs as well and then gets up and goes to the bathroom. He comes back with plasters, lint, Dettol and water in a plastic tooth mug. Kneeling beside her again, he washes the cuts and then goes to the bathroom, gets a towel, dries them. When he's done that, he carefully cuts out pieces of lint, measuring them up so that they will fit neatly. He does a much better job than she could ever do, making sure they're all covered, even the ones which are only scratches.

After that he pulls off his shoes and lies down on the bed, and she lies beside him, that smear of her blood, dried dark now, still decorating his lips. He makes her turn over so that her back is against his chest, her damaged arms carefully folded in front of her.

I don't know your name, she says.

Jay. She repeats the name several times. She feels too drained to think or to talk. The night has that strange stillness which comes with extreme heat. At the window the black of the sky is tinged purple. From somewhere far away the beat of disco music pulses into the night.

Jemmy sleeps and wakes to find that the sun has split open, like the yolk of an egg, turning all the sky yellow. Jay has gone. She gets out of bed, pulls on underwear and a summer dress. Some static fuzz which has always crowded the air has cleared now and she hears clearly. If she listened carefully enough she could hear sap moving up through the trees at the window, sucked up from root to leaf.

She reaches for her cardigan but it's too hot to wear it. And anyway she can explain the cuts. Walking on the Downs, a barbed-wire fence, sharp stones. She stands at the window, stretches her arms above her head, feeling the dressings on them stretch and sting. For a moment, she thinks of Jay. He's somewhere in the distance, down on the seafront perhaps, and he catches sight of her, gives her a wave, turns away. He's released her from prison and so she must leave him behind. He understands that. If they speak, then she might finish up back inside.

Her mobile rings and she looks at the number. It's Bill, the guy from the night before. Her thumb presses down onto the green phone icon. And so she steps into the future, into sunlight. Mercifully, she cannot see a further darkness waiting.

# 52

# Now

## Lara – Brighton, May 2003

Lara sits at the table in the Roma Street sitting room and emails Greg. Then she checks her watch – it's ten o'clock in England so it's midnight in Baghdad. Will anyone have their phone switched on? She tries Patricia, the Spanish journalist, but is redirected to voicemail. She tries some of the other numbers – journalists, protesters, the landline of one of the families he's visited. No one answers. She leaves a voicemail message at the British Embassy in Iraq although they've never returned any of her calls. Then she phones the Stop The War office in London. She wants to phone again and again and again until she gets through to someone but she doesn't let herself do that. Wait one hour, she tells herself.

She imagines Baghdad, cooler now that it's night-time, but the air still full of gunshots, people hurrying from one street corner to the next, restless nights spent on mattresses laid out on concrete floors. She doesn't want those images in her head and so puts on the radio, starts to make herself a coffee. Picks up that book of Jay's about conscientious objectors in the Second World War. She remembers now that he asked once about his great-grandfather, the one killed somewhere near Dunkirk. She hadn't been able to tell him anything, of course. And now the book fails to keep her mind steady so she lays it aside.

Oliver? She wonders if he ever went to the hospital. When she went to find him the glass doors of the Community Centre were closed up with a padlock and chains and she'd had to bang on the door for ten minutes to get him to come down. When he did finally come he looked crippled and raw, about half his usual size, and talked about a break-in at the church, something to do with a dog. Mindless vandalism, she'd thought, but hadn't really listened because she needed to tell him about Jemmy.

And she'd been sure he would help – but she was wrong. He'd insisted that he could do nothing, said again and again that he was not a faith healer, never really had been. You care for this girl, he'd said. You can probably do as much yourself. With this break-in. We've got to be careful. There's been a problem with a stray dog. I don't want you to be hurt.

Also he couldn't go in her car. He never went in cars, never. The roads are horribly dangerous. One never knows the dangers. She should be careful when driving. *I don't want you to have an accident in the car. I really don't want that. The road to London, the M23 is particularly dangerous. So many accidents there.* Finally they'd finished up having a row and she'd said unforgivable words.

Look, all this stuff with your wife, I'm really sorry. Awful that she died of this allergy thing but you're letting that ruin your whole life. Why? Why can't you just try and help? I'm not saying you're responsible, of course you're not responsible.

He was like a deflating balloon, crumpling to nothing.

I couldn't save her, he said.

Well, so what? Anyway, as far as I can see, you didn't even like her that much.

She'd thought at that moment he might hit her. But then everything changed because it turned out that he knew Jemmy, or half knew her. *A young girl, piles of dark hair, a coat with flowers stitched on it?* Apparently she went into the church sometimes to light a candle. So he'd said he would go to the hospital, that he'd walk, but Lara still doesn't know whether he did. When she left he was still talking about the break-in, the dog, how they all needed to be careful.

She is still angry with him, although she realises that she shouldn't have lost her temper. The worst of it is that she cares for him – deeply. He's her friend, a proper friend, but still there's no hope she'll ever understand him. Why didn't he want to help? Only twenty minutes have passed but still Lara picks up the piece of paper with Patricia's number on, reaches for her phone. But before her hand touches it, the phone comes to life. The screen lights, the ringtone rattles through the room. No number shows on the screen. Lara pushes the green phone icon, the line clears its throat and she hears a voice.

Oh thank God. I was looking for your number. But I just don't know anything more for the moment.

What? Lara says. Patricia, is that you?

The line makes a noise like the jumping of a vinyl record.

*Sí, sí.*

I was trying to call you.

Yes, yes but my mobile phone was stolen two days ago. That number is no good. So I'm calling you that our friend Hans is heading to the hospital and he's going to let me know.

What? I don't understand.

Someone called, Patricia says. I don't know who it was.

Listen. I'm Jay's mother. You remember?

Yes, I know. Of course, I know.

What are you saying? Has Jay been injured?

I'm sorry. I thought someone called you. Yes. We think that Jay has been hurt in an explosion but we don't know. They said a young English man.

Oh my God. I didn't know.

Lara feels her whole body drop. It's as though she has fallen but is still standing.

Hans called me and so he's going to the hospital. I don't know. I'm going to call as soon as I find out anything. I promise I'll call straight away. I'm sure he's all right. There was a big bomb but that was yesterday evening already. Maybe it's all a mistake.

I'm going to drive to London, Lara says. If he's injured I need to come.

Wait, wait until we know.

Lara rings off, stands in the middle of the sitting room, feels her blood thump in her head. She hurries to the bedroom, starts to packs a bag, tries to think what she might need. Credit card, passport, hat. In the bathroom, she shifts through the contents of the medicine cabinet, tries to decide what to take, then grabs a plastic bag from the kitchen and tips everything in.

Finally, finally, the months of waiting are finished. She's going to see Jay soon. If he's injured, they'll have to bring him home. An injury? That could mean anything. It could mean he's lost an arm or a leg, it could be that he's in a coma. Lara goes through all the options in her head as she pushes bras and knickers into a canvas bag. But at least there's no more waiting. Something is going to happen now. He's going to come home. She feels sure that he'll be all right.

Jeans, T-shirts, the charger for her phone, her passport. Thick socks, a jumper. In Baghdad it can be cold at night. She grabs her coat, and bag, Mollie's car keys. Thank God she has the car here already. Outside the night is gleaming, indifferent. She gets into Mollie's car and checks the petrol gauge. She has easily enough fuel to get her to Heathrow. She feels Jay close to her now. Darling, I'm coming. It won't be long now. Please wait for me.

The engine roars and the car rabbit hops up the street. But then she calms herself, drives like someone practising for a driving test. Amman, she'll have to fly there, not Baghdad. But there'll be no flights to Amman now until morning so there's no rush. Just drive slowly. The night is plum-blue, sprayed with stars, topped by a cardboard-cutout moon. Briefly the car headlights touch on a roadside shrine – a limp football scarf, wilting flowers. Lara imagines the messages tied to those flowers, their felt-tip grief half washed away by seeping rain.

Briefly she thinks of Oliver – the road to London, the M23 is particularly dangerous. So many accidents there. What was he talking about? She pulls out onto the main road and keeps her foot down. Car headlights flash into her face. The car rattles and groans. She opens the window and feels the air on her face. Wait for me, Jay. Wait for me please.

She knows that the American or British military can airlift people out of Iraq. She's sure they'll do that for Jay. He knows a lot of people, the journalists will find a way of helping him. It may be only a bad cut or a broken arm but still it'll be reason enough for him to come home. She knows that he'll come now. He needs to get out of there. And they need time to talk, mother and son. To talk properly, in the way that they've never done before. Things will be quite different when she gets him home. She wishes she'd taken a little more time to prepare that bedroom but she'll ring Mollie and ask her to do it.

The drive is long, the road dips and turns. The car chugs in the slow lane. Headlights blind Lara and she concentrates on breathing deeply. *Yea, though I walk through the valley of the shadow of death.* She tries Jemmy's trick. Start at four hundred and count backwards. Junctions pass, she stares at signs, Haywards Heath, M23, Crawley, Dorking. At least the M25 will be clear at this time of night. 379. 378. Breathe deeply. 375. Should she head straight on to Heathrow or stop for a break somewhere while she waits for dawn?

In her mind, Lara tells the story to Jay as she'll tell it to him when he's home, when he's safe, when they sit together in front of the fake gas fire in the Roma Street flat. As she'll tell it to him sometime in the far distant future, when he's married and has children himself. A well-worn story, a part of their family history. A story to be told in the way that a mother sometimes tells her child the story of his birth. Fondly, full of wonder, gasping at the strangeness of things. *And then I came to find you, got in the car and drove all through the night, took a plane from Heathrow, drove through the desert. Coming to find you, at last.*

# 53

# Now

## Mollie – Brighton, May 2003

La-la-la-la. Mollie tips her head back to look at the stars. As they left Eastbourne, Rufus had folded back the roof of the Daimler. But then a sudden shower of rain had come and he hadn't stopped to put the roof back up and so now they're soaked – and laughing. The rain's stopped again now but the air is cold. Mollie loves the rush of it, loves to see the stars above tip and wobble overhead. The vast steering wheel twists in Rufus's hand as the car roars on. She sits on a cushion which covers the handbrake and Rufus's arm is around her, pressing too hard against the cast on her wrist.

They danced all evening amidst the high white columns and giant potted palms at the Grand. It's the only place left which still has a proper band on a Saturday night. They used to go often, with their professional dancing shoes, and sometimes they were the only couple dancing, and often people came to watch them, and clapped as they finished, or came to congratulate them afterwards. Rufus knows the barman, as he was one of the stage managers at the Devonshire Park, many years ago, and so there are always memories and jokes to be shared, and plenty of drinks on the house.

The road is almost deserted and stretches out ahead of them, silver fading into black. Seaford, Newhaven. A distant flicker of white cliff. The ancient engine stutters and roars as Rufus changes gear. *Hey-ho, the wind and the rain.* Mollie feels that she has once again taken possession of the landscape of her own flesh. She notices the scar left by a burn on the back of Rufus's hand, made by a hot iron, which she had accidentally dropped on him soon after Lara was born. And the cufflinks he's wearing – ones with blue stones in them. A fiftieth birthday present. She found them in some antique shop – Sheffield or Leeds? And the familiar pattern of the wrinkles around his eyes, one eyebrow permanently slightly higher than the other. Together they start to sing – *Paradise here, paradise close, just around this corner.* She's cold, even wrapped up inside her old fur coat, but she feels Rufus's arm steady around her. Don't let the police catch us, she thinks, because Rufus is way over the limit and already has nine points on his licence. Above her the stars turn as the road curves.

Rufus brakes and the car slows as he pulls his arm out from behind Mollie's back, and steers the car down a lane which runs between tall hedges. The sky narrows overhead and the air is darker. The engine of the car stutters and throbs. Ahead of them, flickering in the car headlights, a fork appears in the road. Rufus takes the right-hand fork and the car bumps along a farm track. The landscape opens out again and below them they see the lights of the road, the distant shapes of the villages out towards the coast. Peacehaven, Rottingdean. Cliffs moonlit and solitary, an endless blackness where the sea must be.

Rufus staggers out of the car and pulls Mollie with him. Her bones are stiff from the dancing, and the cold, and her head spins so that she can hardly stand. Rufus pins her against the side of the car, and slides her onto the bonnet. His huge, cold hands fumble under her dress. His fingers digging between her legs and she leans forward to kiss him. He struggles with his belt and gets his trousers halfway down. Then he pulls her legs apart and presses himself against her but cannot enter her. Instead his hand fumbles and he kisses her hungrily, his other hand gripping the back of her head. Suddenly he begins to cry – a raucous, bubbling sob – and Mollie pulls her arms tight around him, remembering all the nights of their marriage when she lay in bed, longing for him to get back from the theatre, every nerve alive.

Really, we are a pair of disgusting old people, she thinks. But still she's awash with wonder as she holds him there, and stares out over his shoulder at the purple sky and lights draped like necklaces over the land. He pulls her off the car bonnet and they dance, slowly, on the verge of the farm track, beside a field of new corn. They stumble on rough earth, and brambles rip at Mollie's ankles but he keeps tight hold of her. They sing 'The White Cliffs of Dover' and 'Down by the Salley Gardens' and 'My Love is Like a Red, Red Rose' as they sway over the rutted earth. Then they sit on a bank, and smoke a cigarette, and faraway the hem of the sky is pink from the lights on the coast. The night smells of dew and cut hay and petrol from the car. Then Rufus says – Isn't it time to be getting back? Is there any bacon and egg in the fridge? I'm absolutely starving.

The car rolls back along the main road and into the outskirts of Brighton, through Kemp Town, across the back of the town, and towards Union Street. Mollie longs for bed now – bacon and egg and a cup of tea and then shut the bedroom door and don't let anyone disturb you until at least halfway through the afternoon. Then perhaps a walk down the pier and a bit of supper out somewhere.

Rufus says, Once we hear, I'm quite happy to drive up to London to meet the flight. Typical Rufus, offering too little assistance with too greater show of magnanimity, and at a time long after help was actually needed. Mollie doesn't fool herself that anything will change now that he's home. Early in the evening, he'd talked long and loud about giving her some help with DIY and maintenance. He may even have meant it but it'll never happen. Mollie thinks briefly of Lara, sees an image of the family as a dance – people taking different partners as the music twists and turns. Brief, unlikely alliances before a more familiar pattern returns. Or perhaps a game of musical chairs. Who will be left standing when the music stops?

Rufus parks the car in front of a neighbour's garage, which will cause a row later, but to hell with it. He helps her out of the car and she staggers up the front steps, enjoying the sharpness of the dawn air, the silence of the sleeping houses around her. Pray God Mr Lambert isn't home. Even at three o'clock in the morning, he's quite capable of trailing down the stairs and starting on about his piles.

Silence. Peace. Not a sound from anywhere. What bliss. Rufus says that he's damned if he's sitting in that musty old kitchen downstairs. Why not sit in the sitting room for once? Get the fire going? Have breakfast at the table in the bay window up there – why ever not? Mollie agrees that they should do that. After all she can tidy up the room again later. Why do they always keep it for the guests when they never go in there anyway? The fire is already laid and while Rufus kneels to light it, she lies down on the sofa. Her head is heavy and she wonders if she'll manage to cook the bacon and egg before she goes to sleep. Better perhaps to have a little rest first. Rufus swears as he burns his finger on a match. The fire smokes, crackles, catches.

A while later Mollie opens her eyes and sees Rufus spread out in front of the fire, dozing, his head on a sofa cushion. Behind him the embers glow. At the window the darkness still presses in. Mollie realises that she must have slept but has no idea what time it is. She wonders vaguely about Jemmy lying asleep upstairs in bed. That girl needs to get out more, be more positive. You can only do so much for people. Mollie knows that, because she's had an experience similar to Jemmy's, this makes her less patient than she might otherwise be. Understanding should lead to kindness but sometimes it merely causes one to feel frustrated. Ah well, hopefully Mollie will be pushing that baby out in a pram some afternoon soon.

And Lara – has she found out what time the flight will come? Mollie feels that she should get up and find something to eat, or at least go up to bed, but she's so warm and comfortable that she doesn't want to move. It would be good to stay like this forever, in this moment of night, when the house and the street are quiet. When Rufus is sleeping peacefully and the fire radiates a comfortable heat.

# 54

## BEFORE

### Oliver – London, September 1998

Grace does have her blower with her and her medication. Oliver has checked. And they're off for the weekend, driving from his parish in Whitechapel down to the sea, to Brighton, Grace's favourite seaside town. It's been hard for him to get away and so it's gone ten at night as they leave the suburbs of London behind. Grace suggests they should swap places, offers to drive, since he's exhausted. He isn't sure that she is any less tired. She's just had an exhibition. He's been healing, as always, and filling out grant forms late into the night, trying to get money to rebuild the north wall of the church – although Grace and he agree that the whole place is an Edwardian monstrosity which should be bulldozed.

Grace insists again that she should drive. He doesn't want this but knows she won't give up. And so finally, when they reach the M23, they pull into a lay-by and swap places. And she drives as she always does – a little too fast, but skilfully. And he tells her to slow down and she laughs, starts to annoy him by driving with exaggerated care. It's a night of continual rain, thick and dark as tar. He is lulled by the frantic, mesmeric scraping of the windscreen wipers. And she talks about what they'll do the next day – a walk on the beach, a cup of tea. She hopes the hotel will have a dirty-weekend look about it, has insisted on a room with a view of the sea. She wants fish and chips for supper, she wants to paddle. More than anything she likes a seaside wind which tugs and whips, stings salt on the lips. He wishes she would stop talking and let him sleep.

He will never know how it happened. Afterwards the police will make a call for witnesses, they'll carry out a mechanical assessment of the car, they'll erect a sign on that stretch of motorway asking anyone with information to come forward, they'll examine the surface of the road. It's autumn and it may be that wet leaves made the road slippery but this can hardly be the case. There are no trees nearby and anyway the leaves have not yet started to fall.

And, of course, they ask endless questions about the allergies, the idiopathic anaphylaxis, even though the paramedics have confirmed that what happened had nothing to do with that. Finally, no reason can be found. Oliver asks himself again and again if there was a noise, a bump, the sound of something giving. But all he can remember is her sudden laughter, a sense of the car turning, lights swirling, his body flung sideways, his head smashed against the side window. Then a buckling and crashing and a scream and then a thump and the blare of car horns and a smash from somewhere far away and then a gaping stillness. And he raises his bruised head and says – Grace, Grace. Then he feels the door give beside him and a man is there with a torch.

My wife, he says. Get my wife. He can't see her in the darkness. He doesn't know if his head is pointing towards the sky or the earth. He hears instructions being given. Someone is shouting about the danger of fire, the need to get everyone clear. Pain shoots through his leg. He finds himself pulled out of the car, drags himself upright and staggers around the wreck. Two men have pulled her out and she's lying on the tarmac. The light of a torch shines down on her. Oliver kneels. Her face is calm and unmarked, as innocent as a child sleeping. And he waits for her to jump up and laugh but she doesn't. And then he sees how much she's bleeding. A voice tells him that an ambulance has been called. Traffic still buzzes on the other side of the motorway. A woman is crying. The rain beats down, soaking Grace's hair and her clothes and mixing with the running blood.

He knows what he has to do. It's quite simple. It's said that he's cured people with terminal cancer and so, with the grace of

457

God, he should be able to do this quite easily. He spreads out his hands and lays them on her. He concentrates on his own heart, his own breathing, and waits for his life to be transferred to her. All you have to do is to want – entirely and absolutely and with a great force – that someone should become well and it will happen. All he has to do is to reduce the bleeding for a while and the ambulance will be here. He looks down into her face and tells her that she won't get away with this. And he waits.

But nothing happens. His hands are only hands. They contain nothing beyond flesh, blood, muscle, bone. And around him only tarmac, the rain, the tight-fitting darkness, the shadowed faces, the man with his half unfolded warning triangle dangling from his hands. He waits again, applies all of his mind to her. Make her live. Make her live. But there is nothing there. He is quite alone, just a man on a motorway in the dark with his hands resting on the body of a woman. Nothing more. And it's never happened to him before that he can do nothing. Now, when he's needed, when he has to stop the bleeding, he can find no way of doing it. And he's struck by a freezing fear. He feels her going from him, knows that she will die.

People around him are telling him that the ambulance is on its way. It will be with them any minute. But he stands up and moves away from her because she's already gone. He felt it – spirit, as light as a shadow, slipping past him, crossing some unseen barrier, dissolving soundlessly into the night. And the woman on the ground is no longer her. The white face is empty, the rain-soaked hair an irrelevance. He moves away from the circle of watchers and stands staring at his own hands. Then he climbs up the bank beyond the hard shoulder and sits down in the wet grass, wiping rainwater from his hair and face.

And then the ambulance men come with giant lanterns and a stretcher and they bend over her and people call for him, and climb up the bank, come to tell him that it'll be all right now that the ambulance is here, but he knows that it won't. And down below he watches the vast pantomime of their efforts as though it's all happening some miles away. Equipment is brought and instructions are given and the ambulance men are continually bending over her. A policeman comes up to him and asks questions but he can't understand what's being said. He knows that he should stand up and go back down the bank but he can't do it.

And then another policeman comes and two paramedics and they help him to get up and he realises that all the power has gone from his leg and that he's bleeding. They take him down the bank and sit him in a chair and they tell him that the paramedics have been able to do nothing, although he already knows that. And they take him to hospital and dress his leg, although later he can remember nothing of this.

All he can remember is being driven home to Whitechapel through the dawn by a policeman and all the time he keeps the bag which contains the blower and the medication with him, in case she should need them, in case she should stop breathing. And when finally he lies down in bed, he puts the bag carefully on the bedside table. Because he takes great care in this matter. And he hates her for her bloody carelessness, and her laughter. And she'll be laughing now somewhere else, that same abandoned mirth, without any thought for him. Having a good day. And he'll be left holding the blower, in case she should happen to need it. A day at the seaside, Brighton. Fish and chips, a cup of tea, a seaside wind which tugs and whips, stings salt on the lips.

# 55

# Now

## Lara – Brighton, May 2003

There will be no flights to Amman now until morning so there's no rush. Just drive slowly. *Wait for me, Jay. Wait for me please. 256. 255. 254.* Rain is thrashing down across the windscreen, the lights of the motorway shatter and then come back together again as the wipers move. Lara can't breathe any more, fear is choking her. The dawn must come – that's all she can be certain of now. Time to stop for a coffee but no signs for services appear. Why hasn't Patricia rung? It can't take that long for her to find out. Again she thinks of that distant city, the dark streets, the terror and confusion at the hospital, bloodied people lined up in corridors, wailing children, a young Spanish woman searching through the wards and beds, trying to ask, not understanding. There will be no anaesthetics there, hardly any disinfectant, no beds, no clean needles.

A car cuts in and Lara brakes, swerves towards the hard shoulder, presses her hand down onto the horn. Bastard. Briefly she thinks of Oliver and all of his mad warnings about cars, the danger of the road. She should be touched that he cares about her but her anger has not yet entirely turned to ash. Her shoulders are locked tight as she leans forward, staring into the curtain of rain. Her eyes touch for a moment on the sleeve of her jacket. That green suede jacket with the upside-down horseshoe-shaped stain. The Liam jacket. It was wrong of her to lie to him, to tell him that she'd had a miscarriage. He'd tried a couple of times to get in touch in that first year but she'd never returned his calls.

Could she now ring him up and say, *OK, Liam in Los Angeles. Put down that cordless hoover, which costs only forty dollars and will transform your life. Because I need to tell you that actually you have a son.* No, she can never do that.

A coffee, something to eat. Staines. She pulls off the motorway. Surely somewhere must be open around here? It's hard to think about food but she hasn't eaten since breakfast. She's going to need all her strength. She comes to a twenty-four-hour petrol station attached to a motel and a supermarket. A tiny Asian man guides a mop across the floor. At a till, a young woman sits with a nodding head waiting for customers who don't come. The lights are violent and piped music tinkles. In the café, groups of night-dazed travellers sit blinking at plastic tables. A businessman reads through some papers. Three young men slouch, gathered round a radio which plays scratchy music.

Lara records every detail so that she can tell the story to Jay later. Printed words appear abnormally large – Coca-Cola, Nespresso Coffee, No Smoking, Two for the Price of One. *I was endlessly waiting for the call, I was so sick with fear I couldn't breathe.* She looks up at the board and tries to decide what she should eat. The girl serving behind the counter is lost in rolls of flesh, a pert white cardboard hat sits on top of her greasy face. Lara asks for coffee and a cheese sandwich. She doesn't usually eat cheese but here it looks like the most edible option. The girl serves the coffee and takes out a white baguette sandwich from the cold cabinet. Lara takes money from her purse, finding it difficult to get a grip on the coins. The girl places the sandwich and coffee on a plastic tray and Lara picks it up.

And then the phone rings. Lara tries to grab it but it's stuck in her bag, behind a book, a notepad, a case containing credit cards. Her hand fumbles through her bag. She needs to put the tray down and use both hands but she can't do that. A scream is rising in her throat. Eventually her hand closes around the phone and her finger clicks. She hears the voice at the other end. On the tray, the cup of coffee starts to slide. Lara watches it. She needs to adjust the angle of the tray but the coffee cup is still sliding. It waltzes down the tray, followed by the sandwich. Lara tips her hand one way and then the other. But still the whole lot goes. The steaming coffee splashes down her T-shirt and her jeans, and the sandwich breaks in half and slides to the floor, spilling slivers of cheese.

*And there I was in the service station when the call came.*

The voice on the phone crackles and hisses. The girl looks at Lara, raises her eyebrows, sighs. Still holding her phone, Lara bends down and starts to pick up the empty cup of coffee. But as she gets down towards the floor something breaks inside her. She gasps and drops forward onto her knees, draws in a snatch of breath, wails. The businessman looks up and starts to move towards her and then stops. The three boys with the radio stare then look away. The serving girl has moved out from behind the counter. Even the Asian man with his mop has stopped to see what's going on. Lara switches the phone off and starts to pick up the cheese sandwich. The girl is straining downwards, breathless, trying to help.

The music still rattles from the boys' radio as they leave and in the distance a till drawer closes with a ring. Lara feels the heat from the coffee scalding her leg. She must drive on to the airport now and sort out a flight. Of course, there may not be one until later in the day. Not many people fly to Amman.

And then she realises there's no reason to go there any more. She feels herself suspended, unattached to anything or anyone. She wants to scream or to wail but no sound will come. The fat girl moves, and her huge arms come down, and Lara finds herself enveloped in flesh, lifted onto a chair. And the Asian man comes with his mop and starts to clear up the mess. The businessman wipes uncertainly with paper towels at the place where the coffee went down the front of the counter. The serving girl goes to get another coffee and a sandwich and stands them on the table in front of Lara. And the Asian man is down on his knees now and the businessman looks awkward and twists the napkins around.

And then the girl leans over and tries to take hold of Lara in an awkward hug. And the four of them stay there, just like that, a tableau of incomprehension. Lara and the fat girl and the Asian and the businessman. While the piped music tinkles and the lights glare down onto the witnesses of this moment.

*And this is where I was, my darling, the night when they told me you were dead. I was sitting on the floor of a service station and this man was trying to wipe up coffee with a piece of tissue. And this tiny Asian man was kneeling down, with his forehead pressed against the floor. And the music still went on playing and the cup of coffee was still there for me to drink but they'd told me you were dead. Oh do not leave me. Do not leave me now, my love.*

# 56

# Now

## Jemmy – Brighton, May 2003

The lights hover above her like vast suns, bleaching everything, stinging her eyes. Jemmy stretches a hand towards the plastic armchair beside the bed, moving carefully, feeling a tug deep inside. Her fingertips close around her dark blue T-shirt and she pulls it over her eyes. Words float in and out of her mind and she tries to catch hold of them but they go swishing past like shoals of fish, quick and silver, flashing in the light.

It must be the pills.

Bill is somewhere not far away. She can hear his voice but not the words, only their rise and fall, their insistent rhythms. He's complaining to one of the doctors. Jemmy must be moved to another hospital. Not enough is being done. Soon Bill will start worrying about whether she has clothes, her sponge bag. Like the reports he writes at work – damp in the bay window, rotting floorboards in the attic, a crack of structural significance in the back wall at the northern corner of the property. Underpinning required.

Jemmy is no longer angry. What he's doing is useless to her but this is what he can offer. Maybe love is worries about nightdresses and sponge bags. She should have known this before. Romance has gone but a tired and tarnished love still remains. And yet she is twenty-three years old.

Twenty-three and old. Maybe she's always been old?

That man was here earlier – the man from the church with the red-eyed dog – she can't remember properly. She may have spoken to him but she may not. He'd stood by the bed, tall and solid but transparent also, so that she'd expected to see straight through him. It had seemed that he shone bright yellow but it must have been the lights. And she'd breathed him in like peace and silence. She can't remember now. He'd said Laurie's name and also – Sebastian.

And she'd heard big words floating past like God and love. She herself has always been sure that salvation is only kindness – dropped like a stone into a pool, its minor disturbance spreading endlessly in concentric circles, seen and unseen. But now she is certain that the red-eyed dog man brought with him something more, something beyond. So hard to remember. He was the one who saved Sebastian, she is sure of that. It had turned out that the first doctor had been wrong and now she's been told that Sebastian can stay inside her for a while longer. The situation isn't any worse and it might even improve yet. She has more days, more time. Precious, precious.

She drifts towards sleep, the T-shirt still pressed into her eyes and Bill's voice continuing its fish-like progress somewhere far, far away. Jay is with her as well, out there in the far distance, on his way home. He's been with her all the way, always will be. She lies on her side and her hands are held tight around Sebastian. Occasionally she feels his tiny movements like a summer wind brushing against leaves. Bill comes to sit beside her and fish words flash. She moves the T-shirt from her face, reaches out, takes hold of his hand, kisses the end of his fingers, keeps his hand pressed against her cheek.

# 57

# Now

## Oliver – Brighton, May 2003

Oliver sits on a bench just outside the entrance to the hospital, his head down, his shoulders sagging. When he raises his head briefly to look at his watch, he finds that it's now three o'clock in the morning but his exhaustion has little to do with time. He needs to walk home, go to bed. Gradually he summons the strength to stand, sets off down the road. The surfaces ahead – roads, roofs, the bonnets of cars, the lids of dustbins – are touched with a dull silver sheen from that shower earlier in the evening. He concentrates on putting one foot in front of the other. Through Kemp Town and into Edward Street, past the closed shops, the sleeping houses, disturbed only by the bark of a dog, the roar of an engine.

He thinks of the girl in the hospital bed. Jemmy. They say that's her name. Those marks on her arms – scars. Showed up like silver threads in the frost-white light of the room. As he walks, his energy returns and gradually he raises his head, looks around him. The night is nondescript, nothing but a blurred backdrop. But the air feels settled now, peaceful in a way that it hasn't done for many long days. Something dislocated has fallen back into place. Muscles and sinews gasp a sigh of relief. The pain eases. He thinks of the hospital. He might ask – why now? Why not then? But he doesn't want to attach any significance to what happened. He has always refused to believe that God should be merely fickle.

Dislocated. Fallen back into place. He looks around him tentatively. Yes, there are balconies but nobody stands poised, ready to throw themselves down. And people walk along pavements but they will not step into the path of a car, or be hit by falling masonry. Oliver can't make the adjustment. Without The Dying, the world looks naked. A balcony is glaringly empty without a figure who is about to jump. Cars are strangely innocent, they roll down the street quite merrily, harmless, jaunty even. People no longer glitter with the nearness of death. They're merely people, ambling along, quite safe, stripped of risk and unpredictability. Oliver doesn't trust this. Soon the images will start again. The world will reveal itself as it truly is – infinitely dangerous and unpredictable.

He walks on, hears a distant roll of thunder. Spots of warm rain fall, then stop, then return, gathering force. He comes towards the centre of the town, takes the road towards the church. The balconies remain innocent, the cars continue to smile. He watches, endlessly watches, but the world remains brazen in its newfound kindness. Eventually he reaches the end of his street. The rain still drips but he notices also that he's covered in sweat. It runs from every pore, soaking his shirt, his chest, his hands, running down his face. His eyes blur as sweat runs into them.

He's insubstantial, free. Someone has cut the guy ropes and a breath of wind could carry him away. He shrugs his shoulders, rolls his jaw, shakes his hands loose. *He who saves the life of one man.* Strange that he never believed that, even though he pinned those words on his wall. He reaches the church, unlocks the padlock on the door to the Community Centre, steps inside. Upstairs in his room, he strips off all his clothes, finds a flannel, washes the sweat from his chest and arms. He takes a clean T-shirt and pyjama bottoms from a drawer, pulls them on. How? How has this happened? This should be about the hospital, about Jemmy and Sebastian, the return of God. But instead it's about Lara – who understands nothing at all, takes care to understand nothing. A joke with a weak punchline. But still he knows that it was Lara, with her brutal lack of tact, who released him. He should not be surprised. He's always known that sometimes that which damages also heals.

He never liked Lara but now he loves her.

A wave of rain washes against the window again, thunder whips and snaps. He wants to be outside in the innocent and safe world. He wants to feel the newness of it, the glamour and comfort, the luxury. He pulls open the windows and feels the shivering air come in but still that's not enough. Without stopping to put on shoes or a coat, he turns and heads downstairs, undoes the padlock again, opens the doors, steps out. Under his bare feet the doormat is spiky. Moving out into the road, he feels water rolling down onto him, washing him clean.

He stands there for hours, minutes, days, lets the rain run down onto his face, fall down into his mouth, splash into his eyes. And now, again, he's filled with the love of God – but of a small, misguided God. Who moves through the world like a heaving bull, spectacular but clumsy. Full of love and all the many errors that it brings. God may not be good but it's possible to cooperate with the goodness in Him. He must be forgiven his failings now. The relative size of things has changed. If the smallness of God is acknowledged, then the vast, surprising expanses of man must also be recognised. Oliver's greatest sin has been the attempt to be small.

In truth, he can be proud of what he's done for Lara. He and this new God, this small and uncertain God whose canvas is so limited. Those great epiphanies and redemptions for which one waits. They turn out to be nothing more – nothing less – than the forgiving smile, the hand on the shoulder, the muttered word of encouragement. God as the sum of all the unselfishness in the world. Ideas like that would once have been an insult to the Almighty but now it seems possible that the grand is trivial, the trivial spectacular. Oliver shivers, stares upwards through the rain. It's always been said that the devil is in the detail, so perhaps it's not surprising that God should be there as well. A curtain has lifted, the night is fierce, the world charged with an infinite, crackling energy.

# 58

# Now

## Lara – Brighton, May 2003

The first morning without him. It's half past seven in the morning but the Guest House is crowded. Rufus and Mollie. Wilf, Spike and Martha. Upstairs Stan, Stan and Stan hang around in the hall and the sitting room. Mr Lambert has put on his best frock, done his make-up, is clearly making an effort not to talk about his minor ailments. Everyone moves with an underwater heaviness, rehearsing the steps of a slow dance, behaving towards each other with exaggerated respect, looking for some comfort they can offer, some service they may render – but there's little to be done. Lara watches, thinks, the whole house and everyone in it is made of cut glass. Take care or it will shatter.

Phones ring – Lara's or Wilf's mobile, the house phone. At first Lara had answered all the calls but now she sometimes hands the phone to Martha. Greg rang earlier and swore viciously, then started crying, the sound like a saw going back and forward through wood. Others have also rung from Iraq, speaking in foreign accents, raging and weeping, spluttering incoherently. Some of them Lara doesn't know but they must be friends of Jay's. Hans – who she had always assumed to be middle-aged – sounded fourteen years old and she'd found herself speaking to him as she might have spoken to Jay, becoming a mother now, too late.

Around her a web is being spun, a story created. Wilf and Spike say, Jay made the final sacrifice, he gave his life for others and for the cause of peace. Lara is grateful for this, but the truth is he just happened to be in a marketplace when a bomb went off. Wrong time, wrong place. No one knows who planted the bomb, of course. It seems that as many as thirty others were killed. Lara had at least wanted Jay to have his own personal death.

Rufus stands by the kitchen window, staring up, silent. Mollie moves towards him, takes his hand. They are both old now. The text of life itself has become so powerful that neither of them have need to embroider it now. For Lara, love is still more than she can manage but forgiveness is possible. Her mind moves back a few hours to the moment when she opened the sitting-room door and found them there, sleeping like children beside the fire. Rufus lying on the hearth rug, snoring and dribbling slightly onto a cushion. Mollie like an injured animal under a blanket on the sofa. Lara had sat down, waited a while before waking them, giving them a few moments more of innocence, protecting them, watching them as a mother watches over a sleeping child, as she had once watched over Jay. After she told them, she'd waited for her father to wail and curse and fall on the floor. She'd needed him to do that, since that was how he always behaved.

But instead he'd cried like a child, standing against the curtain with his back stiff and his hands over his eyes. Rufus weeping for the baby he didn't want to be born, and for the young man who he raged against. For the boy who provoked him, and criticised him, and needled him, and deflated him. For the boy whose love he couldn't bear. And Lara had felt then that she was seeing her father naked, newborn. And it made her realise that he'd always lived inside a thick shell, and that she and her mother had helped to keep the shell in place so that the naked thing inside him wouldn't be seen by the human eye.

Now someone guides her to the kitchen table, sits her down, puts a bacon sandwich in front of her. Strangely she's hungry and begins on the sandwich with enthusiasm, licks butter from her lips. Wilf and Spike sit down as well and the tomato ketchup is passed. Lara drinks tea, feels her body unfreezing. Of course, Jay isn't really dead. Soon they'll be told it was all some mistake.

Martha pours more tea for Spike and says, Of course, it wasn't like this when my daughter died, not really.

Lara stares at Martha, bacon sandwich suspended, but Martha has turned away to get the milk. Oh that too, Lara thinks. How come she never knew that Martha had a daughter, a lost daughter? So many things she never saw. But still she's hungry enough to go on with the sandwich. Her mobile rings and Rufus answers it. She drinks and chews hurriedly now, knowing that the end, another end, is coming. Sorry, Rufus says. It's the Foreign Office. I think someone should. They want to know about the body.

Lara looks at him and realises that Jay is dead.

Bacon drops from the sandwich, Lara's hand grips her mouth. She thinks she might vomit.

All right. OK. OK. Tell them to ring back. Or—

Spike eases the phone from Rufus's hand. Don't worry. I'll sort it.

Lara feels panic rising. He's dead, he's dead.

She turns and sees Oliver at the kitchen door, walks into his arms.

I have to go out – now.

She finds herself handed up the stairs and wrapped into a coat. The front door is opened and she feels Oliver's hand on her shoulder as she steps out into the ordinary morning street. A man pushes himself at her, armed with a microphone. She retreats, falls against Oliver, tries to get back into the house. Rufus strides across the hall, passes her, steps out onto the doorstep, bawls with such force that the reporter staggers back down the steps, falls into the street. Despite it all, Lara looks up at Oliver and half laughs. Sometimes it's good to have Rufus as a father.

Oliver guides her out of the house again and they escape down the street, untroubled. The man from the Foreign Office shouldn't have asked those questions because Jay is still alive, or at least he's somewhere close. When she answers those questions then Jay will be absolutely and conclusively dead.

It isn't yet eight o'clock but other people are already out on the beach, walking dogs or swimming in the rolling grey surf. Lara strides forward, feels Oliver following her. Occasionally she stops, tries to talk, but the breath jerks in her throat and she heads on, up and down the same stretch of beach. Finally she slows and wanders down to the water, sits down on the sea breakwater and looks over at Oliver. He takes his shoes and socks off and his long white feet stretch out on the wet pebbles.

I never thought, Lara says. Every day I imagined, but still...

Her breath keeps coming up into her throat in a strange gasp, somewhere between a hiccough and a dry sob. Her muscles and sinews have disconnected from each other and she's just a sack of rattling bone. She stares out across the beach to where a dog jumps for a stick, leaping into the sunlight, its body snatching as it pulls the stick out of the air. She's shocked by how calm she feels.

It was arrogant, Lara says. To think I could bargain. Even when Greg said he couldn't find Jay, I wasn't worried. I thought I'd be repaid. I thought if I just had the courage to let him go completely then he would come back alive. But it doesn't work like that?

No, sadly it doesn't.

She's become part of Oliver's club now, a club which nobody wants to join, a club where the entrance fee is beyond what anyone should have to pay. She thinks back to all the things she's said to him – things which were deliberately rude and insensitive. She'd said those things so that she wouldn't have to consider what it must have been like for him when Grace died. She'd said them as a means of avoidance, of distraction. Now she's going to have her face pushed down into pain until she's choking on it. Anything else can be mended, but this is for ever.

I don't understand, she says. I don't understand.

But there is nothing to understand. Her mind is like a car with a broken steering wheel. She tries to drive straight, but the car veers from left to right, might dive into a ravine or meet with a brick wall. It takes all of her concentration to keep it on the road. She doesn't want to think about the way he died, the moment of his death, his flesh blown apart, burnt up. What was it he saw?

A sudden light? A dull thud into nothing? She tries not to let the scene unravel in her mind but still she glimpses parts of it.

I don't know what he was doing, she gasps.

He was just in the market. Wandering. Wearing a black New York T-shirt.

She wonders how Oliver knows this, what he sees. Maybe someone just told him earlier. But who? When? She stares down at her feet, watching the water draw up the beach, stop, fall back.

You know I've missed the point so many times, she says. I always wanted it to be about something else, some grand story – him dropping out of university, Rufus, Liam, Mollie. But perhaps for him it wasn't about any of those things. Not Iraq as a symbol for something else, just Iraq. The people he cared for dying, a country tearing itself to bits. He said he wanted me to let him exist. But it was only recently that I— and now it's too late.

You can still get to know him, Oliver says. Not in the flesh perhaps.

Lara shivers and swallows, stares out at the sea.

Do you think his life was wasted? I mean, I know that his death won't alter anything in Iraq – nothing at all. But all the same. I think something—

Yes, Oliver says. Yes, of course. She knows from his voice that he's doubtful but she's grateful to him for trying. She herself is doubtful but now hope must be stitched together from the most meagre corners of cloth.

He lived as he wanted to live, Oliver says.

Yes. Yes. And of course, I'm going to go on. Working with Wilf and the others. Because although the war was apparently won, everyone knows, don't they? That slowly but surely, over the years, it will be lost. Perhaps we'll raise money for the families of the others who died. That's something we could do. And maybe the money won't get to them, or will be lost in administration or stolen. But that's the only thing left, isn't it? Either that or hatred and anger – and there's no one in particular to be angry or hateful against really.

She swallows a sob, wipes her sleeve across her eyes. Jay was so many things to her, the son she fought for, the son who was a burden, who was a fool and then a hero. He's been all of those things but still she has no idea who he really is, was. The cornerstone, the scapegoat, a bone for them all to fight over. *Will the real Jay please stand up?* But he's slipped away out of the back door, down an alleyway, over a wicket fence, across someone's vegetable patch. Gone.

What hurts the most, she says, is the fact that maybe none of it matters that much. He was just one boy. There is this view that human life has such great value but does it?

He was important to you, Oliver says. To me. To us.

He is putting on his socks now, easing them up over wet toes.

Why do I feel – excited? Lara asks.

You do, at first. Fresh grief does bring a rush of energy and hope. When death still has some glamour.

And then?

Eventually – grinding, mundane, tedious.

The day is clearer now. The town is visible in sharper focus. Lara can't believe that the news isn't emblazoned on posters all along the seafront. Of course, people will know soon, when she goes and answers those calls. And there'll be articles in the newspaper, and moral outrage and calls for this and for that. And people won't know whether to call him a hero, or a saint or a lunatic. Some will be mourning and others will be muttering a different story behind their crooked hands. *Of course, he was mad, I blame it on his mother, they were always an odd family.* But even that will only be for a week or two and then everyone will forget. Except for the few – Mollie and Rufus, Oliver, Jemmy. It's only now she thinks of Jemmy.

Thank you for helping her, she says.

I didn't do anything.

No, I'm sure you didn't, she says. She knows now that this is what she must say.

You know Jay was important to Jemmy, Lara says. In the hospital, she told me.

Looking at Oliver, Lara realises how he has changed. His hands have stopped moving around so much. He's calmer, settled. She also realises she loves him. Not in the romantic sense, of course. Those emotions are an absolute irrelevance in the world they now inhabit, a luxury far beyond what they can afford. But she loves him for his courage, for the way that he tries so hard to supply hope to other people, while having none himself.

Lara stares out across the sparkling water, towards the grey oblong of a distant ship. Briefly an image appears, a memory she didn't know she had. Jay turning cartwheels somewhere. Not on this beach, in a park maybe or in the garden of some long-gone holiday cottage. Burning through a dew-glittering morning like a Catherine wheel, spluttering and splashing, the light of him dazzling. *Oh my darling – how I loved you and I never knew, you never knew.*

The ship – it's low on the horizon, barely more than a smudge. But moving surely, heading on somewhere. Grief is out there as well, beyond that distant horizon, but drawing in towards them. Her mobile phone will still be ringing at the Guest House, the administration of death continuing. She longs to stay here a little longer, with Oliver, in the morning freshness. She looks down and sees that her jeans are still stained by the coffee she spilt on them at the service station. This is the place before the storm breaks. When she has to return those calls then Jay will start to be dead. But she's needed there. *Oh give me some of your courage, my love. Remind me that even this day I must live a life on fire – because you're not here to do that.* She leans across to Oliver and kisses him. He holds her against him. Together they walk up the beach, towards the waking town, the Guest House.

Ahmed has returned from washing up at the hotel. She hears his voice as she enters the kitchen. No. No. She can face anything but not Ahmed. For a moment she turns back to Oliver but then forces herself into the room. She is guided to a chair, shrinks into it, knows there can be no escape. Ahmed comes straight to her, kneels down, takes her hand. She forces herself to look at him. If only he would call her a selfish bitch – that she could easily stand.

I am sorry, he says. I am very, very sorry.

Please, Ahmed, don't. It's kind of you but really – Jay made his choices.

But still he holds her hand, and says again that he's sorry. She's never noticed before that he's beautiful – his face dark and feline, the features painted in with the finest lines of the brush. Slowly she unfolds, lays her head against his shoulder, feels tears spilling onto her cheeks. But she isn't only crying for Jay, she's crying for the gulf which divides her from Ahmed and always will. For despite his dignity, despite her head, briefly, awkwardly on his shoulder, she can never understand. Even though Jay is dead that makes no difference. Still Jay will have to be put aside, cannot be compared to the loss of half a family, a whole life. A country where story has broken down into strings of meaningless events, a cacophony of senseless babble. Once she would have hated Ahmed for this and still the embers of hate burn – but she also knows that it's right that she should always stand aside for him. Even grief has its leagues and now she sees that may be part of its value.

Jay made his choices, they all did. And what's happened is due to the squalid little mistakes and petty grievances of their lives. And there is no bridge to be built. No lessons to be learnt, although they may create some. She – and all of them here – have been given the bright and brilliant gift of the day, the fact of being alive. And this is the way in which they have squandered it. Affluence and security have led them to nothing but folly and trivia. Lara sees all this but surely she must have atoned enough by now? She was only ever an averagely bad mother.

Martha appears holding Lara's mobile. Patricia, she says. Lara takes the phone. Patricia's voice is calm, distant, stretched thin as silk. She confirms what Lara's already been told about the bomb and the market. So he'd been dead all of yesterday and nobody knew. At the hospital Hans identified him because of the T-shirt, Patricia said. There was no doubt. If only there could be some corner of doubt. But he was wearing this T-shirt, black with the Empire State Building and – New York, New York. He was given it by an American soldier. And Hans spoke to the doctor, who said that it would not have made any difference when they took him to the hospital because there was no hope.

Lara clenches her teeth. She wonders about the T-shirt. Was that the only way they could identify him? And there had never been any hope. What did that mean? For a moment, her mind fills with shattered bone, fragments of flesh, dismembered limbs, organs crushed like over-ripe fruit, pools of blood – but she pulls herself away. She will not ask, not now.

Patricia says, Someone here said it is like he committed suicide slowly. But this is not right because he was very happy when he died. I saw him that morning and he was happy like a lamb in spring. He has gone running into death with his eyes and his arms wide open. I told him many times that he would die and he knew that and he said he felt no anger for anyone, only love and that if the time came he would go quite willingly.

Lara clenches her teeth, whimpers inwardly. She says thank you to Patricia, assures her that she'll call soon to let her know. But let her know what? What is there now to know? Lara hands the phone to Wilf, bites back a wave of pain. Around her old patterns are re-establishing themselves. Martha and Mollie are competing over who should make the tea. Mr Lambert can't be expected to hold out much longer. And Mollie is starting to talk about the Coventry Blitz and a white house with the back window blown out but a woman and a child still asleep in the bed. Mollie doesn't understand what has happened, of course. But right now they all need to fail to understand. The era of being irritated by Mollie's tepid washing-up water is at an end.

And as Mollie speaks, Rufus is firing himself up, as he must do, so that Mollie can be more than the outline of a person. For a moment, Lara thinks back to that evening when Rufus and Mollie found out that she was pregnant with Jay. This morning at least is not like that. The difference matters. Lara asks herself yet again

– what happened to my mother? Why is she only the outline of a person? So vivid and present and yet not here? Was it all to do with that earlier war, Coventry? Lara will never know. She sees her parents now as very young people – blameless, and ignorant. Unprotected. Just starting out in the world. As though the years have peeled away from them and left them all quite fresh again. With skin almost too sensitive to touch. This is what Jay has done to them.

You can have them operated on, Mr Lambert says to Martha. But a friend of mine went down that road and he's never been able to sit down again.

Terrible, Martha says. Tea? Coffee?

Coventry? Could you just shut up about Coventry? Rufus says.

But Lara can feel none of the old anger now. In this new and brutal landscape the old patterns are comforting. All of them now have crossed into a world where kindness, forgiveness, is all that can save them. They at least owe Jay that. Lara remembers his letter – *all I know with certainty is that every day you make the choice.*

I've warmed up that bacon sandwich for you, Martha says.

Oliver comes to sit beside her, lays his hand over hers. Yes, kindness. Perhaps that's all God ever was. Jemmy's courage, Rufus's glorious fit of temper, Sebastian alive still in his watery world, Martha with the warmed-up bacon sandwich which Lara will never eat now. And the woman in Baghdad singing a lullaby to her children, the old man who befriended Jay, close to death but joyful. Here it is possible to find a small and failing God in whom they can all trust.

# ACKNOWLEDGEMENTS

This book took an extremely long time to write and so I am grateful, first and foremost, to all those kind friends who tactfully decided not to question my sanity as year rolled on from year and no book emerged. I am also truly grateful to all those people who pledged for this book through the Unbound website. Without your generosity, support and enthusiasm, I would not still be writing. There are also many who are not able to offer financial support but, nevertheless, cheer heartily from the sidelines. I am equally grateful to them. In particular, I should like to thank John Boyle, Loretta Stanley, Jeannette Cook and Martin Westlake of the Brussels Writers Group. Susannah Rickards patiently read many drafts of this book and Clare Andrews was also a committed early reader. Kathleen Jones always offers a word of wisdom when I need it and Clare Dunkel regularly comes out with brutal but necessary comments on the challenges of being a writer. Caroline Sanderson, Paola Schweitzer and Amanda Holmes Duffy are endlessly supportive. The title of this book comes from a poem by Naomi Shihab Nye called 'Kindness'. I would like to thank her for that poem and for all the thoughts that those wonderful lines inspired. I am also grateful to everyone at the Quaker Meeting Houses in Brussels and Nailsworth and to my colleagues on the Oxford Master of Studies in Creative Writing. My agent Victoria Hobbs at A. M. Heath is always there when I need advice or help. Mark Ecob was responsible for creating a cover which I absolutely love. My family doubtless find it impossible to live with a writer in the house but manage not to say so. Thank you to them for their patience. Finally, of course, I owe a huge debt of gratitude to all those at Unbound who have made this book possible – John Mitchinson, Dan Kieran, Anna Simpson, Imogen Denny, Xander Cansell, Amy Winchester, Georgia Odd and Caitlin Davies.

Unbound is the world's first crowdfunding publisher, established in 2011.

We believe that wonderful things can happen when you clear a path for people who share a passion. That's why we've built a platform that brings together readers and authors to crowdfund books they believe in – and give fresh ideas that don't fit the traditional mould the chance they deserve.

This book is in your hands because readers made it possible. Everyone who pledged their support is listed below. Join them by visiting unbound.com and supporting a book today.

Clare Algar
Giampi Alhadeff
Clare Andrews
Nick Andrews
Ange & Kate
Lesley Angus
Youssef Arif
Rosie Arkwright
Jarrett Arp
Arvon Foundation
Charlotte Ashby
Tim Atkinson
Jane Bailey
Kim Baker
Sue Barrance
Katie Beringer
Florence Berteletti
Lorraine Blencoe
Jo Bloom
Emily Bolton

Estie Boshoff
John Boyce
John Boyle
Wendy Brandmark
Richard Brass
Carys Bray
Anne Brichto
Julie Cain
Pauline Camacho Fielding
Isla & Una Campbell
Susie Campbell
David Camplin
Carly, Martin, Zephyr & Sol
Kate Carpenter
Louise Cartledge
Barbara Castelein
Paloma Castro
Alison Catchpole
Taiita Champniss
Eliza Chisholm

Julian Clyne

Vanessa Cobb

Malinda Coleman

Ali Coles

Michael Collins

Debbie Condon

Stephen Connolly

Jeannette Cook

Elly Cooper

Helen Craig

Samantha Curtis

Alex Dampney

Judith and Geoff Dance

Sara Davies

Anja de Jager

Michael Dickson

Shuna Dickson

Sian Digby

Jenny Doughty

Cressida Downing

Simon Dowson-Collins

Jane Draycott

Clare Dunkel

Robert Eardley

Gillian Eastwood

Vincent Eaton

Lucy Morgan Edwards

Katharine Elliott

James Ellis

Jude Emmet

Jennie Ensor

Felicity Everett

Mandy Fenton

Katie Fforde

John Fieldhouse

Angela Findlay

Daisy Finer

Caroline Foster

Sally Frapwell

Jan Frazer

Friction Talks

Swithin Fry

Paul Garner

Jamila Gavin

Kim George

Rose Gerring

Lyndall Gibson

Julia Gilbert

Graham Gilby

A.J. Grace-Smith

Voula Grand

Amelia Granger

Peter Green

Anthony A. Gribben

Marilyn Griffin

Eva Grut-Aandahl

Wesley Gryk

Sam Guglani

Lorna Guinness

June Hall

Sara Hammerton

Rob Hanley

Kiran Millwood Hargrave

Simon Hargreaves

Lindis Harris

Sophie Harris

Sarvat Hasin

Clair Hector

Per Hellstrom and Kristina
    Nordlander

Linda Hepper
Helene Hewett
Catherine Higgins-Moore
Amanda Holmes Duffy
Antonia Honeywell
John James
Lisa Jenkins
Kathleen Jones
Nina Jorgensen
Rachel Joyce
Kyra Karmiloff
Elena Kaufman
Nik Kealy
Dan Kieran
Michael and Micheline
  Kingston
Stephen Kinnock
Andy Kinsella
Joan Kinsella
Stephen Kinsella
Tony & Angela Kinsella
John Kjellberg
Helene Kreysa
Milan Kristof
Roman Krznaric
Alison Layland
Marti Leimbach
Aliki Levi
Jacqui Lofthouse
Loose Muse
Sally Lovell
Jo Lowde
Susan Lynch
Eileen Maguire
Kate Mallinckrodt

Sarah K. Marr
Virginia Martin
Maya Matthews
Anna McCulloch
Sarah McKenzie Wylie
Marilyn Miles
Martin Mills
John Mitchinson
Virginia Moffatt
Bel Mooney
Sasha Mordaunt
Peter Moseley
Indu Muralidharan
Richard Nash
Carlo Navato
Annemarie Neary
Alexandrine Norton
Jamie Nuttgens
Peter Oliver
Monica Parle
Tim Pears
Irene Pinner
Justin Pollard
Irena Postlova
Sue Prain
Sarah Pullen
Martina Pulver
Tam Purkess
Belinda Pyke
Fergus & Griet Randolph
Kate Riordan
Cari Rosen
Julie Rosenberg
Caroline Rowland
Jan Royall

Rebecca Rue
Mark Russell
Helen and Richard Salsbury
Caroline Sanderson
Paola Schweitzer
Stephanie Scott
Ruth Sessions
Tamsin Shelton
Audley & Amanda Sheppard
Sarah Shilson
Ian Skewis
Heather Speight
Stephen Spinks
Loretta Stanley
Catherine Stewart
Jemima Stratford
Anne Summerfield
Katie Sutcliffe
Emma Sweeney
Siobhan Taylor
Laura Theis
Jackie Thomas
Betsy Tobin
Peter Touche
Sarah Towle

Louisa Treger
Caroline Tuke-Hastings
Sam Urquhart
Kerri Vermeylen
Meg Walker
Annabel Wardrop
Caroline Watkinson
Laura Watts
Emily Webb
Barbara Weightman
Liz and Martin Whiteside
Glynis Whiting
Joanna Whittington
Naomi Wildey
Miranda Williams
Paul Wilmott
MaryRose Wood
Madelaine Woodford
Anuita Woodhull
Yvonne Woods
Peter Wragg
Linda Youdelis
Mary Young
Nicole Zabbal